BODY
SURFING

BODY SURFING

A NOVEL

Dale Peck

ATRIA BOOKS
New York London Toronto Sydney

ATRIA BOOKS

A Division of Simon & Schuster, Inc.
1230 Avenue of the Americas
New York, NY 10020

This book is a work of fiction. Names, characters, places, and incidents either
are products of the author's imagination or are used fictitiously. Any resemblance
to actual events or locales or persons living or dead is entirely coincidental.

Copyright © 2009 by Dale Peck

All rights reserved, including the right to reproduce this book or portions thereof
in any form whatsoever. For information address Atria Books Subsidiary Rights
Department, 1230 Avenue of the Americas, New York, NY 10020

First Atria Books hardcover edition February 2009

ATRIA BOOKS and colophon are trademarks of Simon & Schuster, Inc.

For information about special discounts for bulk purchases, please contact
Simon & Schuster Special Sales at 1-800-456-6798 or business@simonandschuster.com.

Designed by Davina Mock-Maniscalco

Manufactured in the United States of America

10 9 8 7 6 5 4 3 2 1

Library of Congress Cataloging-in-Publication Data

Peck, Dale.
Body surfing / Dale Peck.—1st Atria Books hardcover ed.
p. cm
1. Teenage boys—Fiction. 2. High school students—Fiction. 3. Best friends—Fiction.
4. Demoniac possession—Fiction. I. Title.

PS3566.E245B63 2009
813'.54—dc22
2008015496

ISBN-13: 978-1-4165-7612-9
ISBN-10:   1-4165-7612-6

The author would like to extend a special thank-you to Josh McCall and Jeremy Somer, who provided assistance and insight at every stage of this novel's composition.

For He had commanded the unclean spirit to come out of the man. For it had seized him many times; and he was bound with chains and shackles and kept under guard. And yet he would break his bonds and be driven by the demon into the desert.

And Jesus asked him, "What is your name?" And he answered, "Legion," for many demons had entered him.

BODY SURFING

Prologue

The centurions captured the boy in a raid on his family's home somewhere in Gaul—even he didn't know the exact location, maps being not particularly common in his part of the world, or reading for that matter. He'd been ten at the time of the attack, perhaps eleven (calendars were also scarce): too young to fight, which was the only thing that saved his life during the initial raid, but still lissome, and the conquering soldiers thought he might fetch a good price in the slave markets back home. Either in the Coliseum, if he toughened up during the thousand-mile march to the Eternal City, or, if they were lucky, as a sexual servant in one of the decadent wealthy houses that had multiplied like the pox with the empire's ever-expanding power. Along with their gods and their architecture, many noblemen in the new Rome had embraced the ancient Greek custom of regarding women as cattle: necessary for breeding, but not much else. It was a boy to whom one brought one's most ardent—and adroit—lovemaking. It was said Nero himself enjoyed slitting a boy's throat as he sodomized him, so that his death throes would cause his anus to contract around the royal member, and bring the emperor that much more pleasure.

But six months of forced marching took their toll on the boy's physique. By the time the colonnade reached Rome, a slave trader flipped up the tatters of his tunic and pronounced his ass too stringy to appeal to anyone, let alone the emperor. Into the ring he went. If he was too stringy to be a prostitute, he was too small to be trained as a gladiator. His only role was to run around screaming until he was cut down. To a boy who had never seen more than a hundred people gathered in one place, the roar of the crowd was disorienting and terrifying. Add to that a host of lions and tigers, water buffalo and elands, a pair of rhinoceroses, half a dozen cobras, and one enraged elephant, and all he could do was dodge, jump, run, fall, roll—and scream. Fifty armed men slashed and stabbed at each other, while another hundred—barbarians and Christians and other undesirables—were added to the mix, primarily for the sake of volume.

People died to his left and right, gored by horns, slashed by jaws, disemboweled by claws, swords, staves. But even as the boy did his best to escape the hundred deaths that stalked him, a part of his attention was consumed by the canopied emperor's box. For six long months the Roman soldiers had filled his mind with gruesome stories of what their depraved ruler was going to do to him. The great Caesar was insatiable. He consumed aphrodisiacs from the deserts of India and jungles of Africa to keep him potent, and was even rumored to refuse to spill his seed so that he didn't have to wait the minute or hour it might take him to recover his virility. Perhaps the strongest proof of the centurions' stories was the fact that none of the soldiers bothered him, since the emperor was said to pay a premium for virgins. And even now, while wholesale slaughter took place in the arena below him, he was being attended to. A succession of boys, girls, and women took their turns rubbing his feet and shoulders, fanning him, bringing him food and drink, or simply fellating him. Beautiful women placed their breasts in his mouth one at a time, so that his view of the ring wasn't spoiled. His mother and sister—both of whom were said to have shared his bed—flanked him, and occasionally received the attentions of one of his slaves after he or she had serviced the most powerful man in the known world.

The sandy floor of the ring became gooey with blood. Whether it was because he was fast or small or just very, very lucky, the boy continued to elude sword, tooth, claw. There were fewer than a dozen men left, fewer than half a dozen. A tigress, bleeding from a long gash in her flank, nibbled at the copper skin of a Scythian, while other beasts, still in battle frenzy, pawed and sniffed at the bodies to see if any were merely faking death.

One of the rhinoceroses had been killed, and the boy hoisted himself atop the mountainous corpse, hugged the leathery hide like a monkey clinging to its mother's back. His eyes were screwed shut, but he had the strangest feeling someone was looking at him. He slitted his lids, and there he was. The emperor. Undisputed ruler of *Mare Nostrum* and all the lands that broke upon it. He was shaded beneath his striped awning on the far side of the ring, yet his eyes seemed to bore into the boy's—glowing eyes, filled with a liquid, luminous intelligence that seemed not of this earth.

The boy couldn't move, couldn't look away. When a lion sniffed at his foot he didn't even flinch.

One of the emperor's hands rested on his scepter and the other rested on the head of whoever serviced him—boy or girl, it was impossible to tell. And then the emperor did the strangest thing. He smiled. Smiled, and nodded, and closed his eyes. White-knuckled fingers pressed on the head of the body kneeling before him.

The boy closed his eyes too as the lion's teeth sank into his ankle and, with a flick of its powerful neck, threw him a dozen feet across the ring. But even as it leapt after him the boy felt a strange sense of peace fill him, of strength and speed and power. It was as if molten iron were being poured into his veins and leaching through his skin, rendering him invulnerable yet still mobile. Pain vanished. So did fear. The boy rolled out of the cat's way and found his fingers closing around the hilt of a sword, flipped it like a kitchen knife and hurled it directly into the lion's throat. The beast vomited blood and bile and dropped in a convulsing heap to the ground.

The crowd's roar was so loud that even the animals stopped. They looked up to see if a storm were coming, an earthquake. But then they turned back to the ring. To the lone figure still standing. Not just standing, but taunting them. Goading the animals and goading the crowd too. *Show me what you've got*, he seemed to say. *Give it to me. Give it* all *to me.*

The animals circled warily. Humans didn't fight this way. Not when they were alone. They cowered or ran or hid in trees. But this one screamed at them, ran after them. Weapons littered the floor of the ring, swords, lances, maces, and the boy jumped from one to the next, handled each as if he'd been trained in the art of war by Alexander himself. His actions were deliberate and fearless—and completely inexplicable to the person doing them, who seemed a spectator to himself, as distant from his own flesh as the throngs in the stone benches all around him. One by one the beasts fell, the lions, the tigers, the buffalo and elands. The boy's arms were gory to the shoulders with blood and bone and offal.

It was pure chance that did him in: he stepped backwards onto a trampled cobra, which had just enough bite left to sink its fangs into his ankle. In an instant his leg went numb, although the poison's flow seemed to stop in his thigh, not reaching the vital muscles of diaphragm and heart. He was still standing but was unable to run or dodge. His breath was labored, spots danced before his eyes. Still, he taunted the animals. *Come on!*

The rhino answered the challenge. The charging ungulate slammed into the boy's body and its great horn—longer and fatter than the boy's arm—pierced his abdomen. The boy gouged out the animal's eyes with his bare hands and continued to jab at the pulpy sockets until the beast shook its head so violently that the boy's body was ripped in half, torso flying in one direction, legs in the other. Even then he didn't lose consciousness. Even then he fought on, dragging himself with his fingers toward a dagger glinting in the bloody sand. The boy had the disjunctive experience of watching a pair of hyenas rip his legs one from the other even as his fingers closed over the dagger's hilt, but before he could tighten his grip it bounced from his fingers. The boy rolled himself over, just in time to see the charging elephant rear up on its hind legs, and then a foot the size of one of the columns that held up the Temple of Jupiter came down on his head.

For months afterward, audience members swore that he continued to fight right up to the last moment—that he crossed his arms over his head as if he could sustain the weight of an elephant with his bare hands. The emperor, asked to award the fearless barbarian posthumous freedom, remarked enigmatically, "We are both free now." But the slain boy came to him in a dream that night, told him that death's freedom was something no one, not even an emperor, could command with certainty. As it happened, Nero would die by his own hand less than a year after the boy did, and Rome itself fell three centuries later. Emperor and empire achieved immortality in the minds of future generations, however, acquiring dominion over an area a hundred times larger than that of Caesar's realm.

As it happened, so did the boy.

1

Land of the Living

"If one does not understand how the body that he wears came to be, he will perish with it."

—The Gnostic Gospels

1

The woman at the bar of the Hotel Acropole leaned on her elbows and scanned the dim room. At not quite six feet in battered, American-style cowboy boots, Ileana Magdalen (that's what the name on her passport said anyway) was taller than just about everyone else in the dingy establishment. There were no other women in the bar, although countless numbers passed the open French windows in their head scarves and flowing robes, more than a few concealed from head to toe by brightly colored *burqas*. Ileana looked down at her sweat-stained tank top. Her nipples protruded through the wet ribbed cotton, and she had to fight the urge to cross her arms over her chest. Fuck it, she thought. It's too goddamn hot for a bra. And besides, if she had to put one more *ounce* of clothing on, she was going to kill the wrong man.

Ceiling fans swatted the hot air. Outside, slender Africans and lighter-skinned Arabs milled along the sweltering streets of Omdurman, a working-class neighborhood in Sudan's sprawling capital city, Khartoum. The predominant language was Arabic, but Ileana caught snatches of Chinese, Hindi, Russian, staccato dialects she didn't recognize. But the most persistent noise was the whine of traffic: horns, brakes, screeching tires, revving engines. Backfires that sounded a little too much like gunshots for comfort. Oil had made Africa's largest country a thriving nation by regional standards. Unfortunately, a

significant chunk of its newfound wealth had been spent massacring
its non-Islamic citizens. Ileana had seen the devastation firsthand.
She'd just completed a two-week tour of the western province of
Darfur with Francois Dumas, a French epidemiologist with the World
Health Organization, after which she and Dumas had driven six hundred miles in an ancient Land Rover whose sprung shocks amplified
every ridge, bump, and pothole—minehole, Dumas joked, and Ileana
didn't bother to point out that the oblong craters looked like they
were caused by mortar fire rather than land mines, whose blast radius
tends to be perfectly circular.

The journey across the Sahel had left them parched, and they
came down to the bar to wash the dust out of their throats. Ileana arrived a few minutes after Dumas, found the Frenchman looking skep-
tically around the seedy room. But after a brief exchange in broken
English (along with the "gift" of a few American dollars) Ileana convinced the Acropole's barman to produce a bottle enigmatically la-
beled Cocker Spaniard. "Kentuckessee whiskey," the barman said.
"Number one brand." Despite the fact that Ileana paid for it, he
handed the bottle to Dumas.

"I'm impressed." Dumas squinted at the label, which looked as if
it had been written by hand. "I think."

Ileana popped the cork and poured them each a drink.

"Save the compliments till you've tasted it." She held up her
glass. "Death is in my sight today." She tossed her drink back and
closed her eyes, shuddered pleasantly as the gasoline-colored liquor
stung its way down her esophagus. She ran her tongue over her tingling lips to savor every last drop of the burn.

When she opened her eyes, Dumas was staring at her with more
than scientific curiosity.

" 'Death is in my sight'?"

"Something a friend taught me." Ileana's tone discouraged further questioning.

Dumas nodded, held his drink up.

"To friends," he said, casting another glance at his companion.
"Old and new."

The epidemiologist downed his drink. When he could speak again, he cursed: in French, English, and a language Ileana didn't recognize. Spaniard? she thought with an inner laugh. Kentuckessean?

The scientist excused himself to go the washroom. "I hope it is safer than the alcohol," he panted, mopping his brow with his handkerchief.

Ileana glanced around as her companion tottered off. The rundown room certainly seemed an unlikely place for a pair of international aid workers to end up. The sawdust on the floor was stained with spilled drinks, the air clogged with sweet-smelling *shisha* smoke wafting from an enormous hookah on a corner table. After the devastation of Darfur, Ileana would have preferred to sip a chilled lychee martini on a palm-shaded verandah with the majestic Nile in the background. But the Legion's last known twenty for her target was here, and the front desk had confirmed that a guest by the name of Antonio Soma had checked in several days earlier. The clerk declined to mention the room number aloud, so Ileana folded a blank piece of paper into an envelope, scrawled Soma's name on it, and watched as the clerk slipped it into a cubbyhole. 206.

In truth, Ileana hated knowing the name. Wished all she had was that number. Names made it harder. More personal. More human. Some members of the Legion hid behind words like "ichthys," "mandorla," or "vesica pisces," archaic terminology that attempted to draw a philological distinction between target and host, but Ileana had no time for compartmentalized thinking. Her quarry was formidable enough as it was. She didn't need to distract herself with mind games and rationalizations.

But still. She hated knowing the name.

Unfortunately, her mobile phone wasn't receiving pictures, so "Antonio Soma" was all she had to go on. Her contact had described him as "on the tall side," slightly built, with dark hair, dark eyes, olive skin. Not exactly novel features in an Arabic capital. But there were other things more telling than hair or eye color, or names for that matter. That had been Alec's first lesson, all those years ago.

Some two dozen men were scattered around the bar. Ileana ignored the groups, confining her attention to the single men. Her target would not want to make friends. She judged each sidelong glance for an appetite that betrayed a more than carnal hunger. She made no effort to conceal herself. There was an invisibility in being watched: no one would suspect the most conspicuous person in the room of engaging in subterfuge. She smoothed her dark blond hair into a ponytail, fished a rubber band from a pocket. Her bare arms moved dexterously, the skin so taut it revealed the action of the muscles beneath. Deltoid, triceps, and biceps flexed and stretched, augmenting the action of the rotator cuff in one of those miracles of human anatomy that go unnoticed on less refined specimens. Few would have guessed she was over thirty, and not just because of her lithe body. Her face was as smooth as a teenager's. Some would've said it was because she rarely smiled—no smile, no smile lines—and only a blind man could have denied it was a beautiful face, with its Slavic cheekbones and almond-shaped gray eyes. But it was a cold beauty, aloof, untouchable. Not that many men hadn't tried—and at least one succeeded, if the watch on her left wrist was any evidence. The band was an intricately woven platinum braid, the face broad, thick, unadorned. A man's watch. Ileana had been rubbing it unconsciously for the past several minutes. She caught herself now, smiled at the watch wistfully, gave the knob a couple of turns.

When she looked up she saw Dumas returning from the washroom. The scientist's presence caused a chain reaction throughout the room as, one after another, the men looked away from her. She suppressed a frown. Dumas was genial, but she'd hoped to ditch him so she could concentrate on her hunt. But apparently her companion was not to be deterred. The tuft of dark hair that showed in the gap between the top two buttons of his requisite UN-issue khaki shirt made Ileana's chest tighten. Was Dumas actually going to make a pass at her? But all the Frenchman did was pick up his glass with a theatrical air of trepidation.

"This stuff is absolute poison."

Ileana didn't take her eyes from the room. "Probably made from rotten yams and siphoned gasoline."

Dumas swirled the liquor in his glass. As Ileana watched his fingers, she remembered how delicately he'd probed patient after patient in the refugee camps. A true healer's hands, nimble and nurturing, attuned to the flesh beneath the fingertips. She tried to think of the last time she'd felt a man's hands on her body, then tried even harder to forget. She reached nervously for her watch, then jerked her hand back to her side. This is no time to get distracted, she chastised herself, let alone sentimental. *Focus.*

Her contact had said Soma was clean-shaven. That could change in a week, of course—hell, the target's sex could change in a week—but even so, she ruled out all the men with long beards, which took care of three-quarters of the room. In fact, there was only one patron about whom she had any lingering suspicions, a young man, little more than a boy really, who wore his wispy mustache with the pride of someone only recently able to grow facial hair. He couldn't have been more than eighteen or twenty. His dusty gray business suit was too small for his long legs, but he wore it as he did his mustache, with an air of adolescent panache. More to the point, he seemed to be checking Ileana out. She couldn't be sure because of the pair of knock-off Ray-Bans that covered his eyes, despite the dimness of the smoky room.

Beside her, Dumas sighed heavily. "What I wouldn't give for a nice glass of Pernod."

Ileana ignored her companion. She stared into the reflective black lenses and made a silent offer.

"A chair at a cafe in Montparnasse. Paris, you know, in the springtime . . ."

The boy bit. He took his glasses off and glanced at her once, then quickly looked away. But the glance was all Ileana needed. The adolescent shyness, the nervousness of a john. The poor boy seemed to think the brazen Western woman in her revealing (if not exactly feminine) attire was for sale.

Ileana nearly jumped at the sound of her own sigh of relief. Calm down, she told herself, or you'll be useless when Soma really does show. Easing onto her stool, she turned and gave her attention to Dumas.

"Paris." She forced a laugh. "You would settle for the Seine when you have the Nile—the three Niles—at your disposal?"

"It's true, the Seine is a trickle from a rusty tap compared to the Father of All Rivers. But the liquor—" Dumas held up his glass "—makes up for the lack of scenery."

"I would have thought your work had inured you to the need for such creature comforts."

Dumas laughed mirthlessly. "I do not think anyone ever becomes inured, as you say, to such . . . things." His English was good, but Ileana had to admit it was hard to come up with synonyms for what they'd seen in Darfur. "Such . . ."

"Atrocities?"

Dumas's expression wasn't so much unsympathetic as resigned. "The brutality of war is old news, no? Especially this kind of ethnic war?"

"I'm Croatian," Ileana murmured. "I know."

"Ah!" Dumas didn't heed the warning in her voice. "I have been wondering about your accent for the past two weeks." He smiled a little too eagerly. "I did two years in Bosnia and Herzegovina with *Médecins Sans Frontières*. Doctors Without Borders. Ninety-three and '94. Believe me, I understand."

Ileana nodded, but doubted that even someone who'd pulled bullets from flesh and sewn up limbs ravaged by shrapnel could understand what she'd endured. She poured two more shots. Alcohol offered its own kind of understanding, and she touched Dumas's glass with hers and swilled the fiery liquid as though it were a toast to the fallen.

Dumas shuddered as the whiskey went down. "Are you sure you're not Russian?" he said when he could talk again. "You drink like a professional."

"Self-discipline." Ileana smiled. "Self . . . possession," she added, but so low the last word was inaudible.

2

Caitlin Reese's parents had been planning their twenty-fifth anniversary for the past six months. They'd booked a suite at the Waldorf-Astoria for the weekend—where, unbeknownst to their daughter, they were entertaining a fifty-seven-year-old Russian and his nineteen-year-old girlfriend, who referred to themselves in certain online forums as "The Master and Margarita"—leaving Caitlin to throw *the* blow-out party of the year. Almost everyone in the senior class at Dearborn Academy was crowded into the Reeses' prim, two-story Shaker and neatly manicured backyard. There were kids playing quarters and spin the bottle, boys passed out on couches, a claque of girls gathered around the keg and snickering each time someone worked the pump too vigorously and ended up with a cup full of head. The usual couples were pressed into corners or trashing the flowerbeds or wrapped in the pile of jackets on Caitlin's parents' California king, although the clear award for Most Original Place to Do It had to go to Stan "the Mandible" Sabory and Lipless Leslie Barton, who had folded themselves into Caitlin's little sister's Preschool Playhouse and rocked it so hard that it fell over—a fact that, judging from the continued rocking, neither of them noticed.

Jasper Van Arsdale tried to slip into the party surreptitiously, but his best friend found him almost immediately (at the bar, duh). By way of greeting, Q. wrapped Jasper in a headlock and pulled him through the sliding glass doors into the backyard. They stumbled past the steaming pool and the vibrating Playhouse toward a neglected-looking swing set. Before Jasper could say anything, his friend pulled out a bottle of–Scotch? yeah, Scotch–and held it out to Jasper. Q.'s hand quivered, though Jasper didn't think it was from drunkenness. Preternaturally calm Mohammed Qusay Jr., insulated from the banal troubles of adolescence by a bottomless reservoir of wealth, good looks, and charm, actually seemed nervous–worried even–though it didn't make up for the fact that he'd been acting like a complete ass-hole lately.

"You know," Jasper said, waving the bottle away, "you've been kind of a jerk the last couple-a days."

"Jesus Christ, honey, I'm not asking for sex. I'm just offering you a drink."

For the past week, Q. had shown up drunk to school, picked fights with jocks, grabbed random girls' asses, and graffitied just about every locker and stall door he passed–in Farsi no less, although fuck if he'd tell anyone what he'd written. On Thursday he actually brought a flask to school, pulled out a book of matches in third period and tried to light his burps on fire. Mrs. Rinaldi, the geriatric (and generally oblivious) human sexuality instructor, had been forced to take notice. By rights she should have sent Q. to the principal's office, but that would have meant certain expulsion. Rather than hang him out to dry, Mrs. Rinaldi merely gave Q. detention. Any-body in his right mind would have counted his blessings, but appar-ently Q. wasn't in his right mind. Instead he stole a Bunsen burner from chem lab. Hapless Buckwheat Johansen had been the peer mon-itor that afternoon, and as soon as Mrs. Rinaldi waddled off to her Neon, Q. unscrewed the burner's lid and poured its contents all over Buckwheat's shirt, then stood over him smoking one of his dad's Montecristos. Q. had threatened Buckwheat with an even worse fate if the boy told on him, but the story had made its way through the student body with the speed of a flash fire.

"Oh come on," Q. said. "Have a fucking drink. We're celebrating."

"Celebrating what? The fact that Buckwheat got away with nothing more than an alcohol rash?"

"Sure," Q. shrugged, "if you think that's worth celebrating." He took a drink. "And the conclusion of four years of high school mendacity." He took another drink. *"And"*—speaking over Jasper's opened mouth—"an end to the insanity. For I have seen the light and am about to return to my old, placid, rule-abiding self."

"About to? When might that be?"

"Soon. Very soon. But not in the middle of a party, retard."

Jasper glanced at the bottle. It *had* been a long week, full of finals and devoid of college acceptance letters, not to mention sex.

"I don't really like Scotch."

"This is not just Scotch. This is an Islay single malt of the rarest appellation, filched directly from Mohammed Qusay Sr.'s panic room."

"Aren't Muslims supposed to eschew alcohol?"

Q. waved the notion away. "The vagaries of religion are beyond me, but I'm pretty sure the Quran provides dispensation for quality beverages. And this, my friend, is quality with a capital Q. If I do say so myself." Q.'s teeth flashed in the light glinting off the pool. "It cost the Sheik six hundred bucks."

"I'm a redneck, remember? I'm sure I couldn't tell it from Wild Turkey."

"Well, in that case." Q. reached into his bag and pulled out two plastic soda bottles. "Wanna Fanta? Or do you prefer a more healthful Gatorade?"

"My friend, you *are* profane."

The cocktail tasted sort of like cough syrup—or syrup that made you cough. It was sweet and sharp at once, so fiery as it burned its way down Jasper's throat that he could feel it moving into him like a demonic possession.

"Well, I think that deserves a 'shit.'" He took one more sip. *"Shit."* He picked up the bottle, squinted at the label. "It's pronounced 'I-la'? I always thought it was 'I-slay.'"

"I slay, you slay, we all slay. Who the fuck cares how you say it, as long as it does the trick?" As Q. drained his cup and tossed it into the rhododendrons, Jasper noticed a flash on his friend's wrist.

"Yo, what's with the bling?"

Q. held out his arm to Jasper. "A pregraduation present from the Sheik. Patek Philippe. Sweet, huh?"

The wide gold band hung casually on Q.'s wrist, yet had an air of importance about it. Gravitas. *Money.* Jasper looked at Q.'s face.

"How much?"

"You don't wanna know."

"How much?"

"Twenty-nine."

Jasper's eyes bulged. "Hundred?"

"Thousand."

Jasper tried to whistle but couldn't. "Jesus Christ. Is it a watch or a religious icon? I feel like I should pray to it."

"Time is expensive, my friend. Time. Is. Expensive." Q. tapped the Patek's thick face. "Speaking of time. Tell me something, Jazz-man. What would you do if you knew you were out of it? If, say, you only had twenty-four hours to live?"

I'd tell you never to call me Jazz-man again, Jasper thought. I'd pawn your watch and fly to Vegas. But something about the earnest tone in his friend's voice kept him from joking. For whatever reason, a memory of his most recent fight with his dad flashed in his mind, and, somewhat sheepishly, he said, "I dunno. I guess I'd tell my dad I love him."

Q. blinked. Let his eyes stay closed. Pretended to fall off the swing. Really *did* fall off the swing. His lanky form lay stretched in the grassless furrow that Caitlin Reese's Mary Janes had worn over the course of countless afternoons. Without bothering to open his eyes, he said, "Oh—my—*God*."

"Fuck you. What would *you* do?"

Q. smirked, opened one eye. "I'd steal my old man's Porsche and get Sila to blow me in the front seat, then drive it into a cliff at a hundred miles an hour."

Jasper forced a laugh. "You'd let Sila out first, though, right?"

Q. shrugged. "Yeah, sure. And you? Come on, my man. Twenty-four hours. With whom would you spend your last day on earth?"

Jasper didn't answer immediately, but his thoughts weren't hard to read.

"Michaela, huh?"

"Maybe she'll finally take pity on me. When she finds out I'm dying."

"Uh uh. No pity fucks. You can't tell her you're gonna die."

"Whatever. Our one-year anniversary's in a couple of weeks–"

"You don't *have* a couple of weeks!" Q.'s hand on Jasper's ankle almost made him jump out of the swing. "You have to act *now*." Q.'s skin was hot, his grip tight as a bear trap. But just as suddenly as he'd grabbed Jasper he let go. He stood up and hurled the half-empty bottle at the stockade fence. Three hundred dollars' worth of Scotch made a sickle-shaped shadow on the slats. "Twenty-four hours. No more, and–" Q. actually looked at his $29,000 watch "–no less."

Q.'s face seemed feral, his teeth shiny, sharp, *hungry*. Jasper could imagine what he must have looked like when he stood over Buck-wheat Johansen with that cigar. And the way he'd looked at his watch? As if Jasper really had twenty-four hours to live? How creepy was that?

"Q., what the fuck? Tell me you aren't about to go Columbine on me."

"Don't make this about me. Answer the goddamn question."

Jasper stared at him blankly, then chugged the rest of his drink. "Whatever, dude. I see the asshole days aren't over yet."

He started to walk inside, then stopped. Michaela stood in the doorway, staring at the boys with an uneasy expression. There was a clock over her head: 8:47. Its little pendulum swayed back and forth with hypnotic rhythm, and it was a moment before Jasper could look away. He started to walk toward the house, when Q. blocked his way.

"What the fuck, Q.?" Jasper drew himself up to his full height. He and Q. had had plenty of scuffles during the course of their ten-year friendship, but they'd never actually thrown down. Q. was taller but Jasper was thicker, more of a weightlifter than his track-running friend. He stepped so close to Q. that their chests were nearly touching. Jasper could feel the heat coming off Q.'s body, smell the cloying mixture of Fanta and Scotch on his breath. "This is getting old. Now get *out* of my way."

Q. looked at Jasper sizing him up. "Gonna kick some A-rab ass, Jazz-man? Gonna finally give the ol' towelhead what he's got coming?"

Jasper glanced at the door, saw Michaela still staring at him. Maybe it was the light behind her, outlining her body: her delicate neck, the thinness of her waist above the swell of hips, the hollow between her thighs. God, Jasper thought, she's so beautiful. So fucking beautiful. He suddenly asked himself why in the *hell* he needed someone to talk him into sleeping with his girlfriend.

Q. saw where he was looking. "Play your cards right and you won't have to live till your anniversary. *Wait*, I mean. You won't have to *wait* till your anniversary. Think of it as a test of character."

Even as Q. spoke, Michaela melted into the party. In the moment of silence between Usher's "Yeah" and some extra-crunky Ying Yang Twins, Jasper heard the faint sound of moans coming from the Playhouse across the lawn.

"How's this for a test of character? *Grow the fuck up.*"

His friend no longer blocked his path, but Jasper shoved him anyway, jogged into the house. He'd show Q. what he was made of. Show them both what he was made of—Q. *and* Michaela. Fuck if he wouldn't show them.

If he'd looked back he might've seen his friend smile. A curious, wistful, patient smile that looked about nineteen hundred years older than the face of the teenager on which it appeared.

Then again, if Jasper had looked back, his friend probably wouldn't have smiled. He would have just looked at his watch.

Twenty-four hours.

And counting.

3

I should have written something on the note, Ileana thought to herself. I shouldn't have given the clerk a blank note, which would only make her target suspicious. An elementary mistake. Alec would never have done something so stupid.

It had been more than an hour since they'd arrived. Still no sign of Soma. She thought about retrieving the note, but Dumas's hand fell heavily on her knee. Cocker Spaniard may have tasted like shit, but it got the job done: the Frenchman's conversation had acquired the volubility of the intoxicated, and more than once over the past hour he'd found it necessary to put his hand on her leg.

Ileana sighed, crossed her leg so it was out of Dumas's reach. The note would have to wait. She tried to concentrate on what her companion was saying.

"It is like 1918 out there. Or worse. The plague. With bureaucrats blocking every attempt at aid, and the international community devoting all its attention to the war on terror, there is little we can do besides bury the victims."

Ileana nodded. The last stop on their tour had been a refugee camp where rampant dysentery left corpses so dried out and blackened they looked like pieces of charred timber, and a virulent strain of flu snuffed out life after life with the kind of ruthless efficiency one associated with the guillotine.

"It seemed to me especially tragic," she said now, "the way the diseases seemed to target the children."

Dumas peered at her. "But this is the way it always happens. I'm surprised you do not know."

Ileana rubbed her watch nervously. Yet another thing Alec had been better at than she was. Maintaining cover.

"As I said before, my organization formed less than a year ago. This is the first real catastrophe we've dealt with."

"Ah yes, your 'anonymous American billionaire.' I had forgotten. It is so hard to believe you could be inexperienced at anything." Dumas gave her a meaningful smile. "Influenza almost always affects the young the worst. Older people have stronger resistance. Their immune systems are fully developed, perhaps they have had flu one or two times before. The children are virgins, as it were. They have no such defenses."

"Virgins," Ileana echoed, then added quickly, "And the other . . . symptoms?"

"Mon Dieu, yes. The other symptoms, as you say. It is enough to make one crave even this poison. Well," the Frenchman shrugged, "the other symptoms are not so unusual, either, I suppose. We were both in Yugoslavia, no?"

"I don't just mean the rapes." Ileana's voice was brittle as glass. "The sexual activity was more widespread than that. Almost as if there was an epidemic of lust, despite the horrific circumstances."

Her question seemed to touch a chord.

"Despite? Or because?" The Frenchman touched the taut flesh of Ileana's upper arm. "I became a doctor because of my fascination with the human body. Its strength, its frailty. Its mystery. But my years with *Médecins Sans Frontières* and WHO have made me more and more fascinated by the mind that dwells within that body. How is it that this seemingly mechanical accumulation of a hundred trillion cells produces something as intangible as consciousness? As, if I may take a small leap, the soul?"

Ileana smiled a bit uncomfortably. "I'm afraid I don't quite follow."

"A thousand pardons, mademoiselle. It has been so long since I have had a like-minded conversational partner, and such a lovely one at that." Dumas blushed. He fumbled in his pocket, pulled out paper and a pouch of tobacco. "What I meant to say," he continued, nimbly rolling a cigarette on his thigh, "is that this is not the first time I have seen such behavior. Indeed, I have encountered it so often that I've done a bit of research. The Bible tells us that the hedonistic perversity of Sodom and Gomorrah only increased as God's wrath destroyed the city, and Homer writes that the Greek armies were able to storm Troy because the inhabitants of the city were engaged in orgiastic celebration, despite the pyres still burning outside the city walls."

He finished the cigarette. Ileana produced a lighter, sparked it.

"Take Boccaccio's *Decameron*," the Frenchman continued, his words acquiring a professorial air. "The predecessor of Chaucer's *Canterbury Tales*, in which a group of people hiding from the *Yersinia pestis* bacterium—the Black Death—hole up and tell each other tales to while away the time. Many of their stories are quite ribald, licentious even."

"Dirty," Ileana cut to the chase.

"Indeed," Dumas's hands plucked at his pant legs. "Dirty. *Cochon*. Historians believe these tales are a reflection of actual behavior that Boccaccio was forced to couch at a narrative remove, so as not to offend conventional pieties. But there is in fact a documented case of a large monastery in the south of France. When the plague swept through, it killed some three-quarters of the monks. Later, a nun found the survivors engaged in what could only be described as a bacchanalia. Their attentions were focused not just on each other, but on their servants, their livestock, even the decaying bodies of their dead brethren. The nun herself claimed to have been violated by no fewer than seven of the anchorites before she could make her escape, and, though her attackers disavowed any memory of their actions, or claimed that 'the spirits of the dead' had taken control of them, the Holy See concluded they had in fact been agents of Satan and burned them at the stake." Dumas paused, smiled grimly. "They burned the nun as well, of course. Just in case."

Ileana had to fight to keep her face impassive. In fact she knew this story. Knew the nun's name, and the monks'. Knew exactly how close Dumas was to the truth. How close, and how far.

"And the refugees? You think perhaps they were just trying to fuck the pain away? Pardon my French."

Dumas found the joke entirely too funny, and his laugh rang out in the bar.

"Since the beginning of time, sex and death have been inextricably linked in the mind of man. Indeed, in France we still refer to orgasm as *le petit mort*. The little death."

Ileana looked at the tuft of chest hair. A wave of nausea churned her stomach. "We're not talking about a seduction that takes place over a fine Bordeaux. We're talking about bruised, battered, diseased refugees copulating next to corpses. That is not exactly *le petit mort*."

"No no no, you misunderstand me. Certainly I do not think there is anything romantic or erotic in what is going on in Darfur. But the universality of the symptoms suggests we must broaden our focus. I was in Iran after the 2003 earthquake, in Indonesia after the 2004 tsunami, in New Orleans after the 2005 hurricane. I have been in Bosnia, Rwanda, Afghanistan. In all of these places, in the midst of unimaginable devastation, I have seen a version of this epidemic of lust, as you called it. I have come to believe that death on such a scale fractures the societal restrictions that normally curtail man's desires. The beast within is loosed. And the beast wants to, to . . ."

"Fuck?"

"*Oui.*" Dumas pulled at his open collar. "To fuck."

Again, Ileana marveled at how close to the truth the epidemiologist was.

"So you think it's just psychological? The id asserting itself in the breakdown of superego control?"

"Sex and death are the polarities of physical and psychological existence," Dumas answered. "The natural reaction to such horror is, in some way, a turn to life, although not necessarily in a loving or even positive way. Neither ovum nor spermatozoon knows from morality, after all."

"You mentioned the soul earlier. Do you honestly believe we do nothing more than enact the dictates of the animal—the physical—mind? Is there nothing of the infinite in this kind of behavior? Of God, or his adversaries? *Listen,*" she said over Dumas's opened mouth. "The monks you mentioned earlier spoke of demonic possessions. Many of the refugees talked the same way. As if an alien consciousness had forced them to commit such strange acts. The Zaghawa have a word. *Ogbanje.* It refers to an evil spirit who returns to the womb each time it dies, possessing an unborn child so it can inflict a new cycle of misery. And Arabs speak of *afrit* and *ghul,* male and female djinn who inhabit humans and force them to commit acts they would never do otherwise. And the medieval Christian belief that witches were in fact hosts of Satanic agents led them to execute hundreds of thousands, possibly millions, of suspects over the course of three centuries. Can you really accept that so many similarities across such disparate cultures and religious traditions are purely chance?"

Dumas's lips pursed as he put his glass down and regarded the woman beside him frankly. "*Ogbanje? Afrit? Ghul? Demons?* Apparently you were gathering more than statistical data in your interviews." He laughed nervously. "I am suddenly reminded of your inexperience. You are not the first novice to run after a spiritual explanation for atrocities such as those being committed in Darfur. But I am a scientist. An empiricist. Where some people see God's hand, I see only the slavish devotion to one tradition, one institution, rather than another. Fractured human psyches reverting to more primal expressions. And yet . . ." For the first time the look Dumas gave her was less lustful than sad, as though he wanted to agree with her, but couldn't. "Though I do not believe in 'the soul' as such, I cannot deny that there seems to be more to this body than a finite number of cells."

"Consciousness," Ileana reminded Dumas of the word he'd used earlier.

The Frenchman nodded. "We know consciousness is an electrical phenomenon. A measurable current moving within the environment of a single brain, a single body. We can prod that body with drugs, poke the brain with needles, and, within certain parameters, predict what the effect of our stimuli will be. And yet we have never been able to duplicate a single human thought or emotion. We can break the body down into organs, break the organs into cells and cells into their component parts. We can even break apart molecules and atoms, but we cannot locate the moment at which the inorganic becomes organic, the instant that a collection of cells acquires the ability to think and feel. I must admit that when I look at a ditch filled with thousands of corpses, I sometimes find myself taking comfort in the hope that consciousness comes from somewhere outside the body, and that it returns to that place after the flesh that housed it has been so brutally destroyed. But it is just that. A hope. A comfort. It is only a matter of time before science solves even this mystery, and the miracle of the soul is reduced to a series of ones and zeros equally at home in a motherboard as in mother nature."

Dumas looked at Ileana self-consciously after this speech. In fact she was a bit surprised by what he'd said. There were gatherers in the Legion who said much the same thing, although their conclusions were based on rather different data from what Dumas had at his disposal.

She reached for the bottle, but just as she was about to pour another round a young man entered the bar. He was tall with dark skin, but something about his manner and dress—louche, studiedly careless—suggested the European rather than the Arabic. Italian perhaps, maybe Spanish. He paused in the open doorway and surveyed the room, looking at each and every person in turn, but also, and quite ostentatiously, allowing himself to be looked at.

Dumas saw where she was looking. "Do you know him?"

"I'm not sure." She didn't turn away from the newcomer, whose eyes had already found hers. "Do you?"

The connection was instant. Almost electric. The man smiled, then turned and walked back out of the bar.

"I have encountered him here and there. He writes for the yellow press, going from famine to war to earthquake the way certain types of lawyers run along behind ambulances. His name is Antonio So—"

But Ileana had already slid from her barstool. Dumas could only watch in confusion as she left.

"The maids have been telling stories of that one."

Dumas looked up to see that the barman had reappeared.

"He is a wild one. A real demon. Your friend does not know what she is getting into."

Dumas took one last look at Ileana as she left the room. Her hands were crossed behind her back, and one of her fingers had slipped under the band of the man's watch she wore, rubbing the skin beneath.

"Somehow," he said, turning back to the barman, "somehow I think she knows *exactly* what she is getting into. Oh well," he sighed, "at least she left me the bottle."

And, shaking his head in amused regret—a true Frenchman, he was honest enough to know when a woman was out of his league, although it never hurt to try—he poured himself one last drink.

4

The sound of water dripping into the spaghetti pot woke Jasper the following morning. The drops *ping*ed on the base of the empty pot with a crisp metallic sound, meaning the water had only now managed to work its way through the loose shingles of the roof and the large patch of mildewed plaster that hung over the teenager's room like some crumbly French cheese. From long experience Jasper knew that meant the rain had started about an hour ago: April showers blah blah blah.

He opened his eyes briefly. Painfully: how many cups of Caitlin Reese's bathtub punch had he been stupid enough to chug last night? Gray light the color of old gym socks illuminated a tattered carpet of clothing: T-shirts and boxers and T-shirts and jeans and T-shirts and sneakers and still more T-shirts. The clouds made it impossible to tell the time. Six in the morning? One in the afternoon? Jasper's throbbing head didn't care. He pulled a pillow over eyes and ears and tried to go back to sleep.

Ping!

Ping!

Ping!

The trickle of water pricked at Jasper's headache like an electric charge. But then the pain disappeared beneath a memory that washed over him like a pot of boiling water. A dark closet, the smell of moth-

balls, shoes that could use a shot of Dr. Scholl's. Fingernails scraping
his back, a pair of voluptuously soft breasts. Moist breath in his ear:
"Fuck me!" A tug at his zipper. Then: darkness, warmth, confusion;
pleasure, need, release. It all sounded great, save for one troubling
detail: Jasper was pretty sure the girl hadn't been Michaela. Oh God,
he thought. What the hell did I *do* last night?

Just then, his dad's voice cut through Jasper's hangover like a
bandsaw. "Rise and shine, buddy boy," John Van Arsdale called in his
best imitation of country geniality. "Weekend's getting away from us,
we got work to do."

A groan escaped the pillow as Jasper remembered that his dad
wanted him to turn the garden over today. Like most things on the
Van Arsdale farm, the rototiller was broken—had been for, oh, seven
or eight years—which meant Jasper would have to work the quarter-
acre plot with a pitchfork.

Ping!

Ping!

Ping!

Quarter acre; pitchfork; rain. All that, plus a hangover. It was
shaping up to be a *stellar* day.

"Ahem. Jap?"

Jasper pulled the pillow from his face and saw his dad in the
open doorway. John Van Arsdale wore an old flannel shirt and
threadbare overalls, one strap left undone in a gesture that was probably meant to be jaunty, boyish even, but was undermined by the
salt-and-pepper stubble grizzling a face that was entirely too creased
for its forty-three years.

Jasper, on the other hand, was completely naked, and he yanked
the blanket over himself.

"Dad! You can't just barge in here like that!"

John Van Arsdale didn't try to hide his grin. "Door was open,
Jap."

A steaming cup of coffee tilted precariously in his dad's right
hand. As Jasper smoothed the blanket over himself, he wondered if
the stale smell of alcohol came from the cup or his dad's skin—or his

own. God, he must've been *trashed* last night. He never slept naked,
let alone left his door open.

"How many times do I have to tell you that Jap is just not cool?"
he said now, hiding his embarrassment behind condescension just as
he'd hidden his morning wood beneath the blanket. "It's racist and
anti-Semitic and, given the fact that I am neither Japanese nor Jewish—nor, for that matter, female—particularly inappropriate."

John Van Arsdale's jaw muscles tightened as he stared at his an-
noyingly articulate son. "Your ma called you Jap," he said finally, and
turned from the room.

Jasper threw his pillow at the empty doorway.

"Cheap shot!"

Cheap maybe, but effective. Jasper's mother had died when he
was barely out of diapers. He couldn't remember her face, let alone
what she'd called him, and at the lowest points in the teenager's tem-
pestuous relationship with his dad—which is to say, about once a
day—the elder Van Arsdale was not above throwing that fact in his
son's face. John Van Arsdale acted as though Jasper's intelligence and
eloquence were an indictment of his own failure to raise himself in
the world, and all too often Jasper played into his dad's inferiority
complex by talking down to him like some smarmy district attorney
grilling a country bumpkin on the witness stand. Why couldn't he
have said "Fuck you" like a normal teenager?

But in another minute the boy's anger had faded to its customary
level, and he fished a pair of boxers out of the general disarray on his
floor, did thirteen quick pushups (he had a thing for prime numbers),
then hopped in the shower. As he washed, he searched his body for
clues to what had gone down at last night's party: hickies, love bites,
bruises, maybe a phone number Magic Markered onto his palm or
the shaft of his penis. But, physically at least, there was no evidence
anything had happened. The most distinct memory Jasper had was of
something warm and round and full in each hand. Whoever she was,
she'd had good tits. Michaela had good tits. Please, Jasper thought,
please let it have been Michaela.

A good half hour after his dad woke him, the teenager shuffled into the kitchen dressed in a pair of green nylon mesh shorts and a wrinkled T-shirt that had seen cleaner days. A tattered Dearborn sweatshirt hung on a chair where he'd tossed it after practice yesterday, splotches of mud on the chest, a jaundiced stain prominently ringing the collar. As Jasper pulled the fragrant garment over his uncombed mop of brown hair he promised himself that he really *would* do laundry this weekend, or at least get Michaela to do it for him. Assuming she was still talking to him.

Mincing across the cold linoleum on his bare feet, he made his way to the counter. He poured himself a cup of coffee, then offered the pot to his dad. The pot wobbled in his hand, and a few drops of coffee added themselves to the panoply of stains on the linoleum, but neither man noticed. Jasper was staring at his dad and his dad was staring at his paper. For a long moment the only sound in the room was the hum of the refrigerator.

Jasper caved first.

"Top you off?"

Van Arsdale didn't look up.

"Why, thank you, son."

Jasper poured his dad's coffee, then made himself a bowl of cereal and sat down at the table. A tall glass containing a single purple daylily sat in the center of the table—a slightly incongruous detail in what was obviously a bachelor pad, and a rough one at that. It made more sense, however, when you realized the elder Van Arsdale bred *Hemerocallis* varietals and sold them to the second-homers who made the two-and-a-half-hour trek up from New York City on the weekends. Jasper knew he was supposed to comment on the flower, which was not only the first of the season, but one of John Van Arsdale's own creations besides. *Hemerocallis* "Amelia V.A."

Jasper stared resolutely at the purple, gold-fringed petals as his dad's chair scraped back from the table. The rubber soles of Van Arsdale's Bean boots squeaked on the linoleum, and then there was a clunk as his dad set his cup of coffee on the counter. He opened a cabinet, pulled down a bottle, poured a finger of applejack into his Folger's. Faint clinks as he stirred the liquor into his coffee as though it were milk.

Jasper waited. A sip. A sigh. Then:

"Cold out today. Wet. Need a little something to warm me up."

"*There* we go." Jasper stood up so suddenly his chair tipped backwards and the flower wobbled in its glass. The glass didn't fall but the chair did, and Jasper kicked it out of his way.

"What the—" Van Arsdale almost spilled his coffee, but didn't. "What the hell're you shouting about?" He put one hand on the counter, shielding the unlabeled bottle filled with ruddy brown liquid.

" '*Cold out today*.' God, you don't even *try* anymore."

"Jap?"

"Don't *call* me that!"

Jasper kicked the back door open and grabbed the pair of mud-encrusted running shoes on the top step. The wet grass was cold and slick beneath his bare feet, and he slipped more than once as he made his way down the hill. But he didn't stop to put on his shoes.

He waited for the screen door to slam behind him. It didn't.

Fuck you, Dad, he thought. I'm *not* turning around.

"I'll be in the field if you need me," his dad called after him finally. "I picked up some cold cuts for lunch. They're in the fridge."

As opposed to the linen closet, or the washing machine. No, Jasper added to himself. Those were good places to keep bottles of liquor, not lunch meat.

"Cakes said she saw a suit at the Thrift might fit you," Van Arsdale spoke into his son's silence. "For your graduation. Said she put it on hold if you want to try it on."

Great. The *perfect* cap to a *perfect* fucking morning: Cakes. His dad was dating a forty-seven-year-old peroxide blonde who called herself Cakes—who was now, apparently, picking out secondhand suits for him to wear to his own graduation. *Cakes*, for God's sake.

As he stepped into the dusty air of the barn, the screen door finally slammed. In his kennel Gunther barked once, and then there was just the rain, throbbing on the zinc roof. Jasper dropped his shoes on the ground next to one of several wooden barrels:

Van Arsdale Home-Brewed Apple Brandy
Distilled from His Own Orchards

There was a slug in the right shoe, and it exploded around Jasper's toes when he shoved his foot in. Jasper would think of that slug just before he died—the coldness of its innards, the antennas feebly twitching—but that was still a long time in the future. It was barely nine o'clock in the morning, and, if Q.'s $29,000 watch had been right, he still had ten more hours to live in his mother-born body.

5

Ileana checked her pulse as she walked after her target. It was her first hunt in more than a year. More importantly, it was her first hunt on her own, and she was going to play it by the book. Every time she complained that the Legion was taking too long to come up with a new partner for her, she was told someone was "looking into it." It was "a slow process." There was "a dearth of suitable candidates" but one would be selected as soon as "humanly possible." Ileana suspected the truth was that the Legion was losing interest in the hunt. It was prohibitively expensive, for one thing, not to mention risky—and not just for the hunters, as the circumstances of Alec's death testified.

She drew a circle in her mind now, of the kind witches were said to use to contain demons when they summoned them. A thick ring of powdered gypsum made iridescent by a tincture of silver dust (not plain blackboard chalk, as so many movies depicted it). Within its protective boundary she allowed certain memories to take shape. Memories of that terrible day in 1992, of the incomprehensible feeling of being a stranger—a prisoner—in her own flesh, a helpless observer of the depraved, degrading acts her flesh performed. The things her hands reached for, the objects she put in her mouth. On the worst days, the days when her own continued existence seemed too oppressive to contemplate, she forced herself to think of all the reasons she had to go on living. In the years before Alec died she'd always managed to come up with three or four, sometimes even half a dozen, but since he'd been killed she found herself falling back on just one: revenge. But now, as she checked her pulse against the second hand of the watch he'd given her, she put aside ideas like *hand*, like *mouth*, let go of words like *revenge* and *reason*. She forced herself to reach past the limits of bone and blood, of muscle, tendon and ligament. Any athlete could train those parts of the body. The real key was endocrinology. The glands, the hormones they secreted. Before Francois Dumas had poured himself another shot of Cocker Spaniard, Ileana's liver and kidneys had neutralized the alcohol she'd consumed, even as her pineal and pituitary and thyroid glands replaced it with a finely calibrated chemical cocktail no mixologist could've dreamed of, let alone concocted. Epinephrine to boost her heart rate and insulin to stimulate the metabolism of glucose, endorphins to increase her resistance to pain and serotonin to keep her focused.

If you could somehow distill the microliters of fluid she produced in the few seconds before she entered the hotel lobby, they wouldn't have filled a teaspoon. Yet by the time she entered the room Ileana had become as taut as a wire, knew she could outrun an Olympic sprinter, outbox a heavyweight. For the next several minutes at least, she was a match for any human being in the world, save perhaps Antonio Soma. Her only real advantage was that the Mogran didn't know that.

Mogran was another word she tried to avoid, at least while she was hunting. She thought of him only as a demon—a demon whose circle of protection just happened to be a human being named Antonio Soma.

When she emerged into the lobby, however, her quarry was already gone. Damn it, she cursed. She swung by the desk and shot a glance into Soma's cubbyhole. The note was still there. That, at least, was good news.

She went up to her room and took a moment to collect herself. It was every bit as important to power down, as it were, as to prepare for a fight. To neutralize the chemicals that had been released lest they leave her nervous system so highly strung that it crashed. There was a liter bottle of water on the dresser—a local brand, Source of the Nile—and she opened it, drained half at a gulp. Sinking on the bed, she closed her eyes and reviewed what she knew about this particular demon.

It had first surfaced in Singapore. It was a hard place for a white face like Ileana's to disappear, but the demon had been in the grip of the frenzy, and she knew it wouldn't be paying much attention to the local scenery, archaeological or human. But it had been difficult to pin down for precisely the same reason. It must've jumped twenty times in half as many days, leaving behind a trail of bruises and broken bones, STDs and traumatized psyches—some merely battered and confused, others permanently unbalanced. It had only killed once though. Twice if you counted the man who was executed—hanged, in public—for a crime he professed no memory of, right until the noose was slipped around his neck.

After that she lost it. She used the downtime to interview some of its victims—those that could still talk anyway. Most had no idea what had happened to them, and, as a consequence, no real under-standing of what they were telling her. Possession had been a jolt to their mental processes so extreme it registered as little more than am-nesia or nightmares. But a few remembered what they had done, the inexplicable violence and even more incomprehensible fucking, and one or two told her about extraordinary acts of strength and agility, perceptions that seemed beyond human ken. One or two even spoke of memories that couldn't have been theirs. It was these last she fo-cused on, using everything from feminine wiles to hypnosis to POW interrogation tactics to glean whatever residue of its own identity the demon had left in its victims' minds. She cross-referenced the snip-pets of information she extracted with the Legion's database until fi-nally one name emerged.

Malachi.

When Ileana first reviewed the data, she was amazed he hadn't been eliminated already. He was sloppy, almost tauntingly so. Left traces of himself everywhere. As far as she could tell, the only things that saved him were the speed of his frenzies and the length of his lulls—he could go through fifty bodies in two months, then hole up in one poor soul for half a century. But that was getting ahead of the story.

In the beginning, he'd been nothing more than the son of a seventeenth-century cobbler in Old Salem, Massachusetts. At the ripe old age of nine, the boy had been caught *in flagrante delicto* with his own mother. Believing only witchcraft could cause such aberrant behavior, mother and son had been tried by the traditional method: they were sewn into a sack and tossed in Steney's Pond. According to legend, if the suspect drowned, it was taken as proof of innocence, and he or she was given a proper burial in the cemetery at the base of Gallows Hill. But if after three minutes the accused was still alive, then demonic aid was clearly present; the witch would be pulled from the water, and promptly burned at the stake. In Malachi's case, he and his mother both drowned. The mother, whose name had been lost to history, remained dead. But the son . . . the son came back.

Perhaps because of the horrific nature of his death, the beginning of the demon's reign looked more like revenge than the typical random frenzy: the Legion suspected him of being behind more than a dozen cases of supposed witchcraft in and around Salem—fourteen people executed for pranks Malachi had pulled while in possession of their bodies, before he suddenly abandoned his hometown and melted into the larger world. Every seventy-five to a hundred years the trail would get hot again. There was persuasive evidence he'd spent time in France during the Revolution, in America during the Civil War, in Germany during the Holocaust. He liked judges, generals, camp directors—people who held the power of life and death over masses of individuals, rather than just one or two. For that reason it was impossible to pin down his body count, but even by the standards of the Mogran he was a vile specimen.

By comparison, his recent behavior was low-key, almost lethargic. After leaving Singapore, he'd reemerged in Sydney, then Cape Town,

Lagos, Fez. Fez is where he'd taken Soma. The fact that he was still in Soma's body in Darfur was a good sign. Suggested the frenzy was winding down. Ileana had moved in quickly. For two weeks Malachi stayed one step ahead of her, but for whatever reason he hadn't jumped, and now, finally, she had her chance.

She opened her eyes, slipped a finger under Alec's watch. Her pulse was a steady thirty-five beats per minute, her senses as sharp as if she'd awakened from a full night's sleep. In a moment she'd changed from fatigues and tank top to wraparound skirt and spaghetti-strap top. The skirt reached past her knees, but it had a long seam that would allow for easy kicking should it come to that; the top was yellow, and had a tiny silk flower sewn between her breasts. Something to draw the demon's eyes, keep them from hers. She put the boots back on though. They were a bit clunky perhaps, but the right had a sheath stitched inside it that held a five-inch stone blade. The knife was Aztecan, had once been used to cut beating hearts out of living victims. If all went well, she'd put it to its ancient use in a matter of minutes.

She slipped her finger beneath Alec's watch one last time. Not to check her pulse but to stroke the scar that transversed her wrist beneath its wide band. It was Alec who dragged her back to life after her own demon had shed her flesh like a butterfly abandoning its cocoon, and Alec's memory that kept her going still. A wave of longing washed over her, of loss and love followed by hatred. She would make the Mogran pay. Malachi and every other one she could sink her blade into, until they were gone.

All of them. Gone.

Only then would she lose the taint her own demon had left beneath her skin fifteen years ago. Only then would she know peace.

6

The rain let up as the sun rose. Bands of steam hung in the hot, windless air. In short order Jasper shed both sweatshirt and T-shirt, but perspiration still rolled down his skin. But, though the teenager would've never admitted it (at least not to his dad), there was something pleasurable in his task, despite the repetitiveness and muscle ache. For Jasper, moving–action–playing–*work*–was a joy, whether it was climbing trees or playing baseball or that modern dance class he'd taken on a dare from Q. Even turning over a quarter acre of wet soil with a pitchfork. His body never failed to surprise him with the things it could do. Had never let him down either, as both the shelf full of trophies in the living room and the smoothly turned furrows of earth attested.

Jasper worked patiently on the garden, distributed each heavy load evenly between shoulders and biceps, hamstrings and thighs. By lunchtime he'd fallen into a stabbing, hip-thrusting rhythm that had more than a touch of the sexual to it. God, he was horny. He was seventeen years old for fuck's sake. Was it any wonder he'd ended up in that closet last night? And why *wouldn't* Michaela put out? It's not like he just wanted to use her or something. He *loved* her. Had already made a pact to go to the same college with her, share an apartment, desired nothing more than to make her breakfast and serve it to her in bed every day for the rest of their lives. Meanwhile, Q. and Sila had been doing it just about everywhere for the past year. On her bed. On his bed. On her parents' bed. On his parents' bed. Hell, they'd even done it on Jasper's *dad's* bed, while he and Michaela sat downstairs and tried to watch a DVD. It wasn't fair. It wasn't *right*. Of course, even less right was the idea that he might've finally had sex with her and been too drunk to remember. Or—the ultimate disaster—the idea that he'd had sex with someone else, *and* forgotten about it too.

The garden was only half finished, but Jasper figured it was well past noon, and he'd put off talking to his girlfriend long enough. He needed to find out what had happened last night. He stabbed the pitchfork in the earth and headed down to the river to make sure he wasn't disturbed—his dad had checked on his progress twice already—but well before he reached the water, a voice floated to his ears.

"'Ere we go!"

There was the *pop* of a carbonated beverage and, a moment later, a long "Aahh!" The voice was male, loud, off-key; the "aahh" sounded more like a mating cat than lip-smacking satisfaction.

Jasper would know that voice anywhere. It could only be Mason "Jarhead" West, a twenty-something gas jockey who worked at the Stewart's on Route 9H, where he sold beer to high school kids in exchange for invites to their parties. For such a big man, he was surprisingly genial—docile when sober, positively puppylike when drunk, which was most of the time. He wasn't "short-bus stupid," as Q. had once put it, but it did seem to take an effort for him to close his mouth. The impression wasn't helped by the fact that he was also partially deaf, and had the hard-of-hearing's habit of tonelessly shouting everything he said.

Jasper peeked out from behind a clump of mountain laurel. Jarhead had one foot on top of a Styrofoam cooler, his love handles spilling from the ragged remains of a Hudson High football jersey.

"You gotta thread it *through* the body, Danny. Damn fish'll just nibble it off if you do it that way."

Jasper noticed the second person now, a tall skinny boy—no, a tall skinny girl with dark hair cut in a retro '80s wedge that angled in front of her right eye like a pirate's patch. She was hunched over something, a fishhook apparently, and her tight gray T-shirt had rolled over her waist, exposing a couple inches of pale taut tummy. When she glanced up Jasper saw that she was *way* too hot for Jarhead. Must be his sister, he thought. Or a dyke.

"Fuck you, Jarhead," this girl—Danny—was saying. "Where'd you get these worms anyway? They keep breaking."

"What?" Jarhead threw his head back, drained a good third of his can.

"I *said*," Danny shouted, "the worms keep *breaking.*"

"*Breaking?*"

"Breaking, ripping, whatever. They tear in half when I stick the hook in."

"That's why I said you gotta thread 'em *through* the body. What are you, deaf?" Jarhead's donkey laugh echoed over the water.

"Whatever." Danny looked up again, and from his hiding place Jasper saw that her face was almost as angular as her haircut: long chin, sharp cheek and jawbones. Too severe for him, but still, he knew she was the kind of girl some guys cream over. Nice tits too, especially for such a thin chick. "Keep it down, would you?" Danny said now. "You'll scare away the fish. And gimme a beer already, for Christ's sake."

Jasper waited until Jarhead bent over, his pants riding dangerously low and exposing two half moons of pale ass cheek. He cupped his hands over his mouth and boomed in his best megaphone voice: "Attention poacher! You are in violation of local ordinance OU812! In compliance with state law YRUGay, I am hereby placing your hairy ass under arrest!"

Jarhead stood up so quickly he knocked over the cooler and sprawled in a spray of ice water and silver cans of beer. Danny jerked up, and, judging from her high-pitched yelp, caught her finger on the hook she'd been holding. Jasper stumbled out from behind the bush, laughing hysterically.

"Oh, I got you bitches. I fucking got you good!"

"Who—Jasper?" Jarhead said, eyes narrowing, jaw hanging lower than ever. "Man, you fucking scared the shit out of me!"

"You know this idiot?" Danny stuck her bleeding finger in her mouth, then spat it out again. "Aw, fuck. Worm guts. Fucking *gross.*"

Jarhead joined Jasper in a fresh round of laugher. "This is Jasper, man. Jasper, this is Danny. She works down at Stewart's with me. Hey, how 'bout that party at Caitlin Reese's last night? The bitches was off the hook!"

Danny rolled her eyes. "Jarhead, don't talk black."

"Don't talk back?"

"Don't talk *black.*" Danny wiped blood and fish guts on her jeans. "It's uncool when white guys talk black. Cute stunt," she added, walking over to Jasper and sticking out her hand.

Even in sandals she was about a half inch taller than Jasper. Her shirt had rolled even higher on her wasp-thin waist, showing off a sliver of navel ring. Jasper found himself tempted to grab it rather than her hand.

"Sorry 'bout that," he said, blushing a little. "Didn't realize there was a lady present."

"There are ladies around?" Danny let out a long, practiced burp. "I had no idea."

"Shit, man!" Jarhead said now. "Who was that shortie you dragged into the closet last night? I bet *she* was a helluva ride."

At the mention of the girl in the closet, Jasper pulled his eyes from Danny's and stood up straighter.

"Don't talk shit about my girlfriend, Jarhead."

"*Girlfriend?*" Jarhead's shout could've been heard on the other side of the river. "Don't tell me that was Michaela. I ain't *that* stupid. Not unless you turned Michaela into some hot ass Indian chick. Woo-hoo!"

Jasper felt all the blood drain from his head, even as Jarhead laughed and tossed him a beer. It banged painfully off his kneecap, which sent Jarhead into a fresh fit of braying laughter. But Jasper hardly heard him.

Indian? Really? *Indian?*

There were exactly two Indian girls at Dearborn, and only one of them was in the senior class. Only one of them had been at the party last night.

Sila Patel.

Q.'s girlfriend.

Jasper and Danny bent over at the same time to pick up his beer and came dangerously close to bumping heads. Danny grabbed the silver can and held it while Jasper opened it. White foam bubbled out over both of their hands and Jasper felt his cheeks go bright red.

"Girlfriend, huh?" Danny smirked. "What a lucky, lucky lady."

Jasper jerked awake when his cell rang. The sun had moved behind the hilltop at his back. He must've been asleep for hours. His first thought was of the half-finished garden. Great, he thought. One more thing for his old man to get on his case about.

The phone rang again.

"Fuck," Danny hissed. She held a long fishing pole deftly in her hands, looked like Huck Finn crossed with a runway model. Jasper clapped his legs shut to hide his hard-on, but Danny seemed intent on the river. "Answer that thing before you scare off the fucking *fish*."

Jasper pulled his phone out. "Q BALL." Somewhat nervously, he flipped it open.

Q.'s voice sniggered into his ear in a broad imitation of an Indian accent. "Who is a naughty boy then?"

Jasper felt a moment of hope. Q. wouldn't be teasing him if the girl in the closet had been Sila, right? It's not like Jarhead West was the most reliable witness in the world.

"Oh man. What did I fucking *do* last night?"

"Fuck," Danny hissed again. "The fucking fish. *Dude.*"

Q. dropped the fake accent, and Jasper's hopes went out like a match dropped in a toilet bowl. "Don't worry, buddy. My girlfriend, your girlfriend. Why should I care who you fuck? Last day of your life—anything goes, right?"

"Oh fuck, man. I'm sorry. I was just so drunk. *Fuck*. Do you know if Michaela saw me?"

Q. laughed into the phone. "Why don't you ask her yourself?"

"What? She's there?"

Instead of Q's voice, Jasper heard Michaela's, faintly, as if from a distance. "Fuck off, Q. I don't want to talk to the prick."

The Indian voice came back.

"The little mistress is sorely aggrieved. Methinks you will very much have to make it up to her in person. I shall convey her to your crappy abode in my chariot of Porscheness in three shakes of a water buffalo's tail."

"Q., no," Jasper said, and heard Michaela's voice say the same thing in the background (or backseat apparently). But Q. spoke over him.

"Get ready for the ride of your life, buddy boy."

With that, the line went dead.

7

Ileana looked both ways before stepping into the hallway, then headed toward Soma's room. She paused outside the door. Even as she reached for the handle, however, she heard a creaking floorboard, then noticed a crack of light emanating from within, crossed by a flickering shadow. Her hand snaked toward the blade in her boot. Epinephrine, insulin, serotonin flooded her bloodstream.

The door swung open. Ileana jerked back, but it was only a maid, leaning heavily into a cart of cleaning supplies. The girl was pleasant looking, with rich dark skin and full breasts—which Ileana couldn't help but notice because the girl was in the act of tucking something into her bra. Ileana gave her the benefit of the doubt and assumed it was a tip, and not a theft.

She cleared her throat quietly. The maid gasped, looked up, then cast her eyes to the floor. Ileana wondered if perhaps she'd been too generous in her assessment.

"Excuse me, ma'am. I was only–"

But Ileana didn't care what the maid had been up to. Gesturing silently for her to pass, she stepped out of the way. She waited for the cart to round the corner before nudging the door open with her boot.

The chamber was a mirror of anonymous hotel rooms around the world. A pair of double beds, a desk with a glass top protecting the wood, a small TV hanging from a ceiling bracket. A dim lamp on the table between the beds cast a sulfurous glow in the center of the room, but the corners were steeped in shadow. The near bed, she noticed, was crisply made up, but the other was wrinkled. Not unmade, but rumpled, as though someone had lain atop it. Odd, Ileana thought, given that the maid had just been there. But perhaps Soma had told her to leave it. And where *was* Soma anyway? If she'd waited too long—if she had let the demon get away yet again—she would never forgive herself.

Soma's bags were on the far side of the bed, unpacked. The clothes were in the dresser drawers, various documents stacked atop it, but as she sifted through them for signs of an itinerary she heard the faint lap of water and froze in her tracks.

There was a louder splash, unmistakable this time. Someone was in the bathtub.

She cursed under her breath, reminded herself she was on her own. No partner, no backup if she got in trouble. She headed straight for the bathroom, where Antonio Soma lay naked in the tub.

"Remember me? From the bar?"

Soma's eyelids fluttered, as though he'd fallen asleep in the bath. *"Qué?"*

Ileana took a step forward, exposed a generous portion of thigh. "I was able to persuade the clerk to tell me your room number."

A wondrous, slightly greedy smile smeared itself across the journalist's face. His body, lean but muscular, was deeply tanned, and his elbows hung casually over either side of the tub. He didn't bother trying to cover himself. Ileana wondered if this was the demon acting, or if Malachi was allowing a bit of Soma's own personality to come through. Mogran loved to do that. Release—augment—certain urges already present in their host's psyche, especially when they wanted him to remember what he'd done after the demon had vacated the premises.

Ileana sat down on the edge of the tub. She felt Soma's eyes devouring her body, settling for a second on the flower between her breasts, then flitting to her face, her eyes.

"Well, *hello*."

Damn he's good, Ileana thought. *It's* good. *It* is not human, not anymore, and *it* wants me to like Soma.

She reached down, trailed her fingers through the warm bath water. Soma's stomach was firm beneath her touch. She let the fingers of her left hand walk south, never taking her eyes from his, even as her right slipped toward her boot, seeking the familiar feel of the bound leather strips of the knife's handle.

Soma closed his eyes. His hips swayed beneath her touch. "I feel as though I have been dreaming, and have awakened into an even better reality. *Dios mio!*" he hissed, as her palm glided over the tip of his cock. At least *that* part of him was showing signs of waking up.

"I hate to disappoint you, Antonio, but this is your worst nightmare."

Ileana's hand closed around Soma's penis. She lifted him from the tub as though the swollen member she clutched were nothing more than the handle on a cumbersome suitcase. Soma's head fell back, snapping against the rim of the tub.

He screamed—squealed really—even as his eyes flew open, their dreamy expression replaced by one of concentrated horror.

He saw the blade in her hand.

"No! Por favor, no!"

The basalt knife was six hundred years old. It was brittle and razor thin but sharper than steel. It would have snapped if she'd hit the pelvic plate, but Ileana knew exactly where to strike, what angle to turn it. With a deft motion, she plunged the blade into the groin and opened Soma's femoral artery. The penis, half severed from the body, and a six-inch fountain of blood shot up between her fingers, spurting in time with her victim's beating heart.

She dropped Soma back in the tub. His head hit the rim again but he didn't cry out. His skin had already gone ashen, his eyes cloudy, confused. In seconds his body was concealed beneath the crimson water. His mouth opened as if to speak, but Ileana struck again, this time driving the blade through the thick cartilage of the esophagus, through the hollow of the jawbone and up into the oral cavity. The pressure of the blade caused Soma's tongue to stick out of his mouth obscenely, and all he could do was sputter cupfuls of blood and bile. His arms lifted weakly, then fell back. A last breath rattled from his throat, and he was still.

She leaned in close. "That was for Alec." Then, in a solemn voice, she said the words he had taught her:

"Death is in my sight today, like the clearing of the sky.
"Death is in my sight today, like sitting under an awning
     on a windy day.
"Death is in my sight today, like the smell of myrrh and
     the perfume of lotuses.
"Death is in my sight today, like the well-trodden path by
     which a man returns home."

The poem was culled from an Egyptian prayer, older than the pyramids. The hunters' psalm, Alec called it. Lest they forget the true nature of what they did. Ileana recited the penultimate line:

"Malachi and Antonio Soma. Though you are dead, your names live on."

There was one more line, but that would have to wait until her last hunt. Until the last of the Mogran had been killed.

Beneath the armor of the chemicals augmenting and guiding her own body, Ileana felt a trace of pride. Her first hunt without Alec had ended in a clean kill. He would have been impressed. He would have also told her not to lose focus. She wasn't done yet.

She steeled herself for the last part. She pulled the plug, let the bloody water drain from the tub. Soma's body was milky white beneath its pink tinge, like an Easter egg dipped in a cup of red dye. She severed penis and testes first, then, holding the torso upright by the hair and allowing the serrated edge of the stone blade to do the work, she removed the head from the neck. She worked slowly, never hacking or sawing. Slicing. Dissecting. This was surgery, not mutilation. Alec had referred to it as insurance. The demons could repair extraordinary damage, but no one had ever heard of them regrowing an organ, let alone a head. She would have preferred to burn the corpse, but there would be no good way of getting it out of the hotel unnoticed.

As she stood to wash the blood from her hands, she caught a glimpse of her own reflection in the mirror. The cold eyes, the expressionless face. She hadn't even broken a sweat. This was what her work had done to her, she thought. Was it worth it? She caught a glimpse of the carcass in the tub and had to wonder. Her mother had wanted her to be a nurse. Ileana supposed you could call this a kind of palliative care.

She wrapped Soma's head in one towel, his genitals in another, drew the curtain on the tub. He deserved that much privacy, even if the Mogran didn't. Some blood had seeped into the links of Alec's watch, she noticed, and she sifted through Soma's toiletry bag until she found his toothbrush, squeezed a little Crest on the bristles and used it to scrub the watch clean. The carrageenan brought up the shine on the silver.

Almost unconsciously, she checked her pulse as she worked. It was already down to fifty beats per minute. Forty. Thirty-eight. Even by Legionnaire standards, Alec had told her, she had a heart like an elephant.

8

Up at the house, Jasper put on a pair of blue jeans and the only long-sleeved T-shirt he could find that didn't actually stink. On its front was a picture of a man skiing off the side of a mountain. The logo read "Dead Man's Sportswear: Fit for Your Own Funeral," which made Jasper think about Q.'s stupid game from the night before—a game that, apparently, he was still playing. Had he really stolen his dad's $250,000 Porsche? He must genuinely have a death wish.

He paused at the top of the staircase, listening for any noise from the first floor, then tiptoed down the steps. He was about to slip outside when he heard the familiar *clunk* behind him in the darkened living room. Glass bottle, wooden table, the quiet sigh of addiction appeased one sip at a time.

Jasper froze. His eyes rested on the dingy white wall, on which hung a school picture of himself in ninth grade beside a faded photograph of his mother holding an infant Jasper in her arms. Next to them was his dad's diploma. Greenville High, not Dearborn—not that "fancy-pants academy" his "scholarship boy" attended. The little white rectangle was wrinkled and mottled with beer stains from a graduation party twenty-six years ago. For the first time in years Jasper noticed how the stains blurred his dad's name on the diploma: "John Van Ars–e."

For a brief moment Jasper felt the weight of the future pressing down on shoulders that were still sore from turning over wet earth for four hours. He made himself the kind of promises that only a seventeen-year-old can make. That he would not end up like his dad. That he would be different. He would not be—

There was a second *clunk* behind him. A second sigh.

He would not be Jasper Van Ars—e.

A moment later he'd slipped outside. A sickle moon hung low on the horizon. How had it gotten so late? If this *was* his last day on earth, he'd pretty much wasted it. Turning over soil, knocking back a few cold ones, sleeping the afternoon away. Not exactly *memento mori*.

Bluish light outlined the budding branches of the two huge beeches that overhung the driveway, and the wet air smelled fecund, primordial even. Heavy, like soil, but also full of promise. Maybe the night would turn out okay. Maybe Michaela would give him a big kiss, tell him last night was her fault for holding out so long. Maybe Q. would pop in the White Stripes or D12 and they'd cruise Main Street with the bass turned up so loud the windows in the shops would rattle in their frames. Yeah, and then maybe he'd come home and instead of finding his dad passed out on the couch, the old man would be sitting at the kitchen table with Jasper's Harvard acceptance letter, along with the notice that he'd received a full scholarship, all he had to do was show up in the fall with a suitcase and a smile . . .

Yeah, right.

He heard the car before he saw it, the engine cutting through the curves like a power saw. Q. hadn't been kidding. He'd actually taken his dad's Porsche. Jasper could have sworn the wheels were off the ground when it crested the hill north of the Van Arsdales' driveway. When it landed, the car flattened itself on the roadway and shot toward Jasper.

Jasper put his hand out as though he were thumbing a ride, then flipped his palm at the last minute and stuck up his middle finger. Brakes squealed; antilocks held the car in its track like a jetfighter landing on an aircraft carrier. Jasper half expected a *Back to the Future* hiss to escape the car with the rolled-down window, but all he got was a driving beat—Danger Mouse or DJ Shadow, some overproduced crap like that.

Q.'s smile was wide, his teeth white and sharp in his light brown face. Sila sat in the passenger's seat, Michaela in back. Both girls refused to look at him.

"Feldspar!" Q. shouted over the bass.

"Mohammed."

"What? Real names? *Some*body's in a mood."

"Whatever." And then, steeling himself. "Hey, Sil."

Sila pushed the door open. The expression on her face was tortured, embarrassed, pissed off, apologetic.

"You want the suicide seat?"

Jasper walked around to the passenger side. He tried to catch Michaela's eye as he walked, but she turned her head. "Nah, I'll, uh—" He nodded at the back. In the shadowy compartment behind Q., Michaela hid her face behind her dirty blond hair.

"Yo, Jasper," Q. said from the driver's seat. "In or out, buddy. This baby wants to *fly*." He stomped on the accelerator, bathing Jasper and Sila in a cloud of exhaust.

A moment later the new antiques stores on Catskill's Main Street were whizzing by the Porsche's windows, Louis Quatorze fading into French country faster than you could say "guillotine." In the minuscule backseat, Jasper could feel the engine's throb in his prostate. His spine was curved into a capital C, his knees wedged against the back of Sila's seat and rubbing against his cheekbones. He and Q. had been lusting over Mohammed Qusay Sr.'s 500-horsepower fiftieth-birthday present to himself for the past six months, but this was hardly the introduction he'd been hoping for.

"Yo, Q. You didn't tell me you needed to know yoga to get in the backseat."

Q. turned the radio down. "Look, everybody. The Jazz-man makes a joke. He fucks my girlfriend in a closet and then he makes a joke. Now *that's* what I call a friend."

"We didn't—"

"One-oh-five! One hundred and fucking *five* on Main Street! Dude, this car is better than sex! Now you've even got a basis for comparison, Jasper. Ain't that fortunate?"

"Q." Sila tried again, but this time it was Michaela who spoke over her.

"Hey, Q." She leaned into the space between the two seats. "Maybe you want to head to the Thruway or something, get away from all this traffic?"

As she leaned back, Jasper looked at her.

"Hey."

The Porsche's backseat was only slightly wider than a bathroom stall, but a third person could have fit between Jasper and his girl-friend. Michaela made a sound that could have been "Hey" or "Hmph" or "Fuck off, you fucking cheating bastard," and pulled her hair back over her face.

Jasper stared at her a moment longer, then looked out the window at the landscape speeding by. He remained lost in his thoughts until he heard his name, and realized Q. had said it several times.

"Aw, is Jasper mad?"

Q. had adjusted the rearview mirror so he could look into Jasper's eyes.

"Is Jasper giving Q-ball the silent treatment? Maybe Jasper wishes he was in his drunk daddy's white-trash pickup instead of his sand nigger best friend's Porsche? Huh? Is that what Jap-Jap is thinking?"

Jasper smacked the back of Sila's seat in frustration.

"Look, man, what's up? Have you lost your fucking mind? Seri-ously. You need to tell me what's going on before I go ape-shit on your ass."

Q. reached for the radio. Trippy beats filled the car's interior. Jasper recognized the song after a moment. DJ Shadow. "Blood on the Motorway."

He squirmed forward between the seats. "Q." he said in a danger-ously flat voice. "If you don't turn that fucking radio off and *talk* to me, I swear to Christ I will punch in the goddamn console."

His hand balled into a fist, but Q. beat him to it. He punched the radio, and in the sudden silence his slightly high-pitched "Mother-*fuck*!" had a boyish ring to it. "God *damn* it," he said, laughing ruefully, shaking his hand.

"Q., baby," Sila said, her voice neither gentle nor cold. "You're bleeding."

She reached for his hand, but Q. slapped it away.

"Don't *touch* me, you fucking whore! Don't fucking—aw, fuck!" Q. punched the console again. "Fuck fuck fuck!" he yelled, punctuating each *fuck* with another punch. Plastic cracked. Something went flying. When Q. reached up to the rearview mirror, Jasper could see a line of blood snaking down the back of his hand and smearing the thick gold face of his new watch.

Q. fixed Jasper's eyes in the mirror.

"You fucking *fucked* my girlfriend last night."

Jasper thought about telling Q. he hadn't meant to, that he didn't even remember it. Somehow he didn't think that would help. In the silence, Sila whispered, "We didn't fuck, okay?"

"Damn, Q.," Jasper finally said. "I'm sorry, man. Really sorry."

"Aw, don't worry about it, Jasp," Q. spoke as if all he'd lost was a round of bingo. "You were just acting like it was your last night on earth, right? Nobody wants to die a virgin. I guess my girlfriend's just easier than yours."

"Q.," Sila said exasperatedly. "We *didn't*—"

"Yeah, yeah, yeah," Q. cut her off. "Whatever, babe, it's the thought that counts." He looked back at Jasper, and when he spoke again there was a strangely melancholy note in his voice, as if he were almost sad his best friend and girlfriend hadn't actually hooked up. "Sil tells me you passed out before anything could happen. Normally I'd be insulted on her behalf, but considering the circumstances I guess I should say thanks for following in your old man's drunken footsteps."

The car was approaching the tollbooth to the Rip Van Winkle Bridge. The Hudson rolled lazily in the moonlight, rent here and there by the wake of a late fisherman heading in for the night.

The dark water reflected the white fishhook of the moon so sharply that Jasper felt he was racing high in the sky, the earth receding below him like a pebble dropped into the infinite ocean of space.

"Hey, why don't you stop at that Stewart's where Jarhead works? He'll sell us another six, we can park somewhere, get buzzed, what do you say?" Jasper didn't mention that Jarhead was probably still drunk on his dad's property on the other side of the river. If he could get Q. to stop the car, he'd call up Michaela's dad. Mr. Szarko would come pick them up, no questions asked. He was good about that kind of thing.

Jasper could see his friend's eyes sharpen in the mirror. "Nah. I don't feel like getting drunk." He had to wipe blood off the face of the Patek Philippe to see what time it was. "We've only got a few minutes left. I wanna have all my wits about me."

"Yo, cut it out with the twenty-four hours thing. It's seriously not funny anymore."

Suddenly Sila turned to Q. "Jesus fucking Christ. It's your fucking fault all this happened. I had no idea it wasn't you until Jasper said *Michaela's* name. You told him she would be in that closet, didn't you? You set the whole thing up. Why in the fuck would you *do* something like that?"

Again, silence filled the car. Jasper could see that a muscle in Q.'s cheek was twitching.

"Maybe I wanted to save him," he said in a funny voice. A voice that didn't sound like Q. at all. "Maybe I didn't want him to suffer my fate."

"What the hell are you—"

Sila was cut off by a snuffling, snorting sound, and Jasper realized his friend was fighting back tears. Sila's eyes widened. She put her hand on Q.'s cheek and he shrugged it away, but the gesture was more petulant than angry. She put it back and this time he let it stay. A few seconds later, she took off her seatbelt and leaned over to hold Q. "Baby," Jasper could just barely hear her over the engine. "Oh, my stupid, stupid baby."

A second snort broke from Q.'s mouth, followed by a loud guffaw, and in a voice Jasper almost didn't recognize Q. said,

"Suck it, bitch."

"What the—"

"I said *suck it*." A half-scream escaped Sila's mouth before Q. smashed it into his crotch. "Don't fucking tell me you didn't know. You've wanted to get in Jasper's pants since fifth fucking grade. Now shut up and suck my dick, or I swear to *God* I will drive this car into a fucking tree!"

Q. stomped on the gas and the car surged forward. Trees crowded in close like pylons on a slalom course, and the darkness between them seemed every bit as solid as the trunks. He took both hands off the wheel and the car veered into the left lane. Somehow over the engine's roar Jasper heard the distinct sound of a zipper opening, and then Q. grabbed the wheel and jerked the car to the right. The Porsche fishtailed, the tires screeching across the asphalt.

"Jesus Christ, Q.!" Michaela screamed. "Stop!"

Q.'s eyes—wide, crazy, absolutely alien—found Jasper's in the mirror.

"Listen to me carefully, Jasper."

"Q., stop the car—"

"I said *listen*, Jasper. Go home."

"Q., just stop the car and we'll—"

"*Home*, Jasper. There's no place like home. Home sweet home. A man's home is his castle. *Home*. Go there."

The Porsche picked up speed. The bright digital display read ninety-six miles an hour. 97. 98. 99. Choked sobs came from Sila's body.

I'd steal my old man's Porsche and get Sila to blow me in the front seat, then drive it into a cliff at—

100.

"Q., please. Stop. *Please*."

Q.'s eyes were lidded, a guttural moan came from deep in his throat. The knuckles of his bloody hand were white in their grip on Sila's hair. And then suddenly his eyes snapped open and he slammed the back of his head into the seatrest again and again.

"Remember, Jasper! Home!"

For a moment, Jasper didn't recognize the face in the mirror, so distorted was it by an unfathomable mixture of hatred and ecstasy. With a grunt, Q. jerked the wheel to the left, hard, then let go of it.

"What the–?" he screamed. His hands flew up to cover his face. "No! No! *No!*"

The tail of the car spun beneath Jasper. Panic clutched his guts. But then a strange, almost numbing peace seemed to flood into his body. Time thickened, slowed. Milliseconds fell through eternity like drops from a roof with a hole in it. The engine screamed, the tires squealed. There was a *thunk!* as something broke beneath the chassis.

Yet Jasper felt safe, as though he were cocooned inside a fluid-filled bubble. He heard Michaela scream. He heard Sila scream. He heard Q. scream. They were all screaming, but he was just looking. Looking out the Porsche's tiny window at a solid wall of stone that filled his plane of vision. He could see every striation in the schist, every quartzite crystal and fossilized tree root, every dark vein of granite and sparkling fleck of mica and creamy blue seam of jasper.

The word jogged something in his memory. Jasper? What–*who*– was Jasper?

He felt something squishy between the toes of his right foot, and remembered the slug that had been in his shoe that morning. Remembered the star-shaped violet flower that sat on the breakfast table, the one his dad had bred in honor of his mother, and then he remembered that he hadn't told his dad he loved him. He hadn't told his dad he loved him and he hadn't had sex with his girlfriend– hadn't had sex with Q.'s girlfriend for that matter–and it was this latter fact that sealed his fate. Jasper Van Arsdale was going to die a virgin, and he was going to have eternity to contemplate his mistake.

9

Ileana packed quickly. Exchanged the heavy boots for a pair of huaraches, moved the stone blade to a garter beneath her skirt. The rest, what little there was, she tossed in her duffel.

She never carried much. A change of clothes, her cell, the most recent passport the Legion had issued her. The briefcase she'd lugged through the refugee camps had been a prop for Dumas's benefit—she'd stolen it from a businessman in Fez and had no idea what was inside it. The stone blade was a sentimental accoutrement, but it was easy to transport—it didn't set off the metal detectors at airports. Like the watch, it had been Alec's, but unlike the watch, he had given it to her when he was still alive.

The sound of distant sirens snapped her from her thoughts.

She went to the balcony and peered through the curtains. Two, no, three Sudanese police vehicles squealed to a halt in front of the hotel. It seemed unlikely some other disturbance had brought them here. But how had they discovered Soma's body so quickly?

Ileana stepped back from the balcony. She hurried to the door, cracked it open. The main stairs led to the lobby, but there were fire exits at either end of the hall. As she trotted toward the one on the right, she could hear booted feet on the tiled floors downstairs. There were shouts and cries as guests were confronted by the police.

She reached the stairwell, eased the door open. A pair of uniformed officers were guarding the lower exit. One of them glanced up and started shouting. She jerked back as a hail of bullets ripped through the plaster over her head.

She ducked back into the hallway. She could hear the police galloping upstairs. She ran down the hall to the other fire exit. Just as she was about to duck through the door, a guest came into the hallway in his bathrobe and slippers. His eyes went wide as he saw Ileana running toward him.

"Sorry about this."

"*Pardon*—?"

Ileana took him down with an elbow to the jaw. He dropped like a sack of potatoes. She pulled him through the stairwell door and wedged his bulk against it.

"A piece of advice," she said to the unconscious body. "Next time you hear gunshots, head the *other* way."

She ducked through the far door. The first three rooms were locked but the fourth was open. She slipped inside. She had only a minute or two before the police got the stairwell open. Then, when she whirled around to scan the room, she realized her minutes had been reduced to seconds.

A man and a woman lay on the bed, naked, their mouths already open.

Instinct took over. She reached beneath her skirt and pulled the knife from its garter. She didn't speak, just put the index finger of her free hand to her lips.

The couple stared at her in terror. The man pulled the sheet up to cover his companion's breasts—a touching gesture, considering the dainty little whip and neatly stacked pile of cash on the dresser.

Ileana went to the balcony. The alley appeared to be deserted, but it was still a fifteen-foot drop, and she wasn't Mogran. She couldn't keep flooding her body with hormones without expecting to pay a price.

Someone—the man or the woman—let out a low moan.

"Quiet! Just be quiet and no one will get hurt. Do you understand?"

The couple stared at her blankly, their mouths open as if they were screaming but someone had muted the volume.

Ileana gauged the distance, wondering if she could jump to the next building. Probably not from a standing position, but if she got a running start . . .

Just as she turned to assess the length of the room someone began pounding on the door.

"*Shorta!*" the man and woman began shouting in chorus. "Police! Help!"

Ileana tossed her bag to the street and vaulted over the railing after it. She landed hard but managed to tuck into a roll. She heard her knife clatter across the alleyway, wasted precious seconds groping through the gravel until her fingers locked onto the leather handle. A sentimental accoutrement. But Alec had given it to her.

She grabbed her bag and ran for the far end of the alley. She could feel her system overloading. If she didn't stop soon, she was going to pass out—if her heart didn't simply burst. She gritted her teeth and ran.

"*Tawaqqafa!* Stop! Stop!" Shots rang out. She was so high on endorphins she didn't think she'd know if she'd been hit. Her legs continued pumping, so she assumed she was fine.

She was nearly out of the alley when a vehicle screeched to a stop, blocking the exit. Ileana couldn't tell if it was a cop or not. The breath tore raggedly from her mouth. She didn't have the strength to turn around, let alone attempt to dodge the bullets that waited there.

"Ileana!"

The door swung open, an interior light came on.

Dumas.

"Get in! Now!"

Ileana fell into the Rover as Dumas stomped on the gas pedal. The vehicle lurched forward. The open door smacked into a pylon and slammed shut just as Ileana pulled her leg in.

"Christ," she said, gasping for breath. Her heart was pumping so hard she thought her ribs would crack.

Dumas glanced over and smiled. Her senses, still hyperacute from the hunt, could smell the alcohol on his breath. She hoped he wasn't too drunk to drive, but was far, far too tired to care.

As if reading her mind, Dumas said, "Don't worry, my dear. Everything will be fine."

When the engine cut out she jerked her head up. The lights of downtown Khartoum twinkled on the far side of the water. To her right, a jet hung low in the sky, coming in for a landing at the airport. Somehow—miraculously—they had gotten away.

With an effort she lifted Alec's watch, glanced at the phosphorescent dial. Just after seven. The first thing she'd done when she checked in at the Acropole was find out what flights headed out tonight, so she knew there was a 9:35 to London, where the Legion had arranged a safe house. It would take a little finessing, but she was pretty sure she could get on it.

"Pardon me if I seem ungrateful. But why did you help me? And . . . and *how* did you know I needed help?"

In the long pause before Dumas answered, Ileana registered a change in the car. Realized she couldn't smell the alcohol on Dumas's breath anymore. When he spoke, all trace of an accent was gone.

"Were you aware that this area is known by locals as al-Mogran?"

No, she thought.

"It is an ancient word, referring to the union of the Blue and White Niles to form the single river that was the lifeline of the world's oldest and most enduring civilization."

An image of Soma's mutilated body flashed in her mind. Dear God, no, Ileana thought. It can't be.

"Thousands of years before your paltry Legion began referring to us as Mogran, that is how the Egyptians knew us. As the union of two entities to form a third that was greater than either of them. They worshipped us as gods, which you would do, if you had any sense."

Dumas flipped on the overhead light and turned to face her. The night was nearly as hot as the day, but his face and body were dry, as if he had grown immune to the effects of the desert. A light swam in his eyes, shifting, swirling, as though they were hollow globes filled with luminous fish. She searched for even a trace of the man with whom she had spent the past two weeks but instead saw a nine-year-old boy, bound in a sack with his mother, struggling to hold his breath as silty water seeped through coarse fabric.

"Malachi."

"Huntress," the demon said. "It is so nice to finally make your acquaintance."

10

It was like swimming.

I am thrilled to announce the latest addition to the Cantor family
of fine porcelains

No, not swimming. Drowning.

Ever since I saw taking my own life as a viable option I cannot
say the word

Drowning in words. But not just any words. Thoughts.

There are five thousand men wearing uniforms who are not army but
Even though he has a sister Geoffrey has a special place in my
We are programmed to believe compliments and avoid pain

Other people's thoughts. Jasper's brain had become its own spam
email. But through it all, one word screamed louder than the rest.

Singing is a gift from God and when you say I can't sing
I want to feel that golden pleasure flow all over my
It has been said by some that God is just a

These are the best books for my very short
We settle into a rut and the excitement
It's kinda hard to take him too serious
What I could use right now is some
Let me know if you can come to my
I want to get fucked up nasty and
I was only a month pregnant so I
He was in the flower of youth
If you see Brittany wish her
Hey at least this one looks
It's all about the hair
I transformed my
It's the truth

He had to go home.

The words pressed down on Jasper, choking him.

Give it up man, the fish keep eating your worms right off the hook. I told you, you gotta thread it through *the body.* Through *the body.* THROUGH—

Summoning all his strength, Jasper blew the strange words away. Blew them out like candles, plunging him into a silence that was also a darkness. He felt as though he'd been poured into some peculiarly shaped vessel, all nooks and crannies, bulbous projections and strange indentations, that his liquid form couldn't resist fitting itself to. But at least the voices were gone, save for one faint echo.

"Eye *seh,* wuh *tie* you wahna go *hoe?*"

Jasper blinked. No, that wasn't quite it. He *made* himself blink. He felt the muscles in each of his eyelids squeeze shut. They stayed that way until, with a second effort, he opened them. It took an even greater concentration to focus, but when he did the dark world snapped into view as if he'd donned some kind of night-vision goggles/binoculars/microscope. Each tree leaf seemed sharp-edged among its thousands of neighbors. The whitecaps of rolling black water crested in discrete drops, each and every drop briefly, perfectly distinct before his eyes. He could see fish swimming a few feet below the surface of the river, bats wheeling through the blue-black sky and snapping at insects on the wing—mosquitoes and mayflies mostly, aphids, weevils, moths. But the more clear it became, the less sense any of it made.

"Yarheh? Yarheh? Err to Yarheh!"

That one voice. It wouldn't go away. But Jasper couldn't quite make out what it said. It was like plugs had been stuffed into his ears. He concentrated. Felt his ears move, pivot, like a dog's. Seemed almost to feel the minuscule bones reorient themselves within his inner ear. What were they called? Hammer, anvil, stirrup? Actually, the problem was in the cochlea, but the names didn't matter. What mattered was fixing their relationship to each other, aligning them properly so that—

A claxon sliced through his thoughts: "Earth to Jarhead! I said, what *time* do you want to go *home*!?"

Jasper turned his head. It felt thick, heavy, as if coated in wet plaster or Play-Doh. He took in the grass, the darkness of the river beyond. The white face somewhere between the two. Danny. *Danny?*

"Jesus Christ, Jarhead. I know you ain't *that* drunk. I've seen you knock back twice as many in half the time."

How in the hell had *Danny* gotten here? And why was she calling him Jarhead? And . . . and what the fuck was *he* doing here? What had happened to the car? To Q. and Michaela and Sila? To the fucking mountain they'd slammed into at a hundred miles an hour?

He remembered the impact. The unique sound of metal tearing like tissue when you blow into it too hard. And then silence. A breathtaking silence, as if he'd been thrown from the car all the way to the bottom of the Hudson. And then those voices. Those . . . thoughts. Other people's thoughts, in his head. And then—

A chuckle pulled him back to the real world.

"Confused?"

Jasper looked up. Again he felt the weird sensation of having to concentrate, as if his mind had disconnected from his body, had to be refastened to it one synapse at a time. Danny was standing up, brushing the dirt off her ass with a fastidiousness that had nothing to do with the girl who'd just asked what time Jasper wanted to go home, let alone the hot tomboy who'd wiped worm guts on her pants earlier in the day.

"You beat me here," this new Danny was saying. "I'm impressed. I guess you really *did* want to get home."

For a moment Jasper stared at Danny in confusion, then turned and saw the lights of the little house at the top of the hill, a shadow moving around inside it.

His house.

His dad's shadow.

Home.

Jasper turned back to Danny, who was walking toward him with her hand outstretched. For someone who'd been drinking all day, her steps were steady and strong.

"I knew you were the right one," Danny was saying, almost to herself. "I could tell you weren't done with this world yet. That you would run back here like a chicken looking for its mother's wing. Death is a big, cold, dark place, no? Plenty of time for that later."

Danny had reached Jasper by that point. She stood there, sober, self-possessed, radiating an otherworldly strength. The spitting image of the person Jasper had met a few hours ago—the sharp-featured face, the high, firm breasts, the pirate patch of hair hanging over one eye— but still, something older and far more serious radiated from the eye not covered by the wedge of hair. It was almost luminous, as if glowing fish were swimming in its depths.

"Cat got your tongue?" Danny's laugh was deeper than Jasper remembered, ageless. "Well, come on then. Rise, Pinocchio." She took hold of Jasper's arm and hauled him to his feet as though he were a wooden doll.

Jasper felt as though his body belonged to someone else. He still had no idea what was going on. How he'd ended up here, when the last thing he remembered was being in a car crash on the other side of the river. Maybe he'd been in a coma? He had amnesia? He'd been walking around not knowing who he was and now, somehow, his memory had come back to him? Somehow he didn't think he'd become a minor plotline on *Days of Our Lives*.

Danny led him to the river like a mother teaching a toddler to walk, jerked her thumb at the dark water.

"This should help."

Jasper didn't understand. Did she want him to splash some water on his face? He sank to his knees—God, it felt like he was carrying an extra hundred pounds—cupped two palmsful of freezing water, buried his face in it. But almost immediately, he jerked his hands away. His cheeks felt strange in his hands. Puffy, swollen. Misshapen. Maybe he'd been disfigured in the accident?

He could feel his heart begin to beat faster. What is happening to me? Slowly, nervously, he separated his hands, waited for the water to still. It was dark and the moon was thin as a fishbone, but there was enough light for him to see that the face staring up at him was . . .

was *not* . . .

was not *his*.

It was Jarhead West's.

Jasper threw himself backward as if he'd seen a shark in the water. He nearly hit Danny, who leapt nimbly out of the way, her laughter echoing across the river.

"Freaky, right? God, I can barely remember the first time I looked in a mirror and saw someone else's face. Well, that's not true. I can remember it perfectly. But still. I'm almost jealous."

Suddenly a thousand memories collapsed on Jasper's fragile psyche. Only they weren't his memories. They were Jarhead's. A lot of them involved eating, or drinking, or jerking off. A mother with a lumpy ass and loud voice. A father, rail-thin, a shot glass glued to his right hand. A dining room table on which dishes of moldy leftovers mingled with fresh bowls of spaghetti, macaroni, mashed potatoes—all the colorless starchy foods of the lower classes. The garage smelled of grease and stale beer and a catbox that needed to be cleaned. The bedroom reeked of unwashed clothes and more beer, a single bed, its worn mattress pushed against the far wall. The springs protested when he fell on the bed in a drunken sprawl, then began rhythmically creaking as he reached inside his boxers and—

Jasper shook his head, but the memories didn't go away. Instead, more came. Impossibly precise, detailed memories from all the moments of Jarhead's life. He remembered the sensation of beer in Jarhead's mouth at Caitlin Reese's party, felt it sliding down his esophagus, filling his stomach, leaching through intestines into kidneys, liver, bladder. He remembered breaking his wrist in a football game when he was a junior: he'd arm-checked a linesman from Troy and his radius and ulna snapped like a pair of chopsticks. He remembered the sweet fetid smell of the dead mouse that had been in his desk on the first day of fourth grade, remembered a stomach full of mashed apricots and peas when he was eight months old. The warm slide of shit into his diaper, the bright blurry shapes of the mobile hanging above his crib, the terrifying squeeze of the birth canal on his head and the insistent, latex-gloved hands of the doctor pulling him from the safety of his mother's body.

He remembered it all, not just at the sensory, but the cellular level. It was as if Jarhead's body had been digitized and downloaded directly into Jasper's brain. Except—except *he* was in Jarhead, not the other way around.

Jasper opened his mouth to speak, but nothing came out. He forced himself to crawl back to the river. Jarhead's face still stared back at him, looking every bit as confused as Jasper felt.

He closed his eyes, opened one of them. So did Jarhead. He stuck out his tongue. So did Jarhead. He said, "Holy fuck," and so did Jarhead, except Jarhead didn't make any noise because he was only a reflection.

A reflection of Jasper.

Who, apparently, *was* Jarhead.

He turned his head slowly. Danny had sat down, was examining her hands, legs, stomach as though she'd never seen them before. She looked up and smiled—a patient yet somehow slightly greedy smile.

Jasper looked down at his hands. At Jarhead's hands, doughy, dirty. His, but not his. They did what he told them to do but only when he *told* them to, as if Jasper worked his body through a video game controller. He looked up at Danny pleadingly.

Danny pursed her lips, nodded benevolently. "Ready to ask?"

Jasper swallowed. "What–what's happened to me?"

"Isn't it obvious?" Danny gave her head a little toss, and now both of her eyes were visible, glowing, amused, all-knowing. For the first time Jasper felt more than confused. He felt afraid.

"Jasper, my friend: you're dead."

11

Dumas–Malachi–glanced at the hand Ileana was slipping toward the seam of her skirt. He shook his head. Without taking his eyes from hers, he reached beneath her skirt and lifted the knife from its garter. His fingers were cold, businesslike. Her thigh could have been a mannequin in a department store.

The demon brought the blade to his nose. Sniffed. "Ah, Antonio. Even your blood was spicy!" His eyes shifted to Ileana's. "The most annoying thing was that I *liked* Soma. I was going to rest in him a while. But you had to ruin it." He let the knife fall to the floor. "Aztecan, no? That's so like you hunters. To cloak your killing in history and myth, as though it were a sacrifice and not simply murder. You hunters, and your foolish, misguided Legion. You think your dim memories of union allow you to second-guess our actions and outmaneuver us. We are Mogran, Ileana. As old as this river, as beyond your comprehension."

Not a trace of Dumas lingered in the voice, the eyes. Malachi's control was total. Ileana had seen this kind of possession before. Knew that even if she could get the Mogran to jump, Dumas's psyche was unlikely to recover. That made killing him easier, at least on an emotional level. Overpowering the Mogran was another question.

"How did you get out of Soma anyway?"

Malachi laughed gleefully. "The maid, of course. I used her for the exit, then borrowed her body just so I could see the look in your eyes as you went in to kill the wrong man."

Ileana remembered the expression on the maid's face, the wrinkled bedspread. Remembered the confusion and terror in Soma's eyes as she killed him. Her heart pounded, and she fought to control herself. There would be time for remorse later.

"And Dumas? Did you take him, too?"

"I have you to thank for that. He was all revved up after a few drinks with, how did he put it, 'a like-minded conversational partner, and such a lovely one at that'? He practically seduced the maid himself." The demon put a smirk on his host's face. "You would be proud of your epidemiologist. He wore a condom and everything."

"It's a shame there's no prophylaxis against you." She looked the demon full in the face. "But why come to my rescue? Perhaps–" she arched her back and pushed her breasts in his face "–perhaps you feel the need to give Dumas what he really wanted?"

Malachi looked at her tits as though they were a couple of scoops of ice cream and he already had a banana split in each hand. His laugh was the laugh of a nine-year-old bully.

"Do you actually think you can *seduce* me?" With blinding speed, he grabbed her wrists, pushing her back into her seat. "I can hear your *heartbeat*, Ileana. Can hear you revving it up, trying to flood your tired muscles with oxygen. I can smell the hormones you're so desperately manufacturing to give your body one last burst of speed and strength. Do you honestly believe that will help you against *me?*"

The demon held her effortlessly, and Ileana suddenly felt defeated. She turned her head from Malachi's, if only to escape his hot breath, his mesmerizing stare.

"You know I'm the newest." The demon's voice was filled with self-love. "The youngest."

She closed her eyes. She had heard these speeches before. The self-justifying rhetoric of an overconfident Mogran who thought your life was in his hands. But she was tired now. Alone. She had killed an innocent man. Maybe it was time for the hunt to end, or at least for someone else to take over.

She wasn't scared. Not of death. The idea that all life must come to an end was simply a fact of the universe. To remember it, to live with that knowledge, was what made you human. Forget it, and you became what this creature was. A cosmic leech. A demon. No, the only thing that twigged her conscience was the fact that she would leave the hunt unfinished. She didn't believe in an afterlife, but if there was a heaven, if Alec was there waiting for her, she would be ashamed to tell him she had not managed to exterminate every last Mogran.

The demon leaned closer. "I want you to hear this. I want you to go to your grave with the knowledge that you failed."

Ileana almost nodded. She had failed. This demon's judgment couldn't hurt her. Only Alec's mattered.

"Ileana, Ileana, Ileana," the demon crooned in her ear. "The Alpha Wave is active again."

Ileana's eyes snapped open. *"What?"*

The demon's smile was practically luminescent. "Have I got your attention?"

Ileana shook her head angrily. "The Alpha Wave is something the gatherers dreamed up."

"I thought so too, but it's very real. And now one of the nine has taken it upon himself to break the Covenant—"

Ileana's heart knocked against her ribs. "Another tall tale."

"—and tell me the secret."

"What secret?"

The demon smiled smugly. "Oh no. That would be giving you too much."

Ileana tried to mask her desperation. If Malachi's secret referred to what she thought it did, then everything really was doomed. Not just the work she and Alec had done over the past ten years, but the future—the future was almost unimaginable.

"What's the harm? You're going to kill me anyway."

"Who says I'm going to kill you? Maybe I'm just going to possess you, reduce you to depths you can't imagine." He laughed as Ileana launched into a fresh bout of struggling. "Death doesn't bother you, does it? But to be a host again—*that* would kill you. Especially know-ing I could never leave, no matter how many, what kind of creatures I forced you to copulate with. Men, women, dogs. *Corpses.*" He shifted position now, so that he held both of Ileana's wrists in one hand, used his free hand to stroke her crotch as though brushing the wrinkles from her skirt. "I know about the sigil, of course. So yes, I am going to kill you. But part of the torture of your death will be knowing that you failed, but not *how* you failed. Foras told me I talked too much. But this is one secret even I know better than to spill."

"Foras? One of Solomon's demons?"

The demon winked. "Oops. There I go again."

He paused. For a moment Ileana thought she saw a glint of Dumas in the eyes, but then it was gone. But the demon had caught her reaction, and he turned it back on her with pinpoint accuracy.

"Francois's ideas were interesting, weren't they? About the soul. Electricity. Some within your organization share his belief, don't they? Of course, they're the same ones who believe King Solomon had a jar in which he kept seventy-two demons he controlled through use of magical signs. I do wonder though." With revolting noncha-lance, Malachi stroked Ileana's groin. "I wonder what our scientist would have done. If he'd actually managed to get in here. Do you think he would have been repulsed by your little *alteration*? Or would it have turned him on?"

Ileana turned her face away from the demon's leer. The look of gloating he put on Dumas's kind face was more than she could bear. The hand holding her wrists tightened, and she felt the links of Alec's watch bite into her skin. She started struggling again, but Malachi didn't budge.

"Tell me more . . . about the Covenant." She writhed in Malachi's grasp. "The Alpha Wave."

The demon held Ileana as if she were nothing more than a strug-gling baby. "Ileana. Please. Go peacefully. It is so much more digni-fied."

Ileana squirmed that much harder. She was banking on the fact that Malachi didn't realize she wasn't trying to get away. All she wanted to do was—

bend—

her—

wrist!

Malachi's eyes went wide. A second later, his grip slackened and he slumped over. An inarticulate moan warbled from his throat.

"Foras was right," Ileana said, bending over him and retrieving the stone knife from the floor of the Rover. "You talk too much."

"Ungh."

Malachi's body shivered, but Ileana knew the twitching was purely autonomic. She pulled the demon's head back by the hair, exposing the pale throat. Dumas had been shaving with cold water for the past two weeks, and a rash showed through the thick shadow of stubble. She let the knife trace the stubble as though all she were going to do was razor it off.

"The blade *is* Aztecan," she said, almost gently. "Six hundred years old. And the curare in poor Francois's palm has been used by South American hunters for thousands of years. But the pressure-activated mechanism in the watch is strictly twenty-first century." She turned the demon's head toward her, looked deep into the terrified eyes. "There's enough alloferine in your system to paralyze a whale. More than even *you* can neutralize, at least right away."

Ileana looked deep into Dumas's eyes, found Malachi lurking there at the bottom. The few people who had learned to see a Mogran inside its host always described it the same way: a light shining in the eyes like phosphorescent fish swimming around a bowl. Malachi's light was darting about frantically, as though he were trying to jump out of the water. "You see," she cooed, "we *do* know some things about you."

Dumas's hand twitched. It could have been another muscle spasm or it could have been the demon, already regaining control. Ileana didn't wait to find out. With one motion, she cut a hole the size of an apple out of Dumas's throat. A torrent of blood spewed onto the seat.

The Mogran's eyes grew bright, and his body began to convulse. There was no mistake this time. No escape.

A moment later the light was extinguished, and only Dumas's lifeless orbs stared up at hers. Ileana dragged the body from the car. She removed head and genitals, then, as an added precaution, siphoned a couple of liters of gasoline out of the tank and poured it over the corpse. The same lighter that had lit Dumas's cigarette less than two hours ago now sparked his funeral pyre. As the smell of roasting flesh filled her nostrils, she recited the psalm, trying not to think about the fact that she'd said it a mere half hour ago, over the body of the wrong man. An innocent man. A bystander.

"Malachi and Francois Dumas. Though you are dead—" Her voice broke, and she took a moment to steady herself. "Though you are dead, your names live on."

The scent of burning flesh tickled her nostrils as she waded into the waters of the Nile. The place where the Mogran had put Dumas's hand tingled as well, as if he had shocked her. She put her own hand there. Let her finger trace the mutilated flesh.

Alec had watched as she made the cut herself.

"You are a hunter," he said.

"I am a hunter. I will never be prey again."

The flesh beneath her hand was bumpy yet waxen, like the droppings of a burned-out candle. She couldn't feel her own fingertips but she could feel the ghostly prickle of the Mogran's touch. She scratched, but the itch refused to go away.

12

I . . . *died* . . . in . . . the . . . crash."

Jasper had followed Danny up the bank to the stone staircase that led to his house. The short walk had settled him somewhat: in half a dozen steps he'd taken firmer control of Jarhead's body, fixed his posture, smoothed his gait. For her part, Danny moved like a cat on the prowl, each footfall landing silently in the loamy grass, her ass riding up and down as though she might pounce on a hapless vole or mole at any moment. Jasper couldn't keep his eyes off it. Who knew death was such an aphrodisiac?

Oak and ash trees rustled above them; the water that had shown him his new face lapped quietly against the bank.

"I died," Jasper repeated, "and now I'm in Jarhead West." He looked over at Danny. "This gives a whole new meaning to the phrase 'Hell is other people.' "

Danny's giggle was anything but girlish. "Hell is a word made up by priests and monks. Did you know it shares a root with cell, the place a prisoner lives—or a monk, for that matter."

"In hell," Jasper shook his head. "Danielle Thatcher is a linguistics instructor." He wondered how he knew Danny's full name, then realized it was Jarhead who knew it.

"Danielle Thatcher, like your friend Mason West, has stepped away a moment. Or rather, they're both temporarily hidden behind stronger personalities. Namely, ours."

"You're not Danny?"

Danny threw back her head and laughed hysterically. "Good God, no. No more than you're Mason. She's a nice body to hang out in though." She ran a finger beneath a breast, then nodded knowingly. "He's still there, you know. Go on, look."

"Look—?"

"Don't overthink it. *Look.*"

Jasper tried to figure out what Danny meant, but even as he did the answer came to him. Or, rather, Jarhead came to him. It was as though Jasper had flipped a switch in his brain and a darkened room filled with light, and there was Jarhead: sagging jeans, filthy jersey, dopey, benevolent, needy smile. When the light went on, the former linebacker seemed to look directly at Jasper, confusion giving way to delight.

"Jasper!" he brayed in his deaf man's voice. "Why is everything so *loud?*"

Jasper snapped the light off. He felt an electric shock in his—in Jarhead's—brain, as though some circuit had been fried beyond repair.

"He can *see* me."

"Well, you are in his head after all. It only seems fair."

"Fair." As though possessing someone were nothing more than a schoolgirl's game, hopscotch, tetherball, four square. Was that the right word? Possession?

"Of course, you can hide yourself from him. Or, more accurately, you can make it so he can't see you, by turning him off. But that's likely to do more damage."

"Damage?"

"This is the universe, Jasper, metaphysical or not. The same Newtonian rules apply: for every action, an equal and opposite reaction. You got a second chance in Mason West's body, but you had to die first. And Mason gets to play host to your psyche, but not without a few, shall we say, residual effects."

Jasper shook his head. His host's head. "I don't get it."

"Imagine Mason's brain is a forest. His consciousness is like a deer path, a single meandering thread of daylight amidst a world of dark trunks and leaves. Then in comes *your* consciousness like a bulldozer, widening the path, straightening it, but only by plowing under a significant number of the trees. You're the bull in the china shop, Gulliver trying to have tea with the Lilliputians: things are gonna get broken. Once you acclimate you'll realize you can do far more with Mason's brain and body than he ever dreamed, but when you leave him, well, he'll find he's not exactly the person he once was. How different he is will depend on how much crashing around you do in there."

Danny paused. The look she gave Jasper had nothing to do with metaphysics or consciousness or deer paths. It was pure sex. The kind of look Michaela had never given him. Jasper thought that if he put his hand on the breast Danny had just touched, she wouldn't brush it away the way his girlfriend did. She would guide it where she wanted it to go, put her own hands on his body. It was only when he thought of her touching his body that he ran into trouble, because it wasn't the body he knew. It was Jarhead's. The thought of Danny having sex with the gas jockey's lumpy limbs was anything but a turn-on, but it wasn't quite enough to turn him off either. He almost had to sit on his hands to keep from grabbing her.

Suddenly a thought came to him. If he wasn't Jarhead, and Danny wasn't Danny, then who was she? How did she know all this?

"How—I mean, well, who *are* you?"

"I was wondering if you'd ever ask. My name is—or was, a thousand lifetimes ago—Leo. But you might just want to think of me as your guide. Your Virgil, to lead you through this treacherous passage to safety."

"I thought you said your name was Leo."

Danny—Leo—rolled her eyes. His eyes? "The Virgil thing was a metaphor? An allusion? What do they teach you in school anyway?"

"Leo? Like, um, Leonora?"

Danny shook her head. "Lesson number one, Jasper: gender

doesn't matter. Not anymore. Who or whatever I am, I'm in this body now. This very lissome young female body. Should you touch me—" she took Jasper's hand and put it on her thigh "—this flesh is all you'll feel. And this flesh, I'm sure you'll agree, is all woman."

It was harder for Jasper to take his hand off Danny's—Leo's—thigh than it was to bench 225. But he made himself do it, because he sensed there were more important things going on than the throbbing he felt in his—no, Jarhead's—pants.

"Don't worry," Danny/Leo spoke to Jasper's crotch. "We'll get to that part eventually. Right now I'm going to let you know what's going on, and then"—the snigger that came from Danny's mouth sounded anything but girly—"we can attend to more pressing matters." She squeezed Jasper's leg tightly. "Okay?"

Jasper's leg twitched. He didn't trust himself to speak. Just nodded meekly.

"Okay," Leo said. "Here it is. You ready? Because you died a virgin, your spirit has come back to correct the error. Once you have sex in the body you now inhabit, you can pass into the wild blue yonder."

Jasper bit back a laugh. "You're kidding, right?"

"Think of it as the golden rule: you gotta fuck, either in the body you were born with or in one you borrow. It's called unbinding the soul."

Jasper couldn't suppress his own snigger. "That's it? No big secrets? Just—just sex?"

Leo plastered a knowing smile on Danny's innocent face. "Oh, there are secrets, Jasper. Mysteries and covenants to which only a very few are privy. But these are material phenomena. The universe is exactly as it appears to be. The senses you were born with, the eyes and ears and mouth with which you experience the world, the carnal appetite that drives you, these are all you need to get to the next plane of existence."

Jasper tried not to gulp. "What *does* come next?"

"Well, I guess that's secret number one. If God didn't see fit to tell you, then far be it from me to spoil the surprise."

"God didn't tell me I had to have sex, either."

"He didn't?" Leo narrowed his host's pretty eyes. "Has there been a day, an hour, a sweaty teenage second that you haven't thought about getting your rocks off since you were, hmm, Jasper, how old? Thirteen? Twelve?"

Jasper would've blushed, but it seemed a little complicated in Jarhead's body.

"Eleven."

"Eleven. So for six years dipping your wick has been a pretty much constant desire. Do you really think that was an accident?"

Jasper didn't answer. The truth was written all over his body. Or, rather, in one specific place on his body. He didn't want to say it out loud but felt he had to.

"So you're saying that if I . . ."

"Fuck."

"If I fuck you . . ."

A lift of the eyebrows. "Or anyone else."

"If I fuck, I can leave. I can . . ."

Again Leo came to his aid. "Die."

"I can die."

"Remember, Jasper, you're already dead. This just seals the deal." Leo paused. Then: "She wanted you, you know?"

"She?"

"Danny. She thought you were hot."

One of Jarhead's memories flashed in Jasper's mind: Danny looking over at his—at Jasper's—sleeping body where it lay on the bank, and telling Jarhead that she thought he was hot "for a kid."

Leo slid closer to Jasper on the bench. "In a way, you'd be giving her what she wanted." His host's voice was husky. Hungry.

But it wasn't true, Jasper thought. Danny thought *Jasper* was hot. But he was in Jarhead now. And there was another memory: of Jarhead making a drunken grab for Danny's ass one night and Danny playfully but forcefully batting it away. She didn't have any desire for this body at all.

"So, what's it gonna be?" Leo said impatiently. "Miss Thatcher's flesh is starting to chafe on me, and I can see you're a little antsy too." Danny's hand fell on Jasper's crotch, and Jasper figured out how to blush pretty quickly. With a single contraction, the hand squeezed all of Jasper's scruples away. He was dead, after all. He was hardly accountable for his actions.

He nodded rapidly, tried not to gulp.

"Okay."

"Okay?" Leo teased him. "No wonder you died a virgin. Your seduction method leaves something to be desired." He stood up and peeled off Danny's shirt in a single smooth motion. "Come on, Jasper. Show me how badly you want it."

Jasper stood up and fumbled at his belt. It was only the unfamiliar roll of flesh at his waist that slowed him down. Every action reminded him that this wasn't his body. His head was spinning. Just a few more seconds, he told himself. A few more seconds and he would be out of this foreign flesh, and this strange sense of dislocation would be gone forever.

He avoided looking at Danny's face. Kept his eyes focused on her breasts instead. Did his best to imagine that they were Michaela's. That the body emerging from the jeans rolling down her long white thighs was Michaela's as well.

Oh God, he thought. Michaela. What the hell had happened to Michaela?

"Something wrong, Jasper?"

Jasper shook his head. He wouldn't be distracted now. He reached for one of the breasts before him, cupped it in his hands. Squeezed. Tried to imagine it was Michaela's breast, then tried even harder not to think about her. Had she died too? In the crash?

"Such a romantic," Leo said drolly, peeling off Jarhead's T-shirt and pressing their naked chests together. "Is this your idea of foreplay?"

"Shut up!" Jasper groaned, mashing Danny's face into his shoulder. He fell backwards onto the grass, pulling Danny's body with him. Her breasts lay on Jasper's chest now, her taut stomach pressed against his, her crotch directly over Jasper's.

"Do it, Jasper. Do it. Let it all go."

He *would* do it, if only she'd shut up. Stop speaking to him in that voice that wasn't Michaela's, and wasn't even Danny's. Wasn't even a girl's when you got right down to it. How were you supposed to fuck the hot chick who was lying on top of you when she kept reminding you there was a boy hiding somewhere inside those acres of smooth white flesh? Not to mention the images of Michaela that were swirling around his brain. Michaela's scream of terror as the car spun out of control. Michaela's body mangled by the impact.

His partner seemed to feel none of these distractions. With robotic precision, Danny's legs opened, and suddenly Jasper felt himself engulfed by a tight warmth. One part of his brain exploded in a thousand fried circuits—good God, he was doing it, he was finally fucking—but the rest of his head was completely preoccupied with Michaela. How could he leave without seeing her one more time? Without saying goodbye? It should be Michaela he was doing this with.

For the next minute or two he just lay there. Not fighting the process, but no longer into it either. His dick could have been a dildo for all the connection he felt to it, Danny's body an image on a computer screen. He looked away from her bouncing breasts at the empty morning sky, wondering if Michaela was up there looking down on him. Or Q. for that matter, or Sila. The moans and groans of the girl riding him seemed faint and far away. Oh God, he thought. Just get it over with already. His erection was starting to droop.

And then a yelp came to his ears, and with a start he realized it *was* over. Because it wasn't Leo who'd yelped. It was Danny.

"Jarhead? What the *fuck?*"

Jasper looked down from the sky just in time to feel Danny's palm smack the side of his face. He knew it was Danny's hand, not Leo's. The Leo had departed even though he, Jasper, was still stuck in Jarhead's body—which was rather embarrassingly stuck in Danny's.

Her bewildered, horrified face stared at him as she wrenched herself off him.

"Oh my God, Jarhead. I *trusted* you."

A thousand memories flashed through Jasper's mind as Danny stumbled backwards. All the little moments that had passed between Jarhead and the confused, terrified girl who kept her eyes fixed on him as she dressed, as if she was afraid he might jump her again if she turned her back. Jarhead wasn't a guy who made friends easily, even less so with women. He'd harbored an innocent crush on Danny for more than a year, and the truth was she *had* warmed to him during that time. They shared a slacker sensibility—not the snotty kind that favored aggressively unkempt hairstyles and unlistenable indie bands, but the kind that thought a six-pack and *Simpsons* rerun made for a perfect night. On more than a few of those nights Danny had curled one of Jarhead's softly padded arms around her shoulders and fallen asleep on his broken-down couch, and Jarhead had sat preternaturally still, not even reaching for his beer, lest the couch squeak at a volume he couldn't hear and wake up his companion. Now, thanks to a decision Jasper had made for him—a single, selfish choice that had nothing to do with Jarhead's past but everything to do with his future—the lonely gas jockey had lost not only any chance he had at dating Danny, but her friendship as well. If she decided to press charges for rape, he might end up losing a lot more.

Trust. Danny's word echoed in Jarhead's amped-up ears like a klaxon. Because it wasn't only her trust that had been violated: Jasper had trusted Leo too. Had believed him when he said all he had to do was have sex and it would come to an end. In his seventeen years on earth, he'd never given too much thought to how the afterlife was going to start, but he was pretty sure he'd never imagined it beginning with a borrowed dick waving in the morning breeze like a flagpole. A flagpole planted in foreign soil and shorn of its colors. Leo had said it was easy, but, as Jarhead's dick was pointing out with irrefutable eloquence, this was hard. Really, really hard.

2

Book of the Dead

"Let no man think he may escape by pleading
ignorance."

—The Malleus Maleficarum

1

The flat in London was nicer than most. The top two floors of a terrace house just off Islington High Street. Four big rooms with white walls, high ceilings, soft yellow light falling aslant pale floorboards every morning. A little Spartan, but luxurious compared to some of the rattraps Ileana had put up in over the last decade. A big bay window in the bedroom overlooked the back garden, where the children who lived in the downstairs flat played every afternoon. A boy and a girl, six or seven years old, possibly twins. They were indefatigable, running and screaming, now laughing, now fighting as they slipped imperceptibly from London Bridge to Ring Around the Rosie to Cowboys and Indians and other games of their own invention.

Sitting in the high-backed rocking chair in the bay window, Ileana felt like a cross between Whistler's mother and Mrs. Bates. She stared through the glass, watching the children innocently playing at death. It occurred to Ileana that demons weren't the only beings to treat mortality as a game. Children do it too. London Bridge: a parable of the rise and fall of Anne Boleyn. Ring Around the Rosie: a dance to the victims of the Black Plague. Cowboys and Indians: a reenactment of one of history's most notorious genocides. God, what a phrase. "One of history's most notorious genocides." As though there were a selection to choose from, like apple varieties or prostitutes.

She identified with the ease with which the children slipped into and out of various identities. She'd introduced herself to their parents as Lana, told them she was in London to set up a branch of a management consulting firm out of Poland. She softened her consonants, played Chopin and Górecki on the stereo; that part was always easy. Becoming someone else for a few weeks or months until the next assignment. But none of it erased the memory of what had happened in Sudan. First killing an innocent man, then taking out Dumas as well. A kind man. A humanitarian. She tried to tell herself that she, too, was making the world safer, more humane, but she still shuddered awake in the middle of the night with the scientist's last gurgling breaths in her ears, the smell of his burning flesh in her nostrils.

To escape those memories she went to an antiquarian bookshop near the British Museum, where she purchased a copy of the *Lemegeton Clavicula Salomonis*—the so-called *Lesser Key of Solomon*. The *Lemegeton*'s primary feature was a list of seventy-two demons said to have been enslaved by the biblical King Solomon, who was also purported to be the text's author (although all evidence indicated the grimoire had in fact been cobbled together in the seventeenth century from works produced during the Christian Middle Ages). The text listed not only the demons' names and dominions, but instructions for summoning them, as well as the metallic sigils the summoner had to wear to protect him- or herself. Among these demons—number thirty-one on the list—was Foras, the name Malachi had mentioned when he let drop his remarks about the Alpha Wave and the Covenant. Solomon was said to have enslaved Foras and the other demons to help him build the First Temple in order to house the original Ark of the Covenant, although whether a relationship existed between the Hebrew covenant and the one Malachi had mentioned remained a mystery.

In 1918, a demon by the name of Beleth (number thirteen on the list) had been killed by the Legion's founder, Jordan David, at which point the *Lemegeton* became for all intents and purposes the Legion's handbook. Despite ninety years of perfervid examination on the part of the gatherers, however, the book had yielded nothing besides the name of the cut the hunters submitted to in order to protect themselves from possession. But in the wake of Malachi's name-dropping, she dutifully pored through every one of the text's numbingly repetitious passages, studied the intricate design and manufacture of the original sigils, scrutinized the seals, circles, and incantations associated with the jar in which the king was said to have kept his demons when he wasn't using them. She paid particular attention to the biography of Foras: "He is a mighty great president & appeareth in ye form of a strong man, he can give ye understanding to men how they may know ye vertues of all herbs & precious stones & teacheth them ye art of Logick & Ethicks." If such hokum had any more significance than the mumbo jumbo spouted by a two-dollar palm reader at a Renaissance fair, she couldn't see it.

But Malachi had said it. And, although the demon hadn't revealed the nature of the "secret" Foras had confided in him, Ileana had a pretty good guess what it was. No one, not even the demons themselves, knew how they came into existence. As Malachi himself had boasted, he was the youngest. There hadn't been a new Mogran in more than a quarter of a millennium. Thus, though it might take a year or a decade to track down a single demon, each individual death was a definitive step toward the Mogran's ultimate extermination.

Of course, if Malachi was telling the truth, then there was the Alpha Wave to deal with as well. And if a member of the original nine was in fact spreading the secret of the Mogran's reproduction, all bets were off. Ileana had her doubts, though. In the first place, why would a species voluntarily conceal the method of its reproduction, and so render itself vulnerable to the elimination, one by one, of their entire population? Indeed, the idea of *any* restriction on the demons' actions failed to resonate with her experiences as host or hunter. Ileana had had a demon inside her. Had felt what it felt: a ravenous loneliness coupled with the need to pervert everything it came in contact with. And even if the Mogran did want to curtail the scope of their actions, the dictates of the frenzy made it impossible.

But.

But Malachi had dropped his bombshell at a moment when he had no need to dissemble. And Mogran rarely played mind games with humans, for the simple reason that they didn't respect humans' minds. For a Mogran to engage in a battle of wits with a single person was a bit like a supercomputer playing chess with an infant. No, there was every reason to believe Malachi had told the truth, or what he thought was the truth: that somewhere in the world, one or more members of the Alpha Wave—the oldest and most powerful of all the Mogran—were locating the last of their kind and teaching them how to breed.

Ileana knew she should contact the Legion immediately. Here was the information she needed to make the far-flung members of the organization realize the hunt was not yet over, the Mogran down but hardly out. If even one demon knew the secret, then the clock was ticking on everything she and Alec had done over the past decade. But something kept her paralyzed.

Soma's face.

Dumas's.

Yes, and Alec's too. Because even worse than not having a partner was the idea that the Legion would finally assign her someone else to work with, at which point she would no longer be the companion of the man who had helped her recover from the horrors of possession. She would be an assassin, nothing more, nothing less. A hired killer who took an innocent life for every guilty party she executed. And so she sat in her rocking chair, the ancient grimoire slack in her hands, and let Malachi's words bat about the tattered web of memories her own demon had left in her mind. But the only thing that came to her were the horrors of that single night in 1992. The memories held her captive in a waking nightmare more terrible than anything she could dream up, and in their grip all she could do was wait for the sun to rise. Wait for the children's fearless voices to remind her there was still innocence in the world, purity, however tenuous or temporary. That's what she was fighting for, she reminded herself. Not her salvation.

Theirs.

2

Sue Miller wondered if she had time for a cigarette as she strode across the hospital parking lot. Three o'clock Sunday morning, pole lamps glowing like fuzzy yellow tennis balls in the mist, a faint scent of flowers wafting through the air. Technically it was her day off. Now, assuming she even got out of the hospital before Monday, she'd probably end up spending the daylight hours in a coma. The least she deserved was a smoke before dealing with yet another crazy hillbilly.

Just as she reached for her pack, however, her thigh buzzed. God, sometimes she hated technology. A cell phone was a snide little angel watching everything you did with a disapproving frown on its face. Whatever happened to privacy? Whatever happened to being alone?

Her thigh buzzed a second time.

"Jesus Christ, I'm *coming*." Her feet pinched as she jogged up the sidewalk. Why on earth had she decided to wear a pair of $750 Ferragamo fuck-me pumps to a three A.M. emergency call? If someone *bled* on them, she'd kill the poor bastard herself.

The phone buzzed one more time as she pulled it from her pants. Mohinder probably. She could swear the rings came closer together when he called. Damn idiot couldn't handle a routine psychotic break on his own. *A most interesting case*, she could hear him saying in that hoity-toity British accent, as if he hadn't grown up in a slummy Mumbai apartment. *I really thought a second consultation was in order.*

"Consult my ass," she grumbled now, flipping her phone open.

She stopped in her tracks.

"Hmph."

She felt a faint tingle in her thighs, as if her phone were still in the pocket of her skin-tight Jil Sanders. Instead of an incoming call, the screen promised "6 NEW MESSAGES." Only one person texted her with that kind of insistence.

Larry.

Lawrence Bishop was an EMT with Riverview, which was less an ambulance service than a hearse-cum–paddy wagon of last resort. He and Sue had been having a thing for almost eight months now, ever since he'd dragged a twitching nineteen-year-old into the ER and said, "Crack or crazy? You decide." He'd helped her wrestle the kid into an examination room, then volunteered to stick around "just in case." She was acutely conscious of his eyes on her—blue eyes, the color washed out from two decades of weed and acid. The teenager was virtually aphasic. The only word he seemed capable of saying was "Beetles!" (or, who knows, maybe Beatles), which he screamed out at irregular intervals. The blistered lips and powder burns on his fingers were more informative, however, not to mention the pipe the EMT had taken off him, and after she sent the boy upstairs to detox she asked the paramedic if he wanted to get a cup of coffee. In answer, he kicked the door closed, then produced a tiny glassine containing a few white crystals. "Is that *crack?*" Sue asked, outraged, but also strangely excited. "It's got a helluva lot more kick than a cup of coffee." The EMT smiled wickedly. "My name's Larry. I'll tell you again when we're finished, 'cause I expect you'll have forgotten by then."

He was the filthiest man she'd ever met. He'd sneak up on her, stick his fingers in her panties and then suck on them like a lollipop, call when he knew she was making rounds and leave long, graphically detailed messages about what he planned to do to her that weekend— promises he always made good on. Sometimes he texted her fifteen-second movies of himself masturbating that he shot while he was driving the ambulance. Given the hour, not to mention the fact that he was working weekend graveyards (which is why, when you got right down to it, she'd worn the Ferragamos and the Jil Sanders), it was one of Larry's videos she expected to see when she clicked on her inbox.

Instead a nearly unrecognizable silver blob flashed on the small screen. A car. The remains of a car. Not a piece of glass was left in the windows, not an inch of metal uncrumpled. The hood itself had been ripped in half, which Sue recognized as the work of the Jaws of Life. Although who could have lived through whatever caused so much damage? The pile of metal looked less like a wrecked automobile than a beetle God had crushed beneath his heel.

The successive pictures each got closer to the vehicle. Sue found herself wondering when Larry had had time to snap them. Hadn't he been saving people? Or had there been no one to save? She saw the oil and glass glistening on the roadway, the blood saturating the upholstery of the seats, tattered bits of clothing blowing through the air like confetti. In one of those small ironies that made you think there really is a god—and that he gets his kicks out of fucking with us—the six empty beer cans that had presumably been the accident's catalyst were all pristine, despite the fact that not a square inch of the car was undented, undinged, or otherwise undamaged.

The last picture was of a pair of stretchers on which two lumpy body bags were laid out like a pair of potato sacks, followed by a final message:

"THE DRIVER HAD HIS DICK OUT!!!! GOD I AM SO TURNED ON RIGHT NOW!!!!"

Sue snapped the phone closed, shoved it back in her pocket. Before she'd taken two steps her thigh buzzed again.

"Fuck you, pervert," she said under her breath. But her leg kept tingling after the phone stopped, and she shook it a little as she walked into the building, to see what Mohinder had found so interesting that he had to call on her day off.

3

Jasper heard every "Fuck" and "Shit" Danny muttered as she ran off. Heard when she stopped and zipped up her pants and then again when she puked halfway up the hill and then finally when she wrenched open the door of her car parked a quarter of a mile away and sped off.

And yet, as disgusted as he was by what he'd been tricked into doing, his revulsion was mitigated by the sense of wonder he felt from his host. For, locked in a little room in his own brain, Jarhead West was discovering the myriad music of the world for the first time: zippers and car doors, vomiting and birdsong, the endless lapping lull of the river. Jasper could feel him hearing it: the pain at destroying his relationship with Danny mixed with gratitude at his newfound ability to hear. Yes, gratitude. Because somehow, just as Jasper was aware of Jarhead's presence, Jarhead was aware of his. Knew it was his ol' buddy Jasper who'd fixed his ears. But as much as Jasper didn't want to be alone right now, he didn't want to be with Jarhead even more, and, concentrating, he drew a veil ever more tightly around his host, leaving him not just deaf but blind. *Sorry buddy*, he thought, and could have sworn he heard a faint answer: *It's okay Jasper. I trust you.* It was more than Jasper could say about himself.

For a long time he just laid there, overwhelmed by his situation. What he wanted to do most was go home. Crawl into bed, hope that this whole thing would prove to've been some crazy dream born of sexual frustration. But even that simple word brought two conflicting images to mind: first was the little house on the hill above him, dark now, his dad having presumably gone to bed. The second was alien to Jasper, yet somehow more familiar: the trailer on the east side of the river that Jarhead had been living in since his own dad kicked him out halfway through his senior year. The dozens of beer cans strewn inside and out, the dirty clothes and takeout food containers, the sagging mattress laid directly on the floor between two stacks of porno rags grown so high that Jarhead used them as bedside tables. He knew that's where this body belonged, but he couldn't bring himself to go there. Jarhead's flesh might have been his, but he wasn't ready to take over Jarhead's life as well. And so he climbed the 492 steps to his own house—his old house, at any rate, the house that had been his when he'd been alive.

Gunther started barking even before he reached the yard. Jasper tried to shush him but the dog had no idea who he was, and when Jasper stretched his hand out—Jarhead's hand, he reminded himself—the rottweiler went into a snarling frenzy, hurling his hundred and twenty pounds of dogflesh at the gate of his kennel. Jasper was afraid the dog would rouse his dad, but when he got closer to the house he saw that Van Arsdale's truck was gone. For a moment Jasper figured his dad was at Cakes's, but then he realized he was probably at the hospital. Or the morgue. Was the morgue at the hospital, or did it have its own building? He should've paid more attention during *Law and Order*, instead of trying to get Michaela in the sack.

Then again, perhaps he should've turned off the TV and tried harder to get Michaela in the sack.

The first thing he saw when he opened the back door was the chair he'd knocked over at breakfast, the silly flower on the table looking down on it like a mourner. The bottle of breakfast applejack was still on the counter, empty now; a second stood on the table, already half gone. Jasper could hardly begrudge his dad a drink under the circumstances. He'd've poured one himself, but he had no idea what it'd be like getting drunk in Jarhead's body—until he thought of it, that is, at which point every drink Jarhead had ever swilled passed through his mind. It was as if Jasper had googled the words "drunk off his ass" and gotten 29,761 matches in 0.19 seconds. But the memories were followed by even more disturbing sensations: of his host's liver, kidneys, and bladder at work, filtering his blood, neutralizing the alcohol—converting sugar to fat, channeling the ethanol into his bladder to be pissed out. Jasper understood exactly how the applejack would be broken down, how he could maximize the alcohol's effect if he wanted to, or render it harmless. He was so sure of this fact that he picked up the bottle of liquor and swilled it. There was no burning sensation, no coughing, nothing. It might as well have been water.

Just then a car sped down 9G. Jasper started and nearly dropped the bottle. He'd thought it was his dad for a moment, but then he realized it wasn't Van Arsdale's truck, which had a carburetor rather than fuel injection, a worn belt on the alternator that squeaked at a frequency of about fifteen kHz.

But—but how did he know these things? How could *any* human being? The answer to that question was scarily obvious: Jasper wasn't human. Not anymore.

Jasper's head—well, Jarhead's—started spinning. He set the fallen chair upright and sank into it, let Jarhead's face splat on the table. He could hear his father's truck in his mind, could hear every single car that had ever driven past him or Jarhead, could measure the difference in volume and timbre between each of them, discern from the smell of the exhaust the type of fuel they were burning and how efficiently. He could tell that the air in the room was three and a half degrees colder around his ankles than it was near his head, that there was a mouse nibbling its way into a bag of flour in the cabinet next to the stove, that the bathroom faucet upstairs was dripping into the sink at the rate of 13.75 drops per hour. But one thought dominated all these others.

He was dead. He was dead, yet he was more alive than he'd ever been, and it was *scary as shit.*

In his frustration he slammed his fist into the kitchen table. It was made of solid oak—no Formica for John Van Arsdale, thank you very much—but even so, it snapped in half beneath Jasper's fist. The glass with the flower bounced up like one of those spring-loaded bells at a carnival, but Jasper snatched it out of the air without thinking. He stared at the glass in his hand, dumbfounded. The purple blossoms quivered, orange powder dusted his fingers. Pollen. The plant equivalent of jism. Even plants wanted to have sex.

"Oh fuck." Jasper pushed away from the broken table so fast that the legs of his chair snapped off beneath him. He sprawled on Jarhead's fat ass, his right hand holding the flower up like a lifeguard putting a drowner's life ahead of his own. "Jesus fuck." He scrambled to his feet and ran for the back door, which burst from its hinges at his touch. Gunther's hysterical barking bit at his ears as he ran into the dawn, and he was a quarter mile down the road before he realized he still had the flower in his hand. The purple petals whipped about in the breeze but didn't separate from the stalk. They clung tenaciously to life, still spewing pollen in the hope that they might breed before finally giving up the ghost. "FUCK!" Jasper screamed one more time, and, clutching the glass like a relay baton with no one to hand off to, he ran blindly into the light of a new day.

4

1992.

Ileana—or Iljana, as she was known then, Iljana Zanic—had been nineteen. Still a child. Still living with her family in a small farmhouse on the outskirts of Bihac, on the border between Bosnia and Croatia. The country was still called Yugoslavia then, though many people sensed this designation was fast losing any real meaning. It had been a decade since the death of Marshal Tito, and the region appeared to be fracturing yet again along the religious and ethnic lines that had riven the Balkans for at least two millennia.

For weeks she'd listened to the radio for news of the violence exploding across the country. Ileana's family, like a large percentage of the city's population, were Croats, having crossed the river a generation ago to work in the factories that had been built in the Bosnian Republic under Tito. Now they listened with trepidation to reports that the republic's ethnic Serbs had decided to reclaim the city as part of "Greater Serbia." There had already been disturbing stories of Muslims being driven from eastern Bosnia by the predominantly Orthodox insurgents. Ileana's family was Roman Catholic. They hoped this would be enough to protect them, but they kept a few bags packed in the front closet, just in case. Bihac lay on the River Uni, just inside Bosnia's western border. Safety was just a few miles across the river.

But all that was a world away to the nineteen-year-old who donned her prettiest yellow dress for her weekly English lesson with a young man recently returned from college in Canada. Slavs are pessimistic by nature, and Balkan Slavs, whose tiny corner of the world has been the battleground in wars involving every empire from Rome to Byzantium to the Ottomans to the Nazis, are the most pessimistic of all. But the young man had filled Ileana's mind with hope for the future. Perhaps it was just her heart he was filling. He was twenty-one, after all. Lean, articulate, worldly. A poet! Now, sadly, she couldn't remember his name, but at the time she would have believed just about anything he said, especially if he was touching her hand while he said it, or tucking a lock of hair behind her ear.

She'd just passed the ruins of the Hotel Sunce, destroyed in World War II by the Germans or the Allies, no one remembered. Ileana didn't give the hotel a second glance, let alone a second thought. Most of her attention was devoted to turning the wheels of her Communist-era bicycle, a rusting steel contraption that weighed nearly as much as she did. She had to stand to turn the pedals, and the stiff gears whined like a mechanical dog. She only stopped because she was starting to sweat, and she didn't want to be sticky and gross when she arrived at the poet's house. Only then did she notice everyone around her had stopped as well. The old men had turned from their fishing poles, the old women carting water home to flush their toilets had set their buckets on the cobblestones. Everyone stared toward the southeast, where—Ileana's throated tightened, for a minute she couldn't breathe—a thick haze of smoke clung to the horizon beyond the trees.

Ileana straddled her bicycle, her yellow dress riding up her thighs and fluttering in the breeze. She would always remember that breeze, the quality of the air. Warm. Clean-smelling. The scents of spring: flowers, the sun-baked river. It was a day to pull fish from the water, to plant tomatoes and beets or learn English words like "supply and demand" and "free market economics," maybe share a cigarette with a cute boy, or a kiss! But the vibrations she felt through her sandals told her that wasn't going to happen now, and probably not ever

again. The water in the buckets quivered with a regular rhythm, the
fishing rods driven into the muddy banks of the Uni twitched like
the antennas of giant insects emerging from the ground. Ileana had
never heard an artillery column before, yet somehow she knew that's
what it was. The faint sound of gunshots a few minutes later was un-
necessary confirmation—by then Ileana had turned her bike around
and was pedaling for home as fast as the whining gears would let her.

The Zanices lived in the remnants of a collective farm on the
edge of the city. Just the house was left, along with one small barn
and the ice shack, which they used in lieu of a refrigerator. The beet
fields had long since grown in with a grove of alder and aspen bi-
sected by the mile-long stretch of the Zanices' driveway. In the
summer the narrow drive turned into a shadowy green tunnel, and as
a little girl Ileana had often pretended it was a magical path that took
her to the past or the future or some other imaginary place. But it
was still early enough in the season that the noon sun beat down
through the branches, illuminating wide tire tracks gouging the
gravel. Those tracks were anything but imaginary, anything but magical. Ileana was hardly an automotive expert, but even she could see
these were big tires—the kind on a truck, or whatever they were called.
A personnel carrier.

All at once she noticed how quiet it was. No birds singing, no
squirrels chattering as they leapt from one swaying branch to another.
Only the whine of Ileana's bicycle, which suddenly seemed shockingly loud. She dismounted and pushed the bike the last hundred
yards. The chain creaked, the gravel crunched beneath her sandals,
but no one seemed to hear her approach—not even Maja, the family
mutt, who should've rushed out to greet her by now. She must be
sleeping, Ileana told herself, or chasing a rabbit in the woods. That's
what it must be.

She paused a moment before entering the small clearing. The
yard was crisscrossed with tire tracks and her mother's marigolds had
been crushed, but that was all the damage she saw. No smoke, no
broken windows or, God forbid, corpses in the yard. Her grandmother told stories about the last war, bodies left to rot where they

fell because people were too scared to touch them. Maybe they've gone, Ileana thought. Maybe they just drove over the marigolds and left.

Just as she was about to lean her bicycle against the barn, however, a soldier with a rifle slung over his back stepped out of the kitchen door. Even from this distance Ileana recognized the patch on his shoulder, the double-headed eagle beneath the large golden crown.

A Serb.

The soldier didn't bother to find a tree, just stood in the middle of the driveway and pissed on the gravel like a dog marking his territory. Ileana couldn't help but see that the front of his uniform was dusted with white powder. Her grandmother had been baking bread when Ileana had gone out an hour ago, her gnarled hands kneading flour and water with a patience that defied the passage of time. Her grandmother, who had survived Nazis and Communists and everything in between. It didn't seem right that she should fall to such an insignificant boy.

Ileana heard the bicycle whine only after the fact—only when the young soldier looked up sharply, straight at her, his spouting penis still dangling from one hand. He didn't appear embarrassed. Just finished, shook off, tucked himself away. Only then did he swing his rifle off his back.

"*Zdravo sestra*," he called. *Hello sister.* "Why don't you come over here?" The rifle hung innocently under his arm even as he fished a pack of cigarettes from his breast pocket and began to walk in her direction.

Ileana didn't say anything. Didn't move as the soldier walked through the gravel he'd just pissed in. She could see that the flour was especially thick on the knees of his pants, the boots.

"Don't be afraid, *sestra*. We won't hurt you." He laughed quietly. There were handprints on his shirt, Ileana saw, several long white smudges on the left side of his face like a slap.

She thought about making a break for it. There were plenty of trees on both sides of the driveway and he would have a hard time shooting her. But something held her. The flour on his face, his pants. The thought of her grandmother in the kitchen, trying to beat him off. Her mother, her brother and father. She couldn't leave them.

The tip of the soldier's rifle butted her ribs. The metal barrel was cold through the thin fabric of her dress. Ileana told herself that was a good sign. It would have been hot if he'd fired it, right?

The soldier stared into her eyes, yet Ileana didn't feel that he was looking at her.

"*Da.* You want it, don't you, *sestra*? Don't you, you Croatian whore?"

Suddenly his hand was in her hair. Her legs tangled in her bicycle and she stumbled. There was a rip, and the part of her that still believed everything would be okay tried to see where, to see if her favorite yellow dress could be mended, but the soldier yanked her hair again. She cried out, scrambled to her feet. Lost her sandals, lurched barefoot behind him as he dragged her toward the house. There was a warm squelch when she stepped in the place where he'd pissed, and then he was pulling the screen door open and tossing her inside.

Ileana cried out again as she stumbled into the room. Her grandmother lay stretched across the worn tiles, flour everywhere, the old woman a white ghost on a white background, save for a dark viscid roux beside her ear.

She heard footsteps upstairs, the sound of wood splintering, plaster breaking, soldiers ransacking the family's possessions, perhaps in search of valuables, perhaps just to destroy things.

"Iljana!"

For the first time she noticed her father and mother and brother huddled in a corner. She wanted to run to them but the soldier still held her hair.

A man came down the narrow staircase. He was dressed not in combat fatigues like the soldier who held her, but in a colorless uniform with three chevrons beneath the Serbian eagle. A crewcut U of rusty hair sat on his otherwise bald head like a dingy laurel, a fistful of silver chains dangled from one plump-fingered hand. Ileana recognized them as her grandmother's crucifix, her mother's, her own.

"Sergeant Petrovic!" The young soldier practically snapped his heels together. He jerked Ileana's head back. "I found this outside."

The sergeant squinted at the three crosses—Roman Catholic, lacking the second, slanted crossbar of the Orthodox crucifix—then mashed them into a ball as if they were worth nothing more than the silver they were made of, dropped them in his pocket.

"In the corner."

Ileana ran to her mother, who clutched at her, sobbing.

"Listen to me," her father said. "We're nothing. Nothing. I'm no soldier. My son is no soldier. My daughter, my wife, they're innocent. Please. We have nothing to do with any of this."

Only then did the sergeant look up, not at her father, but at the young soldier who'd dragged Ileana inside. Only then did Ileana see the sergeant's eyes. She gasped. It was as if they belonged to another person. His cheeks were florid, his belly strained at the buttons of his jacket, but his eyes were hard and hot as pulsing coals. They seemed to bore right into the young soldier, who stood up even straighter beneath his commanding officer's gaze.

"Corporal Zelimir knows no one is innocent. Isn't that correct, Corporal?"

"*Da*, Sergeant!"

Perhaps it was the English lessons. Perhaps it was the fact that the soldier couldn't have been more than twenty or twenty-one, just like her poet. More likely, though, it was just naivete, or stupidity.

"Zelimir means peace," Ileana said. "Please. Please, don't do this."

The corporal's composure cracked, but the sergeant's eyes held him in place. The expression on the older man's face was thoughtful, as if he were contemplating what Ileana had said. He didn't look at her as he unsnapped the flap of his holster, didn't so much as glance in her direction as he pulled his sidearm out and held it in his palm disdainfully, just like he'd held the crucifixes.

"Peace?" He spoke to the gun, not Ileana. "*Da*. Peace." In one smooth gesture the sergeant shot Ileana's brother in the forehead, then her father. The two men fell like dominoes onto the flour-covered floor, and as the echoes of the gunshot faded from the room her mother's screams reached Ileana's ears.

"Now they are at peace, *da*, Corporal?"

"*Da*, Sergeant!"

"You," the sergeant said now, pointing his gun at Ileana's mother. "Do you still bleed?"

"What? What do you—"

The sergeant squeezed the trigger, putting a bullet in Ileana's mother's thigh.

"I said, *do you still bleed?*"

Ileana's mother seemed too stunned to realize she'd been shot. She looked at the dark patch of blood on her leg and then she looked at Ileana. She reached for her daughter's hands.

"No," she whispered. "No, no—"

Ileana saw the effect of the gunshot before she heard it: a fistful of brain and bits of skull that burst out the side of her mother's head and splattered against the kitchen wall. Then her mother's eyes went blank and she fell into the lap of Ileana's favorite yellow dress.

The sergeant smiled at Ileana.

"They are all at peace now, *sestra*." He put a hand on the corporal's shoulder. "Soon he and I will show you a new kind of peace."

5

Mohinder had been waving the patient's file around for the past hour, as if he only had to shake it hard enough and a medical breakthrough would fall out.

"At Cambridge, I took a lecture on Lorenz. He argued that—"

Sue bit back a scream. She snatched the folder from her colleague's hand, resisted the urge to swat him in the face.

"There's a reason they call it a *briefing*."

She spun on her heel and clicked her way down the tiled hallway. She thought she might duck out for that cigarette, but she had to pass the examination room to go outside. The sight of the young man visible in the window stopped her in her tracks. He seemed naked beneath the blanket that pooled in his lap, but it wasn't his smooth brown skin that had stopped her, so much as the fact that it was splattered with blood from cheeks to toes.

She glanced at Mohinder's report. *Qusay, Mohammed Jr.* The EMTs had cut his blood-soaked garments off to treat what they assumed would be multiple lacerations and found—this. Skin smooth as the inside of a walnut shell. Not just unscratched, but unblemished, as if he'd never once had a bicycle accident, fallen out of a tree, gotten tackled in a football game. Sue had minored in comparative literature in her undergrad days, and a line from *The Thousand Nights and a Night* flashed in her mind. "Those who saw him were

damned for their thoughts." Mohammed Qusay sat on the edge of
the examination table, his blood-spattered torso curved like a half-
ripe pepper. Dark hair clung to his skull in licorice ringlets, his mouth
was purple and full as a plum. Between hair and mouth were a pair of
eyes as dark and deep and oblivious as two glasses of wine.

According to Mohinder, Qusay had no idea what had happened.
Kept insisting someone else had been driving, even though it was his
body that had been pulled from the driver's seat (and only after
sawing off the steering column, which had pinned him in place,
though it hadn't broken a blood vessel, let alone a rib). Mohinder
thought it might be MPD—he was always looking for a case he could
turn into a book, his own personal *Sybil*. Sue had suggested shock,
perhaps a blackout caused by the accident or alcohol or drug con-
sumption. Somewhat smugly, Mohinder informed her that the boy's
alcohol and tox screens had come back clean—sparkling, as if he'd
never touched a controlled substance in his life. "A *most* curious case.
Don't you agree?" Sniveling twat.

It wasn't until she got to Mohinder's line about Qusay's having
been "in a state of partial undress" that she finally put two and two
together, realized the boy on the other side of the glass had been the
driver of the vehicle whose pictures Larry had texted to her phone.
With his inimitable nonchalance, Mohinder had written that semen
had been found in the mouth of the girl in the passenger seat and,
more disturbingly, that bruises "consistent with the dimensions" of
Qusay's hands had been found on the back of her neck, meaning
that the boy in the examination room had basically forced his passenger to blow him, shot his wad, and driven the car into a cliff. The
passenger had been dead by the time Larry and his partner arrived,
as well as the boy in the backseat. The fourth occupant of the car
was in surgery to relieve the pressure on her spinal cord caused by
three crushed vertebrae, faced a likely future as a quadriplegic if she
made it out of the OR alive. It sounded like a suicide pact—something out of a modern-day Goethe novel, or maybe just a Marilyn
Manson song. Sue glanced at the names of the other passengers. Sila
Patel was the girl in the passenger's seat, Jasper Van Arsdale the

second fatality, Michaela Szarko the girl with the broken neck. All four were seventeen. Jesus, Sue thought. This kid had a hell of a lot to live with.

Taking a deep breath, she pushed the door open.

"Mr. Qusay," she said brightly. "I'm Dr. Miller, the psychiatric resident here at Columbia Memorial."

Sue had to fight back a gasp when the boy looked up. The emptiness in his eyes. The innocence. The helplessness. The only time she'd seen a similar expression was during her internship at the VA hospital in New York just after the Gulf War—soldier after soldier who seemed to have left part of himself in Iraq. The part that could remember. The part that could feel.

The boy was rubbing the plastic ID bracelet on his right wrist. She was about to ask if it was chafing when he said, "Do you know where my watch is?"

She took a seat at the desk. "I imagine the EMTs or one of the admitting physicians removed it to, ah, examine you." Although really, she thought, what could they examine? Even a cursory glance revealed that the boy was glowing with health and vigor.

"My dad gave it to me. It was a graduation present. Pregraduation. A Patek. He'll be pissed if I lost it."

A wave of compassion washed through Sue. The technical term was posttraumatic stress disorder, but she preferred the poets' word: shellshock. The poor boy had killed his friends, and he was worried about losing a watch. She wondered if the fact that it came from his father was significant. Daddies rich enough to give you a Porsche and a Patek almost always came with issues.

"I'll speak to Dr. Mohinder about it when we're done. Right now I'd like to ask—"

"It wasn't me! It wasn't me, I swear it wasn't!"

The boy had begun rocking back and forth on the examination table, and the paper crackled beneath him like the sound of a distant fire.

"No one's accusing you of anything, Mohammed. I just want to find out what happened."

Qusay stopped rocking. His eyes fixed hers. "It was him. *Him.*"

Sue fought the urge to look away. "Who was it, Mohammed?"

The boy opened his mouth but no sound came out. His eyes were equally wide, equally silent.

"Mohammed?"

The look on his face made her want to cry out. Such terror, such . . . unknowing. He cinched the blanket around his bloodstained torso, and Sue felt as though she were watching someone wrap himself in his own shroud.

"I can't tell you his name."

Sue had to resist catching hold of the boy's hand. One of her teachers had told her too much empathy made her ill suited for long-term analysis, which was probably why she'd ended up at a hospital in the middle of nowhere rather than with a lucrative Park Avenue practice.

"Let's take it one step at a time, okay, Mohammed?"

The boy took a deep breath, nodded. "Q. My—my friends call me Q."

Sue heard the pause. His friends.

All at once words started pouring from his mouth.

"Have you ever had one of those dreams where you're watching yourself at the same time as you're the person you're watching? It's like you're doing things, saying things, but at the same time it's not you. And you want to call out to yourself, tell yourself to stop, but when you open your mouth only a whisper comes out and no one can hear you. You can't make yourself shout any louder, and you can't hear yourself either."

Sue nodded. "People who find themselves in situations where they don't have control often feel as if they're under the influence of drugs or—"

"It wasn't *drugs*. There was someone else *there*. Someone *in my mind*." Q. shook his head violently, as if he was trying to rattle out the stranger. "You have to believe me. It wasn't *me*. It was *him*. *Him*. He *made* me do it."

"Are you saying you heard voices, Q.? That told you to do things?"

"He didn't *tell* me to do anything. He *made* me. I know it sounds crazy. I'm not crazy, am I? Like schizophrenia or multiple personalities or something?"

"MPD is more common in novels than in real life. In fact, almost all cases have been found to be induced by the treating analyst—a little like the repressed memories craze of a few years ago. Now schizophrenia? That *does* manifest around your age, but . . ." Sue paused, shook her head.

"What?"

"It's just, well, your feeling that someone was inside you isn't typical. Usually there's externalization. Paranoia, aural and visual hallucinations. The patient feels as though the threat is coming from outside—a voice only he can hear, a person only he can see. He's not aware of anything wrong with himself. Thinks he's perfectly normal and everyone else is crazy."

"All he thought about was sex. It was like all he wanted to do was stick my dick in something. But he had to wait till the right time."

Sue noted the disjunction. *He wanted. My dick.*

"What was the right time, Q.? What were you—I mean, what was he waiting for?"

Q. looked at her balefully, as if he thought she were baiting him.

"I used to have a scar."

Sue sat back. The boy's voice had taken an hysterical edge.

"My appendix burst when I was thirteen." The boy touched a spot on his blood-splattered stomach. "There was a two-inch scar there. You could really see it at the end of summer because it didn't tan with the rest of my skin. And now it's gone." Q. touched his face, his torso. "I drove into a cliff at *a hundred miles an hour.* Two of my friends are dead and one's in the operating room and I don't have a single scratch on me. Even my scar is gone. *Don't you think that's funny?"*

"I'm not sure *funny*—"

"Knock, knock."

Mohinder's sycophantic face poked through the door.

"Pardon me for interrupting, Dr. Miller. The boy's father has arrived."

"I'll release him as soon as I've finished my examination, Dr. Mohinder."

"Ah, yes," Mohinder glanced at Q. "It's just that, well, Mr. Qusay Sr. would like to take the boy now."

Something flashed in Sue's mind. Maybe it was Mohinder's stilted manner of speaking, but all of a sudden she thought of her old teacher, J.D. Thomas.

She tapped the clipboard.

"The boy's chart is marked 4-20." Four-twenty being the code that indicated a patient was a suspect in a criminal proceeding, and could only be released with police permission.

Mohinder's smile was almost gloating. "The boy's father has taken care of it."

"Where in the hell did he find a judge at *this* hour?" Sue glanced at Q. "Your dad has some connections, doesn't he? Well, then," she turned back to Mohinder, "get him some clothes. And see if you can find his watch, for God's sake. This isn't *rehab*."

As soon as Mohinder scurried away, Sue pulled a card from her desk, wrote down a number on the back. She was surprised she remembered it after all these years, but Thomas had been important to her. He'd been the one who told her she was too empathic to be a therapist, after all.

"Take this, Q." She pressed the card into the boy's hand. "It's a doctor in the city. He specializes in cases like yours."

Q. took the card, but Sue couldn't tell if he actually noticed it. His eyes were full of a nameless fear.

"What if he comes back?"

"What if–?"

"For me. What if he comes back to finish what he started?"

6

The order went like this: corps, division, brigade, regiment, battalion.

    Two companies in a battalion, two platoons in a company, two squads in a platoon. The squad was the smallest martial unit: only ten men, plus a corporal and a staff sergeant.

Only ten men. Plus a corporal whose name meant peace, and a sergeant with swimming coals for eyes.

They tied her wrists to the posts of her parents' bed. They didn't undress her, but each soldier ripped a little more of her yellow dress away, until eventually there were just tatters sticking to her skin like poorly applied bandages. The corporal dragged in a pair of kitchen chairs, and he and the sergeant commented on this or that soldier's technique or endowment while they waited their turn.

"Don't be shy, Stanko, you're like the bulldozer, you have to open her up for everyone else."

"Vinko, Vinko, Vinko. You have more hair on your ass than on your head. You should shave it off and wear it as a toupee."

"Good Christ, Grigor, is that a foreskin or a garden hose? You could tie a bow in that thing!"

It was getting dark by the time the corporal approached. Maybe it was the whiskey or maybe it was the major's eyes on his naked ass, but the corporal's penis remained soft the entire time, and after squirming on top of her for a few minutes he faked a few groans and rolled off.

"She's got more juice in her than a watermelon."

The sergeant was staring blindly into space, the bottle dangling from one hand.

"*Da,*" he said in a distracted voice. "Close the door on your way out, Corporal. I want time alone with this one."

The corporal glanced back at Ileana. It could have been pity or loathing that he offered her, but in either case he only nodded, then pulled the door closed.

For a long time the sergeant just sat there, twirling the bottle in his hands. At length he brought it to his lips, held it there for a moment before he realized there was no more alcohol in it. He held it up for Ileana to see.

"Empty."

His voice had changed. Had grown older, world-weary.

"Empty. Do you understand?"

By now Ileana was past shock, past pain even. She stared at the sergeant dumbly.

"To me, you are all empty. Every last one of you."

Ileana licked her cracked lips. "Croats? Bosniaks?"

The sharpness seemed to have retreated from the sergeant's eyes, as if the fire within had been stoked but could flare up at any moment.

"Croats? Bosniaks? What do I care of Croats or Bosniaks, or Serbs for that matter? To me, you are all as empty as this bottle, vessels to be filled and drained." He hurled the bottle against the wall over Ileana's head. It shattered, and she closed her eyes against falling glass. Faster than seemed humanly possible the sergeant was on her. She felt his hands on her face, brushing the shards away with surprising tenderness.

"Open your eyes, *sestra*. I want you to see this."

The sergeant leaned over her. His paunch sat heavily on her

stomach, yet he held himself with the grace of a cat. The fire in his eyes was back, burning into hers. The light swirled around like lava flowing beneath the ocean.

"Today we took everything from you. Your family, your country, your purity." He stroked between her legs with his blunt fingers. "But perhaps we gave you something in return."

A groan escaped Ileana's lips, but no words were equal to it.

"*Da, sestra*, I know, I know." The sergeant turned her face to his gently. So gently. "There is nothing more disgusting than life. Nothing save for a new life. Another purposeless existence, born in ignorance, living in squalor, dying in fear. But trust me, *sestra*, there are far worse fates, and today we have saved you from it. When you are moldering in your grave I will remember you, and think how I spared you *my* fate."

Ileana had no idea what the sergeant was talking about. He spoke as if he thought he was doing her a kindness. With tender fingers he peeled the shreds of her dress away, used the sheet to wipe blood and semen from her body. He stroked her arms.

"I will give you strength to punish your enemies."

Ran his palms up and down each leg.

"Speed to hunt them down."

Traced a finger over each eye, around her ears.

"Senses to spy them where they hide."

He was unbuttoning his shirt, his pale flaccid stomach spilling over his belt like an overcooked potato.

"Who knows, perhaps it will be this body you punish first."

She was too sore to feel him enter her—to distinguish the pain of his entry, at any rate, from the general ache that filled her loins. In truth the tenderness of his actions hurt more than the rape itself. He thrust slowly, delicately, as if he were the first man ever to slide into her and wanted her deflowering to be as painless as possible. It was almost like he wanted her to enjoy it.

"Join me, Ileana. Show me what you're made of. What you can do."

She tried to fight, physically, mentally, but his eyes and voice and penis all held her. She felt the burning in her loins change ever so slightly, as pain morphed into a kind of pleasure a thousand times more loathsome.

"No. Please, no."

But it was on her in a way she could've never imagined. Her eyes closed, her mouth opened. Her knees clutched at the sergeant's body as it dove in and out of her.

"No!" she screamed, but it was useless. An orgasm flooded her body, heaving through her in alternating waves of senselessness and self-loathing. It seemed to go on forever, but when it was gone she missed it, because she was still there, the sergeant still atop her, thrusting more violently now, a strangled groaning rising from the back of his throat. The light swirled in the depths of his eyes, and then, with a shudder, it flickered out.

All at once everything changed.

It was subtle at first. Less a flooding than a seeping, like slipping a dry sponge into a sinkful of hot water and feeling it soften in your grip. But the water was *too* hot. Not hot like hot water, but hot like acid. Something utterly foreign was soaking into her, burning her away.

And then it awakened inside her. She felt as if she'd been pushed down a deep well, as if she was staring up the long narrow shaft at an opening that was getting farther and farther away. And then a voice whispered from inside her own head.

Now, Iljana! Take your vengeance!

At first it was the voice Ileana was trying to escape, not the sergeant who still lay atop her, panting, prone. She jerked her arms at the clothesline that bound them. The cord held but the bedposts broke, snapping and swinging through the air. The sergeant looked up just in time to catch one in his face. The blow glanced off his forehead, and he blinked more in confusion than in pain.

"*Sestra?*" He stared at the naked girl conjoined to his body. "Who—who are you?"

"Who *am* I?" Ileana screamed. It was hard to tell what was her and what was the strange force inside her. Her fury was hers, yet it had never burned so pure. And this strength! She grabbed the sergeant by the throat and lifted him in the air as though he were an infant.

"Who am I, you piece of Serbian shit? Who *am* I?" She shook him crazily, his limbs and head flailing about, a choked moan coming from his throat. "How *dare* you!"

"Sergeant?"

Corporal Zelimir had reappeared in the doorway. He stood frozen at the sight before him: the naked Croatian girl swinging the fat sergeant by the throat. He reached for his pistol and Ileana threw the sergeant across the room, knocking both soldiers to the ground. In a single leap she was on them, one man in each hand, pounding their skulls together with a sound like rocks wrapped in cloth. She was beyond speech, just screaming as she beat the life from each man with the other's body.

Shouts from the ground floor, footsteps on the stairs. Ileana dropped the lifeless men and sprang for the window. Her body was rigid as a spear as she dove through the narrow opening, the glass shattering and glancing off her skin, tight and hard as armor. The ground rushed up, and part of her, the part that was still Ileana, braced for impact. But the other part—the part that was in control—tucked and rolled smoothly over the grass, used the momentum of her jump to propel her directly into a run. By the time the soldiers made it to the window the only signs of her were the two bedposts and the frayed cords that had tied her to them.

She stole clothes from a line outside the smoking ruins of a house. Black tights, black shirt, a strip of dark cloth to bind her pale hair like a Bosniak woman. She dressed in a field about a half mile from her house. The field had burned and the ash was still hot, but Ileana's bare feet didn't feel it. She used the ash to darken her hands and face until her exterior was as indistinguishable from the night as the thing inside her.

Bursts of small-arms fire shattered the stillness, tracer rounds arced in the distance; here and there flashes of Serb mortars landed along the edge of town. When a rocket grenade landed a mere fifty yards away, she didn't flinch. Her attention was focused inward, on the wounds she'd incurred at the hands of the soldiers. She set the small lacerations on her face to healing, the rope abrasions on wrists and ankles, the tears in her vagina and anus. She would have liked to clean the revolting remnants of a squad of Serbian soldiers out of her body, but the demon didn't let her do that. When he'd finished recalibrating her system, he made her sit in a squat, only her eyes and ears and nostrils flickering as she gathered data from the night around her. All the while a hunger was growing in her, half lust, half hatred. A desire for the purest form of violence: revenge. Only when the demon felt her actively fighting him—not to be released, but to be allowed to kill—did he let her go.

Hell hath no fury like a woman. Scorned, spurned, burned or bandied about by a pack of Serbian wolves like a hapless lamb. Well, the demon thought, she is the wolf now. The real hunter, no matter what the Legion called its agents.

The demon smiled at his own wit, but the expression didn't reach Ileana's mouth. It remained set in a predatory snarl as, wraithlike, she slipped into the smoking city.

7

Mohinder was unable to find the boy's watch, but he rustled up a pair of scrubs and led him out to his father. After he was gone, Sue began writing up her notes. On the surface it looked like a pretty routine psychotic break—tragic, but routine. But the woman in her, the empathic being who'd survived twelve years of rigorous training whose sole goal was to take emotions and intuition out of the process of caring for someone, just didn't buy it. Q. didn't seem sick to her. He seemed like someone who'd forgotten how to talk to a part of himself. A part he refused to name, lest that name turn out to be his own.

Perhaps that was why she'd thought of J.D. Thomas. A die-hard Jungian, her former teacher had dedicated his life to the study of shadow and anima, the twin selves that dwell behind the screen of the persona. The terms were somewhat analogous to Freud's notion of id, superego, and ego, but Jung conceived of them less as mental forces than quasi-distinct personalities. The anima contained the female portion of a man's personality (women had their own animus), while the shadow, as the name implied, carried the darker urges, the baser ones: for sex, violence, dominance. In extreme cases, one of the two posterior entities could overcome the persona in a manner that resembled MPD, sometimes going so far as to take a nickname to distinguish itself from the primary personality.

J.D., however, had seen the question in more complicated terms. Building on one of Jung's most famous—and most controversial—theories, that of the collective unconscious, he argued that there were *hundreds* of fully fledged personalities in each of us, as well as flecks of thousands more. These personalities weren't subconscious projections: they were in fact our ancestors, their experiences and emotions chromosomally transmitted at the moment of conception. How else is it, J.D. had argued, that all human beings are born with the same feelings? Happiness, sadness, anger, lust? How do we know that crying is a signal of distress, laughter a sign of delight? Few people challenged these basic assumptions, but most biologists attributed them to the same kind of instinct that led a person to jerk his hand from a hot stove. J.D. thought that was a cop-out. Instinct was just a euphemism for thought, and logic implied that if you could genetically encode simple thoughts, then you could encode complex ones as well. Genuine emotions. Ideas even. Memories. Not just your own, but other people's. The human genome was capable of storing extraordinary amounts of information—as yet we couldn't even delimit its scope, let alone guess what all was there. So why not your mother and father, your grandparents, the distant relatives who first made the trek out of the African savannah? You'd inherited your body from them, after all. Why not your mind?

As a grad student, Sue had been enraptured by the notion that her mother and father, both of whom were already dead, were present within her, lending her the benefit of their experience. Seven years at a rural hospital can shatter just about any illusion, but she still remembered that period of her life with nostalgia. Who doesn't get tired of being alone in their skin? Hasn't wished for a companion with whom to bond in permanent, perfect union? Is that what Q. was looking for in his nameless nemesis? Someone to be with him, even unto death?

"Ah, Q.," she said out loud. "What got into you?"

Her words echoed around the little room, and Sue sat up with a start. She had the strangest sense that someone was there with her.

Not looking at her, but listening. The boy's paranoia must be infectious.

She glanced at her watch. Nearly five A.M. She closed the Qusay file and stood up.

Then she sat down again.

Her body felt strange. As though she'd been outside in a blizzard, and was now warming up with a hot toddy. The heat traveled down her throat into her stomach, flowed into her small and large intestines, filled bladder and rectum as though they were balloons. Then it was in her veins, heading for her extremities. Arms, legs, fingers, toes. Her head felt as though it was filled with boiling liquid. Her skeleton crackled with electric energy. Sue was more aware of her flesh than she'd been in years, at exactly the moment she ceded control of it.

Leo was gentle with the woman. Gentler than he'd been with Danny, whom he'd had to take quickly because Jasper had been in such a hurry. Yes, he'd been right about the boy. Such strength, such focus! Such determination! Leo only wished he could've stuck around to see how Jasper handled the poor girl, suddenly come back to herself with her fat friend's flaccid dick in her. He'd find out soon enough, but right now he needed to cover his tracks. It wouldn't do for Jasper to find out that Leo had been possessing Q. at the time of the accident. It might make his claim to friendship a little difficult for the fledgling to believe.

In a moment he'd assimilated every one of Sue's memories from the most trivial to the most traumatic. The time she took the egg from a hawk's nest and tried to hatch it beneath her pillow, and the time her mother whipped her with a wooden spoon until the handle broke. The time she started crying as a patient detailed thirteen years of methodical sexual abuse at the hands of her father and the time she masturbated to those self-same images. My God, she was a filthy one, this Sue Miller—not just dirty but clever enough to make her boyfriend think *he* was corrupting *her*. Leaving her was going to be *fun*.

More importantly, Leo now knew everything Q. had told her in their interview. He wasn't surprised to discover the boy had survived the crash—he'd needed to make sure his host remained intact, just in case he mistimed his ejaculation—but the fact that Q. came through without injury was unexpected. Leo must have recalibrated the boy's nervous system more finely than he'd realized. The boy would live to be 150, barring a plane crash or nuclear war—or, more likely, a shotgun blast to the head, to rid his mind of the guilt that would haunt him for the rest of his life.

Sue, on the other hand, would not have to forget: Leo would take care of that for her. He wiped the interview with Q. from her memory, then sifted through her mind for anything else that might be relevant. He paused over J.D. Thomas. You never knew with the Jungians. And look at this one. Collective memory! Leo hadn't come across that old chestnut in years. It bore all the hallmarks of Legion. Sure enough, when he probed a little further, Leo found that Sue had more than memories of her former teacher. Hypnotic suggestions had been placed in her mind, prompting her to contact Thomas should a patient present with a story that hinted of demonic activity. Thomas's phone number glowed in her consciousness like a Times Square billboard. Oh, yes. Definitely Legion.

This was interesting. It was also annoying. Jasper was at a delicate stage. Confused, apt to frenzy. Leo needed to get back to him before he disappeared. But all this was as new to Leo as it was to Jasper. Like any first-time parent, there were some things you had to learn as you went along.

Leo had been suspicious when Foras first approached him, and told him that if something wasn't done the Legion would succeed in wiping out the Mogran. Foras's revelation about how the Mogran reproduce was shockingly simple: a bound soul—a virgin, in human parlance—was transformed into a demon if it died while possessed by another Mogran. On the one hand, the Alpha's words resonated strongly with Leo's memories of his own metamorphosis. On the other hand, the Alphas had tried to kill him on a dozen occasions over the centuries. If Foras was lying, then any Mogran foolish enough to attempt what he'd just described would die in the attempt. And Foras had no good explanation for why the possessing demon wasn't killed with his host. Leo told the older demon that he wanted to see him do it first. Imagine his surprise when Foras told him he couldn't. When the Alpha Wave forged the Covenant seventeen hundred years ago, they'd needed a way to ensure that none of the nine attempted to create new Mogran behind the others' backs. There was only one way to be absolutely certain. The hunters had their word for it—the sigil—but Foras hadn't bothered to hide behind fancy terminology (or his pants for that matter). Leo had spent a good ten minutes laughing at what the Alpha showed him.

Even so, he was skeptical. Amused: but skeptical. Why, after so many years, had Foras had a change of heart? If the other members of the nine found out, Foras's punishment was likely to be protracted, not to mention very, very painful. The Alpha's reply haunted Leo: for seventeen hundred years the imprisoned demon had been in a constant state of frenzy, with no way to appease it. No amount of endocrinological manipulation had enabled him to regenerate the organs he needed to achieve orgasm. He was stuck. There were times when the need to jump had almost driven him crazy, but nothing he tried had worked. But Foras believed that if there was one exception to a rule, then there must be two. If a demon could exit a host by killing it—assuming the host was still a virgin, still bound—then there must be other exceptions as well. Foras refused to elaborate, but he had come to believe that advances in technology made it theoretically possible for a Mogran to travel between hosts without having sex. However, he said, he needed other demons to test his theories, which was why he'd come to Leo. He would trade Leo the secret of reproduction if, in turn, Leo would generate a few subjects for him to experiment on. Leo had responded by telling Foras he should've struck the deal before giving away his only bargaining chip. He had leapt at the Alpha, but Foras hadn't spent seventeen hundred years in a single body for nothing. Leo hadn't even seen him move, but when he woke up his host's head was facing the wrong way on her shoulders. Round one to the Alpha.

That had been more than five years ago. In the meantime, Leo heard that Kali and Malachi had also been let in on the secret. Kali had fallen to the hunters in Estonia, but to the best of his knowledge Malachi was still out there. An obnoxious child, Malachi. Barely three hundred years old. The most dramatic stunt he had to his credit was a stint as a camp director for the Nazis. Leo had killed more people without getting out of bed. It was sibling rivalry more than anything else that had motivated Leo to try to make the first new Mogran in three centuries.

It wasn't just fear for his own survival that stayed his hand. To be a Mogran was to be possessed (no pun intended) of a most singular fate, and Leo had misgivings about inflicting that destiny on another soul. Yes, he was immortal, and commanded a reservoir of knowledge that rivaled a great university's library. But he had lost something too. Something that the living would call humanity, but that he chose to think of as perspective. He had committed acts that his living self could never have contemplated, let alone executed. Destroyed minds, relationships, families even, sometimes in the name of survival, but more often just for fun. Diversion. Distraction. Every once in a while the impact of his actions caught up with him, though, and during the week he'd spent observing Jasper in Q.'s body, he decided to give the boy one chance. One chance at mortality. But the boy hadn't taken it. Leo believed that unbinding wasn't as simple as losing one's virginity—that there was a psychological component involved in that choice, and that some aspect of Jasper had been unwilling to submit to a single existence, and so had rebuffed Sila in the closet the night before the accident. If anyone was going to be haunted by that decision, it would be Jasper, not Leo.

Now, though, he was wondering if it had been worth it. If he didn't get back to Jasper soon, his fledgling was likely to disappear into the world, and it could take forever to track him down. Meanwhile, Q. had opened a whole new can of worms. Sue Miller, J.D. Thomas, the likely involvement of the Legion—which meant that a hunter was going to be on Leo's trail if he didn't act soon. Like it or not, Jasper was going to have to fend for himself for the time being.

He started with Sue. He chipped at her memories of Thomas, but the synaptic pathways held fast. The psychiatrist's teacher had known what he was doing. He was so good that Leo wondered if perhaps he was a former host himself. In the end Leo had to whack Sue's memories with a mental sledgehammer—in this case, a flood of protein kinase inhibitor so potent it wiped out everything that had happened to Sue between the ages of eight and twenty-six. Middle school to college, long division to conversational French to Melanie Klein and the unconscious battle between Eros and Thanatos. Her mother's death from metastatic lung cancer, her father's suicide, her two-year fiasco of a marriage—all of it, gone.

That left Thomas. Thomas and Q. Leo hadn't wanted to harm the boy because he suspected Q.'s disappearance would raise Jasper's suspicions. It seemed unlikely that the boy would warm to Leo if he knew the elder demon had been the one who ended his mortal life. In time Leo would tell his fledgling—a hundred years from now, a thousand, when Jasper's ties to the world of flesh had long since faded. But Leo couldn't have Q. going to the Legion at this fragile stage in Jasper's development. There was no way around it: Q. would have to be destroyed, along with any evidence that he'd once been possessed by Leo.

The Mogran used Sue's lighter to set Q.'s file afire. As he watched it burn, he felt a similar flame spark in that alchemical synapse where Sue's consciousness met his. As if under his own hypnotic spell, he began to flit about the examination room. Pulled a speculum from a drawer, a bottle of Vicodin, a second of Viagra. Q. and J.D. Thomas receded from his consciousness as the ancient, implacable need took hold. He removed the inhibitions that had kept his host in line for thirty-four years, let her deepest fantasies guide him toward his release. To think that Foras had been unable to appease this urge for nearly two millennia! Leo couldn't imagine how Foras had stood it without going insane.

The Ferragamos made a solid sound on the tiled floor as he walked the psychiatrist down the hallway. The skintight Jil Sanders clung to an ass she paid her trainer $55 dollars an hour to keep nice and firm. By the time she put in a call to her boyfriend, Sue was practically under her own control. Leo was just a spectator, cheering her on. He felt her flesh shiver with anticipation. She fingered the speculum, the bottles of Vicodin and Viagra. She was going to ratchet Larry's asshole open, drop the pills in, fuck them into his system with the vibrator in her bedside drawer, then turn him over and ride him till he passed out. Then she was going to smack him awake and do it again. And again. And again. She only *hoped* he would fight back. That would make it *really* fun.

As she walked to her car, she smelled the flowers she had noticed when she first came to the hospital. The demon gave her the name. Wrote it on her brain in day-glo letters.

"Phlox." Sue giggled like it was a dirty word.

Deep inside her, the demon told himself that Jasper had better be worth all this trouble. If not, he would hand him over to Foras himself.

8

The streets in Bihac were dark, either because the Serbs had cut the power or because the Bosnian government had been unable to provide it. Blackout curtains obscured all but the faintest flicker of candlelight or kerosene lamps, but Ileana saw movement everywhere: rats and mice, feral cats, a dog with a bullet wound in its haunch. The animals avoided her by instinct. Not so the occasional wanderer she encountered.

The first was a Serb. A soldier, but he went down like an old lady with a bad hip. To be fair, he never saw her coming. Ileana jumped him from behind, snapped his neck before he had a chance to cry out.

The next was Serbian as well. His senses were sharper. He heard her footsteps, turned, actually managed to open his mouth—just in time to receive her fist. He had a small mouth, and Ileana had to dislocate his jaw to get her hand all the way inside, then yanked his tongue out by the root. She waved it before his stunned eyes. "Cat got your tongue?" she purred, then left him to bleed out as she sped into the night.

A young man was next, a little older than the poet who taught Ileana English. Ileana could smell the sex on him from fifty feet away, and this only enraged her more. The man started when he saw the dark figure walking toward him, but when he realized it wasn't wearing a uniform—realized it was a girl—he relaxed and smiled uncertainly. *"Sestra,"* he called in a thickly accented voice. And then, in English: "I guess I'm not the only one sneaking out tonight. Matters of the heart," he added, shyly, but proudly too. Ileana's English lessons hadn't progressed far enough for her to understand what he said, but the demon helped her out. Even as she was striking the man in the belly with hard-flexed fingers, an entire language—dialects, accents, the highlights and low points of its literature—filled her brain. The man was English, she knew now, his accent Mancunian but trying for an Oxbridge affect. But only a wordless wheeze escaped his lips as her nails tore through his skin like wet paper. Her fingers burrowed up under the ribs until they found the beating ball of his heart, which she pulled out and held before his blinking eyes. In an accent that perfectly matched his, Ileana said, "Is this the heart you meant?" and squeezed the last of its blood onto his face. She put it in his hands, folded his twitching fingers around it. "Don't let me keep you from it." She was gone before he fell to the ground.

And so on. Four more Serbian soldiers, then a Bosnian militiaman, a pair of local police officers. Scattered in there were three of her former neighbors.

That was the first hour.

The sun was coming up before she'd had her fill. The mortar attacks had ended some time ago, and the town had been eerily quiet for hours. A faint gunpowder tang on the breeze was the only sign of the attack that had happened the previous day.

The demon sat in the back of Ileana's brain. If he'd still had a face there would have been an exhausted smile on it, the face of a teenager dismounting a rollercoaster. God, he loved wars! Ileana's victims lay scattered about the deserted city, but in the coming days they would be catalogued in the laundry list of Serbian atrocities. No one would know better.

A square of light opened in the side of a building. A window blind being raised, brightness radiating into the town. A second blind went up like a sleeper too lazy to open both eyes at once. The demon saw tables stacked on chairs, cakes and pastries beneath plastic covers on a long Formica counter. A restaurant, preparing for business. Only someone as fatalistic as a Slav would open his shop on the second day of a war.

A whiff of baking bread snaked through the air. Ileana's stomach rumbled. The demon didn't need food, of course, but he too felt a rumbling, a hunger. But it wasn't bread he wanted.

The knuckles with which Ileana rapped on the glass door were caked with blood and gore. Ash and blood painted her face like a minstrel.

A man approached, his head crowned by a thatch of hair as bristly and gray as the push broom in his hands. A second thatch, also gray, also dirty, grew between nose and upper lip like a toothbrush used for cleaning the toilet. His apron was an impasto of stains. He looked at the girl warily, shaking his head.

Ileana pounded on the door. The glass rattled loudly, echoing through the quiet streets. She could've broken in of course, but where was the fun in that?

The proprietor hesitated, then hurried forward, one hand digging in the pocket of his filthy apron for a key.

"Are you trying to raise the dead, girl? Quiet down before the entire Serbian army comes running!"

The demon pulled back, giving Ileana a bit of freedom to see what she would do. He held her tongue though, as tightly as her fingers had held the organ she pulled from the Serbian soldier's mouth.

Freedom seemed only to make the girl weak. Ileana slumped into the proprietor's arms, and he had to catch her to keep her from falling. Suddenly his hands noticed what his eyes had missed in the faint morning light: the blood on her skin and clothing. "Good God, girl, what have they done to you?"

Still the demon held her tongue. Ileana struggled against him but could do nothing besides shake her head violently. She shook it and shook it, then began beating it with both hands, but still the demon would not leave.

"*Sestra.*" The proprietor folded her tightly in his arms. "Sweet girl, what's happened to you?"

He took her in back, to an apartment as dirty as his apron. There was a Quran on the coffee table, a bilingual edition in Arabic and Serbo-Croatian, which suggested that the man wasn't particularly devout—an apathy that wouldn't stop a Serb soldier from shooting him in the head three days later, and defiling the pages of the holy book with his feces.

The bathroom was windowless and damp. Droplets of condensation spotted the moldy ceiling, teardrop-shaped rust stains hung beneath the faucets in sink and tub. The only light came from a tall candle in a heavy brass candlestick that the man set on top of the toilet tank. A carpet of shed hair matted the floor.

"I wasn't expecting company," the man said sheepishly. He lowered the lid over the filthy bowl and sat Ileana on it. "So much blood. It's a wonder you're able to walk at all."

He washed her face, dabbing softly at first, then pressing more firmly when he saw there weren't any bruises beneath the dirt and ash and blood. Pink and gray water coursed down her neck, revealing the pale, unblemished cheeks, chin, brow.

"It's good they didn't damage such a pretty face," he crooned, tenderly pulling a piece of debris from her hair, then recoiling when he realized it was a bit of flesh. "My God, what can turn men into such monsters?"

Ileana sat motionless, even as the demon worked busily inside her: dilating her pupils, plumping her lips, allowing the tiniest shimmer of sweat to glisten along her forehead. Her pores radiated chemicals that the man's nose and tongue would register and understand, even if his conscious mind did not.

When his rag strayed to her neck, Ileana straightened her back ever so slightly. Her breasts pushed at the filthy shirt, so wet with blood that they were outlined clearly.

"Forgive me, *sestra*. I cannot get you clean with this . . ."

Ileana's eyes filled with silent pleading. Her arms moved of their own accord, lifting the bottom of her shirt and peeling it off.

The man bit his lip beneath his dirty mustache. "So much blood," he said again, but pity wasn't the only thing in his voice. He wiped her throat and stomach, then rinsed his rag and returned to her breasts. He cleaned one and then the other, lifting them to get at the grime trapped beneath. When his hand brushed against her nipple she breathed in sharply, but that was all the demon allowed her.

"*Sestra?*" The man looked into her eyes.

The demon looked out at him, full of amusement and contempt. Such weak creatures, humans. Slaves to base urges. You didn't even have to possess them to get them to do what you wanted.

It was the man who removed Ileana's pants, standing her up and lowering the filthy garment to the floor. He sponged the right leg, then the left, cleaned each of her feet in turn, around the ankles, between the toes. He turned her around and wiped the back of her legs, the cleft between.

The demon turned Ileana around in a circle as though she were modeling a dress. But there was only the nineteen-year-old body to look at, taut, pale, completely unscathed.

Still kneeling, the man looked up at the girl's face. "There isn't a mark on you. The blood. It—it isn't yours?"

The demon couldn't hold back. He made Ileana grab the man's coarse hair and pull his face into her crotch. The man huffed and blubbered, fought, then gave in. It seemed unlikely he'd ever attempted to pleasure a woman this way. He chewed at Ileana's labia as though it were an unpeeled orange. Ileana felt him gnawing, heard his moans as though they came through a wall. But she could hear her own moans too, and it was the latter that truly disgusted her.

She threw him backwards onto the floor, his head narrowly missing the edge of the tub.

"Whoa, girl, take it easy."

Ileana had to hold the man's stomach out of the way to open his belt. Unlike the hair on his head and face, his pubic thatch was surprisingly well groomed, and the sight of the stumpy penis curled upward like a hitchhiker's thumb brought a smirk to the demon's face.

The man responded with his own embarrassed smile.

"It's not much, I know. But it's all for you."

The demon threw Ileana's head back and laughed. Ileana heard the sound echoing through the dirty little room. Could feel her fingers pulling open her vagina as though it belonged to someone else, could feel her legs buckle as she dropped to her knees and impaled herself on the man's little scimitar. The proprietor let out a short scream, half in pain, half in ecstasy.

"Don't—you—dare!" The demon fixed the man with Ileana's eyes. "I need you to hold on for me. For just—one—*minute.*"

The man's mouth hung open. His eyes were blank as he stared into those of the girl straddling him and rocking up and down violently. A dull moan gurgled out of him.

"Just—one—more—SECOND!"

The last orgasm of Ileana's life was like an icy wind, burning out the strange fire that had raged in her since her rape at the hands of the Serbian squad. All the deadened sensations of the past twelve hours pressed down on her fragile skin. She felt as if a thousand knives were ripping her apart, yet when she looked down at herself she was unblemished. Unblemished, and naked, and sitting astride a—

With a shriek, she threw herself off the man who lay beneath her.

"Who *are* you?" Yet even as she said it she knew. Remembered everything that had happened. Everything she had done. Everything save the why.

"Sestra, sestra." A tired smile played over the man's face. "I'm good, but I'm not *that* good."

Ileana's mouth curled in a grimace of disgust. She hurled herself on the man. She was strong, stronger than she'd ever been, but in her frenzy half her blows struck the tiled floor or the hard cast iron of the tub.

The man threw her off and rolled toward the door. Ileana's head smashed against the wall and she sat stunned.

The man lowered his apron over his open pants. "Has the whole world gone crazy?"

The events of the evening were still scrolling through Ileana's mind, one grisly murder after another. She lifted her hands, looked at them as if they didn't belong to her. How? How had she done such things?

"I'm sorry," the man said. "I don't know what came over me. I should never have done that to you. Not in your state."

A gleam caught Ileana's eye. The long curve of a straight razor hanging just a foot away.

"*Sestra.*" The man saw where she was looking. "*Sestra,* no."

She was entranced by the gleaming metal. Her left hand reached for it slowly. She didn't see the proprietor reach for the brass candlestick on the tank. She stared at her narrow reflection in the blade for one second, then, in a flash, drew it across her right wrist. In the dim light the stream of blood was nearly black.

Then suddenly everything *was* black. Ileana thought she was losing consciousness, but it was just the wick blowing out when the proprietor swung the candlestick through the air. It struck her squarely in the temple. An explosion of sparks, and blessed darkness fell over her mind.

The proprietor dumped her unconscious body on the cobblestones outside his shop.

"Stupid Croatian whore."

Shaking his head, he retrieved his broom and continued getting ready to open. The breakfast crowd would be here soon. People still had to eat, even in wartime.

She felt the pain in half a dozen places when she opened her eyes: her head, her hands, her vagina. But none of them was as bad as the ache that throbbed in her soul.

She was in a hospital ward. Beds, plastic tables, beeping machines. Everything antiseptic and off-white, save for a little blood seeping through bandages here and there.

For the first time she noticed the man sitting beside her. He looked up from the thick silver watch he was winding, saw that she was awake. He smiled, gently, sadly.

"Do you know who did this to you?"

She could see the demon's name in her mind, yet she couldn't bring herself to think it, let alone say it. Slowly, as if it were an experiment, she opened her mouth. Let whatever would come out come out:

"Mogran."

9

The gates of Mohammed Qusay Sr.'s riverfront estate were modeled on those of Buckingham Palace, although they weren't quite as big, or as old. Q.'s dad had built them earlier in the year, after anti-Arabic slurs had been spray painted on his house for the third time since the US had gone to war in Iraq (the local racists apparently being ignorant of the difference between Arabs and Persians). The gold-leafed coat of arms featured a mounted warrior crushing a cobra beneath its hooves. Mr. Qusay had paid a Shia medievalist to design it for him. The warrior carried a scimitar and his shield bore the Islamic crescent and star. If you squinted you could make out a Christian cross on the back of the cobra's head.

Jasper didn't have to squint. He could see the cross clearly, along with the nicks the artist's chisel had left when it etched the design into the iron, and the microscopic traces of oxidation where the glaze over the gold leaf was patchy. He could even tell from the color of the oxidation that the artist had used ormolu, an alloy of copper and zinc, instead of real gold. One time when Jasper was fifteen and working on a book report at the kitchen table his dad had watched a program about gilding on the Discovery Channel, and the information had lodged in his subconscious, hung out there until he could access it again. Of course, he'd had to die first, but why sweat the small stuff?

He blinked, refocusing with a mental effort. Even after a day and a half in Jarhead West's body, he was still adjusting to his new senses. Sometimes he got caught up in the miraculous details available to his eyes and ears, his nose, his skin, would stand slack-jawed in front of a tree trunk like a boy staring at his first pair of naked tits. But he took comfort in these moments too. Knew that the part of him that found his new senses so fascinating was the part of him that was still human. Was still Jasper. Forty hours is a long time to be dead, but it's an even longer time to live in someone else's body. Jasper was amazed at how difficult it was to remember who he'd been, before he became whoever he was now. Whatever he was now. A ghost, a wraith, a—

Jasper knew the word. He tried not to think it, but thought it anyway.

Mogran.

After running from his father's house he'd had no clue where to go. Edwin Crowley, a sometime drinking buddy/moocher acquaintance of Jarhead's, had been crashing on the latter's couch for the past three months, which made Jasper loath to return to his host's trailer. He'd considered going to Michaela's, but he didn't know if she'd survived the crash, and he wasn't sure he could handle it if he found out she was dead. Because if she *was* dead, then, well, she'd be like him, wouldn't she? Out there, in someone else's body, looking for someone to sleep with.

Someone to fuck.

Because that was the one thing Jasper *did* feel: an urgent, almost overwhelming need to fuck someone. Some*thing*. *Any*thing, as long as it was warm, wet, alive. It wasn't lust Jasper felt. He'd been a teenager: he'd lived in a more or less constant state of lust for the past six years. But lust implied an object. A person. Sexual fantasies that involved another body, even if it was only an imagined one. Jasper had none of that now. If he concentrated, he could incorporate Michaela into the feeling. But doing so felt like a violation, because he didn't want to make love to her. Didn't even want to have sex with her. He just wanted to stick it in her. Shoot inside her. Michaela's vagina was less a fleshly orifice than a tunnel through which he needed to journey, to get to whatever lay on the other side. And so, after hiding out in the forest and avoiding all human contact for a day and a night, Jasper decided he had to risk talking to someone. It was Q. who came to mind first, even before his dad. Q. had killed him after all. He owed Jasper one. Big time.

Of course, Jasper had no idea if Q. was any more alive than Michaela, let alone if he'd believe that Jarhead West's body housed the ghost of his former friend. But there was only one way to find out. It was about forty miles from the mountains on the west side of the river where Jasper had hidden out for the past day and a half to Q.'s house in Kinderhook, on the east side. Jasper jogged it in five hours. Not quite a world-record pace, but not far off either. Every new task Jasper attempted made him realize just how complete his control over Jarhead's body was. Hungry? A couple of minor adjustments to the hypothalamus, a small increase in leptin, a decrease in ghrelin, and Jarhead felt like he'd just finished a six-piece bucket of McKennedy Fried Chicken. Tired? Feeling the need for some REM sleep? A bump to his serotonin, cortisol, thyroid hormone, and insulin levels, and everything was right on track. Hand in a campfire? Stimulate white blood cell and collagen production, get those macrophages to work. A third-degree burn would practically disappear overnight.

The fire thing was just a theory—among other things, Jasper didn't need a campfire since he didn't get cold. But he *had* fiddled with Jarhead's broken wrist during the sleepless night. The injury had healed poorly—Jarhead's family lacked medical insurance, and his care had been cursory. The fracture lines in ulna and radius were gnarled with calcium deposits, and the bones were slightly crooked, and ached if Jarhead attempted to lift anything that weighed more than twenty pounds. Jasper couldn't exactly blink them straight, but he could recalibrate Jarhead's immune system to soften the seams, allowing him gradually to realign the two halves of the bones, straighten them, strengthen them. It took all night to do it, but by dawn any trace of the former injury had disappeared. Jasper made fundamental changes to Jarhead's metabolic rate while he was at it, permanently enhancing his host's reaction time, speed, strength and flexibility, increasing his resistance to pain and injury, slowing down the aging process. He'd fixed his hearing already, and now he sharpened his eyesight, his sense of smell, touch, balance. The only thing left to do was add a couple of notches to his belt to keep his pants from falling down. Possession was turning out to be the best diet Jarhead West had ever been on.

A shrieking bluejay snapped him from his reverie. The little bird was hounding a crow across the lawn, diving at it, screaming, and Jasper looked up, found the jay's nest in a locust tree. The downy heads of two chicks just showed above the nest's rim, and as Jasper looked back at the jay on the lawn, fearlessly defending its young, he wondered if maybe he should've gone to see his father. There was something to be said for the paternal instinct after all.

To one side of the driveway was a small box mounted on a pole. The staring orb of a camera next to a single unlabeled button. When he was alive, Jasper had never actually pressed this button, preferring to park outside the gates and call Q. from his cell. Now, nervously, Jasper placed one of Jarhead's plump (but thinning) index fingers over the plastic disk.

He pushed.

Two minutes later, a single syllable emerged from the intercom like a toll ticket.

"Yes?"

Jasper recognized the voice as Miranda, Q.'s mom's English maid.

"Um, hi. I, um, I'm a friend of Q.'s."

Miranda's voice answered him almost before he'd finished speaking. "Master Mohammed has gone away."

He and Q. had always giggled at "Master Mohammed," but now Jasper wanted to cry with relief.

"Q.'s okay?"

"Master Mohammed was unhurt in the accident," the voice said, impatiently but also with a note of awe. "It was something of a miracle."

"Oh thank God," Jasper said, more emphatically than he'd meant to. "Was . . . was anyone else hurt?"

This time the silence stretched on so long that Jasper glanced at the house. Miranda's shadow wavered in the sidelight beside the front door. The window was a good hundred yards away. Jasper adjusted for the distance, compensated for the semitransparent curtain, and all at once Miranda's face sprang into focus. Her slightly open mouth, half-lidded eyes, the finger digging busily in her ear. The maid pulled her finger out, squinted at it, then flicked something away. Jasper was almost relieved he couldn't see the speck of wax on her fingertip or hear it hit the floor. What he did see was that Miranda was . . . not unattractive. Nice breasts in particular. The whole hair-in-a-bun and uniform look was kind of sexy too.

Stop it.

"Master Mohammed had three friends with him," Miranda said finally, her professionally neutral voice tinged with sadness. "I'm afraid two of them didn't survive the accident."

"Jasper?" he prompted, trying to sound as if he didn't know.

"Yes. Jasper. I never could remember that boy's name."

Thanks, Jasper thought.

"And the girl. What was *her* name?"

"Michaela?"

"Yes! No, wait. She's the girl in the coma. The girl who died had a silly name. Sila—that was it!" Jasper could see her blush. "Sila Patel. I'm afraid she and Jasper, Jasper von, Jasper van—"

"Van Arsdale."

"She and Mr. Van Arsdale both died."

"But Michaela's alive?"

In the house, Miranda nodded. "In a coma, as I said. But yes, she's alive. The Qusays have personally seen to it that she gets the best possible medical care," she added in a slightly defensive tone. She smiled benignly at the security monitor. "It's nice that so many of Master Mohammed's friends have come round to see him, instead of just 'texting' the way you young people do nowadays."

She was speaking to the image on the camera, and in her expression Jasper could see the person she was looking at: dopey and unattractive. An object of pity. He could just take her, he thought. Could hop these gates and be in the house before she could dial 911. She wouldn't be able to resist—

Stop it! he told himself. Get control!

"Q.'s friends have been by?"

"Well, just you and Mr. Bishop."

"Bishop?" The name didn't ring a bell with Jasper—and, given his capacity for total recall, that meant something.

"Yes." Jasper could see the maid fiddle with a slip of paper on a table. "Larry Bishop. The assistant coach of the football—pardon me, soccer team."

"Oh right. Larry." There was no Larry Bishop associated with Dearborn's soccer team, no Larry Bishop that Q. had ever mentioned. He sifted through his memories but nothing came up, then tried Jarhead's. There was only one hit: a paramedic who gassed up at the Stewart's, bought twelve-packs of beer and condoms in more or less equal amounts. The paramedic had never introduced himself, but his name tag read "BISHOP" and his partner had once said, "Hey, Lar, get me a case of Red Stripe while you're in there." Jasper had no idea if this was the same Larry Bishop or not, but if he was, how in the hell had he known Q.? Known him well enough to come by and see if he was okay?

Jasper heard Miranda clear her throat through the intercom.

"I'm afraid I really must be getting back to my duties."

"Oh, sure. Of course."

"May I tell Master Mohammed who called?"

Jasper's mouth opened. No it didn't. Jarhead's mouth opened, and there was the rub. It wasn't Jasper who'd come to see Q. It was Jarhead.

"Sir? I really must—"

"Tell Q-ball Feldspar came by."

An image of Jarhead's cell phone flashed in his mind. His host had dropped it in his friend Edwin's car the last time they'd gone out drinking. He'd been looking for it for three days, but Jasper was able to see it the minute he thought about it, one more bit of refuse amid a swamp of empty cans and cups and Ring Ding wrappers.

"Feldspar?"

"Don't worry about it," Jasper said to the intercom. "I'll just call him."

He turned, got ready to run the fifteen miles to Jarhead's trailer. He hadn't gone ten steps when he saw the car.

It was parked—well, dumped really—beside the gatehouse. A tangled mass of metal and broken glass. Jasper couldn't imagine what Q.'s dad wanted with it. To rub it in his son's face, most likely. Mohammed Qusay Sr. was not the most laid-back father in the world.

The ruined Porsche was a sobering sight. It was practically his tomb, after all, and his steps were heavy as he ran toward Jarhead's trailer. But even so, his heart was nearly singing. Michaela was alive! And so was Q.! His best friend was just a phone call away.

The only thing that troubled him was the inexplicable visit by Larry Bishop. Unless he was Q.'s pot dealer, Jasper couldn't think of a single reason a forty-year-old paramedic would pay him a visit at home.

Well, no earthly reason anyway.

10

Alec took her to a farm in the hills of southern Lebanon to recover. The air was sweet with the scent of orange blossoms and tangy with the smoke of cedar burning in the fireplace. From the verandah of the thousand-year-old farmhouse, you could see the glittering Mediterranean, and the sky was a delicate, cloudless blue. There was even a solemn little boy—a deaf-mute named Faroukh—who magically appeared with glasses of lemonade or kefir, bowls of hariri or tabouleh. The atmosphere was so idyllic that Ileana wondered if she'd passed from one kind of madness into another. Only the vultures wheeling lazily over the corpses in the occupied zone let her know she hadn't entered paradise. That and the fresh wound on her wrist.

She didn't want to believe him at first. She'd watched her family killed before her eyes. Had been raped by a pack of Serbian wolves. Her world had gone insane. Why shouldn't she go insane as well? Why shouldn't she take her revenge?

Alec smiled patiently. "You asked me that question in English."

English.

A language she hadn't spoken, before that night.

So she listened. Sipped lemonade, rubbed the rapidly healing wound on her wrist, and listened.

Alec told her that the being that had taken control of her was called a Mogran. It was older than the house they sheltered in, had stolen thousands of lives before hers, was responsible for innumerable murders besides those it had forced her to commit. Once upon a time, though, it had been a person, just like her. A mortal. But through a process lost both to history and to the demons themselves, it had shed its skin and become a being of pure spirit, capable of moving from one body to another—indeed, incapable of living outside a body, like a cosmic parasite, a metaphysical virus. Whether this transformation was accidental or intentional, accomplished individually or with the help of one or more preexisting demons, was unknown. Only two things were certain: first, that it had been a virgin when it died—a "bound soul," to use the demons' own term, still tied to its birth body like every other human being—and second, that it could only leave the body of a given host by having sex: "unbinding," at which point the entire universe was open to it, excluding only those bodies the demon had possessed previously. The rules were specific and incontrovertible: sex, to orgasm, with another person. There was no other way.

Within those parameters, however, a demon's power was prodigious. It began the moment it took possession, when it absorbed the memory of its host. Not just the conscious memories, but the unconscious ones, the incomprehensibly vast amount of data that had flickered past a host's senses during the course of even the most routine existence. Most of us learn to filter out the white noise of modern life, the TVs and radios playing in the background, the billboards passed in the city center, the conversations overheard on sidewalks, buses, trains, airplanes. To a demon, such information was equally as present as the names of its host's parents or children, equally as important.

How it used this knowledge, however, varied from demon to

demon, possession to possession. A Mogran was perfectly capable of assuming control of its host, replacing the native mind with its own. But doing so made an indelible mark on the host's psyche after the demon departed. Left it by turns paranoid, schizophrenic, fractured into warring personalities, sometimes catatonic, sometimes suicidal. It was almost impossible to recover from such an inhabitation, and the Mogran tended to shy away from it, not because of any charitable impulse toward their hosts, but because such behavior led to unwanted attention. In fact, Alec told her, few people were ever aware they'd been possessed, that their bodies had been borrowed, their memories stolen. The demon would hide in the unconscious, poke around in the shadows and use what it found to manipulate its host in subtle, often unnoticeable ways. Lowered inhibitions, nudges to act on urges that normally wouldn't have seen the light of day. The Mogran lacked bodies, yet could not live without one; as such they were dependent upon the human race even as they were complete masters of whichever individual they happened to be housed in. Such a dynamic made the Mogran bitter, malicious even. Their only pleasure was playing with their hosts, messing with their heads, their lives, the lives of the people around them. It was the closest thing to vengeance they could take.

The information it absorbed wasn't merely mental either: it extended to the musculoskeletal level. If a Mogran jumped into a tennis player, say, it would acquire not only knowledge of the rules of the game, but the physical skills to play it. The demon retained all these memories and skills when it jumped from one host to another. When you factored in the thousands of jumps a Mogran made over the course of hundreds of years, you realized that the average demon was an encyclopedia, a library, a veritable internet of its own, capable of speaking hundreds of languages, master of all the arts and sciences, able to fly airplanes, program computers, sculpt with the skill of Rodin. It could make an atomic bomb as easily as bake a soufflé, and both would come out perfectly.

These mental abilities were matched by an equally impressive control over a host's physiology. A Mogran could turn glands on and off like faucets. Could bolster its host's immune system, say, rendering it virtually invulnerable to injury or disease, or sharpen the host's senses, increase its physical strength, even stop the aging process. In extreme cases, demons had been known to change their hosts' hair and skin color, to add or subtract incredible amounts of fat or muscle in a matter of days, even to alter a host's secondary sex characteristics, leaving it unrecognizable to friends and family—and to itself, when the demon left, and the former host found a stranger staring out of the mirror.

Such manipulations had not gone unnoticed at a cultural level. Almost every legendary monster of human or semihuman appearance—werewolves and vampires, yetis and zombies—could be traced back to the work of this or that demon. And, like all those mythical creatures, the Mogran weren't invincible. Immortal, maybe, but not invincible. Severing the head was generally considered adequate, though Alec removed the genitalia as well, as insurance, and burned the body whenever he could. And, as well, the demons had one Achilles' heel. This was the pattern of frenzy and lull that no demon had ever been known to overcome. The frenzy was just what the name implied: a period of intense movement from host to host. The chief aspect of the frenzy was an overwhelming urge to have sex—to jump, as the demons put it—but this was often accompanied by random acts of violence and destruction. A demon at the peak of frenzy was difficult to track because it could blip from one spot on the globe to another in the blink of an eye, but it was also careless, and therefore vulnerable if you did manage to pin it down. It was less concerned with protecting itself than relieving the urge to jump. Alec had once walked into a room where a demon was in the act of raping a victim, and though it had looked him in the eye, it had made no move to protect itself or escape. Hadn't even lifted an arm to ward off the pipe he brought down on its head.

He was a hunter, he told Ileana. A member of an organization called the Legion, whose sole purpose was tracking and destroying the Mogran. He wasn't sure how many members there were. Since the Legion would look like nothing more than a pack of murderers to any law-enforcement agency, they had to go to great lengths to remain hidden. The organization's gatherers—the people who combed newspapers and internet bulletin boards in search of suspicious activity—had never met each other, but communicated electronically, via anonymous email servers and untraceable phone lines. None of them knew each other's real names, let alone the name of the incumbent hunter.

There was only one hunter at a time, Alec told her. And one huntress.

Hunter and huntress were culled from former hosts. Not just because their experiences gave them the motivation to live outside the law and risk death at the hands of the Mogran, but because possession left them... altered. For the vast majority of hosts, these changes amounted to disorientation, blackouts, short- or long-term amnesia, sometimes more serious psychic trauma. Some were plagued by dreams of lives that weren't their own, spoke languages they'd never heard, let alone learned. A very few retained larger amounts of information, even knew they'd been possessed. A few retained physical changes as well. A greater-than-normal resistance to injury or disease, sharper senses, faster reflexes. It all depended on the changes the demon had wrought while in residence. In theory the former host remained exactly as the demon had left him or her, although in practice it was difficult for a hunter to sustain these exertions over long periods of time; the mental effort to regulate the body's autonomous systems was simply too great. But, with a little luck and the element of surprise, it *was* possible for a hunter to overpower even a demon-inhabited body. And, of course, there were always guns, knives, other weapons. Nothing too James Bond, but even the hunters had one or two tricks up their sleeves.

Alec had rubbed his watch here, but it had been several months before Ileana found that it could do more than tell time.

11

Like any child of his class, Q. had been to therapists before. Based on nothing more than his waiting room, Q. could tell Dr. Thomas was going to rank pretty high on the quackometer scale. Two large diamond-paned windows were set in the front wall, but they were shaded by a dense yew hedge whose net of dark needles filtered the interior light to an undersea green. The submerged feeling was reinforced by the room's half Edwardian, half psychedelic wallpaper–burgundy flocking writhing across a muted silver background. But the weirdest thing had to be the deep-voiced singing that rose up out of the floor. It sounded a bit like babies gurgling at the bottom of a swimming pool, and Q. occasionally found himself holding his breath, as if he too were drowning.

He was contemplating making a break for it when the double doors at the far side of the room swept open. The man who stood flanked by the seven-foot-tall mahogany doors appeared to be in his early forties, tall and almost impossibly thin, with narrow shoulders and even narrower hips, so that he seemed less a person than a stick figure whose flesh consisted primarily of his clothing: long black trousers woven in summerweight wool, a dapper gray jacket buttoned despite the warmth of the morning, a scarlet vest adorned with gold embroidery. A pair of piercing gray eyes twinkled behind silver wire-rimmed glasses. Q. found himself standing up involuntarily, a small, hopeful smile spreading across his lips. He stretched his hand out, but the doctor didn't let go of the doorknobs.

"Why don't we talk in the garden?" the doctor said, as if he'd known Q. for years. "It's such a beautiful day, and the pagoda trees are in bud."

"Um, okay," Q. heard himself mutter. Pagoda trees? "Sure."

But the doctor had already turned, and Q. hurried through the shadowy office. Persian carpets on the floor, Turkish kilims on the wall, a marble-topped desk tucked in the darkest corner of the room. His eyes lingered over the couch: it was the kind that only has a single padded arm, with ornately carved feet balanced on brass casters and a gold-tasseled throw decorated with vigorous crewelwork. An odor hung in the air—pipe smoke, but Q. could almost believe it was opium. It was like he'd stepped through a timewarp into the office of a Viennese psychoanalyst in pre-Anschluss days.

Q. pulled up short.

Dr. Thomas turned and peered at him. "Tell me."

"It's nothing—"

The psychiatrist cut him off with a finger. "Don't censor, edit, or contextualize. Just *tell me*."

"A word popped into my head. Anschluss."

The doctor pursed his lips. Waited.

"It's just, well, I don't know how I know what it means. I don't remember learning it."

The doctor stood motionless, considering. Then he nodded his stately, philosophical head. He extended his arm, indicating the open French doors and the large sunny garden. Somewhat hesitantly, Q. made his way to a weathered wooden bench.

"If you'll make yourself comfortable on the Lutyens," the doctor said, settling into an equally worn slant-backed chair set across from it, "I'll just have a seat in the Adirondack."

The doctor's voice had lost its edge, and the fresh air cleared Q.'s head. Almost flippantly, he said, "Does all your furniture have a name?"

The doctor did that thing psychiatrists do, pausing just long enough to make Q. fidget in his seat. Then:

"Everything made by the hands of men has a name, and a history to go with it. Only Adam could name everything in his world, of course. We his children can learn but a fraction of these appellations, and deploy them like sandbags against the ever-encroaching tide of unknowing."

Q. winced. Ask a stupid question . . .

"Take the music." For the first time Q. noticed that the waiting room's weird music—if you could really call it that—had been piped into the garden. "Tuvan throat singers. Recorded three-quarters of a century ago on the Tibetan plateau. A single voice can produce as many as five notes at once. Knowing that fact gives the sound an added depth, don't you think? An added resonance. There are only three men singing, yet they sound like a chorus of angels."

"Or demons," Q. heard himself say, then fell silent again. Demons, like Anschluss, was not the sort of word he used—not in this manner anyway. Not before the accident.

The doctor slipped a hand into a pocket, and the music disappeared.

The movement caused the doctor's jacket to open slightly, and Q. saw the glint of a chain dangling around his neck. The doctor noticed where Q. was looking and, almost as if he'd been waiting for an opportunity, pulled a surprisingly large pendant from beneath his vest. It was a good three inches around, a crudely wrought series of curlicues and crosses and upside down hearts encased within a circle.

"It's called a sigil. In the middle ages, they were considered protection against possession."

Parts of the ornament were shiny and parts were dark, as if it were an amalgam of silver and lead. The morning light traced its contours as if caught within the sigil's curves.

"Each sigil was proof against one specific demon. They were most commonly used by priests performing exorcisms, or by sorcerers summoning dark forces to aid them in foul play."

Q. wanted to ask the doctor which demon this sigil was designed for, but he couldn't think of the words to do so. His eyes seemed to be caught like the light, following the track of the sigil's loops and curves.

A gust of wind rustled the pagoda trees. The shadows cast by their thin branches and budding foliage danced over the doctor's angular face, but Q. didn't notice.

A bird called, another answered. There was the sound of flapping wings.

Q. blinked. A relaxing, almost numbing feeling had settled over him, a sense of slight dislocation, as if his body had retreated a fraction of an inch from the skin covering it. The feeling was weird, but not unsettling. The doctor's garden was so peaceful. What could possibly harm him here?

The doctor's eyes traced the outline of Q.'s body, as if measuring him, taking him in. He tucked the sigil back in his vest.

"Tell me."

Q. tried to say the name, but the same reticence that had prevented him from telling Dr. Miller continued to hold his tongue. When he was able to speak, his voice sounded so distant it seemed to come from a tape recorder.

"I've been having dreams."

The doctor didn't move. His body looked as taut as a wire holding up a bridge, a whip or a snake stretched out to strike. Yet it wasn't a sting Q. felt, a bite, but rather a coolness. The doctor's voice washed over Q. like a breeze. Protecting him and coaxing him at the same time. *Tell me*, Q. heard the doctor say, though he didn't see the man's lips move.

Q. wanted to tell him everything. But how to explain the dreams he'd been having? It wasn't the accident he dreamed of. That would've made sense. But he could barely remember the accident. He remembered everything leading up to it and everything after the paramedics pulled him from the automobile, but the hour or so in between was a blur, punctuated by the sound of rattling breaths as Michaela's blood-filled lungs struggled to fill with oxygen.

But as horrifying as those memories were, the dreams were worse. They were as detailed as memories—more so in fact—but memories that couldn't possibly have been his. The first was of a soldier in World War I, a Kievan peasant who'd taken Prussian bullets in the liver and the right temporal lobe at the Battle of Tannenburg in 1914. Either wound would have—should have—been fatal, and indeed the peasant had been buried in a limepit along with thirty thousand of his countrymen. The lime had eaten coin-sized holes in his skin even as, somehow, his brain and liver repaired themselves, until he was strong enough to mole through a dozen feet of decaying flesh to the surface. Q. even knew the soldier's name, Boris Petrovich Alushkin, and he had the strangest feeling that the words he remembered were in Russian, although his conscious mind didn't understand them at all.

As weird as that was, however, the Quechua Indian who'd slaved in the silver mines of Mt. Potosí in seventeenth-century Peru was a hundred times more perplexing. Q. had never even heard of Mt. Potosí or the Quechua. So how could these images, this language—the official dialect of the Incan empire, for God's sake—be floating around his head, along with a comprehensive mental map of the hundreds of miles of tunnels that laced "El Cerro Rico" ("the rich hill," as the Spanish called Potosí) some four hundred years ago? The miner's name was Chinpukilla, and he'd been caught in a cave-in. For *three months* he languished without food or water beneath tons of fallen rock, slowly, painstakingly clawing his way to freedom, at which point he slipped like a wraith into the darkness.

The final memory was even older. China. The latter Song Dynasty. A ne'er-do-well archer named Zhou Wong had his face blown off when he attempted to demonstrate the virtues of a *huojian*, or fire arrow, filled with the newly invented *huoyao*, or gunpowder. Wong was of high birth, so he wasn't left to die. Instead he was cared for, his face covered with poultices that had more to do with sparing the eyes of the people around him than healing his hideous wounds. Nevertheless, over the course of six weeks the charred flesh of lips and nose and cheeks slowly regenerated, until one day his sister removed the poultices and revealed a visage that was if anything more perfect than the one he'd possessed before the accident.

But the most uncanny detail of the dreams' strangely parallel narratives was the way all three ended: after the men had healed themselves, they celebrated by having sex with the first woman they came upon—at which point all trace of them simply disappeared from Q.'s mind. The disappearance didn't bother Q. as much as the men's ungovernable, irresistible lust, which reminded Q. far too much of how he'd felt in the Porsche, when he simply *had* to have Sila's lips around his dick. And hadn't he healed himself too—or, at any rate, been impervious to injury, even as his friends' bodies were broken, mangled, destroyed? How was this possible? And what could it possibly mean?

As Dr. Thomas walked into his office Q. fell silent, eyes open, a comfortable smile on his lips. The sun filtered through the budding trees, the birds flitted between branches and sang cheerfully to each other. No, the boy thought again, *he* could not get him. Not here.

In his office, the doctor pressed a button on his desk. A flat-screen monitor slid silently from a slot in the side of his desk; a keyboard emerged from beneath the marble surface and automatically adjusted itself to the optimum typing position. Though he loathed technology, J.D. Thomas recognized its usefulness. In a moment, he had accessed the database. *Boris Petrovich Alushkin. Chinpukilla. Zhou Wong.* The doctor had to guess at the spelling, but even so, it took less than ten minutes before a fourth name added itself to the list.

Leo.

On one level, the name was hardly a surprise. There were few Mogran left, so the choices were limited. But something didn't add up. Leo had left the Qusay boy with a brain full of memories, any one of which incriminated him. It was almost as if he'd been in such a rush to get out that he hadn't had time to wipe his host's mind. That suggested two things: first, that the demon was working a larger scheme than playing Russian roulette with a Porsche and a cliff wall. Second, and rather more pertinently—at least for the boy sitting in his garden—that he would be back to finish what he'd neglected. Since Mogran couldn't possess the same person twice, the demon would have to eliminate Q.'s memories manually.

He would have to kill him.

The demon could work though anyone, of course, but he would prefer the most surprising candidate. Someone who knew the boy. His mother, his father, a friend at school. Or someone who knew about the accident. Someone to whom Q. might have told his strange feelings.

Sue Miller. Or—who knows—perhaps Leo would come for him?

The doctor pushed himself away from his keyboard. An amazed smile played over his face. For nearly twenty years he'd been waiting for this, ever since his theories on collective memory had brought him to the Legion's attention. But aside from being granted access to the Archive, he'd never actually met another gatherer, let alone a hunter, or a former host.

He studied the boy's skin through the open windows, un-scratched despite the horrific accident he'd been in just a few days ago. As Q. suspected, his imperviousness, like the accident itself, was the Mogran's work. But what he didn't know was that it could also, with the proper training, be turned against the demon. But such things were beyond the psychiatrist's purview. For this, he would have to call for assistance.

He opened an inlaid cigar box, revealing a phone nestled inside its tobacco-scented interior. The phone was as high tech as the computer, had space in its memory for a thousand contacts. But this number ex-isted only in the doctor's mind. There was a series of electronic beeps and clicks as the call was rerouted a half dozen times, until finally a line rang in who knew what city on who knew what continent. Thomas wasn't sure what he expected a hunter to sound like, but he was sur-prised by the groggy, somewhat grumpy female voice that muttered an indistinct *harrumph*. Apparently he had woken her up.

"H-huntress?" The word sounded anachronistic and slightly silly, even to a man as besotted with apocrypha as J.D. Thomas. "This is . . . this is Legion."

Dr. Thomas could hear the woman snap into focus.

"Do you have a target?"

The woman spoke English in a curiously flat manner—not like a native but like someone who understood what she was saying, though she had never actually learned it. Q. had spoken a few Russian words in exactly the same manner, and the doctor knew that this, too, was the Mogran's doing. The Mogran's legacy.

"Are you there?"

The woman's voice was sharp, and Thomas nodded contritely, even though she couldn't see him.

"No target yet. But the Mogran. It—it's Leo."

A sharp intake of air greeted these words. Not a gasp but a sniff, like a wolf scenting for prey.

"Where?"

"Upstate New York. But you might want to meet me in the city. There's a boy. I think—he might be a new hunter."

For the first time uncertainty came over the line, silent but palpable. Then: "I'll be there in twenty-four hours. Try not to get him killed before then."

"But how will you—"

The doctor stopped when he realized the connection had been severed. He set the phone back on the cradle, closed the cigar box. This was a huntress, after all. She would know how to find him. The only uncertainty, as she'd indicated, was whether Q. would still be alive when she showed up. The doctor stared at the boy in the garden. For the next twenty-four hours, Q.'s fate lay in his trembling hands.

12

Mason West lived in a long squared-off cylinder with a rotted wooden porch and a yard that grew more trash than grass. It took Jasper five minutes of sifting through beer cans, bottles, Solo cups and takeout containers in Edwin's rattletrap Miata to find Jarhead's cell—only to discover the battery was dead. Reluctantly, he headed inside for the charger.

The first thing he heard when he opened the front door was a teeth-grinding moan coming from the bedroom.

"What's your rush, baby?" a woman's voice said. "Slow down, we got all night."

"I'll fuck you through the goddamn wall, yeah, I'll fuck—" The words devolved into a trailer-rattling grunt.

How 'bout that? Edwin's roommate had been missing for two days, but did he worry about where his friend might be? Nope. He took advantage of Jarhead's absence to fuck on something more comfortable than the couch.

Jasper was mesmerized by the sounds coming from his host's bedroom. The smells. The unmistakable aroma of sex, a little tangy, a little rancid. An overwhelming need for release coupled with his host's physical urges, and by the time Edwin's companion emerged from the bedroom in a T-shirt and panties, Jasper was swaying back and forth like a cobra transfixed by a lute.

"Sandra."

The word surprised Jasper—not the name, which he'd known instantly, but the fact that he'd said it aloud. Apparently his control wasn't quite as total as he'd thought.

Edwin's on-again, off-again girlfriend started, then shrugged. It wasn't the first time her deadbeat boyfriend's roommate had seen her in her underwear. She walked to her purse, fished out a pack of cigarettes. She jerked her thumb toward the bedroom.

"Sorry 'bout that. Eddie said you weren't around. We'll change the sheets."

Jasper stood there swaying, stunned by the primacy of his feelings. His need. The way it linked up with Jarhead's feelings about Sandra, running around his trailer with her ass hanging out. She was practically asking for it. Really, he'd just be giving her what she wanted. What she deserved.

"Jarhead?"

Jasper tried to answer but couldn't. Despite the fact that he'd mentally reset Jarhead's broken wrist a day ago, now he couldn't even make his host's erection go down. It felt like it was going to rip through his pants.

Sandra puffed at her cigarette. She was obviously confused, but seemed to think her boyfriend's roommate was just a little drunker than usual. Smiling nervously, she turned toward the bedroom.

"Lemme drag Eddie out so you—"

In a flash he was on her. She seemed to weigh nothing as he threw her the couch.

"Jarhead! What the fuck?"

Sandra's voice grated in his ears. His name was Jasper. *Jasper*. He clapped one hand over her mouth, went straight for her panties with the other. Sandra gnawed at his fingers even as she drove her cigarette into his cheek. Jasper heard the sizzle, smelled the burning flesh. He knew it hurt but it didn't matter. He shut the nerves down and the pain disappeared. Let her burn his host's face off. He would get what he needed.

The panties ripped away like a sheet of tissue, and he pulled so hard at his host's zipper he broke it. He could hear Sandra's gagged pleading in Jarhead's souped-up ears, but only at a remove. All his attention was focused on the space between her legs. On the release that would be his, Jarhead's and Jasper's both. There was a nagging voice at the back of his brain—*this didn't work before*—but he ignored it. He would do it right this time. He would find the way out.

As he reached for his dick, a chair smashed into his back. His forehead knocked into Sandra's, and she went slack in his grip. Jasper was amazed he hadn't heard Edwin coming—then realized he had, but had chosen to ignore it. To focus on the task at hand. Now he looked up, just in time to catch a second blow in the face. Two legs broke off the chair and a thick gash opened up on Jarhead's forehead. Jasper blinked, one slow-willed opening and closing of his host's eyes as he fought to make sense of what was happening.

"What the fuck, man?" Edwin's pimply face was a mixture of rage and fear and confusion. "Have you totally lost your fucking mind?"

The words came to him through a fog. The fog wasn't just Jarhead. It was him. Not Jasper—not the Jasper he'd been anyway, but the thing he'd become. This insatiable, irresistible need for release. The only thing that distracted him was the pain in his head. He almost wanted to tell Edwin to hit him again. To find Sandra's cigarette and burn out both his eyes.

"Edwin?"

"Don't *even*, man! Just get the fuck out!"

Jasper climbed off Sandra's body gingerly. Without thinking about it, he checked her vitals. He didn't have to touch her. Just listened. Her pulse was steady, her breathing even. Aside from the bump on her forehead, she was okay.

"I don't know what to say, man. I'm really sorry."

"I said *get out!*"

"I, um, yeah. I just have to do something in the bedroom."

As he made his way around one end of the couch Edwin looped around the other. Jasper could hear Edwin's heart too, pounding against his ribs, and he knew the skinny boy was too scared to attack again.

"I'll just be a minute. I really am sorry—"

"Fuck! Off!" Edwin screamed, then dropped the broken chair, and knelt down next to Sandra. "Sandy? Baby? You okay?"

Jasper closed the bedroom door behind him, and when he turned around, he caught Jarhead's face in the mirror across the room. He was glad it wasn't his face, because he didn't know how he could've stood the sight of himself. Jesus Christ, what had happened out there? He'd almost raped a woman. If Edwin hadn't clocked him he would've done it without a second thought.

But the worst part was, he knew it could happen again. Knew it *would* happen again, unless he found a way to control himself. The desire was still there. The need. Just thinking about it turned it up again. He could feel Sandra's crotch beneath his. He could just go out there, throw Edwin through the window—

He punched himself in the face so hard he staggered backwards against the wall. In his confusion, it took him ten minutes to find the charger. But he felt himself calming down as he sifted through dozens of mismatched, cheesy socks, discarded pairs of skidmarked under-wear, T-shirts whose armpits were crusty with deodorant. Every item of clothing seemed to have been used as a cum rag at some point or another, and, though Jasper did his best not to visualize these sessions, they were present in all their graphic detail. It was not a pretty sight.

"Jarhead," he said aloud, "buddy, you are one sick fuck." Deep inside him, he could've sworn he heard an embarrassed chuckle.

It was getting better now. Jasper felt almost sane. He found the charger, plugged it in, snapped the phone onto it. His thumb hovered over the keypad. The only time he'd ever dialed Q.'s number was when he put it in his phone book, but it only took a millisecond for him to access that memory now. He punched in the ten digits. The sound of ringing was extraordinarily loud in his ears—Jarhead had, of course, turned the speaker volume up all the way.

"Come on, Q., pick up. *Pick up.*"

"Yo. This is Q. Apparently I'm not in the mood to answer my phone so go ahead and leave a message. I'll call you back, if you're sexy. Peace."

"Fuck!" was the first word Jasper said to his best friend after he died. And then the words started rolling out of him: "Q. Q-ball. It's me. It's Jasper, Q. Feldspar. We met in second grade when Billy Lethem tied your towel around your face with your belt and beat you up till I pulled him off, and the night before you killed me you showed me your $29,000 watch and we drank half a bottle of your old man's Scotch. You had the Fanta. I had the Gatorade."

Jasper caught another glimpse of himself in the mirror. Saw that Jarhead's penis, soft now, was still dangling from his boxers.

"It's really me, Q.," he finished up. "And I really need your help."

13

Miranda Atkins shoved her cigarette in her mouth, punched in the code that set the alarm, and ducked out the front door of the Qusays' eerily empty home. In her haste, she dropped her keys, and cursed loudly in her native Cockney. You had to turn the bolt within sixty seconds of arming the system or the alarm would start blaring, the front gates would seal shut, and she'd have to wait an hour for the local constabulary to show up and free her. She wasn't in the mood to get trapped here again. Not tonight. Not with that *carcass* in the driveway. Really, she asked herself, retrieving her keys, locking the door. What kind of man brings something like *that* home?

She stared at the car as she made her way to her Camry. She couldn't help it. Both doors had been pulled off by what-was-it-called, the Jaws of Life, and even in the dim glow of the low orbs scattered about the Qusays' front garden you could see the blood staining the leather seats. So much blood. Good God almighty, so much blood. She wondered if it would come out. Not that you would ever actually *clean* it or anything. But say you wanted to. Would it come out? She'd recently been turned on to OxiClean, but maybe good old lye would do it. It would be a challenge, that was for sure.

Maybe Borax. Or naphtha.

She was almost past the wreck when she heard the ringing. A faint sound, emanating from deep within the car. Under the bonnet, it sounded like, or in the boot.

A phone. Someone's phone was still in the car.

Perhaps it was the gin fizz she'd sipped after she finished up for the day—no sense paying for it when she had the Qusays' bar at her disposal—or perhaps it was the spookiness of the purple sky, the tendrils of fog rising off the river like the ghosts of drowned swimmers, but her mind immediately filled with an image of a body in a coffin six feet beneath the ground, the face green in the glow of a cell phone's screen, the breath thin and ragged as it prayed for someone to answer, for someone to realize they'd been buried alive. Jasper maybe, or what was that girl's name? She never could remember. Sila! Yes, that was it. Silly name, Sila. Poor thing. Poor dead thing.

"Sorry, luv," she chirped to the ringing phone. "Ain't no one gonna answer *that* call."

14

Q. hated sleeping in his parents' Beekman Place apartment. There was nothing intrinsically wrong with the place: it was a 5,000-square-foot duplex with a pair of enormous terraces overlooking the East River. But his parents didn't maintain an eight million-dollar apartment just so they had someplace to sleep when they came to the city. Oh no. It was their shag pad. Not his dad's or his mom's. No no no. They *shared* it, through a complex arrangement Q. did his best to know nothing about.

But here he was. His session with Dr. Thomas had been—what? A little weird, to say the least. Basically all Q. had done was sit down in the garden and fall asleep. Forty-seven minutes after the doctor said "Tell me" in that Dr. Freud kind of way, Q. felt a little shake on his shoulder. "Time's up, my young friend." A teacup and saucer sat on the wide arm of the doctor's Adirondack chair. There was something a little creepy about a middle-aged man drinking a cup of tea and watching you sleep, but it was by far the most restful three quarters of an hour he'd spent since the accident, so when Dr. Thomas gently suggested Q. stay in the city until their next appointment, he'd thought, well, why not? His dad had flown to Nigeria to discuss security on the oil pipeline, of which he was an investor, and his mother had jetted off to one of her spas—Costa Rica, Q. thought, or Geneva, or maybe Bangalore. He decided to order a pizza, get something off pay-per-view. Something light. Nothing with car chases or naked girls. A real *SIS* night, as Sila would say.

Sila.

Jasper.

Jesus.

The elevator bell rang just as the taxi dropped Tom Hanks off at the Empire State Building. Q. paused the movie but didn't get up immediately. No one besides Lombardi's Pizza knew he was in the city, and the night man should've called before sending someone up. Feeling a little silly, Q. picked up the phone and called the front desk.

There was no answer.

Maybe he was just paranoid after the events of the past few days, but who could blame him? After midnight there was only one man downstairs, and he could've easily been called away by another tenant. Nevertheless, Q. traded his third slice for a brass poker and tried to remember if he'd locked the elevator gate after the pizza came.

As soon as he stepped into the hall a voice called to him. Almost as if he'd heard him, even though the foyer was a good forty feet away.

" 'Lo? Anybody home?"

Q. didn't recognize the voice. It was against building policy to let a guest come up in the elevator unescorted, but the staff was always a little lax with teenagers when their parents weren't around.

"Just a minute," Q. called.

He tiptoed to the foyer, paused outside the door. He could see the elevator gate–closed, but he couldn't tell if it was locked. Couldn't see who was inside either. As he set the poker in the um-brella rack–no point in looking like a crazy person, assuming the guy was just some plumber or electrician–his eyes were caught by the Chinese figurine on a side table. A plump man with upraised arms. A big round face, flowing robes, an enormous headdress that made it look as though his head was haloed in flames. Q. had seen the statue a hundred times before, but now he suddenly recognized it as a Tang Dynasty Lokapala, a Buddhist deity exported to China from India. This was . . . Q. squinted. Virupaksha. The guardian of the west. Of the gates of death. A flash of heat seared his cheeks, as if his face were on fire.

"Hello?"

Q. started, almost knocked the statue off the table. A mahogany Empire table. Probably Duncan Phyfe. Jesus Christ, where was all this coming from? Virupaksha. Duncan Phyfe. Anschluss. He took a deep breath and stepped into the foyer.

"Hey there. I was wondering if you were coming."

Q. looked at the lock on the security gate before he looked at the man. Latched. He tried not to sigh in relief.

"Hey," he said. "What's up?"

There was something familiar about the face on the other side of the metal lattice. Thirtysomething, shaggy bangs, washed-out blue eyes. At least three days' worth of stubble. He was wearing a sloppy version of the building's livery–the jacket was unbuttoned, and there were splotches of something that looked like tomato sauce on the shirt–but Q. didn't recognize him.

"Evening, Mr. Qusay. I'm Larry, the night guy."

"What happened to Ramon?"

"Ramon got called home." Larry mimicked a pregnant stomach. The buttons of his shirt strained across his torso, even though he was junkie skinny. Like he was wearing a shirt that belonged to someone significantly smaller than he was. "Baby number three. Couple weeks early, but everything seems okay, knock wood." He rapped his knuckles on the coffered paneling of the elevator, and the sound echoed sharply into the foyer.

"That's good," Q. said. "So, can I help you?"

The man smiled awkwardly. "That's usually what I say." When Q. didn't respond, his smile turned into a frown. "You buzzed, right?"

Q. furrowed his brows. His brain had been acting weird lately–

Virupaksha!–but he was pretty sure he hadn't called for anything be-sides pizza. "Not that I know of."

"You sure?"

"Well, since they took out the buzzers three years ago, yeah, I'm pretty sure. You just call now."

"Oh yeah, right. Old habits, you know? It's like people saying dial when they call someone, even though phones don't have dials on them anymore. I always liked dials myself but I guess you can't really fit them on a cell, right? Anyway, whatever. We still say buzz, even though we don't have buzzers no more."

Q. blinked. "Look, um, Larry. I'm watching *Sleepless in*–er, *Gone in Sixty Seconds* and my pizza's getting cold."

"Maybe I'd better come in and check the system." Larry scratched nervously behind his ear. "You know your dad. He'll pitch a fit if he buzzes–er, calls, whatever–and no one comes."

When Larry put his arm down, Q. noticed that his cuff rode a good three inches above his wrist. And then he noticed something else.

He noticed his watch.

The Patek.

"Hey! That's my–"

Before he could finish his sentence, Larry had brought one of his battered kicks up and slammed it into the accordion gate. It was a good thing Mohammed Qusay Sr. was paranoid about security: the gate bent, but held. The buttons on Larry's too-tight shirt popped off, and Q. saw that the spaghetti sauce had soaked through to his skin.

He saw that it wasn't spaghetti sauce.

He ducked through the door, grabbed the poker.

"Get back! I'll use this!"

Larry didn't look at him. He merely kicked the gate again. It buckled visibly, but still held.

"Stop! I *will* use this!"

Larry smirked. "Q., Q., Q. You know that won't help you against me." His foot slammed against the gate again.

Suddenly Q. remembered where he'd seen him before.

"You—you were the paramedic. At the accident."

"Forest for the trees, Q." Larry kicked the gate again, and it bent outwards sharply. "You know who I am."

Something had happened to the man's eyes. They were still washed-out druggy eyes, but they seemed to have deepened, grown almost luminous, as if phosphorescent lights were moving about in them. Glowing fish swimming at the bottom of a pond.

Q. almost dropped the poker.

"Leo."

15

Eight years ago Lawrence Bishop had been huffing glue in his cousin's apartment on Union Street and playing a game Trim called What's the Worst That Could Happen? Well, it wasn't a game as much as it was a lecture. Not a lecture really. More like a rant. Or just a foaming at the mouth. It went something like this:

"Celia Ng, right? Hot little Vietnamese chick. Five feet tall, pussy tighter than the nickel slot in a one-armed bandit? I mean, she's got a boyfriend, but what's the worst that could happen?"

"Bam?" Larry said.

"Not yet, man. So she wants to do it in the car. And I'm like hells yeah, let's do it in the car. So we do it in the car. Then she's like, let's do it while driving, and I'm all like w00t! Well, I prolly wasn't w00t! then, I was prolly dope! or shit! or, I dunno, radical!, but still, what's the worst that could happen?"

"Bam?"

"Dude. Not yet. So, like, ninety-five pounds of me-so-horny bouncing up and down on my johnson, and we hit a couple-a parked cars on Allen Street? Totally worth it, right? And then she's like faster. And I'm like I'll go faster, bitch. And then she's like faster you motherfucker! And I'm like I'll *show* you faster, be-atch. I mean, Route 9, right? No traffic, *Use Your Illusion* blasting from the stereo—I don't care what anyone says, Volume II kicks Volume I's ass. A bottle of

Jack Daniel's and a pretty sunset. What's the worst that could happen?"

"Bmmf?" Lawrence Bishop muttered, his nose being stuffed in a bottle of Elmer's rubber cement at that particular moment.

"Dude. Not *yet*. So then she's like pour some-a that Jack on my bush and lick it off. And I'm like two great tastes that taste great together! So now she's got her head sticking out of the sunroof, flashing those little bitty Asian titties at the world, her twat's in my mouth and she's more or less pouring Jack down my throat while I eat her out. And I mean, yeah, the only thing I can see is her navel ring, some cute little purple stone, pale purple, garnet maybe? amethyst? but like, so what? I mean, what's the worst that could happen?"

Pause.

"I said, what's the worst that could happen?"

Pause.

"Larry?"

Larry pulled his head out of the beanbag chair he'd mushed it into, where he'd found the scent of cat piss to be oddly stimulating.

"Huh?"

"I *said*, what's the worst that could happen?"

Larry's blink took the better part of a minute. Then:

"Bam?"

"The *fuck* bam. More like BAM! BAMBAMBAM! Only, fuck, man. I'm still thinking the worst that could happen is I die with whiskey-soaked pussy in my mouth. I mean, totally worth it, right? Except instead I end up in this piece of shit." This piece of shit being the wheelchair Trim had eaten, slept and pissed in for the previous sixteen months. "But hell, man, at least the government pays for it. I mean, what's the worst that could happen now? Dain bramage? The fuck. Pass me that glue, man."

"Seems to me," Larry said then. "Seems to me," he said again, because he'd momentarily forgotten what it had seemed to him. "Oh yeah. Seems to me there's, like, at least one adganvatage to being pazalyred."

"You mean Medicaid?" Trim had the breathless voice of someone trying to keep a hit in his lungs.

"Okay, two adganvatages. Ad-tange-uh-vage." Larry shook his head. "Anyway. Seems to me, no matter how hard someone kicks your ass, it don't hurt."

"Well got-damn," Trim said. "I never thought of it that way." And then: "There's a Louisville Slugger behind the front door."

"You play baseball?"

"Yeah, Larry, I play baseball. Shortstop. Roll my ass around the bases in record time. The fuck, man? It's for security."

Larry sat up straighter, in an instant state of oxygen-deprived paranoia. "You hear something?"

Trim shook his head. "Dude, you are *so* fucked up. I wanna test your theory."

"What theory?"

Trim pushed his torso to one side, showed Larry a bit of pale butt cheek.

"My ass? No pain? Remember?"

And then they started giggling so hard it took nearly fifteen minutes to put their plan into action.

Somehow Trim's ass became Trim's kidneys and then Trim's gut and then Trim's chest and then a couple-a good whacks to Trim's forehead. He survived the various blows, even declined to press charges. "Hell, I told him to hit me," he said when he woke up six days later. "Didn't hurt me none, and the state pays my medical bills."

"What about the blows to the head?"

"He hit me in the head?" Trim ran his fingers over the baseball-sized lumps on his skull. "That motherfucker."

Unfortunately, Larry had fled the scene in his McKennedy Fried Chicken delivery truck. He was still out of his mind on vapors, ended up taking a corner too fast and tearing through the

PathMark parking lot at fifty miles an hour. Clipped some fat-ass woman pushing a shopping cart before driving straight through the plate-glass window of the garden department. The last thing he remembered was the giant chicken on the hood of the truck exploding in a shower of white plastic feathers—that, and the smell of hibiscus, which reminded him of the bubble baths his mother had given him when he was little. The worst that could happen to Lawrence Bishop turned out to be an eight-year sentence for vehicular assault, of which he served three, during which time he only had to take it up the ass twice.

It was Larry's parole officer who'd come up with the idea of being a paramedic. Told him to think of it as restitution. After Larry had figured out the difference between restitution and prostitution, he thought it sounded like a fine idea. Driving an ambulance was less exciting than he might have hoped. Automobile accidents, heart attacks, the various indignities of old age. He found himself handling a lot more feces than he'd expected. Most of the job was downtime. Hours spent sitting in the cab wolfing a slice of pizza or smoking a bowl and watching the sun set over the river. He and his partner, a six-foot-five-inch ex-runningback named Little Johnny, liked to conjure the kinds of emergencies they read about in *Penthouse Forum*. "I'm so sorry to bother you, but I seem to have gotten this zucchini stuck in a very *embarrassing* area." "Thank you *so much* for coming over. I was riding bareback and I think I pulled a muscle in my cervix. Or maybe my coccyx. You'd better check both." "Well, since my husband's dead, do you mind finishing what he started? I'm *sure* he wouldn't mind." But the only attractive women he ever met on the job were the soccer moms who'd just plowed their SUV over some hapless bicyclist. If there were any nymphomaniacs living in Columbia County, they were either preternaturally healthy, or too dumb to remember the number for 911.

But all that changed when he met Sue Miller—a shrink, goddammit, with a $125,000-a-year salary, a TT convertible and a lingerie collection that filled up two walk-in closets. All of a sudden, middle age seemed less scary than he'd ever imagined. He'd been carrying a ring around in his pocket for two weeks now, waiting to pop the question. Hell, he could even imagine having a kid with her. The thought of his prenatal rugrat floating in the womb, looking at the head of Daddy's dick moving in and out of Mommy's pussy turned him on like *crazy*.

Hey, what was the worst that could happen?

Leo had giggled for a good fifteen minutes after he jumped out of Sue Miller and into her boyfriend. After twentysome-odd years of glue, crystal, weed, paint thinner, mushrooms, coke, acid, poppers, peyote, the occasional bottle of Wild Turkey, not to mention pills in every color, shape, size, dosage and combination, Larry's consciousness was like a cosmic Swiss cheese. Leo kept falling down holes into one drug-soaked memory after another, each progressively stupider than the last. When he finally managed to get control, he noticed that his host's dick was rock-hard and had blisters on it from sixteen straight hours of fucking. He could feel the Vicodin and Viagra still coursing through his system, and set about cleaning them out. Although he could appreciate the comic as much as anyone, he saw no need to kill Q. while sporting a woody.

He sat up unsteadily. Sue was sprawled on the floor in her Dirty Nurse outfit, eyes empty, legs V'd out in front of her like a life-sized doll. Her lipstick was smeared around her mouth, which was open in a dazed smile.

"Sue? Baby? You still with us?"

Sue's eyes didn't focus. She played with the pile of the carpet as though it were the most fascinating thing in the world.

"Phlox!" She giggled mischievously.

When Little Johnny came by to pick him up for their shift an hour later, Leo shot him up with 50 mg of liquid Valium and put him in the deck chair by Sue's pool. He shot Sue up too, then strapped her to the gurney in the back of the bus and headed for the city. He couldn't possess Sue twice of course, but he figured it would be good to carry a joint with him—the demons' private term for the body they fucked to get out of the one they were in. He didn't think Q. was going to be any trouble, but if J.D. Thomas really was Legion, then he might have a couple of tricks up his sleeve.

Leo certainly hoped so.

16

Leo.

The man twitched when Q. said the name. His eyes rolled back in his head for a second. Then he smiled.

"Whew. Flashback." He kicked the gate again, not quite as hard as he had before. "That was cool."

"I'm calling the cops," Q. said.

"Go ahead. I'll be gone by the time they get here." He kicked again. "And so will you."

Q. ran into the hall, his socks slipping on the marble floor. He recovered his balance and headed for the stairs. There was a lock on his bedroom door. Maybe it would buy him time.

A crash behind him.

"I'm coming, Q. And this time I won't let you go, Jasper or no Jasper."

When Q. slipped again it had nothing to do with his socks. Jasper? How did Leo know about Jasper? And what could his dead friend possibly have to do with all this?

Just as he slammed his bedroom door he heard a distinctly louder crash downstairs, the *sproing* of metal warping and snapping, followed by the smash of something ceramic falling to the floor.

Virupaksha. So much for guarding the house.

Even as Q. turned the lock on his bedroom door, the *squeak-*

squeak-squeak of rubber-soled shoes running across polished marble made him realize it was pointless. This man—he still thought of him as a man, couldn't bring himself to use the word *demon*—had just kicked down a steel gate. An inch of oak would be useless against him. Q. looked around his bedroom, but there was nothing in the anonymous chamber besides a chair, the bureau, a half dozen books on a shelf. He was pretty sure that pummeling Larry with the leather-bound works of D.H. Lawrence wasn't going to stop him.

He remembered that his father had once kept a gun in his bed-side table. He had no idea if it was still there, let alone loaded, but it was better than nothing. He ran for the terrace, which connected the two rooms, burst blindly through the French doors and slammed into something hard.

Leo.

No other name would do. This wasn't the paramedic. Wasn't Larry. This was the thing that had been inside him. That had driven him to kill his friends.

The demon had taken off Ramon's jacket and shirt. The night man's blood painted the demon's abdomen like a cummerbund.

He held up a gun.

"Looking for this?" Leo tapped his forehead with the gun's barrel. "I know what you know, remember? Every memory of yours right up until—" he looked at the Patek "—fifty hours and forty-six minutes ago." He turned the watch face toward Q., and the boy could see that the crystal was cracked. "Can you believe it? Twenty-nine large and it broke in an itty bitty car accident. Talk about a rip-off. Still, ol' Larry here thought it might be worth something. He snatched it while you were wandering around with your dick hanging out of your BVDs."

Leo turned and threw the gun out over the FDR toward the East River. His arm moved so fast that it literally whistled through the air.

"My kind don't like guns. We like the body." He ran his finger-tips over Larry Bishop's flesh in a gesture that was half lewd, half contemptuous. "We like *your* bodies. Your bodies and your minds."

Q. continued to inch backward. He was on a terrace nine floors up: there was really nowhere to go. But he couldn't stand to be close to this creature.

Suddenly he remembered: the fire escape! It was connected to the far end of the terrace. If he could get there, he could make a run for it.

The demon squinted. "What was that, Q.? You just had a thought."

Q. didn't say anything, just continued inching backwards.

"Don't try to hide it, Q. You blinked. Your pupils dilated. Your masseter twitched. That's the muscle that closes that big dumb mouth of yours, and also makes your ears wiggle just the itsy bitsiest bit." The demon paused. "I'm guessing it was the fire escape, right? You're thinking maybe you can run for it?"

Q. continued to crawl away from him. He was a good ten feet away by then. Almost halfway there.

"I'm disappointed in you, Q. Didn't you learn anything from our week together?"

The demon bent his knees, then shot upward. His jump took him up and over and behind Q.–a good fifteen feet from a standing start. Q. rolled over on his stomach to see what he already knew: the demon now stood between him and his only exit.

"There's no getting away, Q. But before you die, I want you to answer a few questions for me."

In his hopelessness, Q. felt brave enough to sneer. "I thought you knew everything already."

Leo tapped the face of the broken Patek. "Everything except for the past two days. God, you humans can't remember *anything*. Now. Give me straight answers and I'll make it easy on you. Quick and painless as they say. Jerk me around and I'll teach you to hurt in nerves you didn't even know existed. Question one: did you visit J.D. Thomas?"

Q. didn't say anything, but his face must have answered for him because the demon laughed.

"Very good. Question two: what did he tell you?"

Q. remained silent.

"You're gonna have to talk this time, Q. There's only so much I can get from reading the muscle twitches in that pretty face of yours." He took a step toward Q. "Such a pretty, pretty face. You wouldn't want me to rip it off, would you? Have poor old Moms or Dad come over for a fuck-fest and find their one and only's skinless skull giving them the Jolly Roger grin?"

"I–" Q. broke off. "He didn't tell me anything."

Leo shook his head. "Not good enough, Q." He took another step toward the boy. "Think of dear old Mom and Dad, Q. Think of the unbelievable pain I can cause you. The pain I can cause them. *What did he say?*"

"I–I fell asleep. I swear to God. I fell asleep as soon as I got there. I slept the whole time."

The demon stopped walking. He looked thoughtful for a moment, and then he laughed. "You didn't fall asleep, Q. He put you under. *Hypnosis*," he added in a condescending voice. "Do I have to spell everything out? The good doctor put you in a trance." He laughed again. "I've been asking the wrong question. I shouldn't have been trying to find out what he told you, but what you told him. What *did* you tell him, Q.? Did you tell him how much fun we had together? Me and you and Sila and Jasper? Did you tell him about our road trip?"

At the mention of his dead friends, Q. felt tears of frustration sting his eyes. "Why did you do this to me? Why did you make me—make me kill my friends?"

The demon shook his head. "My God, you're clueless. I don't give a rat's ass about you, Q. Prototypical teenaged boy who can't keep his dick in his pants—or, more to the point, out of his girlfriend. It was Jasper I was after. *Jasper.* You were just a means to an end."

"Jasper? I don't understand."

"No, Q., you don't understand. And guess what? I'm not going to provide you any last-minute revelations. Maybe you'll find him on the other side, as they say, and he'll tell you himself. But before that happens you're going to answer my question. What did you tell J.D. Thomas?"

"Why don't you ask *me* that question, Leo?"

The voice came from inside the house. Leo's head snapped in that direction, his eyes wide with surprise. His arm raised, but before he could move there was an explosion of sound and color—the color was red, and it burst from the demon's chest. The demon stumbled backward toward the edge of the terrace. There was a second explosion and he was propelled through the air. His thighs caught on the balustrade, he teetered wildly for a moment, and then—silently, as if he'd never really been there—he disappeared over the edge. But the most unnerving aspect of the whole scene was that Q. could have sworn Leo smiled before he fell off the terrace.

Q. saw the smoking barrel of the double-barreled shotgun even as he heard a crash, and then the keening of a car alarm nine stories down filled up the night.

J.D. Thomas walked out of Q.'s parents' bedroom. His hands were trembling, but a proud smile flickered at the edge of his mouth.

"Come on, Q. It won't be long before he's back."

17

He'd been shot a dozen times before. Fourteen to be exact. Boris Petrovich Alushkin remained the worst. It was really, *really* hard to concentrate with a big hole in your temporal lobe, but two shotgun blasts to the chest was a close second. And then falling nine stories? *Fuck* but that hurt. Thank God there was a Town Car idling on the curb to break his fall.

A small crowd had gathered by the time he woke up. One hundred forty-three seconds. Not bad, not bad at all. By rights he should've taken a couple of hours to repair the worst of the damage before he tried to move, but he could hear sirens approaching. He didn't have the luxury of minutes, let alone hours.

There was a lot of blood spurting from his chest, and he had to push a rib back in before he was able to stanch the flow. Then, concentrating, he eased the pressure from Larry's crushed L2, which was pinching his spinal cord. Feeling returned to his legs *way* too fast, at which point he discovered he'd snapped his left femur in two places. That probably explained why it flopped sideways over the edge of the car like a broken candy cane. It was no fun *at all* setting the bone. He aligned the three pieces as best he could, then sent jets of calcium ions into the semimembranosus and the semitendinosus in back and the vastus lateralis and vastus medialis in front. The calcium caused the actin and myosin muscle fibers to contract tightly, basically mimicking rigor mortis. The rigid muscles held the bone together and, grimacing, he eased off the crushed Town Car.

An old woman fainted. No one noticed.

Leo spat out a mouthful of blood, a couple a teeth. "Somebody help that woman. Good God, were you all raised in barns?"

It was hard to interface with Larry's senses. Sight and sound were particularly fucked up—he didn't even notice the car alarm going off until he was on the sidewalk. By now it had been three full minutes since he'd fallen from the terrace. According to New York City nuisance laws, the alarm should have cut out 120 seconds ago. He bent over, reached past the driver into the crushed cabin. Pressed the button on the keyring that turned off the alarm.

Silence.

"Serves you right, buddy," Leo said to the chauffeur, whose head hung limply off his neck. "Disturbing all these nice people."

He straightened slowly, took a moment to align the five pieces of his shattered pelvis, then began hobbling up the street toward the ambulance.

The broken rib poked out of his chest. He pushed it back in.

A little boy ran screaming.

"Hey buddy," said a guy with a Scottish terrier on a leash. "You just, like, fell out of the sky. Want to sit down?"

Flames came out of the man's mouth when he spoke and his Scottish terrier kept turning into a Dyson vacuum. Leo squinted, decided it was unlikely the man was a demon from hell, and his dog probably wasn't a home appliance.

He felt around the back of Larry's head, found something that felt like a toothpick but turned out to be three inches of antenna. It had punctured his occipital lobe, which played havoc with his visual processing.

Leo looked at the bit of antenna in his palm. It writhed and spat venom like a baby cobra. This is your brain, he thought. This is your brain with a metal spike in it.

"Buddy? You okay?" The Scottish terrier made a whooshing noise as it hoovered up bits of broken glass. Leo would've kicked the dog into traffic if his leg hadn't been broken. He settled for dislocating the man's jaw.

"I got shot too. Dumbass."

He shook his right hand painfully. Turned out half a dozen metatarsals were broken on top of everything else. How do you break a goddamn *fingerbone* without breaking your arm? The universe was so *arbitrary*.

There were no more incidents as he limped around to the front entrance of the building, prying buckshot out of his torso and dropping the pellets on the sidewalk. He lifted himself unsteadily into the seat of the ambulance. Turned the engine over, dropped the bus in gear. Pulled out just as the ambulance that had come to retrieve his fallen body drove up behind him.

If there were a therapist for the Mogran, Leo might've admitted, yeah, maybe he wasn't the best at controlling his hosts' psyches. But there wasn't a demon in history who could manipulate the corpus as well as he could. Hell's bells, he'd just fallen ninety-four feet and taken thirty-three pieces of Number 1 buckshot to his gut, chest, and throat. Name another demon who could get up three minutes after that, let alone drive an ambulance through New York City traffic? Come on, just one.

In fact, it was all he could do to hold Lawrence Bishop's body together, which unfortunately let the paramedic's psyche run rampant. His host's drug-addled memories merged with Leo's in ways that made it impossible to tell what was really happening and what was hallucination. The bulbs at the top of the pole lamps were like yellow whirlpools swirling upside down into the sky. Changing stoplights seemed to open up rifts in space through which he glimpsed other places, other times. In the red light: the court of the emperor of Japan during the time of Genji. In the yellow: Charlemagne walking around in a rusty suit of armor reeking of piss and sweat. In the green: hey, was that Solomon? It was! Talking to those two women fighting over the baby. The wise king threatened to cut the disputed child in half.

"Do it, Schlomo! Cut that little fucker right down the middle!"

The sound of Larry's voice knocked him out of his spell, and Leo shook his head to clear it. Man, *that* was a bad idea. The ambulance veered left and right across the avenue, clipping parked cars on both sides of the street. He stomped on the brake pedal, slammed into the steering wheel, knocked that goddamn rib out of his chest *again*. As he pushed it back in, he repeated something Napoleon had said to him during that long cold march into Russia.

"Slow and steady wins the race, Leo. Slow and steady. Wins the race."

He'd said it in French of course, and he hadn't used Leo's name. Hadn't used exactly those words, but you got the picture.

His name.

The doctor had said his name. So the Legion knew who they were chasing. But he also knew who was chasing him.

What to do, what to do? Go after the doctor and Q., or attend to his fledgling? It was a real pickle—but were *those* real pickles, diving from the top of the building on the corner of 59th and First?

Probably not.

Just then he heard a low moan from the back of the bus. For a moment Leo thought it was J.D. Thomas, but then he remembered the other psychiatrist. Dr. Miller. Sue.

Good ol' Sue.

Good-time Sue.

Good-to-go Sue.

"Gotta go, Sue," he said out loud.

Larry's girlfriend was living proof that things could always turn out worse than you expected.

"Daddy?"

On the corner of 60th and York Avenue, Sue Miller stared at the cable car coming in off Roosevelt Island. For some reason she couldn't sit up. She wasn't sure why. It just seemed like, well, like she couldn't move.

"Daddy, are you there?"

Still, it was a warm evening. The air smelled good and green. Wet.

Whatever she was lying on was comfy. She wanted to touch herself but she couldn't move her hands.

"It's okay, Daddy. I'll be good. I promise."

Her daddy didn't like it when she touched herself. Down there. Like that. But it felt so good! Sometimes she just couldn't help it. Daddy shouldn't have come in when she was taking a bath anyway.

"I won't do it anymore, Daddy. I promise."

Someone in the cable car waved. She couldn't wave back, but she smiled at the angels. Angels in a box waving down at her.

A tugboat blew its horn on the East River.

"Toot toot!" Sue chortled. "Toot toot!"

Just then a car came too fast off the FDR and clipped the foot of her gurney. Sue spun round and round and round. The lights of the city whirled above her glazed eyes like a kaleidoscope.

"Phlox!" she cackled through her smeared smile. "Toot toot! Toot toot!"

18

J.D. Thomas drove a 1933 Pierce-Arrow limousine that had once been owned by Franklin Delano Roosevelt. Or maybe Theodore. Q. forgot more or less as soon as the doctor told him. The doctor's car was fifteen feet long, could seat six people in the cavernous back compartment. The two men rode up front however, where the doctor gripped the enormous steering wheel as though piloting an old-fashioned sailing ship through rough seas.

"You were expecting a chauffeur?" Dr. Thomas said. "Maybe one with an allergy to nuts?"

The enormous car cruised up First Avenue. After ten blocks of silence, Q. said,

"Um, nice ride."

"Why thank you, Q. The shell's authentic, but the engine and the chassis and those kinds of things are new. Cannibalized from a BMW or a Chrysler or something. I love the way these old cars look, but, you know, they don't really drive all that well, unless you make a few adjustments." He patted the leather-trimmed steering wheel. "This baby will do zero to sixty in just over five seconds."

Q. stared at his driver for a long time. Then:

"So, uh, are you going to tell me what happened back there?"

Q. had looked over the railing. Had seen the paramedic's body nine stories down, arms and legs askew on the staved-in roof of what looked like a Town Car. But by the time he and the doctor made it outside, the man was gone. Admittedly, they'd had to take the stairs because the elevator wouldn't move unless the security gate was closed, and the one the paramedic had kicked in wouldn't budge. They'd also lingered in the lobby, where Dr. Thomas clumsily reloaded the shotgun—he put the shells in backward at first—and Q. tried not to stare at Ramon, the night man, who lay behind the desk in a pool of blood, naked except for his underwear. But even so, Q. didn't see how five minutes could make a difference. Dr. Thomas had shot the paramedic in the chest. *Twice.* The man had fallen *nine stories.* He should not be *gone.* But he was. The only signs that he'd been there were the blood that filled the collapsed roof of the Town Car, smeared footprints that tracked through the carpet of broken glass spread over the sidewalk.

The doctor dropped the car in park. He regarded Q. over the barrel of the shotgun that sat between them on the wide leather seat, still emitting the faint tang of gunpowder.

"I can help you, Q. But you must drop the pretense of ignorance."

"Hey, look. You just broke into my parents' apartment and shot a man off the terrace—"

"That was not a man. And you know it."

"What was it then? A *Mogran?"*

Q. started. He had meant to say "demon," but instead that other word came out.

Just then a busted-up ambulance squealed around the corner and roared up First Avenue. The two men sat in silence until it was gone, Q. nervously fingering the door handle, the doctor tapping out a staccato rhythm on the steering wheel. After the siren had faded, he put the car in gear and pulled away from the intersection.

"Answer one question for me, Q. Where did that word come from? Mogran. Or Anschluss for that matter?"

"That's two questions," Q. said. But that was all he said.

The doctor stored his car in a garage on 66th between Lexington and Third. During the four-block walk to his townhouse he kept looking around, but there was no sign of Leo or Larry. Just a bunch of Hunter College students careening drunkenly through the streets, celebrating the last week of the semester. I should be in school, Q. thought. Taking finals, hitting parties, deciding whether to go naked beneath my cap and gown with the rest of the track team. Instead I'm walking up Lexington next to a man carrying a violin case with a shotgun folded inside it. Q. wondered how everyone they passed couldn't guess what the case contained. Hadn't they ever seen a Jimmy Cagney movie?

Q. started. He had never seen a Jimmy Cagney movie. He hadn't, but Leo had.

He turned to the doctor.

"He said you hypnotized me."

The doctor's eyes were invisible behind the light reflecting off his glasses. "I apologize. It seemed the quickest way to ascertain if indeed you had been possessed."

The word hung heavily in the warm air like a streak of fog. *Possessed.*

"How'd you know? I mean, what made you think I'd been . . ."

"The same things that made *you* think you'd been possessed. Your uncharacteristic behavior in the days leading up to the accident, not to mention the fact that you survived the impact unscathed. And then of course the memories, the unexplained knowledge. Anschluss, Mogran, etc., etc. Demons can wreak remarkable changes in their hosts, both to their bodies and their minds."

They walked in silence for a few steps. Q. had so many questions he didn't know where to start. Who, what, when, where, why. But he decided to open with:

"How do *you* know about all this?"

The doctor nodded.

"I am a member—a tertiary member, admittedly—of an organization called the Legion."

"What, like the Foreign Legion? The Legion of Superheroes?"

The doctor laughed. "It is appropriate that you mention comic books, since the Legion was founded by a writer of children's literature. Does the name Jordan David ring a bell?"

Q. wracked his brain. "I don't think so."

"The City of Frozen Souls."

"Oh, right! I read that ten times when I was a kid!" He laughed sheepishly. "I never was very good at names."

If the doctor heard him, he gave no sign. He launched into a speech that Q. sensed he'd rehearsed many times.

"Though he was American, Jordan David was often grouped with Hans Christian Andersen and Lewis Carroll, who wrote before him, and J.M. Barrie, who came after. They were the major propagators of the so-called Cult of the Child, a literature of symbolic, often surreal stories that evinced an enormous fear of, and fascination with, adult sexuality. In their own time, all four men were widely believed to have been virgins, but later evidence revealed all of them were in fact sexual deviants, at least by the standards of their day. Andersen and Barrie were homosexuals, and David and Charles Dodgson, which was Lewis Carroll's real name, were heterosexual pedophiles."

"Um . . ." Q. was stumped.

"It was David's belief—formulated long after the fact, of course— that he, Andersen, Dodgson, and Barrie were all victims of the same demon. I am compressing things enormously here, but suffice to say that after years of investigating, David learned that the demon's name was Karena. The strange acts she forced the men to engage in while she possessed them left them understandably frightened of sexual relations, so they channeled their 'unhealthy' impulses into art. Only David ever figured out that they'd been groomed to do this by Karena herself. For some reason, she hadn't masked herself in him as well as she had in the others, and when writing his book didn't exorcise the unwanted memories and feelings, he devoted his life to researching the possibility of possession. In time he met others who also believed they'd served as unwilling hosts to some alien entity or other, and they banded together to pool their efforts."

"The Legion."

"Exactly. *The City of Frozen Souls* proved enormously successful, and David used the money he earned to fund his activities. Over the years, he and his compatriots amassed a large archive of data about the entities they came to call Mogran. The name was the result of intense hypnotherapy sessions, in which the unconscious levels of former hosts' minds were plumbed for any bit of information they might hide within them. Many current members of the Legion, myself included, continue to practice hypnosis, although I confess this is the first time I've ever used it on someone I suspected might have been possessed."

The doctor broke off. The two men had reached the corner of 70th. Tall trees shrouded the streetlights, and Dr. Thomas squinted into the shadows for several seconds. Q. had been so caught up in the doctor's story that he'd almost forgotten what had occasioned it—what had happened at his parents' apartment, what the doctor was carrying in the violin case. Now he too looked down the dark sidewalk.

A single figure walked the street, so far ahead that it was impossible to tell if it was man or woman, or even if it was coming toward them. It was tall and broad-shouldered, with a head of wild hair, just like Larry Bishop. The two men stared at it until finally it stepped into the ray of a streetlight, and Q. saw that it was a woman. High heels added to her stature, and her shoulders came from pads sewn into her blazer. She crossed the street and headed off.

"A-as I was saying." The doctor's voice shook slightly. "The members of the Legion didn't just interview people who had been possessed. They also engaged in research, both archaeological and academic. An enormous amount of information about the Mogran exists in the public record, in monasteries and museums and even in libraries, but much of it has to be decoded, the speculative separated from the empirical to glean the truth. On some level, the Mogran yearn to be known, though their safety depends on their existence remaining secret. Hence Karena and her writers. In all of their books are journeys in which the body acquires new forms, new powers and perceptions, and then loses them again. A perfect metaphor for possession."

Q. glanced back at the woman, who was just disappearing around a corner. "I don't know if I'd call them powers."

"Pardon me, Q., I don't mean to belittle your experiences, but you got off lightly. Most experts within the Legion believe that Attila—the Scourge of God, as he styled himself—was possessed by a demon of the same name, although his massacres were nothing compared to those of Hulagu Khan, the grandson of Genghis, who slaughtered a million people when he conquered Baghdad in 1258."

"Shit."

"We believe Hulagu was under control of a demon known as Karnok. Before Karnok/Hulagu laid it waste, Baghdad had been the seat of the five-hundred-year-old Abbasid caliphate and was known as the prince of cities. After they were through, it was little more than a smoking ruin and open grave."

Q. laughed sarcastically. "Think Karnok's come back in the Bushes?"

"I have often wondered. Certainly *something* is possessing those men."

Q. had to look at the doctor's face to see that he was joking. The older man winked, then continued.

"In fact, demons do sometimes possess several people in a row in order to achieve a single goal. Take Karena, for example. Then there's the case of Julian, who possessed the Roman emperors Tiberius, Caligula, Claudius, and Nero each in turn, giving the ancient world five decades of violence and debauchery that almost tore the Roman Empire apart."

Q.'s mind filled with an image of the destroyed Porsche. Of Sila and Jasper's deaths. He knew it couldn't compare to the destruction the doctor had just described, but still. They were his friends. It was his life.

"But though the Mogran are usually given to base urges, to violence and sex particularly, they sometimes enter what we call the lull, when they inhabit a single human host for decades at a time. During these periods, they often dedicate themselves to work of enduring social, artistic, or scientific significance. Indeed–"

The doctor broke off. They had reached his townhouse, and he paused on the steps.

"What?" Q. said.

"Well, your demon."

Q. had to force himself to say the name aloud.

"Leo."

The doctor nodded. "We don't know if that's his real name or one he took for himself. For a time we thought he might've even been–"

Q. cut him off. "No! *The* Leo? Da Vinci?"

The doctor nodded. "I tend to think of this as a bit of misdirection on Leo's part. Although da Vinci is found on many lists of history's 'virgins,' the truth is simply that he was gay and, according to our best guesses, involved with a series of his most attractive–and, alas, least talented–students."

"Jesus Christ," Q. said, and then, when the doctor made a funny expression: "Don't tell me." He shook his head violently. "You're not actually defending these creatures, are you? Because they were artists or philosophers or whatever? I mean, whatever was in me, it was *evil*. It killed my friends. The last time I checked, even the greatest artist in the world still goes to jail for killing someone."

"But do the greatest politicians? Progress is rarely bloodless, Q., as our president reminds us all the time."

"I can't believe I'm hearing this. You–"

"Q., please. Try to understand. To the Mogran, good and evil are childish concepts. They aren't interested in right and wrong, only in filling the eternity of their existence. Sometimes their actions have beneficial consequences, sometimes terrible, but in the latter case it is more accurate to think of them as you would a cobra: they don't exist to bite you. They only do it if you get in their way."

The doctor waved away Q.'s protest, then handed him the violin case.

"We should continue this inside. And, as well–" the doctor tapped the violin case "–I would like to replace what's in here with my del Gesu, which is no doubt coming horribly out of tune in this humidity."

Once they were safely in the foyer, the doctor walked into a large living room lit only by the light coming off the street. He spread his arms out, a self-conscious grin turning up one corner of his mouth. The doctor's outstretched arms lifted his sigil out of his vest as well, which added a sixties lounge lizard aspect to the pose, but he seemed unaware of any irony. When he spoke, he deepened his voice, the way you do when you're reciting something important or pretentious:

> "For He had commanded the unclean spirit to come out
> of the man. For it had seized him many times; and he was
> bound with chains and shackles and kept under guard.
> And yet he would break his bonds and be driven by the
> demon into the desert. And Jesus asked him, 'What is
> your name?' And–"

The doctor jumped at a voice emanating from the shadows deeper inside the house.

"And he answered, 'Legion,' for many demons had entered him."

There was the sound of a trigger being cocked.

"Very nice recitation, Doctor. But I'm afraid neither scripture nor sigil will save you now."

19

Jasper swung Jarhead's truck into the hospital parking lot.

"This. Is. *Stupid*."

He slammed the truck into park and bits of glass flew about the cab. Edwin had smashed out the windows in Jarhead's truck before driving off with Sandy in his Miata. Jasper supposed he would have done the same thing. Great, he thought. Now I've deprived Jarhead of not one but two of his best friends, not to mention set him up for a second charge of sexual assault. Somehow fixing his host's wrist and helping him drop a few pounds didn't seem like a fair trade for destroying his life.

He looked up at the hospital entrance. He'd driven by it a thousand times but had never been in it. The only friend he had who'd ever been hospitalized was Q., but his parents had taken him to the city to have his appendix out, not trusting a country doctor to operate on their son. And of course, Amelia Van Arsdale had died there, years and years ago, but Jasper had been too young to visit her.

Really, he thought. The number of things he'd waited to do till after he died was a little out of control. Everything from pressing that button on the Qusays' gate to sex (and sexual assault) to visiting somebody in a hospital.

Well, not just somebody. His girlfriend. Michaela.

One more thing he'd neglected to do while he was alive.

Of course, Jarhead had been there for his wrist, and it was Jarhead's memories that reminded Jasper visiting hours were over. It was, after all, nearly two in the morning. As luck would have it, a paramedic was talking to the blond triage nurse—flirting with her, to judge from the way he leaned over the high counter, or at least looking down her cleavage—and Jasper was able to slip in unnoticed. It was funny how he saw sex everywhere, now that it was the most pressing thing on his mind. The tease and the chase, the call and the response, the stimulations, the artificial aids, and of course the actual act. Had it always been like that and he just hadn't paid attention? He was coming to hate asking himself those kinds of questions, because in his new state they were never rhetorical. His mind sifted, categorized, and prioritized all of his and Jarhead's memories, handed him the answer before he could decide if he really wanted to know it: yeah, it had always been like that. The world was pretty much in a constant state of foreplay.

Whatever. Jasper couldn't deal with sex right now. Even thinking about it abstractly got his blood pumping. Jasper imagined all the sleeping, comatose or otherwise helpless patients who must lie behind every door. How easy it would be to slip in and take one of them, use her for his needs. No, Jasper thought, he wouldn't escape like that. He would douse Jarhead's body with gasoline and light it on fire before he did that.

Jasper assumed people in comas were treated in the ICU, so he went there first. It was a small ward, hand-lettered nametags on plates outside every door. It turned out Michaela was sharing a room with someone named Patricia Myles. He could see the other woman's body on the near bed, a rail-thin form that made almost no impression beneath the blue blanket. What little showed above it—two arms the size and color of kindling, a face so hollow the bones were visible beneath the blotchy skin—was covered in tubes and tape and other medical apparatus. Someone had done the woman's hair though. Curled, set, and sprayed it into a shiny silver orb that haloed her ravaged face in a gentle sphere. Jasper was happy she had someone who loved her enough to come in and fix her up, but at the same time he wasn't sad that *he* didn't have to go out like that. Give him a quick and painless car accident over the drawn-out decay of cancer or Alzheimer's or whatever this woman had any day. But he wasn't there to look at a stranger, he reminded himself. Taking a deep breath, he turned to the bed closer to the window.

Michaela was even more obscured than Patricia Myles. For one thing, her right arm was in a cast. For another, a large brace immobilized her neck. A plastic mask covered her face as well, fastened there with two strips of adhesive gauze that made a crude X over her nose, and a wad of bandages sat on the left side of her head, covering cheek and eye and ear. And her hair—that big beautiful messy mound of dirty blond hair that she loved to flip and chew and fiddle with—had all been hacked off. All that was left was a ragged fuzz crisscrossed by a half dozen deep gashes, each one jaggedly stitched together with black thread that looked like tiny worms writhing into and out of Michaela's skull.

A moan gurgled out of Jasper's throat. This was *Michaela* for God's sake. The person he'd loved so much that when she said "Wait," he wasn't even angry, because he knew sex wasn't the goal of his relationship with her, merely another pleasure they'd have a lifetime to enjoy. He knew everything about her. The way she smiled (the right side curled up tentatively, and then, if she were truly happy, the left followed), the way she ate (staring at her food apologetically, sorry that she had to kill it and grind it up into little pieces between her teeth), the way she yawned (both hands covering her mouth, a remnant of a childhood fear that something might invade her body if she didn't protect it). The way she walked (one leg crossing over the other like a model on a runway) and then again the way she stood still (weight on the left foot, hip jutting out). His hand instinctively curled itself in the shape of that hip, to rest there, to trace the bare flesh above the waistband of her jeans. But . . .

But it wasn't his hand. It was Jarhead's. He curled it into a fist, barely managed to stop himself before he slammed it through the door.

He remembered learning how amputees feel pain in their missing limbs. Invisible arms aching to be stretched, absent calves dying to be kneaded. Jasper could feel the whole of his invisible body. Could map every neural pathway and musculoskeletal millimeter of missing flesh with such microscopic precision that his absent body seemed to pulsate around him like a hologram. But no matter how vivid the mental image, it was still just that: an image. An aura, a shadow. Though he could feel the throbbing need to run to Michaela and hold her in his—in Jasper's—hands, the only body he could bring to her was Jarhead's, and this thought kept him on the far side of the door. Kept a pane of glass between him and the girl he loved. Because, though Jasper Van Arsdale would never hurt his girlfriend, he didn't know what Jarhead West would do to her. What, at any rate, a Jarhead inhabited by Jasper's spirit would do to her.

He could feel the protest deep inside him: *I wouldn't hurt her Jasper.*

I know you wouldn't, Jasper answered. *But we might.*

He let his eyes roam the length of her broken body one last time. Reminded himself that it really *was* her, she really *was* alive, and that's what mattered. He resisted the urge to do something sentimental, blow a kiss or mouth the words "I love you." Just stepped back from the door and turned away. That's when he realized he wasn't the only person who'd come to check on Michaela. He didn't recognize the man himself, but Jarhead did.

"Hey, Jasper," Lawrence Bishop said to him, a crooked smile on his face. "What's up, buddy?"

20

Q. ducked into the shadows of Dr. Thomas's foyer just as a woman stepped into the living room. In the dim light from the streetlamps, he could make out dirty blond hair, a slim, strong-jawed face, a long, taut body practically pulsing with energy. He also saw a small but impressive-looking pistol in the woman's right hand. Its rectangular silver barrel caught the streetlight and gleamed with singular intent.

The woman wagged her gun at the doctor. "You're Thomas?"

The doctor paused. "My name *is* J.D. Thomas," he said finally. His voice seemed calm, but his eyes blinked rapidly behind his glasses. "I'm sorry I wasn't here to welcome you into my home, but I can assure you the police are on their way to rectify that error even as we speak."

Suddenly Q. remembered he was holding something. The violin case. *Duh*. The gun.

The blond woman laughed and the barrel of her weapon jiggled slightly. "I don't think so. For a man whose house is filled with such valuable objects, you have a remarkably cheap alarm system. No motion detectors, no infrared sensors, just a few trip wires on doors and windows that any eighth grader could disarm." She jerked the gun toward the painting over the fireplace. "Is that a real Lautrec?"

Q. squinted at the painting, even as his fingertips felt for the buckles on the violin case. A clown? Something in a Harlequin costume anyway.

"It *is*." The note of pride in the doctor's voice seemed a bit misplaced, given the circumstances.

"Raku pottery. Yoruba bronzes. A complete *incunabula* of the Psalms. The art is worth more than the house, and I'm guessing the house is worth quite a bit. You need to get yourself a new security service, Dr. Thomas." She leaned in close. *"You are vulnerable to invasion."*

"I'm missing a page, actually. Psalm 23. 'Though I walk through the valley of the shadow.' Probably sold off in the sixteenth century to some aspiring burgher, hung over the dining table or the counting desk." The doctor's voice was hoarse but level. "You've been here a while. The *incunabula* are on the third floor."

Q. folded the buckles on the violin case as softly as he could. First one, then the other. He seamed the case open just enough to reach his hand inside.

The woman brought the gun an inch from Dr. Thomas's forehead.

"I did not come here to appreciate your art collection. You have sixty seconds to prove to me *you* have not been invaded."

"I don't understand—"

"Prove to me," the woman cut him off, "that you are not Mogran."

The doctor's lips trembled as if he wanted to smile but was too afraid.

"H-huntress? How did you get here so quickly?"

Q. paused, his fingers touching the barrel, which was still warm. The doctor seemed to know this woman, at least enough to call her Huntress. The woman didn't move her gun away from his forehead, however, so he continued to ease the shotgun out of the case.

"If what you told me about the boy is true," the woman said, "it is likely the demon will stick close to him. I doubt you have the sigil—the real sigil, that is, as opposed to that trinket on your chest—which means you are as likely a host as anyone. Prove to me the enemy is not simply using you to lure me here, so he can strike back against the Legion."

Q. wondered what a "real" sigil was, as opposed to the doctor's goofy necklace. Something that could actually protect you against demons? What was next, he wondered? Magic wands? Flying carpets?

The gun was finally out of the case. All he had to do was snap the barrel closed. Oh, and aim it. And fire. An image of Leo's chest exploding when the doctor shot him flashed through his mind. The pool of blood that had filled the concave roof of the Town Car.

Dr. Thomas started to nod, but his forehead tapped the woman's gun barrel and he took a quick step backwards. "I understand. You—you have to say my, that is, say *his*, say the, say the demon's name."

"Very good, Doctor." The woman leveled the gun at his forehead. In a deep voice—a voice like the one J.D. Thomas had used to intone the bible verses—she intoned: "Show yourself, Leo."

As far as Q. could tell, nothing happened. The doctor's eyes continued to blink rapidly behind his glasses and the woman still held the pistol to his forehead. After a moment he began to fold the shotgun's barrel into the stock. But even as he did so, the woman dropped her arm. She turned the gun around, offered it handle first to Dr. Thomas.

"You really shouldn't keep these in the coffee jar, doctor. Not only does it gum up the firing pin, it tarnishes the finish. And you," she said, turning toward Q. "If you'd taken any longer with that shotgun, I would have had to put it together *for* you."

21

It wasn't just Larry's smile that was crooked. His whole body seemed slightly off kilter, as if it had been taken apart and put back together by a dyslexic toddler. His torso skewed to the right as it came out of his pelvis and his left leg turned out like a hockey stick. The fingers of his right hand zigzagged crazily at the knuckles. No, not at the knuckles: between them, as if each of his fingerbones had been snapped in half. Ouch, Jasper thought. That must've *hurt*.

Leo waggled Larry's wonky fingers. "Please pardon our appearance while we renovate," he said as he pulled the ambulance out of the hospital parking lot. "Larry should be good as new in a few days. Well, he would be good as new, if I planned on sticking around." He examined his host's crooked fingers in the glow of passing streetlights. "Who knows, maybe he'll get used to them."

Under different circumstances, Jasper might've found Larry's fingers fascinating, but right now other things were more pressing.

"You really expect me to believe someone *shot* you? That you fell off a nine-story *building*? How are you still *alive?*"

Leo laughed. "I'm not, remember?" He glanced at Jasper, eyes twinkling. "Come on, buddy. You been in Jarhead long enough to know the answer to your question. Takes a lot more than a couple-a shotgun blasts to put one of us to sleep. If the guy had aimed for the head, of course, it would've been a lot worse."

"And *why* did this guy shoot you again?"

"Turns out ol' Larry here was having a thing with a mafiosa down in Jersey City. Watched too many episodes of *The Sopranos* or something. Needless to say, Mr. Mafioso wasn't too happy when he came home and found Larry shtupping his wife. Lucky for Larry *I* was there too, or he *would* be dead."

Jasper shook his head incredulously. But there was still one more piece to the puzzle. A piece he wasn't sure he wanted to know the answer to.

"And . . . and how *did* you end up in Larry?"

Leo flashed him another of Larry's crooked smiles. "Well, it's obvious you haven't quite figured this out, as evidenced by the fact that you're still occupying Mr. West's fleshy domicile." He looked Jarhead's body up and down. "Looks like he dropped a few pounds though. Nice work."

"You're saying you came back? For me?"

"Guardian angel Leo, at your service."

Jasper bit back a laugh. Somehow he didn't think Leo had ever guarded anything in his life.

"So, uh, what happened back there? At the river?"

"Well, Jasper, if you need me to explain *that* to you, then the situation is worse than I realized."

Jasper would've blushed if he'd been in his own body. "I don't mean *that*. I know what *that* was, thank you very much."

"No, thank *you*."

"This is all a big joke to you, isn't it? Pulling pranks on people, then skipping out before they can pay you back?"

Leo stomped on the brakes. "Listen, buddy. A practical joke is only funny when there are consequences. And there are no consequences for us anymore. We're dead, remember? It's time you started accepting that fact and stopped acting like a mopey teenager." He chuckled. "The joke was *supposed* to be on Mason and Danielle, but you neglected to play along. You didn't *come*," he added, when Jasper looked at him blankly.

"I didn't come? I didn't *come*? Forgive me for being a bit overwhelmed by the experience, but I'd died about two hours before. Orgasm wasn't exactly my highest priority. Jesus Christ. Why the hell didn't you tell me this?"

"Well, good golly. I knew you were a virgin but I figured you at least understood the basic principle of the sex act. But for the record, orgasm is key. I'll be sure to spell everything out for you this time."

"This time?"

"Yeah, Jasper. You want out, don't you? Out of Jarhead? Out of here?" He waved a hand at the cars and houses passing by the ambulance's windows. "Like I said, Leo's here to help."

22

"We need to go *now*," the woman said impatiently.

"Huntress," the doctor called from the kitchen. "There is nowhere to go. We don't even know where Leo is."

"We know he's not in this living room."

From its perch over the fireplace, the sad-faced Harlequin in the Toulouse-Lautrec painting looked down at the gray-eyed woman pacing back and forth. She had a miraculous body. It wasn't so much sexy as strong. Sinewy, but not stringy like a professional athlete's. Kinetic. Efficient. *Dangerous*. Well, Q. admitted to himself, maybe it was sexy. Just a little bit.

"I'm afraid that doesn't narrow it down much. I don't know how you take your tea," the doctor added, emerging from the kitchen with a silver tray on which sat an ornate silver pot and three delicate white cups, "so I've brought milk and lemon. And sugar. Lapsang souchong. I've heard Winston Churchill took his with Scotch, which I can get if you'd like."

The shotgun sat on the coffee table, and the doctor nudged it out of the way so he could set the tray down.

The woman rolled her eyes and turned to Q.

"You are the boy?"

Q. blinked. "What?"

"The boy. The one the doctor thinks can be the new hunter."

Q. flashed a look at Dr. Thomas.

"It just needs to steep a moment more." He sat down next to the woman. "This is Mohammed Qusay, huntress. His friends call him Q."

"I don't want to be his friend. I want to know if he can help me, either as an assistant or as bait."

"Bait?"

"Pardon me, huntress." The doctor cut himself off. "It feels odd to keep referring to you that way. Might I ask your name?"

The woman glared at him, and the doctor shrank into his jacket. "You can call me Lana."

"Thank you, Lana. As I was saying, I haven't had the chance to tell Q. quite what it is we do."

"What *we* do? You presume much, Thomas."

Q. looked back and forth between the two members of the Legion.

"You told me you track down demons."

"Is *that* what he told you?" Lana's eyebrows shot up. "We do more than track them down. You didn't think the good doctor was just trying to *frighten* Leo with a pair of shotgun blasts, did you?"

Q. turned to the doctor. "You want me to help you *kill* them? But they're in *people*. Wouldn't you have to–" Q. recoiled. "Jesus Christ!"

Lana peered at Q. After a moment, she stood up. "I have to leave. The boy is obviously useless."

"Now look–" Q. sputtered.

"No, *you* look. The Mogran care about neither your indecision nor your confusion. They do not pause to ascertain whether someone is friend or foe or innocent bystander. They act without hesitation and without mercy, and if you hope to survive the hunt, let alone be successful in it, you must do the same."

Q. turned to the doctor. "What the hell is she–"

Without warning, Lana leapt across the table. A stone knife had materialized in her hand and pressed into his chest.

"Do not look to him for help. He is not one of us."

Lana's breath was wet on Q.'s face, seemed to have the smell of meat on it. He could feel the tip of her blade as well. She gave the knife a little push, and Q. felt it pierce his skin. Felt the blood begin to well up around the blade, then soak into the fabric of his shirt.

"Huntress," J.D. Thomas said hoarsely. "Please."

The woman had aligned the knife perfectly between two ribs, just over Q.'s heart. It seemed that with each expansion his right ventricle pushed against the knife's tip. And then something funny happened: Q. saw his heart. He didn't feel it: he *saw* it, floating in the ribcage, held in place by connective tissue, a complex of veins and arteries leading into and out of it. A moment later he'd followed the veins and arteries all the way down to his fingers and toes. Saw the muscles they nourished, the bones, the tendons that connected the muscles to the bones and the ligaments that connected the bones to each other. He saw all his internal organs from the smallest gland to the big purple-brown sack of his liver, pumping, processing, manufacturing this or that chemical or hormone or whatever they were called. He didn't know all the names, but somehow he sensed their functions. What they did. How they could be made to do their tasks most efficiently. He felt himself winding up. Felt a sudden reservoir of energy flood his limbs with speed, strength, precision. He had no idea how long all this took, but the next thing he heard was the soft thud of Lana's knife falling to the carpeted floor. He looked down, saw that he held her hand in his, the wrist bent back at a ninety-degree angle. A grunt came from Lana's mouth, between lips parted in a small, grim smile.

"I would ask you not to break my wrist." And then, in an amused voice: "*Q.*"

Q. wasn't sure what had just happened, but he released Lana's hand carefully. She bent it back and forth a couple of times, then looked over at Dr. Thomas, whose own shaking hands were splattering more tea onto the silver tray than into the three cups.

"Perhaps you were right about this one." She waved away the cup the doctor proffered her, rattling in its saucer. "You can hold the tea. But I will take some of that Scotch."

23

The Aristocrats was a long narrow shoebox of a bar. The booths were cracked and stained from years of fat asses sliding into and out of them, the tabletops covered with drunken hieroglyphics, equal parts penises in various stages of erection and breasts ranging in size from very large to so-massive-light-couldn't-escape-their-gravitational-pull. There were names conjoined by hearts, hearts crossed out and replaced with "hates." The classic: *For a good time call ~~Mary~~ ~~Angie~~ Yur Mom.* And then of course the old standby:

> *God is dead.* –Nietzsche
> *Nietzsche is dead.* –God

The bartender had spiky black hair, an eyebrow ring, a tattoo of a dagger on her forearm, yet somehow this seemed to accentuate the fineness of her features. The softly rolled bottom of her cut-off T-shirt exposed a taut belly with a silver ring at the center, all too reminiscent of Danny's. Jasper's mind filled with a sudden vision of the bartender stretched out on the bar's surface, her back arched slightly, her navel ring beckoning him.

"Yo, champ," the bartender fixed a smirk at Jarhead. "My face is up *here.*"

"Don't worry, buddy," Leo said to Jasper. "First round's on Larry." He limped up to the bar. "Two of whatever you got on tap, baby doll."

Jasper noticed that Leo didn't pay for the beers as he left, just winked at the bartender and patted her on the arm with his wonky hand. The bartender's eyes followed him back to the booth, her mouth slightly open, her rag making lazy circles on the bar.

Leo nodded at Jasper's furrowed brow, slid a beer across the table. "It's all in the eyes. Microadjustments of the pupils and the capillaries cause them to lighten and darken in a manner imperceptible to the conscious mind."

Jasper frowned. "You mean . . . hypnosis?"

"Nothing so crude. Just a bit of extra leverage." He nodded at the bartender, who seemed to have snapped out of her reverie and was rinsing glasses in a tub. "If you can hold her stare, her visual processing center will get so caught up in trying to process the data that it will render her, shall we say, *highly* suggestible. Ain't that right, sugar?"

"Hush," the bartender said. But softly, her eyes fluttering down. Jasper's eyes followed. Saw the navel ring, the low-slung waist of her jeans.

"Eyes front, Jasper. There'll be time for that in a moment." Leo glanced at his watch. "Gwen should be here in about a half hour."

Jasper was going to ask who Gwen was, but he was distracted by the gold band on Leo's host's wrist.

Leo saw where he was looking.

"Something wrong?"

"That—" Jasper found it difficult to talk. "That's my friend's watch."

Leo's eyes rolled upwards, as if he were looking at a filecard in his head. "Qusay, Mohammed Jr.?"

His voice was still light, but there was an edge to it as well. A dare. His eyes were cold and dark, but within their depths something glimmered and danced about.

"How'd you get that watch, Leo?"

"Oh right!" Leo bopped his forehead with his zigzag-fingered hand. "You weren't there. I mean, you were *there*, but you were dead." Leo took a long sip of his beer, almost daintily wiped a line of foam off his lip before continuing. "Larry here was one of the paramedics who pulled you and your buddies out of the car. He helped himself to your friend's watch while he was distracted." He rapped the watch against the table several times. "He should've gone for the cash. Fucker's cracked. Looks expensive though."

Jasper frowned. "That seems, what's the word? Convenient?"

"I understand your concern," Leo said, sounding more and more like a practiced sociopath. "But the whole coming-back thing is influenced to some degree by proximity, to some degree by the people you were close to in life. Most people end up in family members, actually. I guess maybe you weren't so close to yours?"

Q.'s question flashed in Jasper's mind. *What would you do if you knew you only had twenty-four hours to live?* And his answer: *I'd tell my dad I love him.*

Jasper felt a coldness run down Jarhead's spine like an ice cube slipped inside his shirt. He stared at Larry Bishop's face, at his eyes, at the Mogran swirling around in their depths. It couldn't be. But even as he thought that, he remembered the maid's words from earlier in the day:

Larry.

Larry Bishop.

It's nice that so many of Master Mohammed's friends have come round to see him.

It all added up. Added up perfectly, but still made no sense. Because why had Leo . . . ? Jasper didn't even know how to finish the question. Didn't even know how to start it. Why had Leo . . . ? How had Leo . . . ? *What* had Leo . . . ?

"Jasper, buddy? You still in there?"

"I swear to God, if you hurt him—"

"God?" Leo snorted. He banged the broken Patek on the graffiti'd table. "*God?* There are a lot of things I'm afraid of, Jazz-man, but God isn't one of them."

Jasper sat up straighter. "How did you know about that name?"

But Leo just looked at him with that maddeningly impassive expression, and Jasper could tell this was all he was going to get. He struggled for something to say, but only one word came to mind. Well, two:

"Dude," he sputtered. "*Why?*"

Leo took another sip of beer. "Why what?"

"Leo, please. I don't even know how to ask the right questions. I don't even know what I'm trying to find out. I just . . . I'm asking for your help."

Jasper searched Leo's eyes, trying to discern what he was thinking. What he wanted to say. But though he could see Leo glowing behind Larry's eyes, he couldn't even begin to guess what was going through the demon's mind. Finally Leo shrugged, took one more sip of beer. And then, as if were revealing the secrets of Oz:

"Mashed potatoes."

"Huh?"

"Mashed potatoes." Leo sipped his beer.

"Yeah, repeating it's not really helping."

"You like mashed potatoes, right?"

Jasper rolled Jarhead's eyes.

"I betcha Jarhead likes mashed potatoes too."

"Look, Leo—"

"Haven't you ever wondered if mashed potatoes taste the same to someone else as they do to you? If your tastebuds are recording the same data everyone else's tastebuds are, and your brain is rendering that data into precisely the same flavors everyone else's is? Like, say, what if mashed potatoes tasted creamy to you, but to Jarhead they tasted more like a paste? You taste the sugar in the starch but Jarhead tastes the squares of butter he mashes into them with his fork? Or you taste autumn, the colorful leaves on the trees, the playoffs on the tube in the other room, but Jarhead tastes his mom and dad with their faces stuffed full of food so they aren't yelling at each other or at him?"

Jasper squinted at Leo. "What's your point?"

"My point, Jasper, is that now you can taste someone else's mashed potatoes. You can see just how similar they taste to yours, yet realize there *is* a difference. That no two people eat the same mashed potatoes, see the same color blue, hear the same Beethoven's Fifth. You have a unique privilege, Jasper, to see the world through someone else's eyes, to realize that it's a different world than the one you live in—close, but not quite the same thing. Doesn't that pique your interest? Even the littlest bit?"

"Say I was curious. What would it matter? I'm about to jet out of Jarhead's body. Head into the wild blue yonder."

"But say you didn't. Say you decided to stick around for a while."

"And do what? Live someone else's life? That's not fair to Jarhead. I've already ruined his relationship with two of his best friends. It's only a matter of time before I get him arrested. And you know, that's not me either. This—" Jasper waved Jarhead's hands, indicated Jarhead's body "—this isn't me. This is someone else. And I don't want to be someone else. No offense, Jarhead," he said, when a hurt whine floated up from the abyss.

Now Leo rolled his eyes. "Jasper, how many times do I have to tell you to stop thinking like someone who's still alive? Not fair? Fair is for people who have to worry about punching the time clock at 9 A.M., paying the mortgage, remembering to TiVo *Survivor*. None of these things is your concern. You're beyond all that now. You're something else. Don't you think it behooves you to explore this new condition? To be whatever it is you are now, so you don't end up doing what Jasper did?"

"And what *did* Jasper do?"

"Jasper didn't fuck his girlfriend. Didn't fuck anyone, and ended up like this. How do you know there's not something you have to do in this new state, to make sure you don't get stuck again?"

The chill on Jarhead's spine came back tenfold. He had to struggle to keep his voice steady. "I thought that's what you were here to do. Make sure I didn't do that."

"Let's just say," Leo drummed Larry's crooked fingers on the table. *God is dead. God is dead. God. Is. Dead.* "Let's just say I've told you everything I can."

And then, almost as if Leo had planned it that way, there was the sound of traffic as the door at the front of the bar opened. Leo looked over Jasper's shoulder and smiled, and Jasper turned around to see the blond triage nurse from the hospital walk through the door.

"Gwen?"

"As perceptive as ever. You can have her or the bartender. Bubbly blond or Joan Jett wannabe?" Leo smiled wickedly. "Michaela had a navel ring, didn't she?"

24

Lana held her drink up to the two men.

"Death is in my sight today."

Q. shifted nervously on the silk toile of the doctor's couch. The huntress was a bit over the top.

When no one joined her in the toast, Lana shrugged, knocked back her drink. As she poured a second, she nudged the shotgun on the table.

"I'm assuming you don't carry this around on a regular basis."

J.D. Thomas, still shaking slightly, sipped his tea loudly. "No, I–"

Lana turned to Q. "The demon was coming for you."

Q.'s hands were trembling as well. Not with nervousness but with a strange uncontrollable energy, as if he needed to whale on a punching bag for twenty minutes, then run a half marathon. He was acutely conscious of the small red stain on his shirt, the heat rising off his chest. Lana glanced at his hands, then edged a second glass of Scotch toward him.

"Be patient. Eventually you'll learn to control it, but for now you'll have to wait until the energy dissipates of its own accord." She flexed her wrist tenderly. "He made you strong. Very, very strong."

The big clunky watch Lana wore had slipped down her forearm. A jagged scar transversed her wrist, the pale flesh knobbled and delicate-looking, but also resilient. *Healed.* Scarred, but healed. He didn't have to ask Lana how she'd gotten this scar. He knew instinctively. Knew she'd gone through what he had, and come out the other side.

Q. nodded resolutely.

"He was in me for more than a week. I think I was a random choice. He was just hanging out. Letting me be myself mostly, but turning it up a little. Lowering inhibitions and all that. And—and yeah. He was making me strong. I felt solid. Hard. Like bullets would bounce off me."

Lana set her glass down. "I doubt they'll bounce, but—" Before Q. knew what was happening, the huntress had ripped his shirt open like a drunken bachelorette at Chippendales. His face went as red as the stain on the remnants of his shirt.

"What the—"

He was cut off by the doctor's gasp. Lana just shrugged.

"Things continue to look up for your candidate, doctor."

Q. looked down at his chest. The place where Lana had cut him had all but healed. When he flicked off the scum of blood, all he saw was a pink dimple about an inch long. It looked as though someone had cut him a week ago, not five minutes before.

Q. shook his head, half disbelief, half recognition.

"I felt him making me stronger. But that wasn't his main focus. It seemed more like he was looking around for something. Someone."

Lana flashed a look at the doctor, but didn't say anything. Q. took a deep breath. For some reason he didn't want to tell the huntress this next part. He didn't trust her as he did the doctor. She had her own agenda, and it seemed a little more ruthless than Dr. Thomas's. But he knew he had to.

"My friend Jasper has—my friend Jasper had been dating Michaela for a year, still hadn't gotten past second base. I used to tell him he was a leftover Puritan. Anyway, whatever, I could tell L—" Q. had to swallow, force himself to say the name. "Leo found this important. He even tried to trick Jasper into having sex with my girlfriend, Sila, but it didn't work. It was like . . . like he wanted to give him one last chance."

"A chance to what?" Lana's angry tone couldn't quite hide her curiosity.

"To die," Q. said. "To spare him Leo's fate."

Lana's eyes went wide for a moment, then fell closed. Her lips moved silently, mouthing words in what looked like a dozen different languages. Q. glanced at the doctor, who nodded that he should continue.

"He made me steal my dad's car. There wasn't much of me left by that point. I was just watching. I couldn't stop watching and couldn't do anything about it either. I picked up Sila and Michaela. He had it all planned out. Just before we crashed I made–" Q. swallowed again, but this time it was his own emotions that made it hard to speak. "I made Sila give me a blowjob. That's–that's how they get out, isn't it? Sex? He had to get out of me before we crashed."

"It's likely he would have survived the crash even if he hadn't left you," Dr. Thomas said. "As you saw back at your apartment, the Mogran are quite resilient."

Q. shook his head. "No. He *had* to get out. Had to do something before we crashed. Before–before Jasper died."

Lana set the bottle down heavily. "Dear God."

Q. sat back. The tone in the huntress's voice was terrifying, in part because *she* sounded terrified, but also because her voice was so filled with hatred that it stank up the room like a noxious gas. Q. thought God's name had ever been used quite so vainly.

"Huntress?" The doctor peered at Lana. "What are you thinking?"

"Oh, come on, doctor. I know you have a theory. All of you *gatherers* do."

Q. looked at the doctor. "Hunters? Gatherers?"

The doctor blushed. "A joke on the hunters' part. It's their term for people like me, who search out people like you."

" 'Gatherers,' " Lana repeated scornfully. "Rounding up the Mogran's abandoned hosts like stone-age women picking up acorns while their men go out with spears and hunt bears. The gender roles might have softened, but the hierarchy hasn't. Go on, doctor. Tell Q.

your theory. Tell him what you think the demon has done to his friend."

Dr. Thomas smiled sadly at Q. "We understand very little about how the Mogran come into being, but among the most popular theories is that a virgin who is possessed by a Mogran at the time of death will in turn become a Mogran."

"But wouldn't that kill the first one?"

"No one has ever heard of a demon exiting a body without having sex. If this theory *is* correct, it would mean the process of creating a new demon somehow manages to protect the existing demon from the destruction of its host's body. So far no one has been able to come up with an explanation as to why or how this should be. The same confusion is the only thing keeping the Mogran from testing this theory, since, if it is incorrect, the experiment would result in their own death."

Q. shook his head. Not so much because he didn't believe what the doctor had said, but because he didn't want it to apply to Jasper.

"The Mogran have been around for thousands of years. Surely they'd've figured this out. They'd've been in a virgin when it got killed, realized they didn't die. Would've investigated, figured it out."

Lana shrugged. "The Mogran do not die that easily or that often." She turned to the doctor. "You have done your research."

There was almost a threat in her voice, but she didn't elaborate. Instead, she remained silent for a long time, obviously contemplating her next move. Finally, with a contemptuous lift of her shoulder, she turned her back on the doctor and looked at Q.

"The legends of vampires originated with a demon called Varius, a former Roman centurion. Interestingly, he never visited Transylvania or possessed the famous Vlad the Impaler, but haunted Paris for two decades in the mid-sixteenth century, only coming out at night, and biting people on the neck. He would implant neurosynaptic suggestions in his hosts—what you might think of as hypnosis from the inside—so that when he left they were consumed by a thirst for human blood. He also gave them such an acute photosensitivity that prolonged exposure to sunlight actually caused them to die. They were otherwise quite difficult to kill—hence the stake through the heart, which wasn't Varius's idea at all, but sprang up of its own accord. As practical jokes go," she finished up, "it has proven itself rather long-lasting."

"Thanks for the history lesson," Q. said dryly.

"Varius also spread the rumor that a bite from an existing vampire was all it took to create another. From this we can deduce that Varius was at least aware of the legends about how his own kind are created. Nevertheless, he seems never to have put it to the test. Leo, however, appears to have overcome his predecessor's hesitance. And if he has in fact turned Jasper into a Mogran," the huntress raised her voice over Q.'s protest, "he is as lost to you as any vampire. You *must* accept that, Q."

Q. didn't say anything, but his expression apparently didn't satisfy the huntress.

"I'm going to bed. In the morning we will travel to Q.'s *friend's* house. We will look around until we find him. I suspect Leo will not be far behind. We'll see how close the two of you remain, when your friend is inside you. When he uses you as Leo did, for his own ends."

"You're out of your mind! Jasper wouldn't—he couldn't do that to me."

The huntress curled her lip. She picked up the shotgun as she left the room. "I think I'll take this to bed with me. It might as well be with someone who knows how to use it."

"Do you want it for protection?" Dr. Thomas said.

"Is that what they're calling it these days?" Lana sniffed the gun's muzzle. "Sure. That's what I want it for. *Protection*."

25

So you live around here?"

Shawna's silver bracelets jangled as she pushed a rag over the same six inches of bartop.

"Um, yeah. Dutch Village."

"That trailer park on 66?"

"Yeah."

"That's cool."

No two ways about it: Shawna was hot. Hot, and a little intimidating. In Jasper's head, he was still seventeen years old, and Shawna was at least twenty-five, and, to him anyway, possessed an older woman's air of worldliness and confidence.

"So your friend is—"

"Crooked?"

Shawna smiled, stuck out her tongue. A bit of metal glinted. Ouch, Jasper thought. But then he imagined how that stud might feel running over certain parts of his body, and the *ouch* turned to *hmmm* . . .

"I was going to say tall. But yeah, he's a little crooked." She pushed the rag back and forth. *Jangle jangle jangle.* She glanced over at the paramedic, who seemed to have put Nurse Gwen into some kind of giddy, giggling trance. "Apparently he likes blonds too. *Sigh.*"

Jasper glanced over at the booth. Gwen was literally holding up one of her breasts inside her smock, as if offering it to Leo the way Eve had offered Adam the apple.

"Apparently they like him too."

Jangle jangle jangle.

Jasper realized this could go on all night. It's not like she was going to jump on this particular body. Two days wasn't enough to knock off the seventy-five extra pounds Jarhead was carrying. He was going to have to work a little harder to make this happen.

What had Leo said? It's all in the eyes . . .

He took a deep breath, put the broadest smile he could on Jarhead's wide face. He touched the tattoo on the back of her hand. A gold crown, under which was written "Croesus" in Gothic script.

"Nice ink."

"Thanks. My family's Turkish. Just trying to keep it real."

Jasper ignored this arcane reference, instead reached out and touched her chin. Used his finger to angle it up so that she had to meet his gaze. He opened his eyes wide, tried to imagine his pupils expanding, contracting. He knew what this would look like. Like lights were shining in his eyes. Swimming in their depths, like luminous fish. Shawna stared into them, her own pupils vibrating as her optic nerve struggled to follow the micromovements of Jasper's eyes. Her gaze softened just as it had with Leo. The rag stopped moving. A smile curled up once side of her face. A little giggle burst from her throat.

"I don't know what's come over me tonight."

Jasper couldn't help himself. "I'd like to come over you."

Shawna smirked, but didn't look away. She looked up and down the bar.

"It is kinda dead in here, isn't it?"

You have no idea, Jasper thought.

Shawna's hand tiptoed across the bar until it touched his.

"You used to play for Hudson High?"

"Yeah. Linebacker."

Shawna's smile grew wider.

"Well, what're you waiting for? Tackle me."

She took his hand over the bar and led him toward the back of the room. As they passed Leo and Gwen, Jasper saw that the triage nurse was in the process of unbuttoning her smock. Her eyes were fixed resolutely on the paramedic's, and Leo didn't look up, either. There was a greedy, impatient grin on his face.

"Whoever said God was dead," he called as Jasper headed into the stockroom, "wasn't looking at what I'm looking at." And then, in a mocking voice: "See you on the other side, buddy."

I hope not, Jasper thought.

When Shawna bent over to push a case of bourbon out of the center of the storeroom floor, Jasper put his hand on the bare place just above the waistband of her jeans. He slipped a finger in, found the line of her panties. Electric sparks seemed to shoot up his arm as he traced his fingertip over the curve of her ass.

Shawna backed into him. The top of her ass pushed against the base of his penis and she rocked up and down on her toes, massaging it through his pants. Jasper thought he was going to shoot in Jarhead's boxers.

"I don't want you to get the wrong idea," Shawna breathed into the dry air of the storeroom. "I've never done this before."

Jasper whirled her around. "Me neither," he said, barely able to get the words out before his mouth smashed onto hers. He grabbed her beltloops and ground her crotch against his. Shawna grabbed fistfuls of Jarhead's baggy jeans and rammed his body against hers.

Jasper pushed her back. Shawna's mouth hung open, her lips puffy, her tongue protruding slightly.

"Do you like this shirt?"

"Wha—"

Before she could finish the word, Jasper had torn it open. The thin fabric folded back and there were her breasts, small but plump, the nipples hard.

"Oh fuck!"

Shawna grabbed Jasper's hair and pulled his face to her chest.

Even as he took one of her nipples in his mouth her hands went to his crotch. She fumbled with his belt as Jasper went back and forth between her tits as if he couldn't decide which one he liked better. A muffled moan gurgled out of his throat.

Shawna was having trouble with his belt, and he swatted her hands away. He grabbed the tongue and ripped so hard that the buckle snapped off, along with half of his beltloops and the button of his jeans. After the incredible constriction of his pants, it seemed that his penis was floating in space. And then Shawna wrapped her fingers around it and pulled it toward her.

"Oh sweet Jesus!" Jasper stumbled to the side. He deliberately smashed his head into the shelf.

"What?" Shawna said, still pulling.

Jasper couldn't speak. He swatted her hand away. It took all his bodily control to keep from coming. He held up a finger in the universal wait sign.

Shawna's eyes went wide. "Don't you dare!" She fell on her knees. Before Jasper quite knew what was happening her mouth had closed around his dick. He threw himself into the shelf behind him so hard that bottles fell to the floor and exploded, tequila and vodka and whiskey filling his nostrils, as if he could somehow become more intoxicated than he was.

The warmth of Shawna's mouth was amazing. The slickness, the smooth glide of the tongue stud over head and shaft. But if a mouth felt this good, then what was her vagina going to be like?

He couldn't wait. He bent over, lifted her like a doll and carried her to the other side of the storeroom, away from the broken glass and runnels of alcohol. Shawna was pushing at her pants even before she was on the floor. And then. Oh God, and then . . .

Her vagina folded around Jarhead's penis in a way he would've never imagined. Gripped it tightly yet smoothly, seemed to tickle every nerve ending up and down its length. He buried his face in her chest and let himself sink into the slick, enveloping heat. Jesus, did it feel good. Oh Jesus. It felt like *everything*.

But even as he thrust into and out of her, he felt something happen within him. No, not in him. In Jarhead. It was as if Jasper's spirit were retreating inside his host's flesh, becoming smaller. He was no longer able to touch the edges of Jarhead's body. The sensations of sex—not just the warmth of Shawna's vagina, but her nails digging into Jarhead's back, the gritty concrete floor beneath his knees and the heady smell of spilled alcohol—all seemed to be fading. In some remote part of his brain Jasper knew that he was dying. Dying for real this time. He was surprised how eager he was for it to be all over.

He heard Shawna's greedy moans far away, Jarhead's answering grunts as he pounded into her. It was almost all Jarhead now. Jasper was just along for the ride. He felt as though he'd shrunk to a pinprick of light inside the vast interior space of Jarhead's body. Then he realized the light wasn't him, but rather a hole that had opened up between the body he was trapped in and the vast universe beyond. An infinite vacuum sucking him into the void.

Jasper took one last look at the inside of Jarhead's retreating body. It was a cosmos unto itself, splayed before him like an interstellar map. A thousand miles away the muscles in the penis quivered. The prostate contracted, sent its shot of clear liquid into the urethra, the testes pumped their load of semen up the vas deferens to mix with the prostatic fluid, and the seminal vesicles added their load of fructose so Jarhead's swimmers would have food during the journey. From this vantage point it was like watching a star go supernova. Like watching the Big Bang. The end of one thing, the beginning of everything else.

With a start he realized he'd lost Jarhead's body. It was gone, and with it all sensory feeling. He couldn't see or hear or feel. But almost immediately the voices came. The thoughts. The same thoughts he'd heard when he died the first time. They were faint still, but getting louder.

Never seen anything like this before . . . Seems ridiculous to me . . . I hate it when she looks at me like . . . Only a few more hours before I can . . . Look, it's a new media thing . . . I can't wait till the parade next year . . . Next stop Iraq . . . A doughnut? Yeah, maybe a doughnut . . . God, is everything this loser says total BS?

At first Jasper left himself open to the voices, let them wash over him on his way to ... to where? Who knew? He was afraid, yet it wasn't a particularly threatening feeling. Not when there wasn't a body to feel it. This was death. Death was just another step.

He felt simultaneously reduced to nothing and infinitely large, as if he were being squished into a little ball and pulled in a billion different directions all at once. The voices were screaming now, countless voices in countless languages. Not just voices, but entire consciousnesses, entire beings. The things they saw flashed in his mind's eye, the things they heard, smelled, tasted, felt were all present to him, and all at the same time. All their emotions, from the most noble to the most vile. Murders, orgasms, broken hearts and broken minds. All of it, all at once. He felt as though his brain was erupting like a volcano. Dear God, it was horrible. Horrible. *Horrible!*

To fight the feeling, he thought of all the people he hadn't said goodbye to. His father, Q., Michaela.

Michaela. God, how he wished it had been her. Just once. If only he'd made love to her once.

For a moment it seemed to him that he could see her. Not Shawna—Michaela. Her shape seemed to flicker in all that vast emptiness, and he found himself grabbing for it desperately. No, he thought. This isn't right. I'm supposed to be leaving. But he couldn't let go. The voices dimmed as he found himself rushing down on her. He could almost see her now, could almost hear her breathing. Could almost *feel* it. He—he was going into Michaela!

And then, like a punch to the stomach, he was whirled away. *Leo*, he thought, as the voices shrieked back in his head. A picture of Larry's smarmy grin flashed before him. You fucking lied to me again!

And then, just as quickly, the voices were gone.

Silence.

For a moment that's all there was. Pure nothingness. Then feeling began to return. Very human sensation. Jasper saw flesh and bone, the by-now-familiar musculature of his own species. He sensed a dozens points of damage as his consciousness scanned the length and breadth of his new abode. Fractured fingers, a pulverized diaphragm, a deep puncture in the occipital lobe. The right femur snapped in two places. This body had been through the wringer.

Suddenly he realized what was happening. He wasn't dying. He was coming back. He was taking another host, just as he'd taken Jarhead.

And then: light. Bright white light. Jasper blinked. Felt real eyelids open and close. It was a moment more before he could make sense of what he was seeing. A dirty urinal, a set of metal walls. Sticky floor tiles. The stink of urine.

He was in a bathroom.

He heard a moan, looked down to see his own legs, and then another body. Naked. Female. Bloody. Her blond hair lay tangled about her face in clumpy red streaks.

Even as he reached a hand out to pull the hair from the woman's face, he saw his own broken fingers. The broken watch.

Lawrence Bishop's fingers.

Q.'s watch.

As he pulled the bloody hair from Gwen's face, all of Larry's memories crashed down on him like the proverbial ton of bricks. In an instant he knew there'd been no mafiosa in Jersey City. That Leo had in fact taken Larry to New York City in order to kill Q., so that Q. couldn't reveal Leo's whereabouts to the Legion. Leo didn't want Q. to tell anyone that Leo had possessed him in order to kill Jasper, so that he could turn Jasper into a Mogran.

And, as Jasper's consciousness took full possession of Lawrence Bishop's half-destroyed body, he knew that Leo had succeeded.

Jasper stared at Gwen's bloody body for a long time. Leo had beat the shit out of her, and she lay unconscious beneath him. All the sudden he realized he was still inside her and he stumbled backward so fast he almost broke his leg again. Leo had done an amazing job of setting the femur, but the fractures were far from healed. Gwen moaned and covered her face.

Jasper turned and limped out the bathroom door before she woke up. As he passed the table he'd shared with Leo—when Leo was still in this body and he was still in Jarhead's—he noticed that the graffiti had been changed slightly. "*God is dead.—Nietzsche*" was still there, right above "*Nietzsche is dead.—God,*" but beneath that someone—well, Leo, obviously, though he hadn't bothered to sign it—had added a new line:

Nietzsche was Mogran. And so was God.

Jasper didn't know what that statement meant, but he knew it couldn't be good.

26

"Jasper?"

Jarhead West's voice reverberated painfully in his ears. It sounded like a foghorn blaring in his skull.

"Jasper? Where are you?"

"Who's Jasper?" a voice said sleepily.

Jarhead started. He realized he was lying on top of a strange girl. His pants were around his ankles and the girl's mouth was open and hot breaths were panting out of her throat.

Jarhead threw himself off her, struggled to pull up his pants. The girl sat up, all a-jingle.

"That was amaz—"

Without thinking, Jarhead swung. It wasn't the girl he was hitting. It was her voice. Her shrieking voice, slicing through his head like a bandsaw. Her head snapped sideways and she fell backward on the floor. Her flesh hitting the dirty concrete sounded like a bag of bricks dropped from the top of a building.

"Jasper?" Jarhead screamed as he struggled to his feet. "Where are you, Jasper?" He ran the length of the strange bar and burst through the front door, nearly fell over as the noise of traffic slammed into his head like a pair of sledgehammers boxing his ears.

"Jasper!" Jarhead wailed into the night. "Why is everything so *loud?*"

3

The Hunters' Psalm

"Wait, oh wait! There is something yet inside me!"
—The Thousand Nights and One Night

1

The Mogran lies down with the girl.

Scattered contusions on right hemisphere of brain. Minor swelling inside skull.

His touch is more intimate than a mother's, less mercenary than a husband's. It runs the length and breadth of her body, inside and out and in parts that have neither mass nor measure. He feels the injuries and violations, the pain. Doesn't remember—or, at any rate, chooses to forget—that he himself is the cause of that pain.

Three crushed vertebrae in the cervical spine. Pressure on the spinal cord, multiple tears on the cord itself; a swamp of numbness in the limbs below. Already, the muscles in arms, legs, diaphragm have started to atrophy. To decompose inside the girl's skin.

A thousand years ago Zhou Chunhua had comforted her younger brother Wong. Pain, she told him, was caused by a blockage of the vital force, *qi*. She taught him to see his *qi* as a river swollen with spring rains but blocked by debris. The river aches to flow cleanly but can only spread out, stagnate. Wong must visualize the flotsam breaking up, allowing the *qi* to resume its course. He must smash the dam of hurt.

Broken humerus. Dislocated knee. Two cracked ribs, one of which had punctured the spleen. Septicemia would have killed her in three days, if the demon hadn't shown up.

Really, she should thank him.

Wong took his sister's advice to heart. Chunhua was comforted by the calm silence with which her brother lay upon his sickbed, but was shocked when, six weeks after the fire arrow burned off his face, she lifted the poultice and saw his beauty immaculate. Lips, cheeks, nose, eyes: all smooth, supple, flawless. She was even more surprised when her brother flipped her beneath him, pinned her body to the bed.

Where does it go? he whispered into her ear.

Chunhua didn't understand. *Where does what go?*

Rivers flow to the sea, but where does the qi *go? After it has burst its dam. Where does it go?* The rotting odor of burned flesh was gone. Wong's breath smelled sweet as berries.

Chunhua struggled against her brother's weight. *Wong, please. Let me go.*

I'll show you, he hissed, and then he released his pent-up *qi* into his sister's body. What happened after that is lost to history, lost to the demon as well. He has long since ceased caring what happens when he leaves his hosts behind.

Consequences.

Consequences are for the living.

A score of bruises, abrasions, lacerations. The smallest injuries, but the most dangerous. A million bacteria and viruses circle the openings. Armies of macrophages are overcome by succeeding hordes of invaders; pus bubbles from the wounds like sulfuric sludge oozing from a fumarole. The smell of rot fills the hospital room, disturbs even the sleep of the girl's comatose roommate. Death's perfume is sour like spoiled milk: Patricia Myles wrinkles her nose and dreams her husband has left the carton on the counter after making his morning coffee.

It will take days to repair her. To fight off the infections, heal the broken bones, cool the inflamed tissue of her spinal cord and ever so carefully reattach and recalibrate the shredded fibers, returning sensation and mobility to taffy limbs. But he *will* heal her, just as he healed Zhou Wong and Chinpukilla and Boris Petrovich Alushkin and a thousand others, and then he will bring her to Jasper. Orpheus was denied even a glimpse of his Eurydice, but Leo is kinder than the rulers of Hades, understands that a society that has lost its faith but not its fear of God must continually be reassured. And so he will display Jasper's virgin bride to him. Behold! Beauty restored like the frescoes of the Sistine Chapel! And Jasper will finally heed the demon's call, or Leo will show him just what else can be done to his beloved.

Only when the demon settles down to do his work does he notice the hymen. Perforated. Torn neatly along its seam like a chestnut cracked open to reveal the tender meat inside.

"Why Michaela Szarko!" Leo laughs inside his host. "You lying little slut!"

2

Q. lay flat on his back on the tatami floor of J.D. Thomas's meditation room. The echoes of his breath rushing from his lungs still reverberated in the air, which is a fancy way of saying he'd just gone:

"OOF!"

Golden light streamed through amber panels in the windows; an enormous bronze Buddha looked benevolently from a shimmering gold-leafed alcove, along with bamboo-framed haikus rendered in delicate Japanese brush strokes. Q. wasn't exactly noticing all this, however. He was more concerned with trying to breathe against the weight of the huntress' foot on his throat. The Croatian woman's stare was implacable. An impatient frown turned down the corners of her mouth.

"You're not concentrating. That's the twentieth time I've taken you down today."

"Twenty-two," Q. wheezed, "but who's counting?"

Heated voices had awakened Q. the morning after Leo's attempt on his life. Making his way downstairs, Q. had found Lana and the doctor arguing at the breakfast table.

"The boy came to me seeking care," the doctor had cried, face red, fingers trembling. "I will not let you drag him to his death."

"Fine," the huntress replied calmly. "But if Leo escapes as a consequence of the delay, I will hold *you* personally responsible."

They were a mismatched pair, the doctor in his dressing gown, the huntress in fatigues and tanktop. The *Times* lay next to the doctor's plate (London, not New York), folded open to the crossword, along with a fountain pen the size of a fat cigar; the stone knife lay next to Lana, as well as a flint sharpener. A *retoucheur*. One more word Q. had no business knowing.

"Are you going to skulk there all morning?"

Q. started at the huntress' voice, reminded himself that her senses were sharper than a dog's. He shambled into the room, took a seat at the table.

"So, uh, what's the fuss?"

"Dr. Thomas has persuaded me to provide you with some training for our confrontation with the Mogran."

"Training? Like *The Matrix*? Am I going to get a codename? Neo? Hellboy? Demon Killer?"

"Your ability to kill demons remains hypothetical, and, at this point, extremely dubious. But if you want a nickname, perhaps we can call you—" she stabbed, chewed, swallowed. "Chum."

"Chum? Like friend?"

"Like 'bait.' Of course, we could call you *chump* if you prefer." Q. thought he saw a flicker of a smile. "I suggest you eat lightly, as I plan on hitting you in the stomach repeatedly."

During the course of the next three days, Lana had indeed hit Q. in the stomach. And in the face, the arms, the legs, the back, the ass, and, on no fewer than five occasions, the groin. She kicked him, kneed him, tripped him, flipped him, choked him, and, once, when he mouthed off, doused him with pepper spray. She also told him her real name.

"Ileana. Why'd you give the doctor an alias?"

"Because I don't trust him. I don't trust any gatherer. Their interest in the Mogran is tainted by curiosity. He doesn't just want to kill the Mogran. He wants to *know* them. You saw his library: thousands of books on ancient and alternative religious traditions and the supernatural. Vampires and zombies and all the other hosts of undead, from will o' the wisps to Inferi."

"Aren't the Inferi from *Harry Potter?*"

Ileana smirked. "The doctor is nothing if not thorough."

"You don't think he would betray us, do you?"

"I'm Roman Catholic. We believe in both sins of omission and sins of commission. Do I think the doctor will sell us out in exchange for a chance to capture and study a Mogran? No. But I fear his conflicted desires might lead to a failure to act at a crucial moment, and that could prove equally dangerous. We would not be the first hunters to—" Ileana's voice caught, and she rubbed the man's watch on her left wrist convulsively. "We would not be the first hunters to fall because of such errors of judgment on the part of our so-called aides."

"We, huh? Does that mean you're finally starting to think of me as an equal? A peer?"

"Don't get cocky, Q."

"Who's gettin' cocky?" Q. proffered the grin that had charmed everyone from teachers to liquor store clerks to police officers in the act of writing him a ticket.

Ileana, oblivious, or at any rate immune, kicked Q. in the nuts, and he went down like a 10-pin.

"You are."

The doctor and Ileana believed Jasper would stick close to the people he'd known in life. If he didn't jump into people he'd known while he was alive—some fledglings seemed drawn to them, whereas others were equally repelled by the prospect—then chances are he would watch over them in whatever body he did inhabit. Eventually he would move out into the wide world, but for now he would likely cling to his mortal existence—a habit that Leo was also likely to understand, and would make him easier to track as well.

For the hunters, that meant Michaela, John Van Arsdale, and Q. Calls to the hospital confirmed that Michaela remained unconscious, while Jasper's father seemed to be in a perpetual state of drunkenness, (it was the doctor who found this out: he had proven surprisingly adept at posing as a telemarketer, and had already convinced John Van Arsdale to upgrade his cable package and vote against a ballot initiative that would reindustrialize the Hudson River). That left Q. In the midst of his training sessions, the huntress would suddenly bark out Jasper's name to see how her charge reacted. All that usually happened was that Q. would say, "Huh?" and Ileana would take the opportunity to sucker-punch him. It was obvious that the waiting game didn't suit her. Her mood grew more foul, her instructions more terse, her punches harder and harder. Q. was hardly eager to confront Leo, but he was so tired of hitting the doctor's floor face-first that he thought anything would be preferable. He had tatami weave permanently imprinted on his lips.

Just then the doctor entered the room, bearing a darkly lacquered tray on which sat a teapot and a plate stacked with sandwiches.

"There are cracks in the ceiling fresco downstairs. I'm going to have a devil of a time explaining it to my contractor. I do hope all this jumping about is helpful."

Ileana glared at the doctor before taking her foot off Q.'s throat. "The boy has the reflexes of a tortoise."

"Hey! I was All-State fencing. You're, like, crazy fast."

"You're failing to understand, Q. I am 'crazy fast,' as you so eloquently put it, because of what a demon did to me, not because of any innate athletic ability of my own. Your fencing accomplishments will be as helpful in our task as the doctor's saucer of sandwiches. What's more useful is the fact that, though my last punch would have broken anyone else's nose, you didn't even pop a blood vessel."

The huntress's voice softened, and Q. suddenly remembered that Ileana had been possessed as well. Been taken against her will, made to do unspeakable things.

"The taint of the Mogran is something all of us wish we could wipe away. But it doesn't go away. The best we can do is take what they have done to us and use it against them." She pointed to Q.'s reflection in a mirror on the wall. "You have skin like armor. Beneath that skin lie other augmentations. Learn to harness them, and you will have your revenge."

"You don't get it! I *killed* my girlfriend and my best friend. I don't want to 'harness' that ever again."

Ileana blew the air from her nostrils, and it was clear she was fighting more than anger. "I pulled tongues from men's mouths." The words fell from her like clumps of mud, splattering on the floor. "I bit their throats open and drank their blood. Reached under their ribs and squeezed the life from their hearts. Forty-six people, Q. I killed *forty-six people* in a single evening, with my bare hands. Don't play the guilt game with me."

"I want him *dead*," Q. said. "I want to kill him for doing this to me."

"Then you must push through your revulsion and tap into the deepest places in your psyche. Find the traces of the Mogran. The lights he left on in the corners of your body. Access what you see there, allow it to make you stronger and faster. Make him pay for what he's done."

The venom in the huntress's voice scared Q. Scared him, and excited him too. Her hatred was so pure that you believed she could defeat anything. Even a Mogran. Even Leo. If the demon had been in front of him, Q. would have thrown himself on him in an instant. But that was the problem. They had no idea where he was.

"I *hate* waiting. Isn't there some other way to track them?"

"The truth is, I thought he would find *us*. The fact that he has made no effort to kill you in the past three days is unusual. And anything unusual in a demon's behavior is always a bad sign."

Dr. Thomas cleared his throat quietly, reminding them that he was still in the room. The huntress looked balefully at the foppish man and his tray of sandwiches.

"Before he died," the huntress continued, "Malachi told me one of the Alpha Wave has broken the Covenant. Apparently Foras is seeking out the last of the Mogran."

Dr. Thomas gasped.

"Malachi refused to tell me what Foras divulged to him. But it seems obvious, especially in light of what's happened with Leo and Jasper. The question is, who else is out there? Who else do we have to worry about?"

"Malachi? Foras?" Q. looked between Ileana and the doctor. "The 'Alpha Wave'?" Q. gave the words air quotes, but there was a nervous edge to his voice. Up to now the idea that there were other demons besides Leo had been theoretical. Now they had names. Goofy names, but that made them no less real.

"It's simple, Q.," Ileana answered. "Simple and terrifying. Apparently one of the original nine Mogran—the Alpha Wave, as they're called—is tracking down surviving demons and telling them how to reproduce."

"I thought you said the Mogran didn't know how to reproduce."

"I didn't say that. The doctor said that. And the doctor was half right. The vast majority of Mogran know neither how they came into being nor how to make another. But there have always been rumors of a sect within the demons. The Alpha Wave. The first nine Mogran, thousands of years older than the so-called Beta Wave. One of the legends about the Alpha Wave is that they hold the secret of Mogran reproduction, which they have kept to themselves for their own reasons. I myself have always dismissed such theories as idle speculation, but it is looking more and more as if there is some truth to it."

Q.'s mind flashed to the last few seconds before the accident. The demon's intense concentration on Jasper practically glowed in his mind.

"Shit."

"Shit is right." The huntress reached a hand to help Q. up. "The clock is ticking, and we've got work to do."

Q. took Ileana's hand, and she promptly threw him against the far wall.

"Leave the sandwiches, doctor. We're going to be a while."

3

S *o—*
Much—
Sex.

From the time he was eight years old, when his cousin Sylvia had shown him how his pee-pee was like a lollypop, Larry Bishop had stuck his dick in anything that would have him. Fat girls. Skinny girls. Old ladies. Jailbait. Girls who were not quite clean. Girls who were not quite girls. He had done it in positions that weren't particularly comfortable and he had done it in ways that were deliberately painful and he had done it till he thought his dick was going to fall off, but he'd never once failed to have a good time. He'd done many things to get girls in bed—cajoled, wheedled, begged, faked a French accent—but he'd never once forced himself on anyone. In his own humble opinion, the secret of his success was his smile. It wasn't a particularly friendly smile, or handsome for that matter. It was, rather, the smile of a champion pussy grazer. Larry Bishop went down on girls with all the diligence of a suckerfish cleaning mold off the inside of a fishtank. Romantic? Not particularly. But Larry's smile told any prospective partner that he wouldn't quit till she'd gotten hers, and in a world full of one-minute men Larry's track record spoke for itself.

* * *

When he first found himself in Larry's body, Jasper limped out of The Aristocrats and took the ambulance back to Sue's house. As he drove, he sifted aggressively through Larry's thoughts. Pushed passed the naked bodies, the tits, the twats, the asses, jumped the hurdles and pitfalls of all those bad drug trips, tried to zero in on the past two days. He knew he should be better at this: all the memories were there after all, each one simultaneously visible to him. His need to order and work through them one at a time was, as Leo would say, the way the living think, not the Mogran. It was for precisely this reason that Jasper clung to it, no matter how much it slowed him down. In his forty-eight hours in Jarhead's body, he'd felt his old self chip away one fleck at a time, and the jump from Jarhead to Larry had left him even more disconnected. Two entire lives stood between his disembodied psyche and the Jasper Van Arsdale who had walked the earth, and it took almost as much concentration to maintain the connection to his real self as it did to control the myriad of functions happening beneath Larry Bishop's pellet-riddled skin.

By rights Larry was dead at least three times over—the shotgun blasts, the nine-story fall, the antenna spike in his brain—but Leo had managed to hold the man together by dint of sheer willpower. Jasper marveled at what the paramedic's previous tenant had done. Things he'd only theorized about in Jarhead's body were actually in process when he entered Larry's. The energy output of each and every cell had been increased exponentially, as well as the operating capacity of all the organs, the speed with which electrical impulses were processed by the central nervous system. The broken rib, femur, pelvis, and fingerbones had all been set, and Larry's own muscles, made rigid by a flood of chemicals, were serving as the cast. The brain was busily repairing the damaged tissue in the occipital lobe, and even the deepest lacerations had scabbed over. Nevertheless, the bones would take another day or two before they were fully mended, and Jasper sensed that the damage to the brain was going to require precise attention to get it back in working order. The edges of his vision were still blurry, and everything had a greenish tinge to it. And he was *starving*. This kind of work required massive amounts of energy, and Larry was as lean as Jarhead had been fat. Jasper needed to get some calories ASAP, or his host was going to pass out.

He found a bucket of McKennedy's in Sue's fridge and gnawed the meat off six greasy chicken legs, washed it down with a half gallon of milk. Then he shuffled to the bedroom for a change of clothes. The first thing he saw was the dildo that Sue, under Leo's control, had shoved in his host's ass. It took all his self-control to keep from puking up his chicken.

The psychiatrist burned in Larry's psyche as the first woman—hell, the first person—who'd ever understood him. Taken all he had to give and added her own spin to the mix. Jasper patted his host's pocket, found the engagement ring Larry'd been carrying around for the past two weeks. He tried to tell his host it'd be okay, that he would slip it on Sue's finger before he knew it and they'd live out a life of sexually obsessed connubial bliss. But he had a hard time believing his own words. From the trace memories Leo had left in the paramedic's mind, it looked like the demon had performed extreme psychic surgery on Larry's girlfriend. It was unlikely she'd remember her own name, let alone her lover's. But who knows, maybe Larry could make Sue fall in love with him all over again.

Jasper himself was more worried about Jarhead. Now that he was in Larry, Jasper could see the difference between the way he took control of his hosts and the way Leo interacted with his. Despite the fact that this control was greater, Leo's touch was infinitely more delicate than Jasper's, his needs and desires synched up with impulses that already existed within the psyches of the people he inhabited. By contrast, Jasper had simply replaced Jarhead and Larry's consciousnesses with his own. He realized now how difficult it was going to be for them to recover. Somewhere out there Jarhead was probably wondering what the hell had happened to him. Where he'd been for the past two days and why the world and his body looked and felt and sounded so different.

Jasper looked at the cracked face of the Patek. The hands of the watch were stuck at 8:32 P.M. A little window indicated that the watch had stopped on April 18.

With a start, he realized he was looking at the exact moment of his death. He wrapped his left hand around the watch to cover up its macabre message, squeezed so hard he felt the cracked glass shatter beneath his palm. Jesus Christ. He was dead. He was really fucking dead. He was dead, but he wasn't *dead*.

Just then the land line rang. Jasper eyed the jangling instrument warily. It was three in the morning. It seemed unlikely it was a social call—although with a swingin' couple like Sue and Larry you couldn't be too sure. It might be the hospital, of course, calling for Sue, but they'd probably call on her cell. No, somehow Jasper knew this call was for him, although whether "him" meant Jasper or Larry was another question entirely. The one thing he was pretty sure of was that he shouldn't answer.

"Hello?"

"Yes, hello. I'm trying to reach Mr. Lawrence Bishop."

A woman's voice, professionally distant. Only Jasper's sensory control allowed him to hear the tiniest of tremors. Not so much fear as anxiety, as if she were trying to cover something up.

"This is Larry Bishop."

A brief pause. Jasper strained his ears, heard first the breath of a whisper—"It's him"—and then, as if from across the room, a second voice, almost ridiculously by-the-book: "The suspect is in the house. Repeat: the suspect is in the house."

Meanwhile, the woman who had called him was still talking:

"Oh, yes, Mr. Bishop. I'm so sorry to call you at this hour, but, well, I have some bad news about your—"

But Jasper had already set the phone down on the dresser. He trotted outside as fast as he could on his stiff left leg. No doubt the police had found Sue tied to a gurney, her mind shot from what most doctors would probably assume was a combination of drugs and trauma, her vagina raw from hours of fucking, and filled with his host's semen besides. Now they were after her attacker. Her torturer. Her rapist. Oh, and there was Gwen too, a bloody mess on the floor of the men's bathroom at The Aristocrats. Great, Jasper thought. On top of everything else, he was now a wanted man.

He took Sue's Saab. It was less conspicuous than the ambulance, more reliable than Larry's beat-up Firebird. Ten minutes later he was doing thirty-seven in a thirty-five in an attempt to be as inconspicuous as possible. On the quiet country lane, the car's headlights—they came on with the car, and couldn't be turned off—glowed like a beacon. Without taking his eyes from the road, Jasper snapped open the fusebox and pulled the appropriate plug. The car went dark immediately. Larry had only flipped through the owner's manual once (he'd needed to change a burned-out taillight), but every word and diagram that had flashed by the paramedic's eyes burned neon bright in Jasper's mind. He didn't have time to be impressed with himself though. He forced his pupils to dilate, concentrated on seeing in the darkness. Thank God Larry knew how to drive stick. Both Jasper and Jarhead had only ever driven automatic.

As he exited the subdivision, his first impulse was to turn right, toward the Rip Van Winkle Bridge and his father's house. But he found himself turning left instead. Of course. A police station lay less than a mile south of Sue's house. He got off the main road, navigated the back streets by a combination of his and Jarhead's and Larry's memories. At first, he headed back toward the bridge, but then it occurred to him that the police might have put up a roadblock or something. Jesus Christ, Jasper, he told himself. This isn't *The Fugitive* or *Thelma and Louise*. They're not coming after you with helicopters and a fleet of police cruisers. Even so, he decided not to take the chance.

He drove Sue's car to the river to a point about a half mile upstream from his father's house, ditched it in some bushes. He stripped down to Larry's BVDs (which weren't BVDs, but some incredibly embarrassing bikini kind of thing), wadded his pants into a tight ball and shoved them in one boot, stuffed his shirt into the other. He'd pulled Larry's leather belt from its loops first, and now he fastened it around his waist. Using the laces, he knotted the boots securely to the belt. Clad only in his skivvies, a leather belt, and Q.'s broken $29,000 watch—Jesus, Jasper thought, I look like a fucking gogo boy—he contemplated the river. A chilly breeze blew across his skin and he shivered. Not because he was cold—it would take a lot more than a breeze to make a Mogran feel cold—but because he knew he was pushing it. He had a broken femur and a shattered pelvis, both of which were far from healed. There were still five shotgun pellets buried in his chest, one of them in the lower right lobe of his lungs. But crossing the river here seemed the only way to ensure he wasn't picked up by the cops. Taking a deep breath, he dove into the frigid water, and then, well, then he *was* cold.

"Fuck!"

For a moment it was all he could do to tread water. His left leg seized up, the muscles barely able to bend after Leo's artificially in-duced rigor mortis. The plates of his pelvis shifted around like the pieces of a broken chocolate bar still in the wrapper.

"Get it together, Jasper," he said out loud, both to calm himself and to remind himself who he was. Who he really was. He stretched out and began paddling, one arm over the other, his body sluicing across the surface of the frigid water. His arms had to do all the work because he couldn't kick for shit with his messed-up left leg, and it was hard to cup the broken fingers of his right hand. Jasper could feel the water slipping between his splayed fingers, realized he was listing to the left as a consequence. He adjusted his course to compensate and continued swimming. He allowed himself to note everything that hurt—his leg, his pelvis, his hand, the broken rib, the kind of headache that makes you wish someone would just shoot you (he ig-nored the fact that someone had shot this particular body only a few hours ago)—and then, having taken stock of everything, he shut down the circuits in Larry's brain that processed pain. He reminded himself how he'd run forty miles in Jarhead's fat body without breaking a sweat. You can do this, Jasper, he told himself. Like it or not, you are Mogran. This body is nothing but a set of biological gears and levers, and you're the master mechanic. And then, with his broken leg dan-gling behind him, his broken hand contorted into a claw and his splintered rib pressing against the inside of the raw flesh of his abdo-men, he swam.

And swam.

And *swam*.

The river was just over six thousand feet wide at this point. He'd learned this when he was fifteen. Q. had bought a pair of kayaks that he and Jasper raced back and forth across the water nearly every day of the summer. But every time Jasper lifted Larry's head above the water to see how far he'd come, the western bank didn't seem any closer. The eastern edge seemed to get farther and farther away, but this wasn't particularly reassuring. It only made it seem that much less likely he'd make it back if he decided to turn around.

Fuck but he was cold now. Why the hell had he decided to do this? Why hadn't he driven up to Albany, crossed the river by one of the bridges there instead of swimming the ice-cold Hudson in a borrowed body with a broken leg? But Jasper knew the answer to his question. It wasn't the police he was running from. It wasn't Leo he was running after. It was himself. Running from himself, running toward himself, it was all the same. He was running from his fate and he was running toward it at the same time. The person swimming the river in this broken body was the same person who had turned over the soil in his dad's garden with such proficiency. Jasper had to believe that. Had to prove it. He *would* prove it, or he would die trying.

He looked up to see how far he'd come, but his brain was so fried that all he saw was blackness broken only by a flash of gold on his wrist. Q.'s watch. Good old Q. When he first met him in second grade, Billy Lethem had called the dark-skinned new student a towelhead, which Jasper didn't understand but still recognized was worse than calling him a dork or a doofus or any of the other staple insults of a seven-year-old's vocabulary. And right after 9/11 the racists had come out of the woodwork. Jasper had seen the graffiti on Q.'s locker, heard the insults hurled from passing cars, not to mention the occasional beer bottle. But in his wildest dreams he'd've never imagined that his friend would be stalked by an actual killer, metaphysical or otherwise. At least Leo couldn't possess him again.

Jasper started, almost stopped swimming. How did he know that? He wasn't sure, but he knew it was true, just as he'd known that the appropriate thing to do when Billy Lethem called Q. a towelhead was to punch him in the face. So the Mogran couldn't possess the same person twice. That was something. Q. was safe from that threat. But that raised another question: who would Leo take next?

This time Jasper did stop swimming. Only a mouthful of water reminded him what he was doing. He'd seen enough mob movies to know how it worked—do what the bad guy says or your family pays the price. Your family or your friends. His father, in other words, or—

Michaela.

Leo was going to take Michaela.

It made too much sense. There was no one Jasper cared about more. Leo could do incalculable damage to her, and Jasper would be unable to stop him without hurting his girlfriend. The Mogran would heal her injuries as he'd healed Larry Bishop's. He would walk her out of the hospital, and all Jasper would be able to do was acquiesce to the demon's demands. Why in the hell was he swimming to the west side of the river? He had to get back to the other side. Had to get to the hospital, stand guard, It didn't matter that Leo wouldn't be using doors to get to Michaela. Jasper had to get back there. He only prayed it wasn't too late.

He tried to turn around, but his limbs failed him. It was like trying to swim through mud. Jasper thought maybe he'd hit something floating in the water. He was so fucking tired that he couldn't process the more banal reality: he'd reached the other side of the river. His fingers were digging into the pebbly bottom of the western bank.

When he finally understood what was happening, he dragged himself ashore with a sob. All he wanted to do was turn around and swim back to Michaela, but he knew he'd never make it. The pain signals were starting to get through despite his best efforts. The blood in his veins was sludgy as cold gravy. He'd say he was running on nothing but adrenaline, but a quick glance inside his host told him that wasn't quite true. He was running on empty.

He was just running.

The current had taken him about a quarter mile below his dad's

house, and he limped and stumbled his way upriver. Then there were
the steps: all 492 of them. His left leg had tightened up again,
wouldn't even bend at the knee, so he had to take the staircase like a
little kid, lifting up his right foot and pulling his left to meet it, lifting
up his right and pulling his left to meet it, up with the right, the left
beside it. It seemed to take almost as long to climb the stairs as it had
to swim across the river, and he wasn't sure how he made it to the
barn, let alone up the ladder and into the loft. As he undid the buckle
of the swollen leather belt he saw that one of Larry's boots had fallen
off at some point—the one with the pants, and Sue's engagement
ring—but he couldn't think about that. He dropped to the hay-strewn
floor. From somewhere far away Gunther's hysterical barking sang
him off to sleep.

Stupid dog. Stupid fucking dog. Shut the fuck up, you stupid
fucking—

"Ahem."

Jasper started from sleep. He knew in the way the Mogran know
these things that three days had gone by since he'd fallen to the floor.
Knew as well that all the processes Leo had set in motion to fix Larry's body had done their job, and the paramedic was good as new.
Better than new. A single green dot danced around the edge of his
right eye. Jasper concentrated; the dot disappeared. Nevertheless, he
could almost believe he was still hallucinating, save for the fact that
the apparition before his eyes wasn't the kind of thing Larry's punctured occipital lobe had been manufacturing. It was much too concrete. Much too real, and much, much too familiar.

The grizzled visage took a pull from a bottle of brown liquid,
then squinted at the prone figure before him.

"Well, let's see," John Van Arsdale said. "You're nearly naked,
you're covered in mud, and it looks like you pissed your panties
while you was sleeping." He held out the bottle. "You want a drink
first, or you want me to go ahead and toss your ass back into the
river?"

4

S ettle down, Q. You look like you've just seen a ghost."

The boy stared at Ileana balefully. "Very funny."

Such a beautiful boy. The huntress let herself admit it. The time had come for honest assessments, and this was Q.'s dominant feature, if not simply his dominant trait. He was a pretty, pretty boy. A complex beauty to be sure. Anachronistic. The planes of his face— the high cheekbones, the broad, slightly aquiline nose and wide jaw— communicated the haughtiness Herodotus attributed to Cyrus and Xerxes, but the flesh laid atop this severe foundation—the plum mouth, the coffee-colored skin—was almost perversely sensual, as if one of Kayyam's erotic quatrains had been dressed with organic tissue. Then there were the eyes, piercing, wounded. Here was the root of masculine sexual appeal: strength wrapped around weakness. A conqueror's spirit concealing a lover's neediness. Such a boy would have women swooning at his feet for the rest of his life. Whether he would ever do anything to deserve their love was another question.

"You are convinced it is your friend?" Ileana said now. When the boy didn't respond immediately, she said sharply, "Q. Focus!"

After lunch, Q. had gone out for a walk. Though both Ileana and Dr. Thomas adjured him not to contact his family or friends, the boy had apparently bought a prepaid cell phone—a "burner," he called it, citing some cop show or other, "untraceable"—and used it to check

his messages. Apparently, in the midst of well-wishes from various
aunts and uncles and schoolmates, there had been a call from someone claiming to be Jasper.

"He mentioned Billy Lethem. Billy Lethem and the Gatorade
and the Fanta and how much my watch cost."

Such a banal—indeed bizarre—catalog by which to quantify the
infinite. But though it didn't show on the outside, the huntress's
mind was reeling nearly as much as Q.'s. A new Mogran! The first in
centuries. The floodgates had been opened, and who knew how far
the deluge would spread. Killing Jasper would be like sticking a
finger in a dyke. Even Leo wasn't really the problem. Not anymore.
She had to find Foras, and all the Alpha Wave. Despite the fact that
they had managed to stay hidden for almost two thousand years, she
had to find each one of them, and take them out, before it was too
late.

But first she had to give serious consideration to Q.'s prospects as
a hunter. Whatever strengths he had—fortitude of character, superhu-
man resistance to injury—the boy was fundamentally a hedonist. Perhaps that was just another way of saying he was a seventeen-year-old
boy, but it didn't matter how you spun it: Q. liked to be flattered. He
needed to be seduced. Pleasure was his operating principle, his prime
motivator, and that made him susceptible. A threat not just to himself, but to anyone who worked with him.

"It could just as easily have been Leo calling," the huntress told
him. "He would have gleaned all that information from his time in
your mind. Did the caller say anything else?"

"Like what? Hey buddy, let's catch a movie Friday night?"

There was the question of the sigil as well.

Ileana could not imagine that this boy—who, despite the echoes
of ancient Persia in his appearance, was modern through and
through—would ever submit to such a drastic procedure. Look at him.
Rocking back and forth on the silk upholstery of J.D. Thomas's living
room couch, knees clenched together to protect the jewels of his
manhood, eyes full of hopeless pleading. Ileana doubted whether the
fey doctor had ever possessed a set of balls, let alone still had them,

but Q. even in this vulnerable state, was not and would never be a eunuch.

The boy squinted. Ileana knelt down before him. "What?"

"It's probably noth—"

"*What?*"

"I, um, I think I recognized his voice."

The boy waited, as if he wouldn't divulge the name until Ileana asked him to. There it was again. The neediness. The fear of what he knew to be true. Ileana stared at Q. until he said:

"I think it was this guy we knew. Jarhead. Mason 'Jarhead' West."

"Do you know where he lives?"

Q. shrugged. "I'm sure he's in the phone book."

Ileana's nod could have broken a block of wood. "Then we will start there."

She smiled as kindly as she knew how.

Cobras had offered more convincing grins.

5

His dad hadn't fixed the chair or the table. In fact it looked like he'd taken a hatchet to them. Splinters of wood were scattered all over the kitchen. In the place they'd formerly occupied sat a lone TV tray, tin, rusty, dented, a flimsy symbol of how reduced his dad's life had become.

"You want bad luck? I'll tell you bad luck."

The old man sprawled in one of the three remaining chairs, legs splayed, bottle clutched between them in both hands. "Son gets killed in a car accident, and while you're at the hospital identifying his body somebody breaks into your house and destroys your kitchen table. Now *that's* bad luck." John Van Arsdale took a pull from the bottle. "I mean, why the kitchen table? And a chair. Just one chair. *Jasper's* chair. That was my son's name. Jap. Japster."

Jasper's mouth—or, rather, Lawrence Bishop's—was filled with the starchy contents of a Hungry Man TV dinner, which was the only food John Van Arsdale had in the house.

"Bad luck all my life. Lost my wife and daughter in '94. Spent two and a half miserable years in the Navy before that. Got the bends twice and the clap once. My pa left me nothing but debt. My ma run off when I was in high school. Bad luck I tell you. Bad luck my whole life."

"He left you the orchard," Jasper managed to spit out, along with a bit of Salisbury steak. He put the first tray on the floor and picked up the second that waited there, steaming.

The old man stared at the nearly naked stranger in his kitchen for a moment.

"How'd you know about the orchard?"

Jasper's mind raced.

"I saw the signs. On the barrel. 'Van Arsdale's Home-Brewed Apple Brandy. Brewed From His Own Orchards.' " His fork poised over a stack of turkey slices covered in glutinous gravy.

John Van Arsdale seemed to have lost the thread of the conversation. "I'm John Van Arsdale," he said, as if he needed reassurance.

Jasper almost reached out and took his dad's hands. But all he could do was nod his host's head.

"You are. You're John Van Arsdale. Your son . . . your son was Jasper."

A long moment of silence passed between the two men. John Van Arsdale's eyes were glassy and distant. Finally he took another drink, and, fork trembling, Jasper dug into the second TV dinner.

"Hungry man, ain't you?" John Van Arsdale laughed. "Get it? Hungry Man?"

Jasper grunted. "I'll pay you. For the food."

John Van Arsdale waved his bottle at Larry Bishop's nearly naked body. "You got cash hidden on you, I'm not so sure I wanna touch it." The old man stood up. Wavered for a moment, the applejack swishing around its bottle like an agitated genie, then caught his balance. "Hold on a minute."

Jasper had no intention of going anywhere. A third TV dinner was whirling around the microwave even now. His dad's footsteps thumped slowly up the stairs. Jasper didn't really pay attention until he heard him turn right at the upper landing. Besides the bathroom, there were only two rooms upstairs: his dad's bedroom on the left and, on the right, the one that had belonged to him.

There was a bundle of clothing in his hands when John Van Arsdale reentered the kitchen. Faded Levi's, a purplish plaid yoke-back shirt that Jasper had bought at the thrift store for a barn dance. One black sock, one Navy blue. A pair of scuffed dress shoes peeked from within the roll. Jasper would've preferred his tennis shoes, but—but he'd been wearing them when he died.

"You look like you're about his size."

It was a moment before Jasper could speak. "Shorter," he said. "I'm—that is, your son was shorter than me. Almost three inches."

John Van Arsdale looked at the wad of clothing in his arms, looked back up at the stranger in his room. Finally he shrugged.

"Devils can't be choosers. Put these on. I'm tired of having a man in stained panties in my kitchen."

Jasper blushed and took the bundle. There had been any number of occasions when elder and younger Van Arsdale had sat at the table in their underwear, both too hungover to get dressed (although neither of them owned underwear like *this*). Jasper pushed his chair away from the TV tray and began to pull the pants on.

John Van Arsdale watched the stranger don his son's clothes. Jasper's pants were indeed a few inches too short for Larry Bishop's legs, and the old man made a vague sort of gesture at the frayed cuffs. "So. Were you a friend of his?"

Jasper stared fixedly at the pants as he pulled the zipper up, as if it was an alien technology.

"Not really. I knew—I know Michaela."

"Sweet girl, Mickie! How is she?"

Jasper grimaced, slipped his arms into the shirt. Michaela *hated* it when people called her Mickie.

"I was just about to go by the hospital to check on her."

"Why? She back in?"

One of the shirt's pearl snaps sounded loud as a firecracker in the quiet kitchen.

"Back—?"

"Didn't you hear? She got out yesterday. Doctors say it was a miracle she even woke up, let alone walked out under her own steam. I don't believe in miracles myself. Not anymore. But that's what the doctors say it was."

When the microwave dinged behind him, Jasper nearly broke an-

other chair. It took all his self-control to keep Larry's eyes from popping out of his head.

"Look. You've been really nice and all, but I've gotta go."

He stood up, but John Van Arsdale reached out and grabbed his
wrist with an iron claw. *"He had no face."*

Jasper could have tossed his dad off like a child. But he held still,
powerless in the face of the old man's grief.

"My boy had no face. The crash ripped his face right off."

Jasper's arm shook in his father's grip. He tried to make it stop
but couldn't.

"He was seventeen years old." John Van Arsdale's eyes bored into
Jasper's. No, not into Jasper's. Into Larry Bishop's. "Seventeen. He
hadn't even started his life. Hadn't started living. He . . ."

The old man stared into Larry Bishop's eyes. Larry Bishop's eyes,
Jasper told himself. His dad was looking into Larry Bishop's eyes.
Not his. Larry's.

Larry's.

The old man shook his head. A whispered croak slipped from his
mouth.

"I don't believe in miracles."

Jasper opened Larry's mouth to protest, then closed it. He had
almost said, "Dad," but stopped himself in time. But he didn't know
what else to say.

The old man shook his head again. "I don't know who you are,
but you need to get out of my house *right now.*"

"I'm sorry. I didn't mean to cause you—"

"Out!" the old man screamed. And then: "I do not believe! *I do
not believe!*"

The old man lifted the bottle to throw it. For the first time ever,
Jasper saw his dad spill alcohol. It splattered from the bottle all over
the old man's shirt. The tart odor of applejack filled Jasper's hyperacute nostrils, but to him it smelled like gasoline, aching for a
match.

"OUT!"

John Van Arsdale quivered as though the ground he stood on was about to open up and swallow him. Jasper backed out the door, began to walk away. The door closed with a click, but it was enough to set off the usual wave of barks from Gunther. But Jasper kept his ears focused on the house as he walked away. Forty-six seconds later—twenty-three heartbeats—he heard the faint sound of his dad setting the bottle on the TV tray, the creak as the old man's tired bones sank into the chair Jasper had just vacated.

"Cold out today," he heard his dad say. "Wet. Need a little something to warm me up."

"There we go," Jasper whispered in reply. But the only voice he heard was Larry Bishop's.

If Jasper's senses hadn't been so focused on his father, he might have noticed that Gunther hadn't started barking when the back door closed. He was already barking. He'd been barking all morning, and intermittently throughout the night, and most of the previous day—not at the stone dwelling at the top of the hill, nor at the barn where Larry Bishop's body had hibernated for the past three days, but at a tiny structure much lower down the hill, on the southern edge of the property, all but hidden inside a stand of second-growth oak and maple. This was the farm's old wellhouse, unused since 1962, when John Van Arsdale's father, Sam, had finally ponied up the cash to get on city water. The building would have fallen down years ago save for the fact that it was made of bricks—dark brown homemade bricks, which also lined the fireplaces in the house on the hill—and, despite one sizable hole in the ceiling that had allowed a colony of bats to settle in the eaves, it was as solid as it had been when it was built in 1847.

A little over three thousand bats hung from the wellhouse's exposed joists, and a foot of guano had accumulated on the floor. The grayish carpet looked like a moonscape, made even eerier by the half dozen bat corpses scattered about—pups mostly, fallen from the ceiling before they'd learned to fly—but it was actually spongy, and provided a soft bed for the naked figure that lay atop it, snoring fitfully, and starting each time a splat of bat shit fell on its face or torso or twitching legs. The figure's fingers scrappled in the bat shit while it slept, releasing clouds of histoplasmosis that it breathed into its lungs and neutralized almost immediately, but its augmented immune system had more trouble handling the lyssavirus contracted from a bat bite when it had first made its way into the wellhouse yesterday morning, as the bats were returning from their nocturnal hunt. Rabies typically takes several weeks to become symptomatic, and, left untreated, is almost universally fatal; the coming battle between virus and antibody would have been an illuminating gauge of Jasper's ability to make permanent changes to a host's endocrine and nervous systems–that is, if Jarhead West lived long enough to put those changes to the test.

6

"There is Dr. T anyway?" Q. looked around the living room as if their host might be hiding in a corner. "I got the impression he never goes out unless he has to."

Ileana beckoned Q. with a crooked finger. "Come with me."

The door to the basement lay behind a bookcase that opened by pulling on a copy of a fat leatherbound tome called *The Malleus Maleficarum*. Ileana had explained to Q. that it was a witch-hunting guide, a medieval predecessor to *Mein Kampf* that had contributed to the execution of untold numbers of witches—tens, possibly hundreds of thousands—over the course of two centuries. The text's fundamental argument was that a witch had no innate powers, but was rather the host of an agent of Satan—i.e., a demon. As with so many superstitions, the truth of it was fundamentally sound. It was only in the application that it went wrong. Now, as she pulled the leather spine and the shelf slid open, she said,

"Have you noticed how the doctor has internalized the Mogran's *modus operandi*?"

"Have I, um, what?"

Ileana bit back a sigh. Even if the boy had been up to par on other fronts, she would have rejected him simply for the way he spoke. "Have I, um, what?" was not something she was prepared to hear every day for the next several years.

"The false front behind which hides an alien entity. This bookcase, for example. There is no reason to conceal the door to a basement. But the doctor seems to love the idea of something not being what it seems. Or his automobile: from the outside it appears to be an antique, but underneath it is completely new."

Q. turned back to her when he reached the bottom of the steps. "Where are you going with this?"

Ileana leaned over and turned a bottle of Chateau Lafite. "I'm going right here." It lay near the floor of the wine cellar, but even in the oenologically subdued lighting she had spotted it immediately: all the other bottles were furzed with dust, but this one was clean. That had told her something: not simply that the bottle was another of the doctor's secret levers, like the book that opened the door to the basement, but that he turned it often, as if he spent a lot of time here.

A section of cellar wall opened with a barely audible click. Q.'s gasp was not nearly as quiet.

"Ileana!"

The huntress was glad she was looking the other way, because it hid her rolling eyes. Her companion was as hysterical as a little girl.

She took her time standing up, turning to face the room.

"My my my. What *have* we here?"

The section of wall had opened to reveal a twelve-by-twelve cubicle—a bunker really, with cement walls and a single window filled with three-inch Plexiglas. The room had only a single piece of furniture: an elaborate contraption that looked a bit like a chiropractor's chair, save that its movable head-, arm-, and legrests were equipped with steel restraints.

The doctor had spared no expense in building his cage: it was not only escape-proof but soundproof as well, which meant that the doctor's fists beating against the inside of the two-ply Plexiglas window made absolutely no noise in the outer chamber. The silent tableau reminded Ileana of a television her family had owned when she was a little girl, which had a picture but no sound.

"Did you—?" Q.'s face was aghast. "But why?"

"The doctor's part in this hunt is done. I merely wanted to make sure he didn't attempt to join in where he wasn't wanted."

She walked over to a small console and flipped a switch. The doctor's voice echoed tinnily out of tiny speakers.

"Ileana! Open this door immediately!"

"He knows your real name!"

"The doctor knows many things he shouldn't."

"Do you blame me for doing my homework? As you yourself have said, this is a war we're engaged in. The more we know about the enemy, the better our chances of winning."

"And yet almost all of your research seems to have been directed against the Legion." Ileana turned to Q. "For a technophobe, the doctor is a surprisingly good hacker. He's managed to access the accounts of more than twenty different agents, including the personal archives of half a dozen previous hunters. He knows our names, our demons' names, the most intimate details about what the Mogran made us do, as well as the identities of all the hosts we've killed during the course of our hunts. If this information fell into the hands of the authorities, our entire operation would be destroyed."

"Ileana." The doctor's voice had taken on a stern paternal tone that almost drove the huntress into a frenzy. "Look at this room. Look at all this equipment in front of you. Do you think I set it up merely to extract information?"

Ileana's hand reached for the switch. She'd had enough of the doctor's soothsaying. But Q.'s hand swatted hers away.

"I want to hear this."

The doctor turned desperately to the boy. "There are many within the Legion who believe the Mogran aren't supernatural beings. Not spirit, Q., not magic, but simply another kind of energy."

Ileana scoffed. "Listen to him at your peril, Q. He will fill your brain with even more nonsense than Leo did."

"Until now, no one has ever been able to investigate the accuracy of this theory. There was neither the technology nor, more to the point, a test subject. But now we have both. We have this laboratory, and not one but two Mogran within our reach."

"And what if we do catch one of them, doctor? What if your machines tell you that the Mogran are not supernatural beings, but mere physical phenomena? What will that do for us?"

"If the Mogran are in fact beings of energy, then they are subject to the laws of energy. That means there may be other ways of protecting yourself from them besides the sigil. There may be other ways of stopping them, as well, besides killing an innocent person. You could get what you want, Ileana. And I could get what I want. And no one else would have to die."

Ileana's voice was icily flat. "Forgive me if I doubt the sincerity of your motives, doctor. What do you really want?"

For the first time the doctor faltered. "I have never been possessed. I can only imagine the anger you must feel. The sense of violation. But for the same reason, I can see things about the Mogran that you do not. Especially a Mogran such as Leo, born under the reign of Nero, eyewitness to almost two thousand years of history, and possessed of a perfect memory of everything each of his innumerable hosts has seen. If we could convince him to talk"—the doctor glanced at the restraining chair behind him—"his testimony could exponentially expand our knowledge of the world."

Ileana also looked at the chair. Imagined Leo bound by its restraints, the doctor pricking, poking, sawing at him in an attempt to torture his secrets from him.

"Do you really think your cell will hold a demon, Doctor?"

"I think the sigil will."

"You want to trap the demon in a *body?*"

The electronic silence stretched on endlessly as the doctor weighed his answer.

"Michaela Szarko woke up this morning. When the nurses came in to check on her, they found her sitting up in bed trying to peel the cast off her—"

Ileana let go of the intercom button.

"Michaela's awake?" A smile of pure wonder spread across Q.'s face, but just as suddenly as it appeared, it faded. "But that means—"

Ileana nodded grimly. "Jasper. Or Leo."

Something in Ileana's face caused Q.'s jaw to drop. He grabbed her wrist. "Ileana, no! You can't expect me to hurt–not *Michaela*."

Ileana's face went as hard as the bones beneath Q.'s fingers. Only her eyes betrayed her.

"No," she said. "I would never expect you to hurt Michaela."

The huntress's fist slammed into the boy's head with a force that would have crushed another man's skull. Q. bounced off the plexy and slumped to the floor.

Ileana ran her fingertips over his head, was pleased to feel a goose egg already rising from the boy's temporal bone.

"So you *can* be hurt after all." Ignoring the doctor beating silently on the sheet of Plexiglas, she turned the lights off and walked from the room.

7

As Jasper reached for the doorbell of 216 Aitken Street, Q.'s watch flashed on his wrist. *Time is expensive.* His friend's words echoed through his mind, but who had really said them: Q. or Leo? How different such a statement was coming from a Mogran rather than a human. People lost time, but the demons only accumulated it, saved the seconds like pennies until they were billionaires.

The inner door suddenly opened. On the other side of the screen, Mrs. Szarko gasped, and Jasper, taken aback a moment, had to remind himself she was looking at Larry's face, not his. There were dark circles under her eyes, but the eyes themselves were strangely luminescent, as if she'd just beheld something miraculous. Miraculous, but a little frightening. Well, Jasper reflected, her daughter had awakened from a coma and walked out of a hospital that most observers predicted she would have been carried out of in a bag. You could hardly blame her for being frazzled.

"My goodness, you startled me. I was just going to check the—" Mrs. Szarko shook her head. "Pardon me. Jasper—my daughter's boyfriend—had a Dearborn sweatshirt with stains just like those." She pointed at three red spots on the stomach—wine, which Jasper had never really liked. " 'Cranberry juice,' he told me. Teenagers."

Good lord, Jasper thought. The woman has a memory like a Mogran. Before he could say anything, however, a voice rang out.

"It's for me!"

Mother and visitor both froze. Jasper knew they shared the same thought: he hadn't pressed the doorbell, so how had Michaela known there was a visitor? A pair of heavy feet half skipped, half thudded down the steps. Skin swished over floorboards. She's barefoot, Jasper thought. No, *he's* barefoot. Leo—

A pale sliver appeared beside Mrs. Szarko, and all the words fell out of Jasper's brain. Leo or no Leo, this sliver was Michaela.

"Dig the threads, Larry."

Jasper shivered. There was something disjunctive—disgusting—about the words that had come out of Michaela's mouth, like chocolate cake soaked in vinegar. The voice was Michaela's, but the tone, the knowingness, the snide insinuation—these were completely alien to the girl he had known and loved.

The demon's eyes were slitted and sharp, as if he were reading Jasper's thoughts.

"Yup. It's me." Leo did a Vanna White, offered Michaela's body up for inspection. He had dressed his host in a pair of Daisy Dukes and a tight pink tanktop. One of the straps had fallen off her shoulder, and the pale top of her left breast swelled above the fabric. She was braless, and her nipples were visible, and Jasper could have sworn her breasts were bigger too. Could Leo do that? He hadn't been in a woman yet. He didn't know how that worked.

Hadn't been in a woman *yet*. What the hell was he thinking?

The demon held a huge sandwich in Michaela's right hand. Two slices of bread had been placed more or less symbolically around a stack of meat as thick as Larry Bishop's wrist.

Mrs. Szarko—a nice lady, but a bit on the prim side—glanced at her daughter's cleavage.

"Honey?"

"Not now, Madelaine." Michaela bit down on a chunk of meat, jerked her head to rip it off the sandwich like a crocodile tearing flesh from a carcass. "I'm busy."

"Don't you want to—"

"I said *not now*."

Bits of meat sprayed from her mouth, and Mrs. Szarko visibly winced.

"I'll be in the—"

But Michaela had already elbowed her mother out of the way. She pushed the screen door open, let it slam behind her, then stood there a moment to allow Jasper to experience the full effect. It wasn't just the shorts, the tanktop. The swollen breasts. Jasper's nose could smell the pheromones pouring from every square inch of his girl-friend's immaculate skin. The hairs on his forearms could feel the heat radiating from her body. Her eyes twinkled, her cheeks were rosy, her upper lip ever so slightly damp (although that might've just been grease from her sandwich). She oozed sexual energy. Sexual prowess. Sexual conquest. Not even the wad of food in her mouth could diminish her triumph. She bit, chewed, swallowed, threw in a burp for good measure. Leo gloated in his girlfriend's flesh, flaunted her control over it, and over him.

"Bet you wish you'd hit this when you had the chance. Don't you, *Larry?*"

Her eyes glowed like diamonds. No, Jasper reminded himself. Leo made her eyes glow: dilated the pupils, released the tiniest bit of saline from the tear ducts. Just enough to make them glisten. Jasper had to keep reminding himself that it wasn't Michaela he faced. Wasn't just Michaela.

Leo nodded, as if he understood exactly what had gone through Jasper's mind. He grabbed Jasper's arm, steered him off the porch. "Let's go somewhere we can talk."

Jasper let himself be led. Though part of him wanted to rip the demon's head from its shoulders, he was paralyzed by the fact that it was Michaela's head, Michaela's shoulders.

"Tough choice, ain't it?" Leo's voice was muffled by another mouthful of meat. "You're thinking, I wanna kill this motherfucker, but how can I do it without hurting my dear sweet precious Michaela? News flash, Jasper: you can't."

They passed a pair of teenaged boys on the sidewalk. The boys gawked at Michaela openly, and Leo returned their stare with obvious pleasure.

"Hey, babies." Leo arched Michaela's back and her tits strained at the fabric of her tanktop.

One of the boys made a gesture like he was being stabbed in the heart, while the other just stared open-mouthed. Jasper had to resist the urge to pound their heads together.

They came to a silver Pontiac. Leo pulled open the driver's side door. The tinkle of a bell announced that the keys had been left in the ignition.

Jasper finally managed to speak. "This isn't your—isn't Michaela's car. Michaela—"

"Doesn't have a car," Leo said. "I know. Her parents have already promised her one for graduation but that's not for another month. This is the neighbor's."

"How'd you know the keys were in it?" Jasper said as he climbed inside. It seemed quite possibly the most irrelevant thing he could have said, but nothing else came to mind.

"I heard the alert bell when they parked a half hour ago." The demon turned the ignition, dropped the vehicle in gear.

Jasper looked back at the Szarkos' house. It was half a block away. Michaela's bedroom faced the back.

"Yup," Leo said when Jasper turned back to him, "I'm *that* good."

He floored it then, and the car squealed into traffic.

Both Mogran were so focused on each other—Leo in triumph, Jasper in horror—that neither saw the tiny Prius pull from the shade of a large maple and follow the stolen Sunfire down the road.

8

J.D. Thomas noticed Q. was rubbing his temple again.

"I think I'm gonna puke."

The antique limousine glided north on the Taconic State Parkway. Though the psychiatrist's eyes never left the road, his attention was focused on the boy in the passenger's seat. Q. had been nursing his head since they'd left Manhattan, and the doctor was starting to worry.

"You'll be fine, Q."

He glanced at the speedometer. Fifty-seven. He was impatient, but he had a charade to maintain. He eased his foot off the gas the tiniest bit, brought the car down to fifty-four.

"I feel nauseous. Isn't that a symptom of a concussion?"

Rolling green countryside flashed by the Pierce-Arrow's windows: a red-tailed hawk spun delicate spirals through the clear blue sky. A perfect day for a hunt.

"Even if you have a concussion, your body will heal it. As the huntress said, Leo made you strong."

"I don't get it! Why would she *do* that? Lock you up, knock me out? If she was going to ditch us, why not sneak away in the middle of the night?"

"Ileana—" The doctor broke off as a car honked and sped past them.

For the first time Q. took his hand off his head. "Look, if you want me to drive . . ."

"Now now, Q. I'm no Dale Burnheart—"

"Earnhardt."

"No Dale Earheart, but my driving skills are more than adequate."

The ancient limousine shuddered in the wake of several trucks hurtling past them. From the corner of his eye, the doctor saw Q. check the security of his seatbelt. He considered his words carefully. The boy could be a valuable tool in the coming struggle—impervious to possession by Leo, and Jasper's best friend besides—but only if he considered the doctor an ally. And, if Ileana perished during the course of capturing the two demons, he was the Legion's best hope for a new hunter. The doctor needed Q. to think of him as a friend or, better yet, a doddering but lovable uncle.

"As I was saying. Ileana has reason to distrust gatherers. Her previous partner, a man named Alec Wilson, was killed by a gatherer who tipped his hand to a Mogran, and was possessed as a consequence."

Q. had closed his eyes and was rubbing his head again. The doctor frowned but kept talking.

"Alec was unique as hunters go. Indeed, he was distinct as a host as well. His body had served as home to the demon Leilani for an astounding sixty-seven years. When Leilani finally took her leave, Alec's mind retained extraordinary amounts of information. His testimony expanded the Legion's knowledge of the Mogran's history and behavior by more than fifty percent, and gave us more than a few clues into secular history as well."

Q. snorted. "Testimony? Did you have him on the witness stand?"

"Not exactly. With Alec's help, we developed a series of techniques involving psychotropic medication and neurolinguistic programming to get as deep into his subconscious as we possibly could. Some of the procedures were not exactly pleasant for Alec, but he understood that the information Leilani had left in him could serve as the Legion's best weapon against the Mogran. In fact, it was Alec who gave the Legion its first real understanding of the patterns of frenzy and lull."

"But wasn't he, eighty? Ninety? I can't imagine some old grandpa chasing demons all over the world."

"Do you remember the genealogical tables from the bible? 'And all the days of Mahalaleel were eight hundred ninety and five years.' 'And all the days of Jared were nine hundred sixty and two years.' 'And all the days of Methuselah were nine hundred sixty and—' "

"Okay, I get it. But you don't actually believe that, do you? I mean, the Jesus freaks don't even believe that stuff. Do they?"

"The bible has suffered from a deeply politicized canonization process and innumerable botched translations, but it remains a re-markably accurate historical document. With a little investigation—a little interpretation—you can find the truth behind most of what is written there. Some of the more arcane statements can only be taken on faith, of course, but once you know about the Mogran, you can forgo superstition and go straight to fact. We have no reason to be-lieve Methuselah didn't live every bit as long as is recorded, with the assistance of a demon inside him."

"Yeah, whatever. I didn't survive being possessed, not to mention getting my skull smashed in by some crazy Croatian bitch, so I could go back to school. You were telling me about Ileana's partner."

The doctor wondered if the teenager had a crush on the huntress. She was the perfect transitional figure to ease his grief over his dead girlfriend—older, wiser, and dedicated to destroying the thing that had killed the Patel girl, as well as his best friend.

"Alec was a remarkable man. Most hunters are either killed or retire after just two or three years. Alec lasted nearly two decades, during which time he eliminated seventeen Mogran, with only three collateral fatalities—most of which, it must be noted, were probably attributable to Ileana. They were a team unlike any other."

"Were they a couple?"

The doctor let several hundred feet of rolling countryside pass by the Pierce-Arrow's windows before answering.

"For a full decade their fates were yoked together. To the eyes of the authorities, they were serial killers, and their crimes spanned more than a dozen countries. At one point Alec cracked the top ten of Interpol's most wanted, before the Legion orchestrated a convincing masquerade of his death. In addition to living outside the law, they pursued—and were occasionally pursued by—the most devious, most cleverly disguised opponent the world has ever known. How does your generation put it? They were on each other's backs. But their relationship was never sexual."

"Yeah, right. If I was with Ileana 24/7, I don't think I'd be able to keep my hands to myself. *Especially* if I'd had to spend sixty-seven years being celibate."

"Trust me on this one. Their relationship was strictly platonic."

Q. must have heard something in the doctor's voice, because he shot him a look. "Is there like a rule or something?"

"Not exactly. Did she by any chance tell you about the sigil?"

"You don't mean your necklace?"

The doctor tapped his chest, shook his head. "That's where the name comes from, but the hunter's sigil is rather different. You know how demons exit their hosts, yes?"

"You mean sex?"

"The hunters prefer the word breed. What the demons are doing is enacting the biological procedure by which the flesh communicates to the spirit that it has fulfilled its purpose. Unfortunately, the spirit is not quite as cognizant of its physical domicile as you might think. It cannot tell the difference between actual breeding and mere conjunction. So long as there are two bodies involved, and, shall we say, fruition, the body ejects the alien spiritual matter. Yet how is it that a being that can see the inner workings of each and every cell in its body can't tell the difference between a vagina and another, shall we say, less fertile orifice?"

Q. made a face. "Yeah, you don't need to get too specific. But, well, how *does* that happen?"

Again the doctor paused, considering. How much to tell the boy? Finally he decided to go for it.

"You study physics, do you not?"

"Yeah. Why?"

"Earlier today, before Ileana assaulted you, I mentioned that some members of the Legion believe the Mogran aren't supernatural beings at all, but merely electronic entities."

"Electricity that thinks?"

The doctor chuckled. "I know the idea sounds farfetched—"

"I'd've said stupid myself."

"—but is it any more farfetched than thinking that the souls of virgins come back to possess the living?"

"You got me there."

"If we rule out the intervention of a divine entity in the creation process, then we're left with the fairly straightforward assertion that consciousness is essentially an electrical current acting on a closed system." The doctor tapped his head. "The brain is a bit like a home appliance: unplugged, it's no more animate than a computer or a toaster. But introduce an electronic current and it is suddenly capable of the most remarkable feats of cognition. We know also that electromagnetic energy is capable of containing enormous amounts of data, and, as well, that electricity doesn't sit still in space, but, rather, moves rapidly between poles of differing charges."

"Yeah, this is all first-year stuff. What's your point exactly?"

"Simply this: when you apply these 'first-year' concepts to the Mogran, you see they fit perfectly, both as regards the demons' ability to retain the memories of all the individuals they've possessed, as well as their inability to exist outside of a human body. Like lightning, they zap from one to the next in the blink of an eye."

Q. nodded rapidly. His hands had abandoned his head, and were gesturing rapidly in front of him.

"There are a lot of what-ifs and maybes in all that," Q. said, almost as if he were lecturing the doctor rather than the other way around. "But okay. Let's just say you're right. What's that have to do with sex?"

"Sex produces very specific electrochemical activity within the body, Q. My theory is that during the act of intercourse the two bodies essentially become polarized into negative and positive spheres; the orgasm is the jolt that knocks the Mogran out of the host body–the flicked switch, as it were."

"Okay, let's assume you're right. How's the sigil fit into all this? What *is* the sigil?"

"Think, Q. The demons can only exit a body through sexual orgasm."

"You said that, like, twenty times."

"So if the body is incapable of reaching orgasm, then the demon is trapped."

Q. snorted. "How exactly do you become incapable of reaching orgasm? I mean, unless you cut–" Q.'s legs snapped together. "You've *got* to be kidding me. You want *me*–"

A sign appeared on the side of the road, announcing the Hudson exit. The doctor quickened his voice even as he slowed the car.

"The hunters have traditionally used the sigil as a way of keeping the demons at bay. But let us put aside the question of you for the moment. It does have other uses as well."

Q. gasped. "You want to trap a demon. In one body."

"Not just any demon. I want to trap Leo. If our reports are correct, Leo may be as much as two thousand years old. He could provide us with invaluable information. He could also be useful as a, how can I put this delicately–"

"A guinea pig?"

"We are at a momentous point, Q. If the theory of the Mogran's electrical nature is correct, we may finally be able to zap a demon from its host in a simple, almost surgical procedure. We might be able to trap the Mogran in inorganic materials. Who knows, we might even–"

Q. squinted at the doctor. "What?"

"This is the kind of thing that makes Ileana angry."

"*What?*"

"I think we might be able to allow the demons to live within electronic circuitry." He turned from the road and looked at Q. meaningfully. "Not only would we not need to kill the host, but we wouldn't need to kill the Mogran either. They could live on, Q. Forever."

Q.'s eyes went soft for a moment, and the doctor knew he was thinking of Jasper again. His friend. The friend he had killed. Was thinking of resurrecting him. Atoning for his crime.

"No more lives need be lost, Q. But reaching that goal might require more than one attempt. Experiments. And for that, yes, we need test subjects. Guinea pigs."

There was a stop sign at the end of the off-ramp, and the doctor dropped the car out of gear.

"Would you mind opening the glove compartment? My glasses are a bit dusty. There's a piece of felt in there."

Q. opened the glove compartment, handed the doctor the cloth. The psychiatrist could feel the boy's eyes on him as he took his glasses off. He folded the cloth around one of the lenses and began rubbing it smoothly. The glasses sparkled in the sunlight coming through the windshield. It was so easy to do, once you knew how.

"Remember, Q.," J.D. Thomas said in a soft voice. "Ileana doesn't just want to kill Leo. She wants to kill Jasper too. Your best friend, Jasper." His fingers continued to rub the lens back and forth, back and forth. The light blinked in a regular pattern. Q.'s pupils narrowed and opened, narrowed and opened as they attempted to compensate for the rapid changes in photostimulation. "All signs point to the fact that Leo is in Michaela's body. Do you really want to lose yet another friend?" When Q. didn't answer, the doctor knew he was almost under. "Remember, Q." he said in a deep, soft voice, "Ileana is not your friend. But I am."

The doctor stopped rubbing, put his glasses back on. A small smile played over Q.'s face. He was still looking at the place where the doctor's hands had been.

For the first time in three hours, the doctor felt free to floor it. There was no squeal of wheels or smell of burning rubber—at two and a half tons, the Pierce-Arrow was too heavy for that, no matter what was under the hood—but the doctor's head was still pushed back into the headrest. It was a very satisfying effect. Yes, it was.

Very satisfying indeed.

9

Leo parked at the end of a dirt road. A few willow trees waved between them and the river. Why do I keep ending up back here? Jasper thought. I didn't even *like* the river when I was alive.

Leo got out of the car. The alert bell dinged insistently, but Jasper left the keys in the ignition and followed the demon. The bell tinkled faintly after him like an admonition, a tiny reminder of Leo's prowess.

In front of him, Michaela's ass moved up and down in the tiny pair of shorts, but her walk was anything but enticing. Her bare feet crushed pebbles beneath her soles, her hands snapped branches out of her way as if they offended her. When she reached the river, she climbed out on a slanted trunk and stood above the dark water. Her back was to Jasper. Her arms and legs were golden and hairless—flawless, really, but Jasper couldn't find anything sexy in the girl who stood in front of him. Sexuality requires a hint of vulnerability, and there was nothing vulnerable about Michaela. Not with Leo inside her, filling her like a nylon stocking stuffed with pennies. And yet, despite that, Jasper was still filled with desire. The desire to fuck and the desire to kill—equal parts lust and hatred, which, instead of canceling each other out, only made both burn more wildly. This was Michaela. This was Leo.

This *sucked*.

Leo pirouetted to face Jasper and waved Michaela's arms at the expanse of water.

"1609. Henry Hudson ventures up these waters in search of the fabled Northwest Passage. The enormous width of the river is encouraging. This is a mighty stream indeed. But less than thirty miles north the river narrows, and he can go no further. He's forced to return the way he came. A year later he tries again, this time heading much farther north. Hudson Strait and on to Hudson Bay, where his ship becomes locked in ice. He and his crew winter on the rocky coast, living off nothing but dried meat and the occasional Arctic hare. When the ice finally melts, Hudson wants to push on for the Pacific, but his crew mutinies. They leave their captain and his son in an open boat with no food, water, or weapons and turn for home. Hudson dies, of course, but so do his renegade sailors. Only eight of them make it back to Europe, where they're promptly arrested and tried for treason."

Leo paused, and a faint sound came to Jasper's ears: the alert bell in the stolen car. He reminded himself that he had the same abilities Leo had. As the demon opened his mouth to speak again, Jasper cut him off.

"Get to the point. I know you've got one in that sick little brain of yours."

Leo laughed. "My point is that sometimes you're damned if you do and damned if you don't. Sometimes," he stared at Jasper with eyes that did not belong to Michaela, "you're just damned."

Jasper pretended his shiver was caused by the wind off the water. "Yeah, I'm still not getting it."

"Hudson was an explorer. He risked everything—hell, he *lost* everything, including his own son—for the sake of discovering something new. Something about the world, but also something about himself. You, Jasper, have an opportunity compared to which Henry's journey looks like a plastic boat running up and down a bathtub. You're the first new Mogran in hundreds of years. The first *intentional* one in thousands. One day they'll call you Gamma-I. The first of the Gamma Wave. The first of a new generation."

Jasper leveled his gaze at Leo. Leo in Michaela's body. Saw both the conjunction and the distinction. Steeling his voice as best he could, he said, "I won't become you."

"You don't even know what I am. You don't know what *you* are. You are *Mogran*, Jasper. The rarest and most powerful entity this world has ever known. In twenty millennia there have been fewer than one thousand of us. Now there is just you, me, and the Alphas. Thanks to the ridiculousness of the Covenant, we came close to making ourselves extinct. But we can start over. On our terms. We can make a new world."

Jasper opened his mouth, but Leo waved him silent.

"Listen to me, Jasper. The planet was bigger when Hudson sailed up this river. But it was getting smaller every day, thanks to the voracious appetites of men like Hudson and Cortez and Columbus and all those other explorers who risked their lives so that civilized man would know the extent of his material existence. But what's left now? For humanity to discover? For humanity to *do?* Your species has placed its foot on every square inch of the earth's soil. Cooked its oceans as if they were pots of water, pumped its atmosphere full of lead and fluorocarbons as if blowing up a balloon. Now it's time to *make* something. A new world. A new body. A new mankind, living in harmony with the Mogran—who are, after all, an inextricable part of them, born of their minds, incapable of living outside their bodies. Don't you want to be a part of that?"

There were two questions Jasper could have asked. One was human, the other immortal. One implied causality and morality, while the other was merely an inquiry into process, an accumulation of data. Jasper, human still—at least in his mind—did not ask *how*. He only asked:

"Why?"

And Leo, immortal to the core, was caught off guard. A whimsical smile played over Michaela's face. A smile that was nearly innocent as Leo realized that his charge—his creation, his child—had made a choice based on an emotion more substantial than the need to be distracted from the emptiness of eternity.

The demon ran Michaela's hands over her body. Showed it to Jasper in all its teenaged glory.

"I was going to give her to you."

Jasper shook his head. "What are you talking about?"

"Michaela. Your one true love. I was going to make her immortal, just like you. To show you how much I cared. That my intentions were honorable."

Jasper looked at Michaela. From her slightly splayed toes gripping the smooth bark of the fallen tree to the inch of pale blond hair that had grown on her scalp in the last three days. Her legs, still pale and delicate from winter. Her arms, lean, quick, inquisitive, always reaching for something. Her breasts. Her hips. The delicate space between.

Leo, seeing where Jasper looked, shook Michaela's head.

"Is that all she is to you? A body? Have you been listening to nothing I said? I was going to give you *Michaela*, not some flabby piece of *meat.*"

Something happened then. The demon's eyes glazed, and he seemed suddenly smaller. Less sure of himself. Scared even.

"Jasper? I-is that you?"

It was Michaela's voice. Not Leo's. Michaela's.

For one brief moment it seemed to Jasper that his soul exploded through the shell of Larry Bishop's flesh and he stood there not just in his own clothes but his own body, exposed to Michaela's sight. But even as his arm reached out to her, the sleeve of his sweatshirt rode up on Larry Bishop's significantly longer arm, exposing the ruined remains of Q.'s $29,000 watch, and he knew it was just an illusion. His arm, like his head, was rotting in a grave in the cemetery.

Michaela's eyes blinked rapidly. "Who—who are you? What am I doing here?" She looked around wildly, realized she was standing over a river. She screamed, teetered, nearly fell. An instant later she smiled coyly at Jasper.

"Leo," Jasper said. An epithet, an accusation. *Bastard. Traitor.*

"See, Jasper? *That's* Michaela. Not this." He punched his host's thigh, her breast, her head.

Jasper looked at the body Leo touched with such impunity. Call him shallow. Call him a man. Hell, call him a teenaged boy. But he didn't believe the demon. Michaela's flesh was every much a part of her as her love of raucous girl pop or nineteenth-century romances. If her mind were transplanted in another body, she would be a different person. Jasper didn't like admitting that. Not because it made him seem shallow, but because it made him wonder what *he* was now. How much of him was still Jasper, how much was something else.

"You were going to make her like us?"

Leo's eyebrows raised at the word. *Us.* "I was. A present for you. A companion, to make eternity less lonely."

"Don't!" Jasper heard himself say before he knew he was going to say it. "Don't do it!"

"No need for melodrama, Jasper. I couldn't if I wanted to. Your beloved? Sweet, virginal Michaela, who made you wait till you thought your balls were going to burst? She wasn't so chaste, after all. Wasn't *quite* the virgin she made herself out to be."

Jasper's hands balled into fists. "Shut up!"

"Ironic, isn't it? When I decided to give you one last chance at mortality, I set you up with Sila because I thought Michaela was too much of a prude to put out. Only it turns out her precious virginity was an illusion. An act."

If Jasper could have choked Leo without suffocating Michaela he would have. Would have wrapped his hands around the demon's neck and squeezed until his head popped off. But there was no way, and Leo knew it. Gloated in it. Practically danced on the fallen tree in his stolen body.

"Let the record show I gave you a chance, Jasper. To have sex. To save yourself from all this. But you didn't take it. Somehow I think you wouldn't have even if I'd managed to get Michaela in that closet. Would you?" He ran Michaela's hands down her waist, over her hips. "I've been around long enough to know. Call it Freudian, call it Darwinian, call it Mogran, but people understand the implications of sex, even if it's only at the unconscious level. We have sex to breed, and we breed so that some part of us remains after we die. Michaela was ready. So were Q. and Sila. But not you. Oh, no. You'd've held out forever, I think. You *wanted* to be like me. And now you are."

Jasper's hackles went up. It wasn't just Leo's hateful words. Something had changed in the forest. With a start, he realized the alert bell had stopped ringing more than a minute ago.

Leo saw the look pass over Jasper's face but misunderstood it. He reached down and popped the top button of Michaela's shorts.

"Think I'm wrong, Jasper? Lying? Then prove it. Show me you can resist the need to jump. Show me you can resist . . . this."

Thumbs hooked in beltloops. A little shimmy, and Michaela's shorts lowered a quarter inch. A half.

"Right here, Jasper. On this very tree. You don't think I took you here just to deliver a symbolic lecture, do you?"

Leo's voice faded as Jasper concentrated. The sound of the river faded. The forest.

There was the faintest of clicks. The mental processing was immediate. Instinctual.

"This is where your little cock-tease of a girlfriend spread her legs—"

Jasper threw himself to the ground as a bullet ripped through the place where he'd been. The sound of the shot exploded in his ears as a jet of blood shot from Michaela's left shoulder and her body flew backwards into the dark water. Jasper rolled behind a tree as two more shots chased him into the underbrush. But neither the crashing of branches nor the sound of gunfire could drown out Leo's voice.

The demon's final words ripped through his heart like his assailant's bullets:

"It was Q.!"

10

As soon as Leo fell into the water, Ileana turned her attention to Jasper. She squeezed off two more shots but the bullets went wide. The fledgling rolled his host's tall body on the ground and disappeared behind one of those shapeless New World softwoods. Ileana glanced into the river for a sign of Leo, but the dark water had already stilled. Muttering a curse, she took off after the fledgling.

He went for the car first, and she thought her task was going to be easier than she'd imagined. The keys were in her pocket, and even if the fledgling did know how to hotwire an engine, she'd put a bullet in his brain before he could accomplish it. But after a dozen steps he veered back towards the trees. She stuffed the gun in her belt and took off after him.

Mud sucked at her boots and vines tangled around her legs. The demon seemed to take two steps for every one of hers. He made more noise than an ox, though, and she could track him by sound if nothing else. Every once in a while she caught a glimpse of his head as he leapt over an obstacle—at one point she could have sworn he jumped ten feet in the air. It was nothing she hadn't seen before, but she found herself wondering if he'd known how to maximize his host's strength and speed from the moment he came back, or if Leo had taught him. Her mind filled with a horrifying image of Leo training an army of new Mogran, and she thought about turning around, taking him out first. But instinct told her the right thing to do was pick off the weak one first, then return for the leader.

Her target may have been weak in comparison to Leo, but he was getting farther and farther away. He was starting to veer from the river as well. Ileana had passed a small housing development on her way here. The demon could lose her there easily or, worse, take hostages. She began to track left to pick up a little ground, but she knew she didn't have much chance. The demon was already more than a hundred yards away. Well out of range of the ancient, tarnished pistol she'd taken from the doctor's coffee jar. Once he hit open ground he could break into a sprint. He wouldn't even need a car.

The demon cut even further to the left. She saw him look back, gauging her position, and suddenly she understood. He wasn't aiming for the development. He wasn't actually trying to get away: he was trying to circle back to where they'd started from. Of course! He was trying to protect the girl. Leo's host. The fledgling's girlfriend, when he'd been alive.

For a moment Ileana faltered. In ten years, she'd never seen a demon do anything for the sake of a living being—never once heard of a Mogran putting a mortal's life ahead of its own. It occurred to her that the fledgling might actually be different. Might be . . . what? Redeemable? As far as she knew, he hadn't hurt anyone yet. Who's to say he ever would?

But that wasn't true, she remembered. This was already his second host. Somewhere out there was the first. Mason West. Even if the fledgling hadn't actually forced him to do anything reprehensible, he'd still taken his body. And he'd exited it, which meant that he'd made him have sex—and he'd do it again, and again, and again. Corporeal larceny. Spiritual rape. That was reason enough to kill him.

Ileana abruptly broke off the chase. Stopped running, and instead began to sneak as quietly as she could back to the place where she'd shot Leo. With any luck, the fledgling would continue to circle. That would give her time to get to the water before he did. Time to hide. Time to prey on his weakness.

She just hoped Leo wasn't planning to do the same thing.

11

J.D. Thomas heard the first shot over the blasting air conditioner. Weather: yet one more reason why the psychiatrist hated to leave the comfort of his townhouse. Weather, and insects. The demons *would* pick a virtual swamp to have their tête-à-tête.

Two more shots sounded close together, suggesting Ileana was firing wildly. No surprise there. The Luger she'd taken was a stumpy, brutish-looking weapon, the mechanism unoiled in who knew how long. He was surprised it hadn't exploded in her face. Nevertheless, it had served as the perfect place to conceal a tracking device. It was amazing what you could buy on the internet.

The psychiatrist turned to his passenger. "Do you remember everything I told you?"

A tiny smile played over Q.'s face. He ran his hands over the tops of his pants as if he were drying his palms. "Yes."

The boy's voice was trusting, as though he were speaking not to the doctor but to a memory. A pleasant memory—a childhood bath or the first bite into a warm *tarte tatin*. Something sensual but relaxing. The kiss after sex rather than the kiss before.

"Good. Now, when I say your name, you're going to wake up. You'll be aware of everything that's happened since you let me out of the cell, save for the fact that you'll have no memory of being hypnotized."

The doctor gathered himself. Time to put on the mask again. He took a deep breath, then:

"Q.!"

The boy's head snapped in the doctor's direction.

"Were those—?" Q. didn't finish his question. Instead he pushed the door open and ran from the car. "Jasper! Jasper!"

Pollen-heavy air flooded the cabin, and the doctor sighed. He leaned over and pulled the door closed, watched Q. run past the huntress's Prius and the demon's Sunfire before disappearing into the clouds of swirling insects. When the boy was gone, the doctor leaned over, closed the door, opened the glove compartment. Thank God he'd thought to bring repellent.

Panic raced through Q.'s body, and dread, but also anticipation. Excitement. He was going to see Jasper again! His best friend, his dead friend. The friend that he had killed.

But emotions weren't the only things coursing through his veins. Hormones and glucose and various chemicals were also flooding his limbs. All the things Ileana had tried to teach him over the past forty-eight hours seemed to be happening effortlessly. Q.'s body flew over the muddy soil, a good ten feet between each footfall. It must be the context, Q. thought. He always performed better under pressure. And he would *not* let Ileana kill Jasper. Not till he'd at least spoken to him.

And then there was Leo. Leo and Michaela. Leo *in* Michaela. Q. prayed the doctor was wrong, but it made too much sense. Michaela had awakened from her coma and walked out of the hospital four days after breaking her back. Only a Mogran could accomplish that. But what if it wasn't Leo? What if Jasper had gotten to her first? God, what if Ileana killed them both?

The shots had come from downstream. The strip of vegetation that grew along the edge of the river was fairly narrow. He'd spot them if they tried to make a break for it. At least, he thought he would. He'd never tracked anyone in his life. Never gone hunting—

not even a scavenger hunt. He wasn't really sure what you did. Maybe yelling?

"Jasper! Jasper, where are you?"

The only sound he heard was the crashing of his own feet. He broke through the last bit of undergrowth and came to the river. The water ran in gentle dark undulations. He looked down at the ground. It was dotted with footprints. Q. stared at them as if they might tell him something. They appeared to have been made by feet. Feet . . . in . . . shoes.

He decided to try yelling again.

"Michaela? Are you here?"

His only answer was the river's gurgle. Q.'s hands twitched with the energy building up in his body. He couldn't stand still. He turned and ran downriver. He dodged tree trunks, jumped over fallen branches. A skinny branch poked from a tree trunk about five feet from the ground. It would've been simpler to duck under it but Q. jumped instead. To test the limits of his newfound strength. He gauged the distance, paced himself. The muscles of his legs coiled and released, and then he was in the air. He was practically flying. Leo's jump on the balcony the other day flashed in his brain. Eat your heart out, motherfucker, he thought, but even as he cleared the branch it rose up and tangled in his legs. As he fell to the ground he caught a pale blur out of the corner of his eye. Blond hair. Lithe limbs. He twisted, tried to ward off the blow.

"Ileana, it's—"

The rest of his sentence disappeared in a whoosh of air. His head smashed against a tree trunk and stars flashed in front of his eyes. A hand grabbed the back of his neck and shoved his face in the dirt. He felt a knee in the small of his back, and then something sharp—the huntress's knife?—pressed against his skin just to the right of his spine, just over his bladder.

"One word," a voice hissed in his ear, "and you'll be pissing out a brand new hole."

12

The demon was getting tired of people shooting him. It had been nearly a century since the last time he'd been shot, and now it had happened twice in one week. If Jasper would just cooperate instead of being so damn obstinate, Leo could focus his attention on the Legion—on this *very* peculiar psychiatrist, not to mention this most persistent of huntresses. He had to hand it to her: he hadn't seen her before she shot. It took genuine skill to sneak up on a Mogran. Her aim was great too: if he hadn't ducked, the bullet would've gone right through Michaela's heart. As it was, the shell tore through the meat of his host's left shoulder, clipping the bone, but fortunately not breaking it. He stanched the bleeding, set the wound to healing, and put it out of his mind.

The Hudson was only about four feet deep where he fell in. Fortunately, the trunk he'd been standing on was between him and the huntress, and he pulled himself quickly into deeper water. He stopped when he was about ten yards from shore, fifteen feet down. He heard the second pair of shots, but, since Jasper didn't fall in the river after him, he assumed his charge was safe. For now, the fledgling was on his own.

His host's natural buoyancy pulled her body toward the surface, and he had to wave her arms to keep himself from surfacing. Such cumbersome things, bodies. Subject to the laws of physics and the interactions of billions upon billions of molecules. Leo had spent the first several centuries of his existence as a Mogran learning the limits of his control over those molecules, but he'd spent virtually the entirety of his postdeath existence trying to find a way to shuck the flesh altogether. To exist as pure spirit. But that was one rule that wouldn't bend, let alone break. The Mogran couldn't resist the call of the flesh. Could not remain outside a host for more than a moment. He'd learned to be pragmatic about that state of affairs, but that didn't mean he had to like it.

He didn't just have to fight his host's fleshly buoyancy. He had to fight her mind too. Her body had already been underwater for more than a minute, and even though her connection to her senses was muted, the instinctive panic was making her particularly unruly. Unconscious urges were always harder to control than conscious ones. He wasn't as skilled as other Mogran at tracking down every little impulse hiding at the bottom of this or that mental crevice, around the corner of this or that phrenic blind alley. Years ago, he'd managed to track down one of the Legion's agents—gatherers, the hunters called them, which he thought was adorable—and he'd learned that more hunters had been culled from his former hosts than any other demon. The gatherer had called him "sloppy," which word Leo had written in 119 languages on the gatherer's walls, until he finally ran out of blood.

But it was true: even now, lost in his thoughts, he'd loosened his hold on Michaela and she'd made a break for the surface. He snapped back in control, propelled his host's body back toward the muddy riverbed. He could've just beaten her down, of course, crushed and compacted her psyche so tightly it would never open up again, but he didn't want to do that. Not yet. The girl was still his best bargaining chip with Jasper, and he didn't want to throw her away by destroying her mind. Not yet. He could hear her screaming for air, could feel her desperately trying to kick her arms and legs. Her terror was so overwhelming that he could actually feel it: little electrical charges that prickled at his nerves like pins stuck in his skin. Such spirit, this girl. He could see why Jasper was in love with her. He was a passive boy, and she would have dominated him like an Arabian queen lording it over her harem eunuchs.

Speaking of Arabs: Leo chuckled to himself to think what Jasper was going to do to Q. now that he thought his best friend had slept with his girlfriend. Not just slept with her: deflowered her. Lying didn't come naturally to a being with access to vast reservoirs of knowledge—the truth was almost always more powerful. But in this case, a little deception seemed the perfect way to chip away at Jasper's two most powerful connections to the living world: not just his best friend, but his unfaithful girlfriend as well. In fact, Michaela had slept with a boy named Adam McCluskey a few months before she started going out with Jasper. The experience hadn't been a positive one, which is why she decided to wait with Jasper. But he didn't need to know that.

Not even a Mogran could see clearly through a river as silty as the Hudson, but he thought he could make out a sinkhole about a hundred feet upriver. Sinuous shapes writhed through it. Tree roots probably. They'd make good cover to pull himself out of the water. He swam toward it.

When he reached the roots he waited a few more minutes, then slowly surfaced. The hawthorn tree whose roots he held blocked his view of the bank, so he opened his ears and listened. He heard footsteps immediately, then the rasp of breath. He listened carefully until he was sure it was a man. Not the huntress then, and not Lawrence Bishop either—not Jasper. Jasper wouldn't be sucking down air with such ferocity. Who could it be then? As if on cue, a voice called out:

"Jasper! Jasper, where are you?"

The demon smiled. Q. He doubted the boy had managed to track them here on his own. This Dr. Thomas was proving more resourceful with each new encounter.

"Michaela?" Q.'s voice was plaintive, forlorn. "Are you here?"

As quietly as he could—and no creature on earth is as silent as a Mogran in stealth mode—Leo pulled himself out of the water and set out on an intercept course. The sodden tanktop had shrunken and ridden up, enveloping his host's lovely breasts. It was a shame the fledgling wasn't there. Leo would've liked to see Jasper try to fight the urge for release.

When the demon's path took him past a dead oak, he broke a long straight stick off its trunk. The dry wood snapped cleanly from the tree, leaving one end angled and sharp. Q. was moving fast, but making more racket than a pack of elephants. When Leo came to a large poplar he stopped, knelt down, angled his branch into the deer-path the boy was following. He waited.

Q.'s steps grew closer. The demon smiled. It had been a long time since he'd had the chance for this kind of sport.

Leaves crunched under heavy feet. There was a grunt as Q. launched himself into the air. Leo jerked the stick upward, felt it catch Q.'s kicking legs. The boy's body crashed to the ground. In a moment Leo was on top of him. The kick in the gut was just for fun, as was smashing the boy's head into a tree trunk and making him eat a faceful of dirt. It was important to let Q. know Leo was still in control, whether he was inside the boy or not. He poked the sharp end of his stick into the boy's back.

"One word, and you'll be pissing out a brand new hole."

A hand roughly rolled Q. over. The first thing he saw was the nasty gash in Michaela's left shoulder, clotted with blood and silt from the river.

"Michaela! Are you all ri—"

Michaela punched him in the jaw, and the iron tang of blood filled Q.'s mouth.

"I told you to keep quiet." She smiled wickedly, ran a hand over Q.'s chest. "So this is what you look like from the outside? Nice."

Q. tried to jerk free, but the tiny girl held him down as if he were a toddler. She leaned over until her face was directly atop Q.'s, stared into his eyes until the boy could see the demon clearly.

"Leo," he whispered.

Leo twitched at the sound of his name, then nodded, sat up.

"Who is with you? Answer quietly, or I'll twist your arm out of its socket and use it to beat the truth from you."

Q. saw no reason to lie. "The doctor. Dr. Thomas. And Ileana."

Leo's eyes narrowed. "Ileana Zanic?"

"I don't know her last name."

"Croatian? Blond, gray eyes, thirty-four?" Q. nodded, and Leo smiled in amusement. "This is going to be even more fun than I thought."

When Leo didn't elaborate, Q. said, "What're we gonna do now?"

The demon looked down as if he'd already forgotten about Q. The wet tanktop pulled heavily around Michaela's breasts, and Q. hated the fact that he noticed this, and hated even more that Leo saw him notice it. The demon glanced down at the nubile body he'd chosen, looked back up with a smirk.

"We wait, Q. Patiently and very, very quietly. Do you understand?" He dropped his knee heavily on Q.'s groin for emphasis.

Q. fought back a groan. The demon's knee was pressing his belt buckle painfully into his pelvis, but when he squirmed Leo only pushed harder.

A moment later he lifted his head. The demon had slitted his host's eyes. Q. realized the Mogran had refocused his senses, was surveying the forest in search of Jasper and Ileana. The demon's eyes carved lines through the tree trunks, and he made micromovements of his head to adjust the angle of his ears. Even his nose wrinkled as he sniffed the air, like a leopard scenting for prey.

Q. closed his own eyes, tried to slow his breathing, refocus his senses. The first thing he noticed was something moving over the skin of his left ankle. It could've been a spider or it could've been a weed waving in the breeze, but he didn't look. The moisture in the ground was soaking through his shirt, and he started to shiver. He wanted to open his eyes but was afraid to. It was so hard to look at Michaela and think of her as the enemy, and yet he knew he had to. He asked himself if he could kill her to get Leo, but couldn't answer the question—which, when you got right down to it, was basically the same thing as saying no. He couldn't do it. Not Michaela. Maybe not anyone. At the same time he felt guilty, because he knew if he let the demon escape that there would only be more victims. Dozens, hundreds, thousands even, and each of those new hosts would be someone's Michaela. Someone's friend, daughter, wife. For the first time he began to understand why Ileana was the way she was. It was an impossible choice, and yet it had to be made.

But if the doctor was right—if it were somehow possible to zap the demons out of their hosts—it could all change.

If, if, if. Q. told himself to stop dreaming and focus on staying alive. Unable to move, afraid to open his eyes, he opened his ears instead. At first all he heard was his heart thud-thud-thudding in his chest like a drum machine, but then other sounds came to him. Leaves rustling, branches rubbing together with an itchy creak. A bird called, a yakkety-yak sound like a bluejay or a squabbling blackbird. A sigh escaped Michaela's body, and even as he wondered whether it was her or Leo who made it, he noticed that the demon's breathing had grown husky. Deeper, longer, louder, as if the demon's throat were slightly constricted.

All the things Ileana had told him about the frenzy flashed through his mind, and with a start, he realized Leo wanted out. Leo wanted . . . him.

He opened his eyes.

Michaela was looking down at him. Q. looked into her eyes for a trace of Leo, but the demon seemed to have retreated. He knew how this worked. He had felt it when Leo did it to him. Took bits and pieces of his desire for Sila, for his dad's Porsche, welded them together and turned them up until the only thing he could think of was making Sila blow him while he drove as fast as possible. Leo would hide behind Michaela's unconscious the same way. Would nudge here, prod there, augmenting those aspects of Michaela's psyche that best served his need to leave her body. Maybe Michaela had looked at Q. at a party one time and thought he was cute, or maybe she'd thought of him and Sila doing it and wondered what it was like. Maybe she looked at him and thought of Jasper, gone forever. The demon would find these thoughts and tease them out, turn them up. It would be Michaela who put her hand on Q.'s chest, Michaela who undid one button of the Jermyn Street shirt, then another. Q. could do this if he thought of it as Michaela. He could do it with her. *For* her.

"Michaela," he whispered.

"Sshh." Her eyes pierced his, held him still. He saw that her nipples had hardened beneath her tank top, and then he felt them as she let her breasts graze over his torso. Her knee slipped off his belt buckle, slipped down between his thighs. She pushed his legs open and pressed her thigh against him.

"Michaela," Q. whispered again. He had never coveted Jasper's girlfriend, but he knew this was his best chance to save her. Leo would get away, but Michaela—Michaela would live. Not even Ileana would kill her out of spite.

Michaela smiled. It was hard to think it was the demon doing it. She was so sexy, so irresistible. He closed his eyes, kept the picture of Michaela's face in his mind, tried to block out any thought of the beast within her.

He felt her hand on his zipper. She pulled. He groaned. Michaela, he kept saying to himself. Michaela, Michaela. He was doing this for Michaela.

Then: crackling leaves, breaking branches. The stamp of running feet. A scream:

"No!"

He opened his eyes in time to see a blur leap from the forest, and then suddenly Michaela—Michaela and Leo—were gone.

13

It took longer to lose the woman with the gun than Jasper would have thought. She was fast, and smart too. When he angled in to circle back to the place he'd left Leo and Michaela, she cut in farther and made up lost ground. She's done this before, he thought, and then he realized:

She was the huntress.

Thoughts filled his head, and for a moment he was running blind. How had it come to this? How in the space of a week had he gone from being a normal seventeen-year-old to a fugitive spirit trapped in the body of a burned-out paramedic? His host was wanted by the police for sexual assault, while Jasper himself was the target of an organization whose *raison d'être* seemed to be his death. It would be laughable if it wasn't terrifying. If, as the determined footsteps of the woman behind him testified, it wasn't all true.

A part of Jasper wanted to stop. To let this huntress shoot him and get it over with. But there was Larry to consider, for one thing, and Michaela too. He had to live long enough to get Leo out of Michaela. Then he'd try to find a way to end this existence without killing his host.

Gee, thanks, man, bubbled up from somewhere deep inside him. Jasper ignored Larry's sarcasm.

There was Q. to consider too.

Q. and Michaela.

The betrayal was like a knee to the groin. To Larry's groin, and Jarhead's, and his too. It reverberated through all the bodies he'd inhabited, seemed to touch the ether that was all that was left of him. His best friend had fucked his girlfriend. His girlfriend had fucked his best friend. His best friend—who, by the way, had *killed* him—had lured his girlfriend to a fallen tree at the river and poked her like some slutty cheerleader from a visiting school's basketball team. And his girlfriend—whose refusal to sleep with Jasper had condemned him to a peripatetic afterlife of borrowed bodies and eternal flight—had put out like some white trash whore. Jasper wondered what it had taken. A six-pack of beer? Or maybe some more exotic pilfering from Mohammed Qusay Sr.'s liquor cabinet? Maybe all Q. had had to do was ask, which is something Jasper had never done. He'd kissed her, nibbled at her lips and neck and earlobes, rubbed her shoulders, her breasts, put his hands inside her jeans and cupped her bare ass, pressed and pounded their zippered crotches together, and one time he'd laid his face in the crux of her legs, just the thin fabric of her skirt and a virtually nonexistent pair of panties between him and his goal, and he'd inhaled the deep rich odor until he was practically drooling with desire, but he'd never once asked, let alone demanded.

He'd been a gentleman.

He'd been a good boyfriend.

He'd been a pussy.

He hadn't gotten any pussy, but he'd *been* a pussy.

Aw fuck, Jasper thought. Shoot me now. Fucking get it over with already.

But.

But Jasper didn't want to die. The speed with which he was running from the huntress told him that whatever still passed for instinct in him had not yet given up the will to live. However overwhelmed his consciousness might be by the ethical dilemmas of possession, he, Jasper Van Arsdale, only son of John, wasn't ready to give up the ghost just yet. He'd only been on this planet for seventeen years, for fuck's sake. Leo had had no right to steal his life, let alone turn him into a Mogran, but neither did this woman behind him, or the Legion she represented. *He* would decide when he couldn't take being a demon anymore. Not some invisible jury convicting him for crimes he had yet to commit.

While all this was going through his head, Jasper continued to angle back towards Michaela. When he glanced behind him to see how close the huntress was, he realized he'd lost her. He pivoted, made a beeline directly for the place where Michaela had fallen into the water. He would save her first, and then he'd decide whether or not to smack the bitch up for sleeping with his best friend.

His mind was racing in a million different directions, but his body was only going one way: toward Michaela. He realized that it didn't matter if he moved from body to body, didn't matter if he carried the memories of two or two thousand other people with him. He was still just one person. This body he wore was the only body he had right now, and he would triumph or perish with it, through it, because of it. When you got right down to it, the future was every bit as uncertain for him as it was for anyone else. There was only now.

He'd been piloting himself solely on instinct. But they were his new, improved instincts. Landmarks he hadn't even realized he'd noticed—the charred slash where a bolt of lightning had struck a silver birch, an empty bottle of Amstel Light half buried beneath last year's mulch—flashed before his eyes, guiding him directly to his embarkation point. But when he was a couple hundred yards away from the spot where Michaela had fallen into the water, a scent came to him. Ham, mayonnaise, mustard. And then a whisper.

"Michaela."

Jasper veered toward the sound. It was like a magnet—no, like a star, sucking him in with its enormous gravitational force—and then he was upon them. Michaela was on top so it was Michaela he hit first. The fact that Leo was inside her was unimportant at that moment. He wasn't stopping Leo from escaping Michaela's body. He was stopping his girlfriend from fucking his best friend—again.

"No!"

He smashed into Michaela's body and they sailed ten feet

through the air. And then Jasper was reminded of Leo's presence, as the girl in his arms twisted while they were still airborne and tossed him clear with an elbow to the jaw that almost made him bite off his tongue. Jasper's shoulders smashed into a trunk but Michaela was more nimble, managed to curl, roll, land on her feet. She crouched down, hands curled into claws, teeth bared like a lioness, but Jasper was done with her, done with Leo. It was Q. he wanted to punish now.

He scrambled to his feet. Not gracefully, but fast. Incredibly fast. He launched himself at his best friend.

Q. made no move to defend himself. Only stared in confusion at the figure hurtling toward him. Just as Jasper crashed into him, a single word escaped his lips.

"Larry?"

And it was over. For a few minutes Jasper had been himself again. Just himself. His host had retreated from his thoughts, was no more real than a voice coming through a wireless headset. But the name that had fallen from Q.'s lips brought back the reality of the situation. He was Mogran now. He existed only in borrowed bodies, not quite dead, but not really alive either.

He didn't manage to stop himself before he crashed into Q. and knocked them both to the ground. Q. still didn't fight back—seemed, like Jasper, to have given up. Jasper stared at his friend. At his confused, pained eyes, at a little cut on his lip from which flowed a trickle of blood. Even as he watched, the blood congealed and stopped flowing, leukocytes filled the tiny opening with pus, the process of healing began in sped-up motion. But Q.'s eyes remained wounded, and Jasper knew this was what Leo had done to him. He glanced at the demon, who watched the reunion with a patient, curious expression, then looked back at Q.

"Q. It's me."

Q. blinked. He wiped his dirty hands on his pantlegs, then put them down in the dirt.

"Is it—is it really you?"

He didn't say the name. Jasper needed to hear him say it. Needed to know that he existed for someone besides Leo. He waited, his eyes pleading. But like Q.'s "please" of a moment ago, he wasn't sure what he wanted his friend to say.

"Jasper?"

Jasper didn't say anything. Didn't even nod.

"Oh my God, *Jasper?* Is it really you?"

A snide chuckle answered for him.

"Oh, this is rich," Leo said in Michaela's voice. "This is like eating crème brûlée off the hairless pussy of a ten-year-old Thai virgin whore."

Jasper turned to Leo. There was so much wrong with that sentence. Skip the big things: skip the fact that he could hear the fucking diacritical marks in his girlfriend's voice or the fact that the prostitute had to be a virgin, had to be Thai, had to be ten fucking years old.

"Michaela's never eaten creme brulee in her life. She's lactose intolerant."

"Huh," Leo said. His eyes glazed over for a moment, and then they sharpened again. "Not anymore she's not."

Jasper launched himself. His body sprang in the air as if bungees had snapped him up. The haughtiness. The smarminess. He would wipe that smug grin off the demon's mouth if he had to break Michaela's jaw to do it. Leo could just fix it anyway.

But in the fraction of a second all this had taken Leo had rolled out of the way, and instead of Michaela's body beneath him there was—

Q.

His friend's eyes were still glazed, as if he were not quite aware of what he was doing. Yet at the same time he was moving incredibly fast. As fast as Michaela, as fast as Jasper. Angling himself to intercept Jasper even as his hand pulled something from the pocket of his jeans. His thumb flicked off the orange cap. A tiny spike caught a ray of sunlight. A needle. Jasper, still in the air, tried to jerk himself out of the way, but it was too late. He felt the needle prick his ankle as he rolled to the ground, jumped to his feet.

For a moment he thought nothing would happen. Q. hadn't

depressed the plunger or he was immune to whatever was in the syringe. But then he felt icy coils wrap themselves around tibia and fibula, patella and tarsals. They encircled his femur, scaled his newly repaired pelvis like frozen ivy. Before he could recite the names of the rest of the bones of the body, the coils had coated his skeleton in a frigid, numbing net. He looked inside Larry's body, trying to find out what was happening, trying to find a way to stop it, but all he saw was a hundred million crystals of ice.

His vision blurred as he lost control of his eye muscles. By contrast, his hearing grew louder, as the protective muscles of his inner ear softened and sound waves smashed unimpeded against his eardrums. But they were distorted, hard to make out. Birdcalls sounded like fire alarms. A voice—Q.'s? Michaela's?—vibrated like a foghorn. A pixilated brown field filled his vision. He realized it was the ground just before his face splatted into it. His mouth filled with dirt but he couldn't spit it out. The only warmth was a faint sensation around his groin. Something like a groan escaped his mouth as he realized he was pissing himself.

And then, louder than a thunderclap, louder than the slamming of prison doors—or the gates of hell for that matter—a gunshot. By then Jasper was so numb he didn't even know if he'd been hit. Sound faded, the light seemed to flicker and go out. For a moment he was aware of himself, floating in the blackened void that was Larry Bishop's body, and then, softly but irrevocably, like a candle puffed out by a breath, he was gone.

14

Q. threw himself to the ground as the gunshot exploded behind him.

The syringe fell from his hands. The needle missed his leg, which was fortunate. The drop of sea snake venom on the tip of the spike would have killed him in less than a minute. He stared at the little spike in the leaves as a second shot ripped over his head, a third. How in the hell had the syringe ended up in his pocket? How in the hell had it ended up in his hands? J.D. Thomas had said he was an accomplished hypnotist, but really, how good was good? And then, as Q. glanced over at the paramedic's unmoving body—the body that housed the disembodied consciousness of his best friend—he realized that the how of what he'd done was significantly less important than the what. He searched the body sheltering Jasper for some sign of life, but saw nothing. Jesus Christ, he thought. What have I done? But he knew. For the second time in a week, he'd tried to kill his best friend.

The fourth shot brought him back to the situation at hand. Q. heard not just the burst of gunpowder but the whiz of the bullet speeding over his body. Bark exploded where the bullet tore into the meat of a tree. There was a flash of movement as Leo hurtled from the shelter of one trunk to the next.

"Ileana!" Q. yelled. "It's me!" As if she couldn't see him. As if anything could keep her from her hunt.

Another bullet roared over his head.

"I suggest you keep your head down," the huntress called, her voice as calm and flat as a traffic reporter warning commuters about a jam on the Thruway.

There was another flash as Leo rolled behind another trunk. Two more shots exploded in a shower of dirt just inches behind the demon. It seemed to Q. that Leo wasn't trying to get away though. It was more like he was trying to close in on the huntress. The fearlessness, the grim determination, sent chills down Q.'s spine.

"Don't make me kill the fledgling, Leo," Ileana called now. "You've gone to great lengths to protect him. I know he means something to you."

Leo looked at Larry Bishop, lying open and exposed. For all he knew the paramedic, and thus Jasper, was already dead. But if he wasn't, if the doctor had put some kind of sedative in the needle, then Q. would be damned if he'd let Ileana kill him. Jasper was Q.'s prey, not hers. He would decide whether his friend lived or died.

Without giving himself time to reconsider, he flung himself in Jasper's direction. Mud got in his mouth and eyes and he sputtered and choked but continued to roll blindly until he hit the warm mound of Larry Bishop's body. He sprawled across it, head over head, arms over arms, legs over legs, crotch over ass. The absurdity of the situation wasn't lost on him, or on Leo apparently. Q. heard a chuckle in Michaela's voice, and then:

"Oh, Q. What I wouldn't give for a camera right now."

Q. ignored the demon, called instead to the huntress.

"Ileana, don't! He's not like Leo!" It almost seemed as if he were yelling in Larry's ear, as if he wanted Jasper to hear him as much as Ileana.

"Do not fool yourself into thinking that there is such a thing as a good demon, Q. And don't think I won't go through you to get to Jasper."

There was another shot as Leo darted to yet another tree. What the hell is he doing? Q. thought. And then, as another shot whizzed through the air, he understood.

"Ileana, stop shooting! He's just trying to draw your fire!"

But it was too late. Leo darted out and Q. heard one more shot, followed by a sickening sound: not the thud of a bullet smacking into a body, but the quieter sound of a firing pin striking an empty chamber. He caught a flash of a grin on Michaela's face as the demon somersaulted into open space and came up with the very stick he'd used to trip Q. fifteen minutes ago. The spear-length shaft of wood flew from his hand like a bolt of lightning. There was a wet sound, a thud, a thump, as something, presumably the gun, fell to the loamy forest floor. Leo poised on one knee, his arm still extended from his throw. For a moment his face was expressionless, but then a little smile curled up one corner of Michaela's mouth.

"*Zdravo sestra.* It's been a long time."

Q. lifted his head. Ileana sat with her back against the trunk of a young poplar. Her eyes were closed, her legs splayed, her hands curled around the spear Leo had thrown at her, which was buried in her stomach. Already the huntress's hands were so red it seemed she wore gloves.

Ileana's head jerked up. Her eyes opened, her lips curled back in a snarl. Her teeth were outlined in red, and a thin trickle dribbled down her cheek. He's pierced the stomach, Q. thought. She'll choke on her own blood, if she doesn't bleed to death first.

The huntress spat blood. She said something in a language Q. didn't understand, then made a grab for the gun. She cried out in pain as the spear shifted in her gut, and a fresh well of blood pooled around her fingers. Undaunted, she reached instead for her boot and pulled out the stone knife Q. had seen her sharpen every morning since they'd met.

"It's been *too* long," she said, beckoning Leo with her blade. "Come closer so I can give you a proper welcome."

Leo's laugh echoed so loudly through the forest that a bird flapped from a nearby branch, and, calling in alarm, flew away.

"Oh, you are a fierce one, *sestra*. I feel a kind of belated fatherly pride, finding out that this is what's become of you. I only wish I'd known sooner, so I could have followed your progress more thoroughly." He stood up and walked toward the huntress. "You are Athena to my Zeus, after all, a goddess of war sprung fully formed from my head."

Ileana waved the knife weakly. "Let's see if I can cut my way back inside."

Q. glanced around in search of a weapon. He spied the syringe, saw that the barrel was still half full with whatever serum had incapacitated Jasper. Leo continued to advance on Ileana, slowly, savoring the moment.

Q. wasn't going to get a better opportunity. He threw himself off the paramedic's prostrate body and dove for the syringe.

Leo's head whipped around, but even as he started to move in Q.'s direction there was a gurgling scream from the huntress, half rage, half pain, as she used all her remaining strength to hurl the stone knife at the demon. She threw with no thought of her own survival: the shaft of wood in her stomach was literally lifted up by spasming abdominal muscles, and a sludgy river of blood surged from the wound. Her hands fell to her sides, her head slumped forward. It seemed the stake in her gut was all that kept her from falling over.

But Leo had calibrated her body well all those years ago. Q. was well nigh invulnerable, but Ileana was as close to a killing machine as a human being could be. Her aim was true. The throw was hard. Three inches of razor-sharp stone embedded themselves in Michaela's neck, and a fountain of blood spurted from the wound.

The demon stumbled and sank to his knees. Q. grabbed the syringe. He sprang to his feet and lunged for Leo, but the demon was already up. He staggered out of reach. He would've fallen had a tree not been there to catch his host's body. Michaela's body. The left side of her torso was already coated in blood. From ear to ankle she was awash in a pink-red smear. The sight was so shocking that for a moment Q. forgot what was inside her—forgot that he was trying to kill her—and instead almost ran to her aid. But then she reached up and, shakily but determinedly, pulled the knife from her throat. She held it out as if to show Q. just how far it had penetrated, and then her fingers closed around the blade and snapped it into pieces. Her mouth opened, but all that came out was a stream of blood.

Leo beckoned Q. *Come on,* he mouthed through the viscous bubbles that spewed from his lips. *Bring it on.*

Q. advanced on Leo as warily as the Mogran had walked toward Ileana. One step, another. The hand with the syringe shook so badly that he almost dropped it.

A smile parted Leo's bloody lips, and he gurgled something that Q. thought was supposed to be a laugh. He pushed himself off the trunk unsteadily, wavered a moment, then caught his balance. And then he ran.

Q. was about to go after the demon. But then his eyes were caught by the huntress. He had no idea if Ileana was still alive, let alone savable, but going after Leo would almost assuredly mean her death. And there was Jasper to consider, assuming he, too, was still alive.

Q. looked at the demon's retreating form. It seemed that he was moving faster, as if he was already starting to recover from his wound.

"Fuck!" Q. jammed the cap back on the syringe and started toward J.D. Thomas's car.

A groan stopped him. Q. turned, saw that Ileana had opened her eyes. The fingers of one hand beckoned weakly. He ran to her.

"*Go after Leo.*" The huntress's voice was a whispered croak, and blood spilled from her mouth.

"I can't. You'll die."

Ileana reached for Q.'s hand as if to squeeze it, but all her fingers did was graze it and fall to the shaft in her stomach. She groaned and squeezed her eyes shut. It was a moment before she could speak again.

"We are hunters, Q. That's what we do."

"I won't let you die."

With an effort, Ileana raised her head and looked Q. directly in the eye. Her gray eyes were so icy they were nearly silver, but Q. couldn't tell if it was her wound that made them so cold, or hatred.

"I would have. Let you."

Q., frozen by her words, could only return her gaze. But just before the huntress's head fell forward he saw a flash of something. Defeat. Or . . . or regret.

"No, you wouldn't," he said, and turned to run for the doctor.

"Q.!"

The boy turned back. "You've got to conserve your strength."

"You can't trust him, Q."

"He was *my best friend*."

"Not Jasper." Ileana shook her head so violently that she cried out in pain. *"Thomas."* More blood spurted from the wound in her abdomen, and her lips had turned blue. "I want you to . . . have something." The huntress could barely get the words out. "My . . . *watch*."

15

Absolute darkness.

Total silence.

A lack of all feeling.

For the first time in his life Jasper Van Arsdale understood the difference between *nothing* and *nothingness*. Because this was not merely a void, an absence. The emptiness that enclosed Jasper's soul—imprisoned it, entombed it—was palpable, almost solid.

Jasper wondered if he'd finally, really, died.

For a long time that's all there was. But then Jasper had a thought. He thought. *I'm thinking.* And what is a Mogran, he told himself, if not pure thought? Either connected to every consciousness on the planet in the fleeting moments between bodies, or else embedded in the mind of a single being. Since there were no other voices in his head, Jasper assumed he must still be in Larry Bishop. This nothingness that held him—it *was* Larry. Jasper wondered if Larry had died, not him. Was this the hell the Mogran went to—a silent, screaming eternity trapped within the emptiness of a corpse?

* * *

But.

There was that sense of being frozen. Not coldness—Jasper couldn't feel a damn thing. But there was a . . . tightness. A rigidity, as if Jasper had sunk to the bottom of the ocean and hundreds of atmospheres of water pressure were squeezing him from every direction, holding him in place. He remembered the vision he'd had before he lost consciousness, of the molecules of his body being transformed into crystals, glittering and perfect, but entirely immobile.

I am ice, he thought.

I need to melt.

He made himself imagine Larry Bishop's body. Remember it. The way it had looked before Q. jabbed him with the syringe, and then the crystalline network that had spread through him as the toxin snaked its way through his veins, jumped from one synapse to another along the electric pathways of his nervous system. Time was another thing he couldn't sense in that void, so he had no idea how long it took until his before-and-after shots of Larry Bishop's internal mechanics were complete. But once he had them in his mind's eye he began to compare the two images, to look for what was different, how they'd changed. How to change them back.

Like the alloferine-based curare in the spike hidden inside Ileana Magdalen's watch, Erabutoxin B, the venom of the sea snake, binds to the nicotinic acetylcholine receptors on the motor end plate of the victim's muscles. An influx of positively charged sodium molecules causes the end plate to depolarize, which in turn makes the muscle fibers contract. The fibers are prevented from relaxing, however, by a neuromuscular blockade between the phrenic nerve and the muscle tissue. In the case of the diaphragm, that means all the air is squeezed out of the body and none can get back in. Apnea results; the victim suffocates.

None of this meant shit to Jasper.

For one thing, he had no idea that sea snake venom had been in the syringe Q. stuck him with. For another, he couldn't tell a nicotinic acetylcholine receptor from a nicotine patch. His ability to see the workings of his host's body, while prodigious, hardly extended to the molecular level. What he *could* see, when he compared the two mental images of Larry Bishop's body, was that the muscle fibers seemed shriveled and tough, like beef jerky. They needed to be rehydrated. Even Jasper knew that you can't just soak jerky in water and expect it to turn back into steak, let alone a cow. It was going to take a far more labor-intensive process to reanimate his flesh. He stimulated this gland, that organ. Since he could neither see nor feel what was going on in his body, he had no idea if he was affecting anything at all, or if he was merely imagining it. All he could do was wait for a sign that something, anything, was happening.

For a long time—or what seemed like a long time—nothing happened. Part of Jasper wanted to give up, but another part of him remembered the miracles Leo had worked in Larry Bishop's body after he'd been shot and fallen nine stories. I am Mogran, he reminded himself. I can do anything I want with this body. Anything.

He decided to try a different approach. Instead of thinking negatively, of reversing the process of crystallization, Jasper asked himself if there was a positive approach. If, instead of taking away the thing that had caused his muscles to seize, he could add something that would cause them to relax. As it happens, this is how antivenin works: the antibodies race through the body, attaching themselves molecule by molecule to the toxic agent, thus preventing it from binding to living tissue. In Jasper's case, the process was twofold: he had first to get his body to manufacture antibodies to the snake venom, and then—the *really* tricky part—he had to convince the venom to release its hold on his muscles so that the antivenin could do its work.

It was not a fast process, to say the least. Fortunately, between roadwork and an accident just outside the town of Claverack, what should have been a three-hour drive ended up taking five. Or would have, if Jasper hadn't woken up.

The first thing that came back was the smell of leather. Leather, and the tanginess of Windex. Someone kept his glass clean. Heat then, as of light amplified through a shiny window. Was he on someone's couch? A couch pushed up against a wall, just beneath a window? He felt a tingle in the backs of his thighs, his ass. A vibration. I'm in a car, he thought. Stretched out on the backseat. A big car, he realized, because his knees weren't bent and he didn't feel any pressure on the bottoms of his feet or the top of his head.

Suddenly a flood of sound filled his ears:

"La donna è mobile, qual piùma al vento,
muta d'accento, e di pensiero.
Sempre un amabile, leggiadro viso,
in pianto o in riso, è menzognero.
La donna è mobile, qual piùma al vento,
muta d'accento, e di pensier
e di pensier, e di pensier!"

Jasper knew opera had words, but he'd never thought anyone really understood them. You just kind of listened to the sound they made. It was Larry who recognized the music as *Rigoletto,* supplied him with the libretto. He'd developed an appreciation for Italian opera in prison: a Gotti family capo in the cell next to him liked to use Verdi and Puccini as camouflage when he received visits from a certain inmate named Anton Bamberger, who was usually just referred to as CoCo.

La donna è mobile! his host sang to him. *Wo-men are fick-le!*

Jasper thought of Michaela. Michaela and Q. *Shut up Larry*, he told his host. But he knew he was back.

* * *

Larry's body was oxygen-starved, but Jasper fought the impulse to take deep breaths. Just a few more seconds, he told his suffocating cells, just let me get everything in order and I'll give you all the air you want.

He risked opening his eyes. He had to find out sooner or later whether there was someone in the backseat with him. All he saw was another seat facing his. For a moment he thought he might be on a train, but then he realized it was a limousine. The only person he knew who could afford a limousine was Q.

He looked at the back of the driver's head. The hair was brown, not black, straight, not curly. Not Q. then. Jasper didn't know if he was disappointed or not. At least he didn't have to worry about hurting Q. He was pissed at his friend, and was looking forward to punching him in the face, but he didn't exactly want to kill him in a car accident.

The seat opposite him backed against the driver's seat. An empty seatbelt dangled just beside it. *Garrote the motherfucker!* Larry Bishop sang out gleefully—as with Italian opera, he had learned the word from the Gotti capo, who loved to talk about the relative advantages and disadvantages of various methods of "taking someone out" (garrotes were nice because they didn't make a mess, but you had to know you could overpower your mark until he suffocated). Jasper didn't want to kill anyone, but he figured that if he could loop the seatbelt around the driver's neck he'd probably have to stop the car.

"*La donna è mobile,*" the aria rolled around again, "*qual piùma al vento.*" The driver sang along in a rich tenor. The car was awash in sound, and Jasper deepened his breath, giving his muscles the oxygen they craved. "*Muta d'accento, e di pensier.*" He gauged the distance, saw himself move in his head, jumping, grabbing the seatbelt, looping it around the driver's neck.

"*E di PENSIER!*"

He leapt.

*　*　*

He felt the driver hit the brakes even before he landed. Jasper slammed into the back of the driver's seat. He grabbed the seatbelt but it had locked, so he just went for the driver's throat instead. The man batted at him with one hand while trying to steer the fishtailing vehicle with another. With his left hand, Jasper reached into the man's nostrils and pulled backwards, and even as the man screamed he grabbed for his tie. He couldn't get his fingers around the knot, but they closed around something else instead. A necklace of some kind, a pendant dangling by a length of braided leather cord. Jasper grabbed the ornate metal ornament with both hands and fell backward, hanging off it with all his weight.

He found the driver's eyes in the rearview mirror.

"Stop the fucking car, or I'll choke you to death."

The driver's face was already beet purple. His glasses were askew and his hair stuck out in a hundred directions, but he still had the appearance of being poised. In control. He fixed Jasper's eyes in the mirror, and then, grimly, lips already going blue, he smiled.

The car surged forward as he stepped on the gas.

"What the hell are you doing? You'll kill us both!"

The driver managed to nod his head.

Jasper didn't back down.

"I died in one car crash this week. What's a second one gonna do?"

The driver swerved in and out of traffic. He clipped one car, a second. Horns blared. There was a shower of sparks as the car scraped along the median rail that divided the north- and southbound lanes of the highway, and still the car gained speed. The driver's whole face was blue now. His eyes seemed to float a half inch in front of his cheeks, and little balls of light glowed in them.

"Goddamn it," Jasper screamed, "just die already!"

The driver's lip twitched. Jasper thought he was actually trying to smile. His eyelids sank to half mast. One of his hands fell off the wheel.

Without any warning, the median rail ended and the car swerved into oncoming traffic. Jasper saw a larger-than-life Toyota logo just before the Tundra clipped the left side of the limousine. The tail of the car spun to the right, and then the rear passenger door slammed into the next section of median rail and the car caromed into the air, sideways, spinning like an amusement park ride. Jasper held on to the braided cord with all his strength. His legs whipped around, smashing into the seat and window and the roof of the car, but he didn't let go.

There was a crash then, as something (an Escalade, it turned out) smashed into the limousine and brought it to an abrupt stop. Jasper felt something snap beneath the cord and realized it was the driver's neck. His own body flailed and smashed into the back of the seat, but the padding, and his Mogran physiology, saved him. Like Q., he had come through his accident without a scratch, save for several deep lacerations in his hands, where the ornament on the driver's necklace had cut into his palms. He stared dazedly at the ornament's weird crosses and swirls for a long time before he remembered it was at- tached to someone.

He looked at the driver.

One of the struts that held up the roof of the car had raked across the man's face, which was virtually invisible beneath a caul of blood. The top of his head had been folded back like a blanket, but even so, Jasper figured it was probably the broken neck that had killed him. The driver's head looped over the seatbelt like a deflated balloon. His nose was literally touching his breastplate.

Jasper kicked the cracked glass out of one of the rear windows, but before he hoisted himself through he pulled the necklace off the driver's neck. He wasn't sure why. Maybe he wanted a trophy. A me- mento, to remind him of the first person he'd killed. It occurred to him that a more useful item might be the man's wallet, so he fished around his pockets till he found it. But the only thing in the large billfold were ten crisp hundred-dollar bills, which Jasper pocketed along with the necklace, then shimmied out the broken window. He turned around to look at the car he'd just been in. It was some kind of antique, with flared wheel wells and running boards and a huge mesh grille like the front of a locomotive. It was also . . . twisted somehow, like a cruller or a washrag being wrung dry.

"Oh my God, oh my God, oh my *God!*"

Jasper turned and saw a bulbous man running toward him. The man's belly was shaking up and down so rapidly that his shirt came untucked and a distended sheet of pink-white skin quivered like rice pudding.

"Are you, I mean, how did, I mean, I mean, I *mean*." The man shook his head and his jowls flapped like a bulldog's. "Dude. How are you still *alive?*"

Jasper looked down at the man. That's the million-dollar question, he thought.

In the distance, he heard the sound of an approaching siren. There were horns, the screech of brakes, a lone car alarm, and more shouts as other people got out of their cars, but Jasper's ears zeroed in on one sound. The *ding-ding-ding* of an alert indicating someone had left their keys in the ignition.

He spotted the Dodge with its door open.

"Is that yours? The red Charger?"

The man turned, looked. A little smile curled up his face, as he acknowledged the incongruity of someone like him driving a muscle car.

"Yeah. Traded in my Monte—" He was cut off by a fist to the jaw and crumpled to the ground.

"Sorry 'bout that," Jasper said, and ran for the car.

16

Michaela Szarko's room was "in transition."

Her mother had decorated it in full princess motif: striped damask wallpaper, swagged lilac curtains, acres and acres of lace. A plaster statue of Cupid stood on a plinth in a corner, a reproduction of a Degas hung over the canopied bed. Mrs. Szarko had chosen the painting primarily because the ballerinas' pale blue tutus complemented the Wedgwood blue in the wallpaper, but also because the girls' delicately downcast eyes and rosy cheeks fostered the illusion that the angelic creature who slept beneath them would never do anything unbecoming of their gaze—would never read the kinds of books that had to be hidden under the covers, say, or, those images still present in her mind, tweak her nipples until they grew inflamed, or insert her Sonicare into orifices not specifically recommended by the American Dental Association. And of course she would never, *ever* spread her pale thighs for some teenaged boy who, often as not, didn't even wear a clean shirt.

Well. Jasper hadn't succeeded in pinning Michaela beneath the Degas ballerinas (or anywhere else for that matter), but Mrs. Szarko's aesthetic motif had fared little better. The once-pristine enameled frame of the mirror over the vanity table was all but lost beneath a hot-glued archipelago of rhinestones, postcards, fortune cookie slips, beer and soda caps, ticket stubs to movies and concerts, and about fifty photobooth strips of Michaela and her friends in various states of dress-up and undress. A big sheet of black fishnet had replaced the flounced silk canopy that once covered the bed, and various articles of clothing—most of them black and all of them torn—littered the three-inch white shag like a second carpet. A mustache shaded the lip of one of the ballerinas in the Degas print; Cupid's face was smudged with lipstick kisses. It was a room at odds with itself, the maternal ideal of prepubescent chastity subsumed by the adolescent need to rebel.

Like the room whose occupant he inhabited, the Mogran was also in transition. He'd had so many plans for Jasper. Pranks. Games. Chaos. Short and long plays. Yet somehow he'd never actually asked himself why he'd made a companion in the first place. The fledgling's parting question had nagged Leo ever since the boy asked it by the river. *Why?* Such a human question. The kind of question that implied the existence of a subconscious, of a part of the brain not accessible to the decision-making apparatus, the instantaneous and eidetic memory of a Mogran. But the discomfort Jasper's question gave Leo made him realize that he—yes, even he—had motives he wasn't aware of. Secret desires that flew beneath the radar, just like a human being's. Something that wasn't thought, wasn't emotion. Something that you might call personality, or character, or perhaps instinct. To think that he still possessed the same psychological weakness as a mortal was humbling. It was also infuriating.

The question was, what should he do about it? Should he cut bait? Disappear into the world, leaving the fledgling to his own devices? Or should he eliminate him, just to make sure he didn't come back and bite him in the ass (or stab him in the back, as the case may be)? Or should he make a statement? Take Jasper out "with extreme prejudice," as they said? Jasper and Michaela and Q. and J.D. Thomas and Larry Bishop and Sue Miller—and of course the huntress—just to let anyone who might be watching know he wasn't to be trifled with. No doubt the Alpha Wave had its spies, and would find out about Jasper, if they hadn't already. Leo needed to make sure they thought twice about coming after him. Of course once the Alphas learned about Jasper, they'd suspect one of their own of breaking the Covenant. The fledgling could have been created by chance, of course, as he himself had been, but they would be suspicious at the very least. Who knows what kind of grumblings Foras had made in the past. For all Leo knew, he'd tipped his hand already. That could work to Leo's advantage. To have the Alpha Wave fighting among themselves. They'd held sway long enough.

Leo smiled at himself with his host's pretty mouth. He still hadn't answered his question. Why? But did it matter why? Was it worth saying he was lonely? Did you really have to admit such things to yourself—say them out loud, the way Sue Miller's patients bleated out their insecurities and prejudices, as if self-awareness somehow made you a better person? Stronger?

Call him sentimental, but he still believed the fledgling would come round. But it was clear his ties to his mortal life would have to be severed. That meant his father, and Q. And of course the pretty thing Leo was looking at right now.

After six hours, the gash in her neck had closed, but it was still angry and pink, an eloquent testament to how close the Mogran had come to dying today—about three millimeters, if you wanted to give it a physical measurement. It was the second time he'd nearly died in a week—which, after various jihads, crusades, and a couple of world wars, not to mention the usual array of famines, plagues, shipwrecks, cave-ins, and wildfires, was a pretty spectacular feat for one dead seventeen-year-old to pull off.

The demon cast his mind back to his first years as a Mogran. Had it been this difficult for him to make the transition? Before Foras told him the truth, he believed he'd been born a Mogran, or that the overwhelming psychic trauma of his death had triggered some process that enabled his spirit to loose itself from its bodily home. But now he understood what had really happened in the Coliseum. That the emperor had been possessed by the Mogran known as Julian, and that Julian, for whatever reason, had decided to try his hand in the ring. Leo didn't know what Julian's motivation might have been—his progenitor had long since disappeared into history—and, since Julian wasn't an Alpha, it was unlikely he knew that he'd created Leo. Chances are he'd simply relished the challenge of taking on an army of wild animals in the body of a ten-year-old boy.

It took forty or fifty jumps before Leo realized sex was the catalyst for his exit. But with each new host, he learned a little more about himself, and nearly three hundred years after he died he finally learned exactly what he was, when he attempted to jump into a body only to find himself rebuffed by the presence of another demon. By that time Leo had heard the rumors, of course, legends, myths, tall tales. But that day he learned the truth and was sworn by the Covenant to protect it. For sixteen hundred years he'd abided by its precepts, if only to keep the Mogran off his back, but as far as he could tell the only result of his obeisance was a life of solitude while the Mogran were picked off one by one, until there were none left besides him and the original nine.

A more cynical observer might be tempted to think that was what the Alphas had wanted to happen all along.

Just then there was a knock.

"Mickie?"

Eric Szarko eased open his sister's door.

"You still awake?"

Leo looked at his host's little brother. What was he? Twelve years old? Thirteen?

He let his host out, just a little. Just enough to let her see what he was going to do.

"Eric," the demon said. "It's so *good* to see you." He patted the chair beside him. "Come here."

17

Jasper ditched the Charger in some trees about a quarter mile from Q.'s house. As he approached the Qusays' fence, he clocked himself at forty-two miles an hour. The fence was only twelve feet tall. There were nasty spikes at the top but Jasper was pretty sure he could clear them. Deep inside him, Larry Bishop cupped his balls, but Jasper soared over the fence with a good foot to spare, landed on the other side without breaking his stride. He had to admit, there were certain fun parts to being a Mogran.

The Qusay grounds were covered in trees and bushes, and it was easy enough to get close to the house under their cover. Once there, Jasper made his way around the perimeter. Miranda was at work, idly pushing a vacuum over the carpets as she stared at a reality show. Q.'s parents didn't seem to be around, and there was no sign of Q. either, until Jasper made his way to the back of the house. The windows of Q.'s second-floor bedroom were open; some kind of 200 BPM electronica was pouring into the backyard. Jasper had never been able to figure out how Q. could listen to that kind of crap.

He looked up at the window. There wasn't a tree handy, or a good ol' trellis, or some nice ropy ivy to latch onto. Just two-hundred-year-old bricks that had been sandblasted smooth when the Qusays moved in. So how the hell was he supposed to get up there?

Jasper stared at the window for a good minute before he figured it out. Duh.

He jumped.

His fingers caught the sill and he chinned himself up. Q. was staring so intently at his computer screen that he didn't even notice the additional presence in the room. His face was right up next to the screen. He appeared to be studying a series of medallions or insignias of some kind.

Jasper pulled the pendant he'd taken from the driver's broken neck out of his pocket. Like the images on the screen, it was a circle enclosing a collection of crosses and curlicues. He squinted at the text beneath one of the symbols:

> The 5th spirit is called Marbas—he is a great president, and appeareth at first in ye form of a great Lyon: but afterwards putteth on humane shape at ye request of ye Master. He Answareth truly of Things hidden or secreet, he causeth deseases and cureth them againe & giveth great wisdome & knowledge in mechanicall arts, & changeth men into other shapes. His seal is thus.

Jasper looked around. Unlike his own bedroom, Q.'s was immaculate. Not because he was an unusually clean teenager, but because his parents had a full-time housekeeper. Jasper searched for something to throw, finally just settled for picking up a handy physics textbook and dropping it on the floor.

Q. spun his Aeron desk chair around, nearly knocking it over.

"Jesus Christ!"

"Not quite," Jasper smirked, "but close." He smiled grimly. "Hello, Q."

Q. fumbled for a button and the music went off. Jasper pointed at the screen. "So, what's with the magick?" He enunciated clearly to make sure the terminal *k* came out.

Q. blushed. "They're called sigils. They're—" He shook his head. "The doctor said you wouldn't wake up."

"Doctor?" Jasper waved the pendant on its broken length of leather like a hypnotist's pendulum. "Is this his?"

Q. nodded, gulped. He actually gulped.

"Yeah, the doctor's dead." Jasper took a step into the room. "Would you have preferred it? If I hadn't woken up?"

Q. rolled a few inches away. "I didn't want to hurt you. He–he made me do it. He hypnotized me."

"C'mon, Q. This isn't a Bryan Singer movie. You really expect me to believe some shrink programmed you to take me out?"

"You're *dead*. I think anything goes after that."

"You got me there." Jasper sat down on the bed. "Relax, Q., I'm not going to hurt you. I just want to talk."

Q. stared at his friend. At his strange body, his strange face. At his eyes, as if searching for a trace of the person he'd known. Jasper tried to open himself up as much as he could. He wanted Q. to see him even more than Q. did.

"They said I couldn't trust you," Q. said finally. "They said you'd be different now. Now that you're Mogran."

"I don't even know what a Mogran is, Q. And I am different. But I'm still Jasper."

Q. nodded, gulped. "He made me do it," he said again.

"Whatevs, I don't really–"

"*Leo,*" Q. cut him off. "It was him. Driving. The day you died. I would never do something like that to you. You know I wouldn't."

"I–" Jasper waved his hands helplessly. "I know that." He snorted. "You didn't sleep with Michaela, did you?"

Q. blinked, obviously surprised by the turn in the conversation. "What? Of course not."

"Not even before she and I were dating?"

"Jasper, c'mon. You know every girl I've slept with. I wouldn't've– wait, did *Leo* tell you I slept with Michaela? God, what a fucking loser."

"He killed me, Q. And Sila too, for that matter. Like you said, anything goes after that." Jasper waited for Q. to ask him if Sila had come back too. If she were a Mogran. When his friend remained silent, he understood that Q. knew almost as much about Jasper's new state of being as he did. The silence went on for another moment and then Q. laughed nervously.

"So let's see. On the one hand, we've got the hypnotic suggestion to stab your friend with a needle full of poison, and on the other we've got the classic accusation of infidelity to drive a wedge between friends." He grinned sardonically at Jasper. "Do you get the feeling we're being played from both sides?"

Jasper laughed. "I never knew death was going to be this—"

"Complicated?"

"I was gonna say high school, but yeah, complicated." Jasper nodded at the computer. "So what's with the sigils? I'm assuming they're somehow related to all this."

"It's kind of fascinating. The Legion—"

"I've got a lot of questions about this Legion."

"I bet. Anyway, the Legion has this thing they do, it's also called the sigil. It's supposed to protect its members from—"

"Me?"

Q. nodded sheepishly. "Apparently sigils originated in the Middle Ages, when everyone was all obsessed with witchcraft. They're signs, see, you wear them on your chest. They're supposed to protect you from demonic possession."

Jasper held up the doctor's sigil. "This? Can keep a demon out?"

Q. shook his head. "The modern-day version is a little different."

Jasper waited.

"They cut your balls and your dick off. Or, if you're a woman, I guess they just kind of carve you out. Down there."

Jasper opened his mouth, closed it.

"I know," Q. said. "*Ow.*"

Jasper was about to ask why in the hell anyone would do something like that, but then he got it.

"It's so you can't have an orgasm."

There was a beat, as each registered what the other knew about Jasper's new state of being.

"It's kind of like a trap. If one of the dem—I mean, one of the Mogran possesses a hunter, they won't be able to get out. I guess you—I mean, I guess the Mogran are supposed to know about this, which is why they never try to possess the hunters."

"That must've been in the newsletter I didn't get."

"There are news—" Q. broke off as he realized Jasper was joking. His laugh was a short, forced bark. "Anyway." He turned back to his computer. "These are from a book called *The Lesser Key of Solomon*, which is this medieval grimoire—um, spell book—that's all about demons. It's kind of the Legion's bible. Everyone gets all caught up in rendering the design just right, but when you read about them you see there's actually just as much attention paid to the *alloy* the sigil is made out of—very specific combinations of gold and silver, with a little copper and iron thrown in."

Jasper pointed to his face. "This is me looking confused."

"Right. See, the thing is, some of these alloys come very close to being perfect conductors. The silver allows for the highest speed, while the gold helps to prevent oxidation, and the copper and iron give them strength for durability."

"Again, Q., not getting it."

"Okay, let's back up a second. No one really knows what the Mogran are. I mean, obviously they're a disembodied consciousness, but whether that means they're a soul or a force or just a stray electric current—which is basically all consciousness *is*—is pretty much a guess. But look." Q. scrolled through a few pages on his computer. "This is from the preface."

The Definition of Magick

Magick is the highest most absolute and divinest knowledge of Natural Philosophy advanced in its works and wonderfull operations by a right understanding of the inward and occult vertue of things, so that true agents being applied to proper patients, strange and admirable effects will thereby be produced; whence magicians are profound and diligent searchers into Nature; they

because of their skill know how to anticipate an effect
which to the vulgar shall seeme a miracle.

"This got me thinking. I mean, what if the Mogran are just another
natural phenomenon that we haven't learned to understand? The
ancient Greeks used to think lightning was thrown by Zeus and
earthquakes were caused by Poseidon. So let's say that the Mogran
really are nothing more than an electrical current that's somehow
managed to jump out of a person's brain. If that's true, then it's logical
to assume this current is subject to the same laws of physics that apply
to all electromagnetic energy, which means that once it's outside the
body it'd be dispersed more or less instantaneously along the earth's
electromagnetic fields. But electricity's not like water. It doesn't just
spread out. It's actually drawn from one pole to another, negative to
positive, positive to negative. So, after the Mogran leaves one person,
it's more or less forced to—"

"Jump into another?"

"Another person," Q. nodded, "or something that's such a powerful conductor it can direct the energy away from the body."

Suddenly Jasper understood. He held up the doctor's necklace.
"You're saying that these things, which I guess some alchemy guy
cooked up in his medieval lab, actually *worked?*"

"Well, I imagine it took a lot of trial and error. Who knows,
maybe it was just an accident. Maybe a Mogran tried to jump into
some king's head, but he was wearing a gold crown and that deflected
him."

"But how would the king find out?"

"Maybe he didn't. Maybe only the Mogran knew what had happened, and did some investigating, and ended up leaving a few traces
of what he found in someone's head, and over the centuries those
traces morphed into these." Q. pointed to the sigil in Jasper's hand.
"You guys do that, you know," he added in a quieter voice. "Leave
memories behind. When you jump."

"You should see what you leave in us."

Q. nodded. In a voice that was half fascinated, half wary, he said,

"The doctor told me you can remember everything from everyone you've been in. Is it true?"

"I'm not sure if remember is the word I would use. It's more like I can't forget. Even if I wanted to."

"But you're still in charge, right? It's not like you're three or ten or a thousand different people. Right? The others are just, I don't know, data. You're still Jasper, right?"

Jasper took a long time to answer. He wanted to assuage his friend's fears, but he didn't want to lie to him either.

"I'm doing my best, Q."

Q. was silent a moment, then nodded. He turned back to the screen.

"So. We usually just dismiss this stuff because we assume there's no such thing as demons. But now we know there really are demons, and that got me thinking. The way these sigils are made, they'd basically just act as a deflector. They'd shoot the current back out into the world, where it'd just end up in someone else. But I'm thinking that with a little modification, we can actually trap them *inside* it."

Jasper tensed slightly.

"Don't worry. Even if I had one, I couldn't, like, suck you out of Larry." Q. brought up another page. There was a drawing of something that appeared to be an old-fashioned jar on the screen, sealed at the top and covered all over with more funny-looking signs.

"According to the *Key*, King Solomon enlisted the aid of seventy-two demons to help him build the Temple and defend the kingdom of Judea from attacks. When he wasn't using them, he kept them sealed up in this jar. Again, everyone gets all caught up with the magical signs. But the jar itself? It was made of the same alloy as the sigils."

Jasper stared at the drawing. "I don't get it. Wouldn't that just, whatever you said, just suck the demons in and spit them out again?"

"It would," Q. said, "except the jar was coated in a layer of wax, and sealed with it too."

"Wax doesn't conduct?"

"Zip. Zero. And as long as it's kept at a stable temperature, it doesn't break down either."

"So you're saying that all you have to do is dip one of these sigil things in wax, and presto, you've got a demon trap?"

Q. shook his head. "That's the tricky part. If you coat the sigil in wax first, then it won't attract the demon. But even if you could carry around a bucket of hot wax to dip it in when a demon showed up, you still couldn't do it fast enough. The demons would be in and out in the blink of an eye. You need to find something that's basically a one-way conductor. In but not out."

"And you think you can do this?"

"Yeah, I think we can do this." Jasper's friend looked at him. "We can get him, Jasper. We can get Leo, and we don't have to kill anyone to do it. All we have to do is get him out of Michaela."

"And get him to jump into someone wearing one of these."

Q. smiled. "That's the easy part. The Legion's been tracking Leo forever, they know his habits better than he does. He tends to work his way through what they call an affiliated network pretty systematically."

"In English?"

"He sticks with the friends and family of the person he's possessing. I think he's gonna stay close to the people who knew you, and since you were such a curmudgeonly fuck, that narrows it down a lot."

Jasper's eyes went wide. "Oh shit. My dad."

Q. nodded. "But first—first we have to get him out of Michaela."

"How—" Jasper's eyes went wide. "*Oh.* Shit."

Q. put his hand on Jasper's arm. Jasper looked down at his friend's hand. Q. couldn't know how important it was to him, that he could touch him like that.

But Q. wasn't just touching him. He was taking his watch—Q.'s own watch—off Larry Bishop's wrist. It had been through the wringer in the past week: two car accidents, a nine-story fall, a swim across the Hudson River. The crystal was completely gone now, the face stained, the links dented. But the hands were still there, and they still read 8:32 P.M. The time of Jasper's death.

Q. looked at the watch for a long time, and then he held his wrist out to Jasper. A big silver watch sat there.

"I'd put it on, but I already got a new one."

Six hours of heart-to-heart soul-searching conversation later, Q. pulled his car—no Porsche, but a pretty snazzy BMW nonetheless—into the hospital parking lot.

"Tell me again why we're doing this?" Jasper said.

"You need to get out of this body," Q. said. "In case you forgot, you're wanted for about a dozen crimes."

"Including the sexual assault of the woman you want me to go in there and sleep with. What part of that makes sense?"

"Jasper." Q.'s voice took on a slightly desperate tone. "You need to think of your host."

The word grated in Jasper's ears, but he didn't say anything.

"You said Sue was practically Larry's fiancée. If he's going to have sex with someone, it should be her. You need to make this experience as easy on Larry as you can."

"But does Sue even know him anymore?" Jasper said. "Leo wiped, like, ten years out of her mind. What about her?"

"Jesus Christ, Jasper, I'm trying to make the best of a bad situation. I don't know what to do about Dr. Miller. We've got to take care of who we can. And right now that means Larry. After we've dealt with Leo, we can try to find someone from the Legion, see if they can tell us what we can do for Dr. Miller."

"You're right, you're right." Jasper pulled his borrowed cap over his forehead. "So, I guess I'll find you? After?"

Q. grinned. "I won't exactly be able to pick you out of a police lineup, will I?"

Jasper shuddered.

Q. laughed grimly. "Your third time in a week. Who knew death was such an aphrodisiac?"

"Fuck you, Q.," Jasper said, opening the door. "Don't forget I can always possess you."

"Not if I wear this." Q. held up the doctor's sigil, which Jasper had given him, since he was about to ditch Larry's body. Q. laughed nervously, rubbed his new watch.

He pushed the door closed then, and began lumbering toward the hospital to have sex for the third time in his life. *My name is Jasper Van Arsdale*, he reminded himself. *I am seventeen years old. I have—*

He faltered. What did he have anymore? Immortality. The ability to jump from body to body like a frog leaping from lily pad to lily pad on a cosmic-sized pond. A memory that could retain anything it was exposed to, a body that could withstand almost anything that was thrown at it. Yet all that came to him were his father's words.

I have no face.

As Q. watched Larry Bishop walk into the hospital, his new cell rang. He reached for it without the slightest sense of trepidation. It was barely eleven. Miranda had left messages with both of his parents that he was back, and he assumed it was one of them. The caller ID was blocked, but they both had private numbers.

"Hello."

"Hello, Q." came a voice he thought he'd never hear again. "How's Jasper?"

"Dr. Thomas?" Q. said. "Um, *hi*."

18

Madelaine Szarko had chosen a Monet print to hang over the marital bed. Water lilies, natch. The pastel blossoms went perfectly with the delicate toile wallpaper, and the milky water complemented the fabric that covered the chairs and bed. Only incidentally did it occur to her that there were no faces in the painting. No eyes looking down on her, to see what she got up to while her husband was away. He was in . . . Columbus, was it, or maybe—ugh!—San Diego? She didn't pay much attention anymore. She'd read one of her historical romances for half an hour, filled her mind with images of pirates ravaging damsels' purity. She was ready.

She reached for her jewelry box, lifted out the false bottom, and pulled her old friend from it. It was still slightly sticky from the last time she used it, but she was in too much of a hurry to wash it now. She told herself she would do it after.

She slipped her friend under the covers. Pulled her nightgown up. Closed her eyes.

There was a faint hum as she hit the switch. She smiled in anticipation. Lifted her hips and lay the tip of the vibrator against the folds of her vagina. Letting them both—vagina and vibrator—warm up. In her mind she sat astride a sorrel stallion, her arms wrapped around the tight waist of a man whose face she could barely see. The rich smell of his leather jerkin filled her nostrils, the pulsing of the horse's muscles vibrated in his thighs, her pelvis, her—

A scream ripped the night apart. A scream of pure abject terror—panting, gasping, sobbing, desperate. It was the scream Madelaine Szarko had been waiting for ever since her daughter's miraculous recovery from her injuries.

"No! No! No! No! No! No! No! No! No! No! No! No! No! No! No!"

There was the sound of glass smashing, and then the night went silent, save for the faint electronic hum from beneath the blanket.

4

The Solomon Jar

"Where have you been, my long, long love?"
— *"The Demon Lover,"* author unknown

1

The house John Van Arsdale had inherited from his father was a small building made of jagged chunks of brown stone. The building's squatness was emphasized by a low-pitched roof, its window slits so narrow they gave the place a fortresslike air. A metal plaque at the bottom of the front yard proclaimed that the structure had been built "c. 1690," making it, as John Van Arsdale frequently reminded his son, the oldest building in Greene County.

Whatever value it conferred, the plaque did little to disguise the fact that the house was, for all intents and purposes, a dump. The shingled roof sagged noticeably in the northwest face, and the glowering aspect was equally present inside. The ceilings were so low that Jasper had been able to jump up and touch them since he got his growth spurt. Not with his hand—he didn't have to jump for that—but the top of his head. A quintessentially stupid adolescent activity. Slamming your head into the ceiling just to prove you could. Van Arsdale used to scold his son that each of the dozen concave circles in the living room ceiling represented one less IQ point. "I'm just trying to be more like you, Dad," Jasper had responded, brushing plaster dust from his hair. "Another twenty or thirty, and we should be right at the same level."

Holes in the ceiling. That's all John Van Arsdale had now. A bunch of cracked-plaster dents in the house he'd sacrificed everything for, just so he could leave it to his son.

The building's best feature was the land it sat on. A high hill bounced it right into the sky. The Catskill range dominated the western view, and each night a miraculous sunset played itself out in shimmering bands of orange and red and pink that had defied painters' efforts to do it justice for more than three centuries. To the east the vista was subtler but no less spectacular, an emerald swath of lawn that sloped through a dark copse of oak and maple for nearly half a mile before dead-ending in the black swells of the Hudson. Waterfront property along that stretch of the river was a rare commodity, and over the years dozens of strangers had parked their BMWs and Range Rovers behind Van Arsdale's battered pickup and offered fantastic sums of money for the place. Jasper's father had managed to hold out so far. "You don't sell your legacy," he said to each prospective buyer, and, if he was drunk enough, he'd launch into a long-winded story that had been told him by his grandfather, about how the little stone house had been built by the family's Dutch ancestors when New York was still New Netherland. He would invite the strangers inside and peel back the kitchen linoleum or the living room carpet (both had long since come unglued) to point out the fifteen-inch-wide planks on the floor. "Solid maple," he'd tell them, "hand cut," and he'd stomp to show how well the floorboards had endured three hundred years. If it was summer, he'd walk them into one of the seven-foot-tall fireplaces at either end of the house, where they could look up and see a bright square of daylight. "Now *that's* a flue. You can be sure we never smell a lick of smoke in *this* house." Never mind that a glass of water left in the midpoint between the fireplaces would freeze in winter, that snow, rain, birds, and raccoons made their way down the chimney (and sometimes into the kitchen): that flue sucked up smoke like a crack whore working a ten-dollar pipe.

He spoke like a cross between a realtor and a carnie, but the only thing John Van Arsdale ever sold his prospective buyers were his day-lilies, maybe one or two bottles of his grandfather's applejack. The old man had started brewing during Prohibition. Another part of the family "legacy." In fact the Arsdales were English; John's grandfather had added the "Van" to throw off the Keystone Kops of the 1920s, which is also when he bought the house. But four generations was still a long time—fifteen more years and they'd've qualified for Century Farm status, would've gotten another plaque from the state that told the world this piece of property had belonged to the same proud, hardworking American family for one hundred years. John Van Arsdale freely admitted he'd screwed up everything else in his life—hell, he'd drink a toast to it—but the one thing he'd managed to do was hold on to his legacy so he could leave it to his son. Now he lay on the couch at night and stared up at the shadowed dents in the ceiling and imagined the whole place falling down on him, nothing left but that stupid plaque out front. But the house remained standing as it had for more than three hundred years. It was only his son—his real legacy, the one good thing he'd made in this world—that was gone.

2

*M*ichaela.

Explosions in her brain. Images, memories, not her own. Violence, sexual carnage. The smell of flesh in all its violated forms: burning, diseased, rotting, and, most disgusting of all, the reek of its own natural perfume. The genital musk. Warm, wet, salty, with a sharp acidic bite.

Michaela, it's me.

There were a thousand different ways Leo could have destroyed her mind. He could have wiped it clean, or programmed her to run screaming from a random but frequently occurring stimulus—the color blue, the sound of birds singing—or he could have placed a single overwhelming image in her head: a pustuled penis, say, or the sun going supernova, or a little lamb gamboling through a par- ticolored pasture that exploded into 962,347 yellow petals tipped with digitalis that caused the earth to bleed rivers of chocolate and cucumber slices. But he had gone for something more painful. He had crammed Michaela's mind with millions of memories from all his past hosts, and, to make it especially torturous, tagged them spe- cifically to her senses. Every stimulus Michaela received through eyes and ears and skin unleashed a torrent of mental images that she couldn't have processed even if they'd come from her own ex- perience. But the fact that they came from thousands of other lives left her catatonic and quivering with the only emotion that could make itself felt in the midst of so much chaos: pure, unadulterated terror.

Michaela, it's Jasper.

If she felt an itch in her cheek, she had to wade through a thousand personalities, journey across all seven continents (Leo had been to Antarctica in thirteen different bodies) before it occurred to her to raise her hand and scratch it. A more complex feeling like hunger was virtually unparseable. A hundred thousand meals flashed in her mind: tabouli from Syria, arepas from Venezuela, xiao long bao from Jiangsu province, beef stroganoff from Russia, ceviche from Peru, harira from Morocco, gnocchi from Sicily, onion baji from the Indian Deccan, huitlachoche from Oaxaca, baba au rhum from Slovakia, alicha wat from Ethiopia, yakisoba from Japan, lutefisk from Norway, venison jerky from the Algonquin Nation, étouffée from New Orleans, and thousands upon thousands of other dishes, all spewed from a subconscious that had once been a simple dark well in which the usual assortment of painful memories lurked, but which was now a chasm that made the Grand Canyon look like a scratch drawn by a chicken claw. Though her autonomic nervous system might cause her mouth to water, she could never wade through the flood of memories to realize that what she needed to do was eat, let alone articulate that fact, or perform the simple mechanical functions necessary to bring food to her lips.

I'm here, Michaela.

And yet there were things even worse than all that, the memories that were indisputably, undeniably, her own. The memories of the last week. Of the car accident, of her coma and recovery, of that day at the river with Q. and the stranger who had called himself Jasper, and, illuminating all the others like an atomic explosion, of Eric.

Her brother Eric.

Coming into her room, a concerned look replacing the usual mischievous spark in his eyes. For thirteen years he'd been the prototypical bratty little brother who waterbombed her slumber parties, loosened the lid on the salt shaker, stretched cellophane over the toilet bowl. But now, because his big sister had miraculously recovered from injuries that should've killed her, or left her paralyzed and a vegetable, he'd come contritely into her room to let her know he was there for her. That he would help her out if she needed anything. Anything at all. And she had looked at him with eyes that fixed him like a deer in headlights. Her little brother. She had held out a hand, drawn him to her side, and from there to her bed. She had gazed into his eyes until his pupils widened and softened and his free will practically leaked out of him like smoke, and then she had undressed him. She had told him what she needed, and he had given it to her. Told him to think of her body as a gift, and he had taken it. Her little brother. He had mounted her mechanically, and only the sudden onslaught of screaming after she came snapped him out of it. Drove him from her bed and from the room. Not by the door—the window. Now it was her brother who was in the hospital fighting for his life, and she—she would have to live with the memory of what she had done to him forever.

Michaela, I'm here to help you.

And now this voice. Why *this* voice of all voices? Why Jasper's?

Michaela, listen to me. I can help you.

No, she said, though whether she said it aloud she didn't know. *You're not real. No more real than anything else in my head.*

Michaela, it's me. I'm here. I'm really here.

No!

Michaela, you have to trust me. I can get you through this.

She didn't believe in the voice, but focusing on it made all those other voices go away. At least this one spoke English. At least it pretended benevolence.

That's better. I'm getting control now. Just relax.

God, how she wanted to relax. To sleep. Just sleep. Never to wake up again. Never to face the consequences of what she'd done. What she'd become.

Not that relaxed! A chuckle, somewhere inside her. *We've got work to do.*

Could it really be?

"Jasper?" she said out loud.

It's me, Michaela. It's really me.

"But . . . but how?"

It's a long story.

3

The applejack stills were gone too, and most of the orchards. There were about eighty trees left, McIntoshes and Cortlands mostly, which reflected the mass marketing of the apple economy in the sixties and seventies, when growers had to sell in bulk to grocery stores or go bust in the wake of competition from Washington State and China. When Van Arsdale assumed control of the farm in '81 after a completely forgettable three-year stint in the Navy, he'd taken an axe to the worst of them all, the Red Delicious, which in his opinion looked like a bell pepper and tasted like a potato. Three hundred trees his father had planted in 1947: John was pretty sure he made more off the firewood than they'd ever earned from those mealy apples. His idea was to replace the mass-market trees with more rarefied varietals, Mutsus and Macouns, Braeburns and Winesaps, each delicious in its own way, but all difficult to grow, and requiring economies of scale that a small farm like his just couldn't produce. In the end he'd been forced to sell off the land a parcel at a time. There was an estate to the Van Arsdales' south now, some internet millionaire who'd built a Rubik's cube of a mansion that glowed like a lighthouse at night, while Apple Acres, a small condominium development, (Grannysmith Lane, Idared Avenue, blah blah blah) stood to the north. On the rare occasions the elder and younger Van Arsdale were in the same vehicle, the father would point out the bland, vinyl-sided apartments to his son: "See that, Jasper? That's your college fund right there."

Aside from the narrow strip of land between the house and the river, John kept just one four-acre field immediately north of the house, on which he grew daylilies.

"Why daylilies?" was a question he heard often enough (from his smart-aleck son especially) to which he usually answered "Why not?" There were a lot of good answers to *that* question, chief among them the fact that flowers brought in less than apples, and were more work besides. But even before Jasper died and his father found himself in possession of his son's college fund, John Van Arsdale didn't give a rat's ass about money. He'd started growing the flowers after his wife and daughter died. He always said it that way, "wife and daughter," even though his daughter had never seen the light of day. Never taken a breath of air or a drink of milk, never even had a name. There's something profoundly disturbing about a six-months-pregnant woman in a casket, unholy even, and when it's your wife, well, John Van Arsdale was pretty much done after that. No bottle on earth was deep enough to drown that sight. But on the drunken nights immediately following her death, when he'd searched his heart for some trace of Amelia, it was their nameless daughter who came to him. She was a warm weight on his chest, like a kitten curled up to sleep, or a gentle touch at the back of his head. John liked to think she'd been spared the horrors of this world—the farms that went bust and the spouses who died and the sons who were as strange to you as people you passed on the highway. His daughter's comforting presence seemed to tell him that life would go on, that it *should* go on, and he should be a part of it. It was this feeling that had led him to the Beech Blossom only a week after he'd buried Amelia, and from there to the bed of a woman whose name he never could remember (he called her Blossom in his head, after the bar, although sometimes he just called her a Beech). Sleeping with her had been close to a compulsion. It had seemed to him that he was honoring Amelia's memory—she'd been so full of life, she'd want him to be happy—but after it was over he just felt dirty. Guilty. *Empty.* Even the comfort of his daughter's presence had vanished, as if she'd been ashamed of what he'd done in her name. So he'd gone from bar Blossoms to garden-variety ones.

I.e., daylilies.

It was right after Amelia died that he sold the big north parcel to the real estate developers, banked enough money for Jasper to go to any school in the country and set up what was left over to dole out enough to get by on, then started with his flowers. What initially drew him was the fact that each bloom only lasted a day, but, since there were six or eight buds on every stalk and three or four stalks to every plant, you had flowers for weeks at a time. Life's brevity, symbolically speaking, coupled with the endurance of generations, all in one beautiful package. Then, too, there was the fact that daylilies were easy to care for, pest resistant, good in sun or shade, which made them easier to sell than roses or orchids or some extra-fancy flower like that. Only later did he discover that the daylily was a relatively simple plant to hybridize. All you had to do was make a little plant love—i.e., take the stamen of one flower and touch it to the pistil of another, and then gather and grow the seeds that ripened a few weeks later. Cross-pollenization, just like the bees did it, albeit a little more systematically. But if you kept good records and were patient, eventually you would create your very own flower: the color and pattern you desired, the number and type of sepals, the height of the stalk, the frequency of blooms. You could even register its name with the American Hemerocallis Society for the whole world to see. John Van Arsdale had developed dozens of minutely different flowers over the years, but he'd only registered two: *H.* "Baby Jane Doe" and *H.* "Amelia V.A." The former was a simple peony-type double, as full as a rose but much more delicate, with scalloped white petals growing from an iridescent pale yellow throat: a simple, lovely flower, all the more so because it only bloomed at night, opening up like the full moon and withering before sunrise. The latter was much more flamboyant, like Amelia had been: a polysepalous spider, four iris purple petals alternating with four sepals in a paler violet. The sepals were more than six inches long, and—the detail that had won him honorable mention from the AHS for hybrid of the year–they were tipped with long gold hairs, which gave the blossom an air of peacock pomposity. It had taken him fourteen years to breed that flower. Nearly the whole of his son's life. Now he planned to dedicate the rest of whatever time was left to him to producing his final hybrid. He hadn't decided what flower configuration or petal type he wanted yet, but he knew what color the flower would be. The rarest of all daylily hues, the hardest to produce: true blue.

Jasper blue.

Hemerocallis "Jasper V.A."

The morning after he found the stranger sleeping in his barn, he made his way out to the field as he normally did. He got all the way out to the field before he remembered he hadn't fed Gunther. Van Arsdale had gotten the pup as a present for his son two years ago–what kind of boy didn't like dogs, right? But that wasn't fair to Jasper. He liked dogs just fine. But he'd been fifteen, his Timmy-and-Lassie phase long gone. Girls were on his mind now, sports, parties, borrowing the truck. He'd gamboled about with the puppy for a few months but you could tell he was forcing himself, and after Michaela entered the picture Gunther faded from his memory like a Polaroid left in a sunny window. It was all Van Arsdale could do to get his son to feed the dog in the morning.

Now, as he approached the cage, Gunther began dancing around, a line of spittle stretching from lip to earth. The kennel was twelve foot square, nicely placed under a horsechestnut that used to have a tire swing hanging off it. In the past year Gunther had dug the floor of the cage down a good foot and a half. It wasn't right, Van Arsdale thought. A two-year-old dog the size of a mountain lion deserved to run free. Deserved to chase birds, rabbits, squirrels, possums, or cars if he felt like it. Dogs were rangers, marking and tracking their territory. They shouldn't be locked up like this.

The rottweiler glanced up at Van Arsdale anxiously as he opened the door, then turned his attention back toward the river. He ignored the scoop of kibble his master dumped in his dish, the bucket of fresh water.

"Damn it, Gunther. You know I can't let you out."

The dog snatched a bite of kibble, chewed it open-mouthed, his eyes darting between Van Arsdale's face and the wide gray strip of water. Van Arsdale looked at the river. The dog had never shown much interest in it before. Then Van Arsdale realized Gunther was actually looking at the wellhouse off to the side of the property. He wondered if maybe a raccoon had holed up in there, made enough noise to attract the dog's attention. Something about the wellhouse nagged at Van Arsdale's brain, but he was too muddleheaded these days to think what it was.

Gunther flashed his master another look.

"Don't look at me that way, dog. It's your own damn fault. If you could just stay outta trouble we wouldn't have to keep you in here."

Van Arsdale heard the word. *We.* He winced.

Bits of kibble and saliva splattered from the dog's mouth. He deftly evaded Van Arsdale's hand when he reached to pet him. He didn't want a scratch between the ears. He wanted to run. To mark his territory and check for intruders.

"Damn it, Gunther." Van Arsdale stared into the dog's big brown eyes, but what he saw was the stranger's eyes. From yesterday. The eyes that had looked at him as if they knew him. As if he, Van Arsdale, should have known the stranger.

"Fine." He kicked the door of the kennel open. "But don't blame me if someone shoots you in the head."

The dog darted out of the gate before Van Arsdale could change his mind. He tore across the long slope of the backyard, those massive rottweiler shoulders propelling him over the ground like a wraith of black smoke, kettledrum barks erupting from his throat. He made a beeline for the wellhouse, but when a mourning dove cooed its way into the air he veered off to the left, and then a rabbit bolting for a clump of laurel led him further uphill.

"Yeah, you'd better run," Van Arsdale said under his breath, but he wasn't sure who he was talking to: the dog or his prey, or the stranger from yesterday.

Those eyes. The way they'd looked at him. As if they knew him.

Van Arsdale shook his head, pretended he was shaking the memory out of his brain, but as he made his way back to the lily field he saw the pitchfork standing in the ground where Jasper had left it last week. The last day he'd been alive.

The pitchfork! That was it! He glanced back at the wellhouse. He needed to gather a few loads of bat droppings for fertilizer. He usually did it right after Jasper turned over the soil in the garden, but, well . . .

He looked again at the abandoned pitchfork. The upright handle had the air of a signpost missing its sign—an historical plaque like the one in front of the house, or maybe just a crossbar with a name and a couple of dates on it. No need to get any fertilizer now, Van Arsdale told himself. Not till he'd finished turning over the soil. For some reason he thought that might take a while.

Gunther's barks grew fainter as Van Arsdale climbed the stone stairs to the field. He stopped when he came to the loose slate about three-quarters of the way up the hill, remembering how the stranger had stepped over it yesterday, as if he knew just where it was. It was eerie. Goddamned eerie.

On days like today, when he found it hard to concentrate, he didn't try to breed. Instead he worked the soil. Like his son, Van Arsdale enjoyed the feeling of honest labor in his bones and muscles. He'd've broken the ground with his fingers if he could have, if the schist and granite in the soil wouldn't've cut his hands to pieces. He worked till he'd done one hundred-foot-long row, then another, then a third, far more than he'd need for his upcoming plantings. But every time he slowed he had a fierce sensation of eyes staring at the back of his head, and his mind would fill with yet another vision of the nearly naked stranger in his kitchen, eating his food, putting on his son's clothes, staring at Van Arsdale as if he knew him. The way he'd stepped over that loose slate. Without even trying it first! Forget what he said about knowing Jasper, about being friends with Michaela, forget about the possibility that he might've been to the house a couple of times when Van Arsdale wasn't around. Even Van Arsdale sometimes forgot where that step was, and he'd climbed up and down that staircase for forty years. But he had watched his wife rot away from cancer until she was nothing but skin and bones and a grotesquely swollen womb. He had gone to the morgue and identified his son by his clothes and the sickle-shaped scar on his left hip because his face had been ripped off. He did not believe a benevolent deity had sent his son back to him for one final goodbye. If anything had come back, it was no longer his son.

He didn't realize it had been hours since he'd heard any sign of Gunther until a sudden round of barking caused him to jerk his head up, just as the dog burst through a pair of 180-year-old Newtons and tore into the field. Say what you want about the dog (whose smiling muzzle was visibly covered in blood), he knew better than to knock even a single petal off one of John Van Arsdale's flowers.

As the dog got closer, Van Arsdale saw there was more than blood on him. The dog's hide looked like a scratch-n-sniff poster, blotched with what looked like honey, axle grease, fry oil, several different colors of mud, and something that smelled enough like shit that John Van Arsdale shooed the dog away when the animal tried to jump on him to express his appreciation. He glanced up at the sky, saw the evening lightshow just starting over the mountains (*H.* "Catskill Sunset" was a flower he'd been trying to breed for a decade, but so far nothing he'd come up with was worthy of the name).

"All right, Mr. Gunther, let's hose you off and get us both some dinner."

The dog ran ahead of him, still barking constantly. He raced down the hill at such high velocity that he nearly tumbled ass over heels into the river, then came barreling uphill toward a robin that stared cockeyed at the barking dog before lazily taking to the sky and alighting on a branch of a sugar maple.

"You know, if you shut up once in a while you might actually *catch* something," Van Arsdale said to the dog, shuffling up to the hose coiled on a spindle mounted to the barn wall. In answer, Gunther shook himself from stem to stern, bits of blood flying off his muzzle and splattering the barn's faded wood with red drops, as if in direct refutation of his master's claims. When Van Arsdale turned on the spigot the dog launched into a fresh round of barking, snapping at the water with his huge teeth before letting Van Arsdale spray him clean. He barked all the way through the operation, the sound echoing off the wall of the barn until Van Arsdale's ears were ringing.

"Enough already! Goddamn dog. Barking fit to wake the—"

That's when the demon took him.

4

It was hard not to hurt her. To slip in softly, let his essence mold itself to the shape of Michaela's mind rather than smashing it out of the way as he'd done to Jarhead and Larry—unintentionally, but still, he'd done it. But he knew he had to be gentle if he wanted to help her, if he didn't want to leave her worse off than she'd been. He imagined himself as a magnum of champagne being poured into an enormously tall thin flute; he had to trickle from his bottle into the glass or else he'd knock it over and break it or it would foam up and spill over the top.

Then there was everything else. Michaela. Michaela's memories. Michaela's feelings. He told himself he wouldn't look, but he had no hands to cover his eyes. Her whole life lay before him. The car accident and the coma. The sex with Adam McCluskey. The demon's entrance. The demon's exit.

Jasper seethed with rage when he saw what Leo had made Michaela do with Eric. He could practically hear the demon chuckling. *Two lives destroyed for the price of one . . .*

But all of this was scattered, broken up into bits and pieces like a fragmented hard drive. It took Jasper a moment to understand what all the intervening material was, but finally he realized it had come from Leo. The Mogran had dumped the experience of thousands of lives into Michaela's brain. No wonder she was so confused. So terrified.

There were too many external memories for him to wall them off individually. He had to gather them into one unit first, and he had to do it without hurting Michaela. He felt like the proverbial bull in a china shop—a bull dragging a wagon loaded with a pallet of bricks—and he had to do his level best not to chip a single platter, break even one delicate teacup. The whole operation seemed to take an eternity. He was learning that this period of acclimation was the scariest, most vulnerable part of being a Mogran. It didn't matter if it lasted a fraction of a second or a few hours: until he was firmly rooted in his host's psyche he had no way to experience the passing of time, so he had no idea how long it was taking, what was happening to his host's body. He could've been in Michaela for a day or two already, or just a few seconds; her flesh could be on fire, or falling through space. It was all meaningless to him.

Gradually, though, as he managed to shunt off more and more of the wadding Leo had stuffed into Michaela's brain, he began to be aware of her. There were lingering traces of pain: the damaged spots where Ileana's gunshot had clipped Michaela's shoulder and her knife had pierced her neck. But he felt as well the incredible strength Leo had given her to resist these injuries. The demon had practically rebuilt her from the inside out. Again he marveled at what a Mogran could do. She was in better shape than Larry even. Not invulnerable maybe, but as close as a human being could come to it. If he hadn't come along, she would have lived a long and tortured existence with Leo's memories polluting her brain. He only hoped he'd be able to fix that.

Now he became aware of his surroundings. He didn't recognize them at first, had to turn to Michaela for the answer. He was in the attic. Michaela's memories since Leo had left her were especially chaotic, but he was finally able to see that her mother had brought her up here when she'd taken Eric to the hospital. Madelaine Szarko, who'd been known to have a conniption fit when deer ate the buds off her peonies, had taken Michaela by the arm and half carried, half dragged her naked daughter up the narrow attic steps and locked her in, then followed the ambulance with Eric in it to the hospital. Jasper had to admit he was impressed.

It's not that weird. My mother's not completely helpless you know.

Jasper started. He'd forgotten where he was.

"Michaela?"

He could feel her hesitation—her fear that she'd completely lost her marbles, coupled with her hope that it really was Jasper.

Is it—is it really you?

"It is me, Michaela. I'm here. I'm with you."

You're kind of in *me, actually.*

Jasper laughed—and was surprised when the sound came to his ears. It was hard to remember that *he* was the one manipulating Michaela's body. That she was the voice in his head.

Tell me I'm not crazy, she said now.

"You're not crazy," Jasper said, standing up. The attic was huge, a single room spanning the full length of the Szarkos' classic five-bay colonial. Boxes and old furniture and the refuse of a pair of child-hoods lined both sides of the room—hobby horses and dolls and action figures, Radio and Flexible Flyers, outgrown training wheels, abandoned bicycles—with a wide path running between. At the far end of the path a mirror stood, and in its heavily dusted glass Jasper could just make out Michaela's silhouette, naked, pale, ghostly. He began walking toward it. He could feel Michaela see it too. Could feel her seeing the word. *Ghostly.*

Are you—are you like the other one? The one who was here before?

Jasper continued walking toward the mirror.

"I'm not *like* him, Michaela. I would never hurt you."

He stood before the mirror now. He looked at Michaela's body. He had never seen her naked before. He felt her blush inside him. Then:

So you really are *dead?*

He pulled the sheet from an old couch, used it to wipe the dust from the mirror. Just enough to see Michaela's face. He nodded her head, watched it nod in the mirror.

"I'm dead."

He felt Michaela looking at herself though his eyes. Felt her grow shy.

Don't you dare—

But he was already wiping the rest of the dust away. Her neck. The top of her breasts. Her breasts themselves. He had felt them through her shirt and under her shirt, but he had never seen them uncovered. Never touched their flesh and seen himself touching them. He reached a hand toward the glass, and then, laughing slightly, pulled back and placed it on the actual breast. Ran a finger beneath its curve. Traced the nipple with a nail.

Jasper! Michaela protested.

And yet he could feel her enjoying it, despite what had happened only an hour ago with Eric. With a start, he realized that this was what the Mogran did to their hosts. Regardless of what other changes they made, there was always this impulse toward the erotic—the sexual, the release. Full of disgust at what he'd become, he jerked his hand—no, Michaela's hand—from Michaela's breast. He threw the sheet away, left the rest of the mirror, the rest of her body, shrouded in dust. It was only after the fact that he realized Michaela had followed all this. He felt her curiosity even before she spoke.

What's a Mogran? Is it like a ghost?

"I guess so. I don't really know." He thought of the Legion, its hunters and gatherers. "Some people call us demons."

He saw Michaela's head nod in the mirror. Realized it was her nodding it. Realized she could do that, if he let her. If he didn't get in her way.

That one who was here before. He was *a demon. A demon from hell.*

"You're safe from him," Jasper said quickly. "He can never get you again."

He could feel Michaela laugh.

I don't think you have to talk out loud. It might look weird.

He was about to ask to whom, but then he realized Michaela was way ahead of him.

It was him? Leo? In Q.? He killed you and Sila?

Jasper nodded.

We have to stop him, Michaela told him then. *He can* never *do this to anyone again.*

"You realize he made a few changes to your body," Jasper said as he ran to the door at the far end of the room.

What do you me—

Michaela broke off when Jasper kicked the door open. It exploded from its hinges.

Jesus!

He dressed quickly, grabbed her phone from the dresser. Q. answered on the first ring.

"Michaela?" There was a question in his voice. A big question.

"It's me, Q."

It's both of us, Michaela said, *but whatever. You take charge, Mr. Man.*

"Jasper?" Q. said. "Where the hell have you been? It's been *three hours.*"

"I know. I'm sorry. I'll explain when you get here. Just pick me up at Michaela's. No wait, her mom might come home."

"Her mom's here."

"Where—at the hospital?" An image of Eric's body hurling itself through the window flashed through his mind, followed by a stabbing pain of guilt and revulsion. *It's not your fault*, he told Michaela. To Q., he said, "Is he . . . ?"

"Eric? He's okay. A few broken bones, nothing life-threatening. I'm afraid to ask what happened."

Don't tell him! Michaela almost screamed in his mind.

"Ow!" Jasper said out loud. Then, in a quieter voice: "I'll let Michaela explain. Right now you'd better come get me."

"Just one thing," Q. said. "I know where Leo is."

5

The demon slammed into him so hard that Van Arsdale actually fell forward and dropped the hose. Gunther started and jumped out of the way as his master twitched and writhed and beat at his head.

"Go away!" he screamed. "Get out of me! Get out of my head!"

Inside him, Leo was shocked by the vehemence of Jasper's father's resistance. It was almost as if his host had been expecting him, had been prepared to fight him.

But it wasn't the demon's presence that Van Arsdale was fighting. It was the sudden, electric wave of hatred for his own son that flooded into him. All his guilt and feelings of inadequacy as a father erupted inside him, even as his beleaguered paternal love screamed out against the charge. He felt as if his brain had been ripped in half, that a pair of cosmic hands were smacking the two sides into each other over and over again in an effort to stick them back together.

"No! I do not believe! I do not believe!"

It was a valiant effort, but doomed to fail. Leo snapped synapses ruthlessly, slowly but efficiently cutting his host off from himself, imprisoning him in his own body, his own mind. Van Arsdale's limbs slackened and his twitching took on a lazy, swaying quality, as if he were a marionette whose puppeteer had laid down his strings. Leo was so busy trying to assume control of his host's mind that he could barely keep him on his feet. Such a fight he was putting up!

The demon chased the last remaining shreds of his host's free will down one mental back alley after another. At one point he caught a trace of the unborn child, found the comfort his host had taken in her presence and called on those old feelings.

Daddy, he whispered. *Daddy, it's me.*

Van Arsdale was confused. "Baby—baby girl?"

If Van Arsdale had picked out a name for his daughter, Leo's trick might've worked. But Leo had been hasty, and Van Arsdale was confused: his daughter had never called him Daddy, just as he'd never given her a name. In a flash of purely instinctual insight, Van Arsdale realized he couldn't defeat the thing that was inside him. Realized also that if he gave in it would somehow cause irreparable harm to his son. The pleading eyes of the stranger in his kitchen flashed before him one last time. With a final, supreme effort, John Van Arsdale did the only thing he could think of: he threw himself down the stone steps that led from the top of the hill all the way down to the river.

Four hundred ninety-two steps. They—Leo and John—were about a hundred steps from the top, but still, there was more than a quarter mile of hill to fall down. Almost four hundred sharp-ended pieces of bluestone to slam and slice their way into Van Arsdale's flesh. Leo had been too caught up in the mental effort of assuming control, hadn't had a chance to do anything with his host's body. Couldn't protect him—couldn't protect himself. Ribs broke, his hip, his right humerus, the tibia in his left ankle. His skull fractured above his right ear and bits of bone pressed through the meninges into the soft tissue of the brain. It was Van Arsdale's bones that broke, but it was Leo who screamed in pain and rage as the world flashed orange, red, purple and then black.

For the first time all day, Gunther was speechless. He approached the prostrate body at the edge of the river warily, sniffed it curiously. There were a bunch of beer bottles down there, an empty Styrofoam cooler, a man's belt; at the river's edge there were a half dozen rotting fish skeletons as well, dozens of tiny cracked snail shells. Gunther sniffed at each of these in turn before returning to Van Arsdale's fallen body. He licked his master's face and got no response. He whined, yipped, let out one nervous bark. Nothing. A flash of movement caught his eye—a rabbit!—and, barking uproariously, he ran off into the bushes.

A few minutes later, a second, ghostly figured emerged from the trees. Its hands were pressed over its ears and its face was contorted in pain. It lingered a moment over John Van Arsdale's fallen body, then, having determined the man wasn't Jasper—wasn't someone who could turn off the wall of sound that battered his eardrums—it proceeded to the river. This is where Jarhead had last seen Jasper when he was alive, and this is where he'd first seen him after he died. This is where he would see him again, when he returned.

Jarhead waded into the river. The cold water washed the bat droppings from his skin, but that wasn't why Jarhead submerged himself. It was, rather, the protective muffling the water provided. The world had been shrieking at him for two days now, and nothing he did could turn down the volume. Even the bat's creaks pierced his ears, seemed to stab right into the center of his brain. His head throbbed; he was dizzy; he didn't understand how this had happened. All his life he'd wished he could hear like normal people, but if this is what the world sounded like he'd rather be deaf.

The river closed over his ears, proffering its blessed silence. Jarhead pulled himself into deeper water and let his body sink down, his eyes open and staring into the murky depths, giving him the appearance of a fetus floating in its mother's womb. Without thinking he opened his bladder, and a faint yellow cloud stained the water a moment before dissipating. His arms and legs moved slowly, just enough to keep him from rising to the surface, but when a two-foot pike moved in for inspection, Jarhead's right hand darted out and caught the fish just behind the head. The pike's tail churned the water rapidly until Jarhead squeezed so tightly that he shattered the fish's spine. Reluctantly, he made his way to the surface. The cold enveloping stillness was the only thing able to soothe his aching head, but, sadly, he still hadn't learned to eat underwater.

6

Q. stared at Michaela for a long time.

"This is, you know. A little weird."

"You're telling me," Jasper said. "I'm the one who's dead, remember?"

Q. checked his rearview mirror, then turned around to look at the road before he pulled away from the curb. It didn't look like he was checking traffic though. It looked like he was checking to see if anyone was following them. Without looking at Jasper, he said, "So tell me again what happened to Dr. Thomas."

Jasper balled Michaela's hands into fists as he recalled the feeling of the sigil's cord against the psychiatrist's neck. The man had somehow programmed Q. to poison him, had apparently planned some kind of torturous interrogation. But still. He hadn't meant to kill him.

"I told you, Q., it was an accident—"

"I don't care about that," Q. said, heading swiftly out of town. "What I mean is, how dead was he?"

"Huh?"

"Cuz he called me. Right after you went in the hospital. And what I'm thinking is, either you totally misjudged his condition, or a demon jumped in and fixed him up. And, you know, I have no idea how many of you there are floating around out there, but I'm thinking the chances that it's *not* Leo are pretty slim."

Jasper remembered the way the doctor's head had dangled off his shoulders.

Fuck, Michaela said inside him.

"Fuck," Jasper said out loud.

"Fuck is right," Q. said. He looked over at Michaela. Looked her up and down. Touched the spot on her neck where Ileana's knife had sunk in. "Jesus fuck."

"Does he know? That you know he's Leo?"

"I think I played it cool. He said he was back in the city, but who knows if he was telling the truth."

Q. was quiet for a long time. Finally he cleared his throat. "Is she . . . I mean, is Michaela in there?"

Michaela giggled inside him. *Where does he think I'd be?*

Jasper smiled at Michaela's joke. He nodded at Q.

"The reason it took me so long to call you is that I didn't want to hurt her. I mean, there isn't an instruction manual or anything. I just had to go on instinct. Feel my way in. I did okay with Larry, but I think I might've messed Jarhead up a bit."

"So that *was* his voice!" Q. said. "I thought I recognized that bray. The cops came to the hospital," he added in a more serious voice. "They arrested Larry."

Jasper nodded. "You were right, though. Sleeping with Sue—"

There was a protest inside his brain. *Who the hell is Sue?*

Not now, Jasper told her. To Q.: "Is there anything we can do for Larry?"

Q. shrugged. "I have no idea. But I've got some money of my own. I can at least get him a good lawyer."

"It's a fucking mess, isn't it? I mean, all this power, these amazing abilities, and all we can do is screw up people's lives."

You saved me, Michaela said.

"Yeah, but I can't spend eternity running around after Leo cleaning up his messes, can I?"

There was a moment of silence in the car, and then Q. said, "You weren't talking to me, were you?"

"Like you said, Q. She's in here."

"Can she hear me?"

Michaela would've rolled her eyes if she controlled them. Instead she said, *Roll my eyes, would you, Jasper?*

"We have to stop him, Q. He can't keep doing this."

"He's been doing it for hundreds of years. Thousands maybe."

"I don't care! We have to *stop* him."

Q. looked over at the passenger seat. His eyes took in both of them. Mogran and host. His living friend, and the friend he had killed. "You know what that means, don't you?"

Jasper met his friend's gaze. "I know what that means."

"But how do you make that choice?" Q. said. "How do you decide you have the right to kill an innocent person, just because they've been possessed by some asshole demon? Would you kill me if I was Leo's host? Would you kill Michaela?"

Jasper was silent for a moment. Q. had made his point. Then:

"You were talking about those sigil things before. You said there might be a way to trap the demons in them."

Q. shook his head. "That's just a theory. I have no idea how it would work in practice."

"If Solomon could figure it out—"

Solomon who? Michaela said.

"King Solomon," Jasper said out loud.

Q. laughed. "Michaela again?"

"I know, it's confusing me too. Just pretend she's on the phone."

"Right," Q. said. "So look. I have no idea what King Solomon did or didn't do. I mean, somehow I doubt he really had seventy-two demons at his beck and call, and that he kept them in a clay jar sealed with beeswax."

"Forget Solomon. Think physics. You said you thought we, I mean, the Mogran, are essentially electrical currents."

"I said it was a theory. No one knows. I mean, no one's ever heard of an electrical current attaining consciousness before."

"Just because no one's ever noticed it doesn't mean that it's not happening all around us. We just haven't figured it out yet. What did your book say? 'Magicians are profound and diligent searchers into

Nature who because of their skill know how to anticipate an effect which to the vulgar shall seem a miracle.' "

"Nice quoting."

"Yeah, whatever. Anyway, your theory is the best we've got to go on. I mean, if it fails, it fails. But it's worth a try. The question is, is there some kind of device that absorbs electricity but doesn't release it?"

"Sure. A capacitor. Or, you know, a battery. Oh my God!" Q. actually slapped his face. "The Baghdad Battery!"

The what? Michaela said.

"My question exactly," Jasper said. "The what?"

"In the 1930s, scientists found these funny clay jars in a village outside Baghdad. They were about five inches tall, and they contained a copper tube wrapped around an iron rod, but separated from it by asphalt spacers. I mean, it was a perfect model of an electrical generating device. All you had to do was add some kind of acid to it, lemon juice, vinegar, and poof, you'd start an electrochemical reaction. It was tiny, but it was still enough to give you a good jolt."

And?

"And?" Jasper echoed.

"Well, you know, all this made sense in theory. I mean, scientists were able to duplicate the process and show it worked. What they didn't know is what the jars were actually for. They thought they might have been used for electroplating jewelry, but in order to generate enough power to actually plate something you had to string together about a dozen batteries, and there was no evidence this had been done. The most likely explanation for the batteries' use was that priests gave certain privileged worshippers–kings and queens and other dignitaries–a little shock, which the priests would describe as a taste of the power of God."

"Okay, first of all," Jasper said, "did you write a paper on this or something?"

"I *did* write a paper on it. I'm half Shia and half Jewish. Got to give props to my peoples."

Jasper laughed. "And secondly . . ." He broke off. "I'm not sure what secondly is. But I think you know."

Q. nodded. "Well, look. It seems too much of a coincidence that the perfect materials for making a battery all come together in one little package. Everyone's obsessed with the batteries' ability to generate an electrical charge, but the whole point of a battery is not just that it makes power, but that it *stores* it. It's only released if you hook it up to a conductor. Otherwise it's trapped. And the Baghdad Batteries that were found were completely sealed with asphalt—which suggests that the people who built them were using them as power storage devices. But what if it wasn't the batteries' own current the manufacturers were storing? What if the power came from *outside* the batteries, and they just sealed it up?"

"By power, you mean Mogran."

"I'm totally guessing here. Totally guessing. But the pieces fit scary well."

"Eyes on the road, Q."

Q. nudged the car to the right. "The tricky thing is, you can't get electricity into a battery unless it's hooked up to a conductor. But anything that'll let the current into the battery is also going to let it back out. So somehow you have to get the demon into the battery and then disconnect it before he realizes what's happening. I mean, assuming we've got our basic facts right. We still have no idea if it works without testing it. And unless you know of a demon who's willing to be locked into a clay jar with who knows what consequences, then, well, I don't know what we're going to do."

For a long time there was only the faint sound of asphalt whirring beneath the car's tires. Then:

"You said Leo was going to go after my dad."

Q. cleared his throat. "I don't think Leo's gonna stay in Dr. Thomas long. He's in a frenzy right now. When he was in Michaela's body, he almost—well, you saw. It was like he couldn't stop himself."

Jasper suddenly understood. "You want me—"

Actually? Michaela cut him off, *he wants me. Jesus Christ, Jasper, you want me to have sex with that thing?*

"But how can Leo have sex with Michaela? He's possessed her once."

Jasper's senses were so keen he could feel the temperature of Q.'s cheeks rise when he blushed. "It's just, um, intercourse. He won't be going into Michaela. Just out of Dr. T."

"And into my dad," Jasper said.

Q. swallowed. "Hopefully."

"Hopefully," Jasper echoed. "Jesus, Q., that's a scary word."

7

Ileana didn't want to open her eyes. The light hurt them, even through her closed lids, but it was nothing compared to the pain in her stomach. She tried to look inside herself, but it was hard to concentrate. As far as she could tell, there was nothing life-threatening. Not immediately anyway. Not for someone with her skills.

She forced herself to open her eyes. She was surprised to discover that she was in a hospital. Q. His gallantry had probably saved her life, but it made him a terrible hunter.

Even peeling back the blanket hurt. There was a large bandage on her abdomen. Leo's spear seemed to have missed liver, spleen, kidneys. Had nicked the wall of her stomach and lodged in her guts. She knew moving around ran the risk of expelling waste matter from her ruptured intestines into her abdominal cavity, which in turn would lead to sepsis, but she had no choice. Both demons were still loose.

It was only when she started to limp to the closet that she noticed her roommate. An old woman. Asleep, or unconscious. The smell of death was all around her. She picked up the clipboard hanging from the foot of the bed.

Patricia Myles. Lymphoma.

Ileana stared at the woman for a long time. She had often wondered if this was what she wanted: a lingering death after a long life, rather than being cut down in the course of the hunt. She wondered how long it had been since this woman had done anything useful, how long since she'd been able to do something that brought her a joy beyond tepid comfort. How long since she'd felt alive. No, Ileana thought, give me a spear in the gut any day.

She found her clothes. Everything was there except for the knife and watch. It took a moment before she remembered Leo breaking the one, herself giving Q. the other. There was a clock on the bedside table. She had been unconscious for fourteen hours.

She slipped out the door. She wanted to hold her gut but she forced herself to walk normally. She didn't have the strength to argue her way out of here, let alone run. Leo had transformed her into a hunter all those years ago in Bihac. Had sharpened her senses, made her faster, more agile. But he'd done relatively little to augment her resistance to injury or her healing rate. Someone like Q. would have been well on the way to recovery by now, but she was not. But it didn't matter. She had work to do.

She would need a car, and a gun too. Well, at least that part of her task shouldn't be hard. No one seemed to lock their doors in this town.

8

Jasper breathed a sigh of relief as the gilded gates closed behind Q.'s car. He wasn't sure why, since he'd shown just a few hours ago how easy it was for a Mogran to breach the Qusays' security system, but he was willing to settle for even the illusion of inviolability right now.

Michaela's mental gasp almost made him jump out of his seat.

Is that the car?

He looked at the wrecked metal carcass. *Q.'s dad is a little weird.*

Weird? That's just freaky. Then: *Do you remember the accident?*

I remember everything. Even things I don't want to. Do you?

No, Michaela said, then added quickly *Don't show it to me. Please.*

I wouldn't even if you asked.

There was a silence. Jasper could tell Michaela was trying to formulate a question. He did his best not to eavesdrop.

Do you have all those other thoughts too? she said finally. *Like the ones Leo left in me?*

Just Jarhead's and Larry's. A pause. *And yours.*

Will they ever go away?

Jasper shook his head. Her head. *I can help you manage them, but I don't think I could clean them up without hurting you. They'll always be there.*

Jesus. Jasper felt Michaela peek into the abyss. Felt her teeter, and pulled her back. *There's just so fucking many.*

They can be a strength for you one day. You can be a walking, talking encyclopedia.

"–should be getting inside," Jasper heard then. It took a moment for him to realize the voice had come from outside his head. "Jasper?" Q. was saying. "Michaela?"

Jasper blinked. The car was in a garage. Q. was looking at him nervously.

"Are you back?"

"Sorry," Jasper said. "It's a little hard to negotiate sometimes."

There was a long pause. Q. scratched nervously at his watch. He pulled the gun from the glove compartment and shoved it in his pants.

"We should get inside."

Inside the house, Q. tiptoed across the floorboards and peeked around corners.

"You don't think Leo's here, do you?" Jasper said.

Q. laughed sheepishly. "I was thinking about Miranda actually."

"The maid? She's gone. I'd hear her if she was still around."

"God, you're worse than Ileana."

"Shit! How is she?"

"I didn't stick around long, but the doctors seemed to think she'd be okay."

God, you guys sure rack up the body count, don't you?

Jasper laughed grimly, and Q. screwed up his face.

"You know, you could tell me what she's saying. That way I won't think you're laughing at me."

Jasper put Michaela's hand on his friend's shoulder. "Just assume we're always laughing at you, old buddy. It's easier that way. Now, what's your big plan?"

Q.'s shoulder remained tense under Jasper's hand.

"Q.–"

"Look, it's just fucking weird, okay? But I'll deal with it." He shrugged Jasper's hand off and stalked heavily toward the stairs. "Just don't make me regret it."

Jasper followed Q. into his parents' bedroom. His friend walked to one of the bedside tables—his mother's, judging from the stack of romance novels—and picked up a clunky-looking clay pot. Q. took the lid off and turned it over. His mother's diaphragm and a little bag of pot fell out.

"The fact that she keeps those two things together . . ."

Jasper chuckled. "You really think you're gonna put Leo in that? And, like, why this one anyway? Why not one of those vases I saw downstairs?"

"One, because those vases downstairs are seven-hundred-year-old Japanese porcelain. Some of them are worth more than your house. And two, a lot of glazes have metal in them. Just traces, but I don't want anything that can even remotely work as a conductor." Q. shrugged. "It's all guesswork at this point. But it's not like we have anything to lose."

Jasper thumped the vase's unglazed side. "Let's start with how."

"It's easier to show you, I think." Q. led Jasper to the kitchen, told him to wait. For the next twenty minutes he puttered back and forth between the garage and the basement, dropped bits of wire and small pairs of pliers on the counter, something that looked a lot like a light switch.

Don't just sit there, Michaela said. *Make him a sandwich or something.*

"I thought I possessed Michaela Szarko, girl-punk pioneer of Dearborn Academy, not June Cleaver."

Look, Van Arsdale, I'm trying to maintain something like autonomy here. It's a little frustrating being a spectator to your own body. To hear someone else say things with your mouth and watch him touch things with your hands. To feel an itch, and have to wait for him to scratch it.

"Fuck, Michaela, I'm sorry. I'll be out soon."

Michaela's reaction was so violent that her body shuddered. *Yeah. By having sex with—by making me have sex with Leo.*

"Fuck," Jasper said again.

The pun is killing me, Van Arsdale. Killing me dead.

Just then Q. came back to the room.

"I need a circuit board. I guess I could rip open one of the phones or something, but I don't know if they can handle the voltage."

It was Michaela who had the thought; Jasper just relayed it.

"There'll be one in the car."

"In—"

"The Porsche."

Q. made a face. "I guess that makes sense." He grabbed some tools and a flashlight, headed for the front door. As they walked back outside, Jasper asked him again what he was making.

"I don't really know," Q. said. "A sort of cross between a lightning rod, a homemade EEG, and a box trap."

The clouds had thickened considerably, Jasper noted, making the night that much darker. There was a bit of a breeze too, rustling the branches that cast the Qusays' front yard even deeper into shadow. Jasper peered into the gloom, but didn't see or hear anything suspicious.

"A box trap?"

Q.'s feet dragged on the gravel driveway. He left his flashlight off, apparently forgetting that Jasper didn't know his property as well as he did, or else assuming his Mogran senses could see in the night as well as the day. He seemed more leery of the wreck by the fence than what might be on the other side of it.

"You know, when we were kids and we'd prop up a box with a stick tied to a string and wait for a rabbit or a squirrel to go under it?"

"I never made one of those."

Movement flickered in Jasper's peripheral vision. He whipped his head to the left but didn't see anything.

What was that? Michaela said inside him.

Probably nothing, Jasper answered silently.

"Yeah, I only ever tried it once," Q. went on. "Believe it or not, a little bunny rabbit never did hop underneath a cardboard box with a ten-year-old boy lying twenty feet away. Why I think I can get a demon to jump into one is a complete mystery."

Another flash. This time Michaela saw it too.

It ducked behind that tree!

I know, Jasper said. He noticed Michaela's hands were twitching. *Stay calm. We don't want to scare Q.*

Why not? He's got the gun.

That's why.

"Come on, Q.," he said out loud. "Let's get what we need and go back inside."

Instead of proceeding, however, Q. stopped in his tracks. "Jesus Christ, what am I thinking?"

"Q.?" Jasper kept his eyes peeled on the tree where whatever he'd glimpsed had disappeared.

"The Mogran have been moving in and out of people for thousands of years. What the hell makes me think I've discovered the secret to stopping them?"

"But you said the doctor had the same thought. He just needed a Mogran to test it on."

"Yeah, well, the doctor is a little crazy. I'm not sure how much of what he says is worth believing."

Jasper decided he'd get the circuit board himself. He backed toward the car, keeping his eyes on the tree. Just then he spotted movement higher up the trunk. It was so dark that even he had to squint to see that it was a raccoon.

Psych! Michaela said.

Not helping, Jasper said.

"But what about the Baghdad Batteries?" he said to Q. "If those really were Solomon jars, then people have been able to trap Mogran since biblical times."

"Well, how come no one in the Legion ever managed to make one? I mean, these people are obsessed with the Mogran, and I've only known about them for a week."

"For all you know, they tried to make one, but never had a Mogran to test it on. Or maybe, you know, they're all like Ileana. Fanatics who want us dead at any cost."

They were at the car by then. Q. switched on his light and

shone it into the ruined interior. There were tattered bits of clothing scattered around the cab, broken CDs and shards of glass, and of course blood. So much blood, staining the seats, matting the carpets.

Q.'s light flashed over something on the floor. He bent over–the doors had been ripped off–and picked it up. It was his phone.

"Aw, hells." It seemed as though he was about to throw it into the night when he stopped. Looked at the little plastic case in his hand.

"What?" Jasper said.

Q. held up the phone. "We've got our circuit."

"You sure that's safe?" Jasper said. "I mean, we won't accidentally beam him out into the world if someone calls?"

Q. started to laugh, then stopped. "I'll take out the SIM card just in case."

An hour later, Q. had assembled his makeshift Solomon jar. Although what part the jar played was a little unclear to Jasper.

"It's pretty simple. Basically, we attach the electrode to the person's head. The wire runs into the phone, here, and we just use its on-off switch to close the circuit."

The "electrode" was a platinum tiara Q. had filched from a safe in the library. Q. had taken off the back of the phone. A length of wire with an alligator clip at the ends connected the tiara to a loose wire in the phone's innards.

Jasper picked it up now.

"This adds a whole new meaning the term smart phone."

Q. forced a laugh, then got back to business. "Judging from what you've told me, it takes you a minute to assume control unless you slam right into your host. I'm hoping the moment of disorientation is long enough for me to turn the phone off."

Jasper nudged the clay jar. "And what's this for?"

Q. shrugged. "We don't really know what state Leo will be in once we trap him in the phone. Will he just dissipate? Fade away, like a dying battery? Or will he remain intact until the circuit's reopened and he can get out again? I'd bash the phone to pieces, but for all we know exposure to loose ions in the atmosphere will be enough to release him. So I'm going to put the phone in a jar and coat it with about two inches of wax, and stick it in my safety deposit box, where no one ever touches it again."

Jasper's eyebrows went up. "Just make sure you don't forget to pay the bill."

"Are you kidding? I'm gonna pony up for the next couple hundred years. All right," Q. went on. "We've got two jobs ahead of us. One, we've got to get Leo to jump out of Dr. Thomas, and keep our fingers crossed that he goes for your dad this time. And two, we've got to convince your dad to wear this."

Jasper laughed grimly. "That part's easy. Get him drunk enough and he'll do anything."

"Jasper—"

"I'm serious, Q. I mean, he doesn't have to be conscious, right? Can't we get him blind drunk until he passes out, then put the tiara on him?"

"Actually . . ." Q. reached into his pocket. "I was thinking of these." He put a medicine bottle on the counter.

"Sleeping pills?"

"My dad's. He uses them for flights to Asia. Says two'll put you out for twelve hours. You'd sleep through a plane crash."

"That just leaves part one."

Q. nodded. "Are you guys ready?"

Jasper wasn't sure if he shrugged Michaela's shoulders, or she did. "We're ready. Ready as we'll ever be."

Q. nodded. He pulled his phone—his new phone—from his pocket and retrieved the doctor's number.

Jasper cocked his ears. The voice that answered the phone was wide awake. Expectant.

"Q.," J.D. Thomas said, "where are you?"

"I'm home," Q. said, "and I think I know where Leo is."

He looked at Jasper and Michaela one more time.

Jasper nodded. Q. nodded back.

"You'd better come here," he said into the phone.

There was a long silence. Jasper could practically hear the demon inside Dr. Thomas consider his options. Finally:

"I'm on my way."

9

Elizabeth Hogarth, better know to her friends as Cakes, drove fifteen miles an hour slower than the speed limit. It was two-thirty in the morning, the roads were unlighted, and God knows there'd been enough accidents in the last week. In fact, Cakes didn't even like to be on the road after dark, but it was a little hard to avoid when you worked as a cocktail waitress. Wasn't any money in the day shift. Fortunately, it was a Thursday and traffic was light at this hour. No jerk tailgating her or flashing his high beams in her rearview mirror. She was on her way to her boyfriend John's house. He hadn't picked up her calls all day, and, what with recent events, she figured he could use a little checking in on. Poor man kept his feelings so bottled up. Out in his daylily field the very morning after Jasper was buried in the suit Cakes had picked out for his high school graduation. "Plants won't water themselves," he told her when she said he should take a day off. That was New England for you. Keep on keepin' on, or however they put it. Which was why she was concerned about him not picking up his phone. He didn't have a cell, of course, or an answering machine, but she'd called every hour from six on. It wasn't like John Van Arsdale socialized or anything.

John's pickup was parked on the gravel beneath one of the beech trees in his front yard. The house was dark upstairs and down. The front door was unlocked, which it always was when he was home. Cakes turned on the hallway light, peeked in the living room and kitchen first. Right off she sensed something wrong. Wasn't a single glass or bottle in either room. John Van Arsdale had poured himself a drink every day after he finished work for the past fifteen years. She made a cursory check upstairs but knew she wouldn't find him there, unless he was hanging from the rafters—which was unlikely, since the rafters were only six and a half feet off the floor.

"John Van Arsdale, if you did something stupid. I'll kill you myself."

She went downstairs, took herself to the back door. It was a dark night, clouds just thick enough to hide the stars. The only thing she could see was the quarter-moon and its dim reflection in the river all the way down at the bottom of the hill. She was just about to go back inside when she heard footsteps. Heavy, running. Cakes had grown up in the country, knew the difference between human and animal steps. She thought maybe it was a deer or a coyote at first, but then a big black shape hurtled out of the darkness and nearly knocked her over.

"Gunther! Goddamn it, dog, get off me!"

The dog barked in her face, nervous, needy. He was a good dog, Gunther. A big, overgrown puppy who didn't get the attention he needed.

"Who let you out, huh, boy?"

Cakes grabbed the flashlight, headed into the backyard. Figured she'd feed Gunther, put him up, then make a few calls, see if anyone had seen John. But the dog set off down the yard at a run, and for some reason Cakes knew he wasn't chasing a possum or deer that she couldn't see. In a moment he'd escaped the flashlight's thin glow and melted into the night.

"Gunther! Get back here." But her voice was weak. "John," she said under her breath. "Tell me you didn't do nothing stupid."

The grass was wet and slippery so she took the stairs. She didn't like the steps herself. Each one was a slightly different width and height, so you couldn't really get your rhythm, especially going down, especially in the dark, and there was that one loose one. She never could remember where—ah! There it was.

"Gunther! Where are you?"

She flashed her light around, but the night was so big and dark it didn't do much. The things in the light were almost more unrecognizable than the things she couldn't see at all.

She heard a faint scraping to her right, swung her light around. The beam reflected off something on the south side of the property. She held it as steady as she could, but couldn't really tell what it was. Somewhat reluctantly, she left the stairs and began walking that way. The ground this far down the hill was gravelly and she skidded in her slip-ons. Her light wavered, and she had to stop to steady it. It took a moment to find what she'd seen before. Something winked back at her. Was it an animal's eye? Maybe a raccoon in a tree? She took a few more steps in that direction. The trees clumped together here, and she felt exposed.

"Good God, woman. Settle yourself down."

Suddenly she realized what it was: the window in the side of the old wellhouse. She'd forgotten all about it. John said it was full of bats—bats and batshit, which was a good enough reason not to go any closer. But still, that faint snap from a moment ago echoed in her ears. It sounded a lot like a door swollen with rainwater being pushed closed. Should she—?

A bark sounded behind her, and she nearly dropped her flashlight.

"Damn it, Gunther, where the hell are you?"

She ignored the stairs, half walked, half slid her way down the hill. A black shape flashed through her beam.

"Gunther?"

The dog whined but didn't come to her. She had to wave her flashlight around for a good minute before she was finally able to pick him out. His eyes flashed green, then dropped back to the ground.

"Aw, hell, dog, what do you got there?"

Cakes approached warily, just in case whatever it was wasn't dead yet. But then her light caught a hand, a rubber boot.

"John?" She ran forward. "Oh no, John! John, what happened?"

The dog licked her face when she drew close and she clubbed him away. She grabbed John's hand but it was cold. She held her fingers beneath his nose but couldn't feel any breath.

"Oh God, John! What did you do to yourself? What did you go and *do* to yourself?"

With a trembling hand, she brought the light up to his face. His upper lip was split and covered with dried blood and dirt, and there were similarly stained gashes on his right cheekbone and forehead. His right eye was swollen into a dark mound like an unpeeled turnip.

The other one opened.

"John?"

For a moment Cakes seemed to see lights dancing in the single eye, the stars of the Milky Way whirling around. The next moment a fist crashed into her face and snapped her jaw out of socket and she plopped onto the wet grass face-first. Her flashlight rolled a few feet away. Its beam snaked through the grass and illuminated the unmoving pair of bodies. Cakes's face and knees tripodded her body; her hips jutted into the air in a sexual caricature. After a long moment, they fell to one side.

It was another minute before the demon could move. He'd put everything into that punch—had to hit her with the broken arm because she was straddling the other. Now, scrabbling with his host's good arm and leg, he pulled himself from beneath the fallen woman. He reached into her skirt, found the waistband of her panties, pulled them down to her knees. He clambered atop her, his closed, clawed hand on her throat propping him up. He crushed her windpipe to make sure she wouldn't wake up. It was a petty and base act even by his standards. But this petty, base little family had brought it on themselves. The Van Arsdales. Father and son were a pair all right, one worse than the other. He was going to come back when this was all over. He was going to burn down house and barn and obliterate every last trace of this family. But he was going to get Jasper first. He was going to rip limb after limb from whatever poor soul the fledgling was possessing. He was going to torture each nerve ending one at a time to make sure the pain lasted as long as possible. Acid. Knives. Needles. Fire. Who knows, maybe he'd videotape the experience and put it on YouTube. The Alphas would love that.

There was a sound off to his right. The demon had to turn his whole face to see what it was, and even then could barely make out the dog because his command of his host's senses was so poor. The dog too. He'd kill it. He'd kill everything that had anything to do with these fucking Van Arsdales.

But first . . .

Oh, first . . .

With a rush he was out of John Van Arsdale's battered body. The pain fell away, as did all sensation, replaced instantly by the world chorus he'd heard so many times before. He had planned to jump in Cakes but realized he must have squeezed too hard on her windpipe because she was already dead. He spun back out into the ether, was almost caught by a hundred souls scattered over the globe. He fought them all off. Who? he asked himself. Where? What? How would he take his revenge?

Suddenly he was seeing through a pair of eyes. He recognized the gates of Q.'s estate. Someone creeping up on it. The thoughts were muddled and hard to read, but then he realized it must be the doctor. J.D. Thomas. But what if he'd taken the sigil? Leo would be trapped. He paused as long as he could. The earthbound pull was nearly impossible to resist at this point. He pounced—

—and seemed to slam face first into a brick wall. It was like nothing he'd ever felt before. He felt like a baseball hitting a baseball bat. The pain was overwhelming, the sense of being flung away irresistible. He shot back into the void uncontrollably, his consciousness shredded and flailing about like octopus tentacles. If he'd had a mouth he would have screamed in frustration.

He slammed into a body so hard he felt it roll to the ground. It twitched and trembled with the desire to be rid of him. He grabbed at its brain but it was harder to get hold of than Larry Bishop's drug-addled mind. The memories were vague, wordless, overloaded with sensory data. Smells especially. A thousand odors assaulted his nostrils, then an equally loud array of sounds. A moment later a picture was added:

John Van Arsdale, his still-twitching body athwart the corpse of his dead girlfriend.

This was weird.

Van Arsdale seemed to be conscious, but didn't have the strength to lift himself off Cakes's body. Sobs and groans tore out of his throat. But who the hell was Leo in? It wasn't the West boy. There weren't any memories that indicated him. There weren't any real memories at all. Just . . . urges. Not even feelings. Tendencies. Appetites. Not even a name.

This was very, very weird.

Leo heard two sounds then. He heard, first, the snap of branches breaking under a heavy tread, and then he heard a growl, and realized it was coming from his own throat. He whipped his head around, focused his ears on the first sound. Even as he spotted the naked ass of Jarhead West lumbering into the river, he realized that he'd somehow ended up in Gunther.

He was in the dog.

He shook his head, tried to laugh, but all that came out was a sputtering bark. There was a first time for everything, but he thought he'd had all his firsts eons ago. This was as much fun as he'd had in centuries. But it was time for it to stop. Glancing back at the figure disappearing beneath the water, he loped toward the prostrate pair before him. Pulling down a pair of pants with his teeth. This was positively *rich*. Fucking someone up the ass whose dick was in a dead woman's cunt. This was as good as it got. Leo lifted Gunther's muzzle to the skies and let out his best howl as, scratching in the dirt for balance, he began to make his way out of his newest, and most unusual, host.

10

There was nothing for Jasper and Michaela to do after Q. left but wait. They wandered nervously from room to room. Jasper let her choose her own path, but it was his augmented memory that supplied the names of the furniture that sat on the Persian carpets and Turkish kilims: an Empire sofa and a Florence Knoll console in the living room, a marble-topped Eero Saarinen table in the dining room flanked by eight Louis Quatorze chairs. The armoire was Chippendale, the lamps in the library Tiffany, the wicker in the solarium Lloyd Loom, the metal mesh on the patio Harry Bertoia.

Man, Michaela said at one point, *you sure know your furniture designers.*

Jasper laughed. "Comes with the territory. All those facts that flash by your eyes when you thumb through a magazine in the dentist's waiting room or scan a page of Google results? They're stuck in my head forever."

Why are you talking out loud?

"Because I like the sound of your voice."

A tiny inward intake of breath, a thousand wordless nuances of emotion. Then:

So, do you think Q.'s going to be able to get your dad to drink a, what do they call it, a Mickey Finn?

"Q. could get a dog to trade a steak for a hunk of granite. I'm sure he'll have no problem getting my dad to drink whatever he wants him to. Assuming he even needs to wake him up, that is. The old man should be pretty much unconscious at this hour. Anyway," Jasper tapped Michaela's front pocket, "he said he'd call when everything was ready."

They had ended up in the library, perhaps because that room was less intimidating than the others, the furniture being straightforward leather club chairs, the walls lined with books that looked pretty much like the ones Michaela and Jasper had both read.

Hey, what was the name of that writer? The one Q. said founded the Legion?

"Jordan David. *The City of Frozen Souls*," he added, before Michaela had to ask.

Right! Can you—

But Jasper had already scanned the shelves. They weren't in any particular order, but he was able to cross-reference all the editions of the novel he'd seen over the years, and the spine practically jumped out from among its neighbors.

"There it is. Looks like a facsimile edition of the first printing."

"Facsimile edition." My, aren't we fancy?

"Like I said, comes with the territory." Jasper pulled the volume off the shelves. The brittle jacket cracked beneath his fingers, and Miranda's addiction to daytime TV showed in the healthy layer of dust Jasper blew from the top of the closed pages.

Give the woman a break, Jasper. She has to clean this whole place by herself.

Michaela uttered a tiny gasp as Jasper turned the book to look at the front cover. *God, how creepy!*

The design was an illustration of vertically elongated faces lined up so they resembled the crowded buildings of a city. The eyes were all looking upward with pleading expressions on their faces, and they were rendered in dark blue ink, which made them look that much colder—frozen, as the title above them suggested. The words were in a slightly lighter blue, the jagged hand-drawn letters looking a little like icicles hanging from a clothesline or a wire fence.

"Hard to imagine a kid's book with a cover like that today. Everything's so happy-go-lucky and tongue-in-cheek."

The nightmares this book gave me when I was little.

"At least you could sleep. It kept me awake for days."

And according to this Dr. Thomas guy, it came from being possessed by a demon?

"Well." Jasper sifted the pieces of a dozen different lectures he, Michaela, Larry, and Jarhead had all heard over the years. "David was part of the generation that believed childhood was an idyll before the horrors of adulthood set in."

You mean sex.

"*He* meant sex. I always thought sex was kind of fun myself."

Said the man who never did it.

Jasper sat down in a chair, set the book on his lap. On Michaela's lap. The distinction suddenly seemed important.

"Do you think he was right?"

Who? Jordan David?

"Do you think sex is really this dark mysterious force that controls us? Even now? Even after Freud and the Kinsey Report and *Deep Throat* and 'My Humps'? Do you think all the soul wants to do is breed? Breed and then die?"

And everything else is just something to do to while away the time? Michaela laughed. *Death has made you philosophical, boyfriend.*

"It's just that ever since I became a Mogran I've seen the evidence everywhere. So much planning and conniving just to get laid. And how often is the sex just, like, a release more than anything else? Something that just makes you want to do it again, not because it was so fun but because you're hoping that next time actually *will* be fun."

You're starting to sound like a Puritan, Jasper. Look at Sila and Q. Do you really think they weren't having fun? There was a pause. *I'm more interested in Q.'s theory that the soul is just an electrical current. Don't you find that more depressing than the idea that sex is just a compulsion?*

"Well, at least there's something. I was an atheist before this. I'm still an atheist, I guess, but now I know there's something after death. And who knows, maybe there's something after this."

After . . . ?

"Being a Mogran."

Like what?

"I don't know." Jasper ran through the religious knowledge of all his hosts. "Something kind of Hindu, I guess? The idea that each of us has a spark inside us that wants to reunite with all the other sparks. Or, who knows, maybe the animists were right."

Well, I always thought the pearly gates sounded a bit kitschy myself. Streets of gold, choirs of angels. It's just– Michaela broke off.

"What?"

I'll never see you again after this. Never touch you.

"Did you really think that was going to happen anyway? Even before all this happened?"

Probably not. But at least I had the illusion. Now I've got nothing.

"You've got your life, Michaela. You'll fall in love–"

Don't say it, Jasper. Don't even think it.

There was a long pause. Jasper said, "Q. should've called by now. Even if it's just to say he can't get the Solomon jar thingy hooked up to my dad."

Relax, Jasper. It's only been an hour. He's probably still trying to wake him up.

"Yeah, you're probably right." But he couldn't hide his growing nervousness.

He'd been idly flipping the pages while he spoke. Two things happened now. First a photograph on the inside back flap flashed before his eyes, a hundred-year-old sepia-tinted print of the author of the book in his hands. And then there was the faint click of a car door being closed in the driveway in front of the house.

"Oh no."

What? Michaela said. *What is it, Jasper?*

She saw what was on the page first, and then she saw what was in Jasper's mind.

Oh God, she said. *We're fucked.*

11

When Q. pulled into the Van Arsdales' driveway, he found two cars there: Jasper's dad's pickup and another he assumed belonged to Mr. Van Arsdale's girlfriend. He'd heard stories about Cakes from Jasper—mostly pejorative ones, which he tended not to believe, but he still didn't need a bystander.

"Shit."

He looked at the strange device in the passenger seat. A clay jar holding a cellphone connected by a wire to a hundred-thousand-dollar tiara. He shook his head. If this worked, he deserved the Nobel for good guessing. And if it didn't work . . . well, if it didn't work, Q. doubted he'd be around to receive even a booby prize. Leo wasn't going to let him get away this time. There was no Dr. Thomas or Ileana to bail him out.

The lights were off in the house, but according to Ileana's watch it was after four in the morning, so that wasn't unusual. Assuming the watch actually told time, that is. Before she let him take her to the hospital yesterday, she'd shown him how to twist the clasp on the handle to release a poison dart through the watch's knob. The darts were spring-loaded, she explained. You had to keep the watch tightly wound or they wouldn't shoot out. When you shot one dart, you rotated the crystal to set up another and wound the knob to tighten the spring. There were six darts concealed in the body of the watch. The first five contained curare, the last strychnine—itself poisonous, but also useful as an antidote to the curare, should Q. accidentally inject himself. Q. had put the watch in his pocket but Ileana insisted he wear it. "Remember, Q. The demons like to get close to you. And if they do that, this could be the only thing that saves your life."

Now, in the car, Q. couldn't help but laugh. Solomon jars and watches that shot poison darts. It was all too much. But he made sure the watch was tightly wound before he got out of the car. He left the jar in the passenger seat however. Left the gun in the glove compartment too. If he succeeded in drugging Jasper's dad—and Cakes, assuming she was there—he could come back for both of them.

He decided he wouldn't knock. Better to just wake them up and plead some kind of desperation. He'd been wrestling with his story all the way over here and hadn't come up with anything that sounded even remotely plausible. He thought the best thing he could do was cry and maybe get the sympathy vote. Q. wasn't much of an actor, but he figured it would be pretty easy to work himself up, given everything that had happened, and everything that still might.

The front door was unlocked, and he eased it open. The first thing he noticed was a faint light coming in the open place where the back door should have been, and which appeared to have been ripped off its hinges. A breeze gusted through the open door and Q. got a strong whiff of that nasty apple shit Jasper's dad swilled like Gatorade. For a moment he thought all that had happened was that Mr. Van Arsdale had done something in a drunken fit.

Then he turned the light on.

"Man, this *can't* be good."

Debris was scattered all over the kitchen floor, through which tracked hundreds of dog prints. Copious amounts of flour, sugar, and milk had been trampled into a gritty paste studded with an assortment of leftovers—chunks of meat and wilted vegetables mostly—and broken dishes, and over it all hung the sharp tang of apple brandy. Q. saw that the dog, Hunter or Hitler, some kind of German name, he never could remember, had not only knocked the back door off its hinges, but had managed to get the refrigerator open as well. He'd ripped out all the shelves and torn everything in there to shreds. He'd pawed and gnawed open the cabinet doors as well, and not just the ones on the lower level. There were footprints on the countertop, many of them bloody, and runnels of broken glass testified to the dog's carnage of the upper shelves.

"What the fuck?" Had the dog gone crazy? Gotten rabies? He'd never seen anything like this in his life. This was Cujo stuff. Cujo on steroids.

He went back into the hall, turned the light on in the living room. The room was in similar shape to the kitchen: sofa and chairs shredded, television and lamps overturned, the curtains ripped from their rods. Dog prints were everywhere. This wasn't dog-on-a-bender destruction, or even dog-hunting-for-something destruction. This looked *personal*, as if the Van Arsdales' dog had set out to willfully destroy everything that belonged to his master.

Q. glanced up the stairs. There were at least a dozen sets of tracks going up and down the steps. By this point, Q. figured the chances that Jasper's dad and his girlfriend were up there were pretty slim.

"Hunter? Hitler? You up there?"

Silence greeted him. He looked for a light switch to illuminate the stairs, but didn't see one. He took a step up, peered into the shadows of the landing.

"Hunter? Here, dog. Here, boy."

Still nothing. Q. took another step. He could see the first few inches of the landing, but after that all was dark. Another step.

"Hunter?"

Quiet. Too quiet. What did that mean? Q. wondered. Too quiet? Silence was silence. Then he realized he was holding his breath, and let it out with a nervous laugh.

There was a single short scraping noise, and then two pinpricks of light appeared in the shadows. Q. barely had time to realize they were the dog's eyes before 120 pounds of rottweiler crashed into him. The boy went flying backward, slammed on his back on the floor. Momentum saved him: his legs went flying over his head and threw the dog off him. The rottweiler's jaws, which had been aiming for his throat, snapped a half inch away from his face as the animal rolled haunches-over-head across the front hallway.

Gunther, he remembered. The stupid dog's name was Gunther.

The dog's nails clicked and slipped on the wooden floors, which gave Q. just enough time to roll onto his stomach. He didn't have time to think, let alone grab anything. He just punched. His right fist connected with the side of Gunther's head. His paws slipped on the wet floor and he went sliding into the kitchen.

Q. got to his feet slowly. Gunther did the same. The dog eyed the intruder warily, teeth peeled back, a snarl razoring out of his throat.

Q. looked around for a weapon, saw a butcher knife on the floor almost immediately, but it was on the other side of the dog. He tried to gauge the distance to the door behind him without turning his head, knew he'd never make it.

Gunther squinted as if he understood. Even as Q. was wondering if the dog *could* understand him—wondered if the animal facing him was not simply a dog—it charged. Q. swung, but Gunther was expecting it. He ducked, and Q.'s fist glanced off the animal's meaty shoulders. Jaws closed around Q.'s ankle, and he was yanked to the floor.

Gunther jumped on Q.'s stomach and went for his throat with single-minded determination. Q. put the only thing he had between his neck and the gaping mouth closing in on it: his wrist. The toothy vise closed over it and he screamed in pain. But at the same time he felt a dozen different glands activate in his body, a flood of chemicals rush to heal the wound. He suddenly remembered, this was Leo's legacy. This was his only weapon. His ability to heal.

"Choke on it, fucker!" Q. grunted. He managed to twist his arm enough to get his fist in Gunther's mouth. Q. could feel tooth against bone, could hear the sound of flesh being pulped. But he could also hear the animal sputter as it fought for breath.

With a start, Gunther seemed to realize what was happening and tried to back away. He loosened his jaws, but before he could move Q. shoved his fist into the dog's throat as hard and deep as he could.

His fingers closed around something. The dog's tongue. He grabbed it and held on tight.

Blood sprayed from Gunther's mouth as he attempted to shake Q. off. Q. was knocked to the ground, but he refused to let go. The pain in his arm was like nothing he'd ever known. He felt as if he were being flayed alive, as if acid were being poured into the wounds. Spots danced in front of his eyes. He didn't know who was going to pass out first: him or the dog.

His left hand flailed for anything it could find. There was another sharp pain as he smacked his hand into a piece of glass, but it felt like a bee sting compared to the pain in his right arm. He grabbed the shard and stabbed it into the dog's face. He couldn't tell if he was doing any real damage, but he could feel Gunther's jerks slowing down, could hear his nails scrabbling for purchase on the linoleum floor. Q. realized his eyes were closed and struggled to open them. The glass had fallen from his bloody hand, but it had done its damage. One of Gunther's eyes was a bloody pulp. The other stared at him weakly but malevolently. The animal's abdomen was spasming, but only a few drops of bile squeezed past Q.'s hand.

"Fucking die already!"

The dog's back legs fell out from under him. He shook his neck, but it was like he was trying to dislodge a fly from his ear. His abdomen contorted again and again. His eyes opened wide with surprise, and then, almost as if he'd been shot, he fell to the floor with a thud. Q.'s grip loosened, and his hand slipped out, along with pints of vomit.

The boy fell on his back, his own gut heaving as he threw up the contents of his stomach. But at the same time he was wondering what the hell had just happened. Dogs didn't just snap like that. Not overnight. Not even with rabies. There had seemed to be an intelligence to the way Gunther had destroyed the house, the way he had lain in wait for Q. at the top of the stairs. Again he asked himself if the Mogran could possess animals as well as people. It had never come up in his conversations with Ileana and Dr. Thomas, but that didn't mean it couldn't happen. Could he—had he just killed Leo? Was it already over?

He looked at his arm, but it was covered in too much blood to assess the damage. He stumbled weakly to his feet and made his way to the kitchen sink. The cold water stung at first, but after a while it began to feel good. Q. let it pour over his arm until it ran clear, then shut it off. It was only after his arm was completely clean that he saw the watch.

"Fuck," he said, and laughed bitterly. "I let that dog chew my arm off for nothing."

"Well, I enjoyed it anyway."

Q. whirled around.

Jarhead West stood in the door to the hall. He held Q.'s clay pot in the palm of one hand like a bowler at the top of a lane. He wore a pair of John Van Arsdale's overalls, and his bare chest was leaner and more muscled than Jasper remembered it, his gut all but gone. But none of these changes was as significant as the malevolent light that swam in his eyes.

"Jarhead," Leo said, pointing a finger at his host. "Jar of Solomon." And he pointed at the pot in his hand. "I'm impressed you figured this out so quickly. But really, Q.? Did you think you could stuff me in here like a genie in a bottle?"

"Maybe if I rubbed you the right way." In one smooth motion Q. lifted his arms and pointed them at Leo. His right wrist bent, his left hand twisted the watch's clasp. The dart shot out of the knob with a click like a ballpoint pen.

Leo pursed Jarhead's lips, watching the tiny missile fly toward him and fall harmlessly to the floor.

"Huh. That was anticlimactic, wasn't it? Let's see if I can do better."

The demon lifted his host's muscular arm. He tossed the jar in the air once, twice, a third time. Somewhere between the second and third tosses Q. realized he needed to rewind and reload the watch, but by then it was too late. He only managed to give the knob two or three turns before Leo hurled the jar at him. It shot through the air and exploded against his forehead. Q. didn't even have time to cry out. With a splat, he fell face first onto the kitchen floor.

The demon shuffled over and turned the boy over. A mess of blood and bile and milk and flour covered the boy's face.

"Ah, Q.," he said, "who'd want to kiss you now?" And, holding him by his hair, he dragged him from the room.

12

Q.?" J.D. Thomas's voice echoed through the empty old house. "Mohammed? Are you here?"

Where the fuck is Q.? Jasper hissed mentally.

You don't have to whisper, Michaela said. *I can hear you just fine. And Q.'s gonna have to take care of himself. We got problems of our own.*

The picture on the back of *The City of Frozen Souls* flashed in Jasper's mind.

Maybe I was wrong. Maybe it's not him.

Jasper! Now is not the time to get stupid.

Yeah? Well, what is now the time to do?

The bad guy is in the house, Jasper. Maybe we should get out of it.

Jasper tiptoed to the nearest window, started to open it.

Wait! Will it set off an alarm?

Jasper jumped. *Jesus! You don't have to* shout *either.* He looked at the window. *I don't see any sensors. Besides, Thomas opened the front door, and nothing happened. Q. must have turned off the system.* He reached for the window again.

Wait!

What now?

The book. You have to put it back. Otherwise, Thomas will know we know.

Jesus, Jasper said again. He made his way back across the room.

The book lay where he'd dropped it, still open to the photograph inside the back flap. The hundred-year-old picture stared up at him, the face unnaturally stiff, yet also possessing an eerily lifelike quality, as if it could open its mouth and speak. The photograph was captioned "Jordan David (1864–1919) at his Thousand Islands summer home," but the parenthetical remark failed to take into account the fact that the 150-year-old author of *The City of Frozen Souls* was in the Qusays' front hall.

Jasper peered at the picture, desperate to convince himself he was wrong. But though the man in the photograph lacked Thomas's spectacles, and the hair that protruded from his tophat was longer and curlier than what the doctor wore now, it was unmistakably him.

I don't get it, Michaela said. *Does he* want *to get caught?*

Well, we don't know that David was possessed when he wrote this book. It could have happened after.

But it's a reprint. Michaela tried to reach for the book, but she didn't control her arms, and Jasper had to do it for her. *Look: 1997. Thomas put this picture on himself.*

It's "The Purloined Letter," isn't it? Hiding in plain sight? And besides, who would believe it? They'd just call it an uncanny resemblance.

Whatever. We'll figure it out later. Just put it away and let's get the hell out of here.

Jasper slipped the book on the shelf, went back to the window. The sash stuck, and he had to wiggle it. It squeaked slightly as it went up.

Sshh!

Not helping, Jasper said. He hoisted one leg over the window and dropped as quietly as he could to the grass outside. He looked up to see if he could close the window, but it was too high. He turned, wondering if he should head for road or river.

"Going somewhere, Jasper?"

Jasper whirled around. J.D. Thomas stood on the lawn before him. He wore the same clothes he'd had on in the accident, ripped and soiled with blood, and yet he still managed to look completely composed.

Jasper! Michaela shrieked in his head. *It's him!*

Still not helping, Jasper said, trying not to wince.

Thomas squinted.

"Is Michaela there too? My goodness, only your third host and already you're experimenting with peaceful coexistence. How enlightened of you."

Jasper remembered how Thomas's scalp had been ripped open, the bone glinting through shredded tissue. Now there was only the faintest of seams along the doctor's hairline, and his neck, which had been so hideously elongated, was as straight and solid as a tree trunk. He'd even retied his tie. Compared to what Leo had done to Larry or Michaela, this was Superman stuff.

He began backing away. Thomas watched him, unconcerned.

"It won't work, you know."

"What?" Jasper said guardedly. "Running? Or peaceful coexistence?" He continued to back away, his eyes darting around for the best escape route or something to use as a weapon.

"Your consciousness is simply too strong for hers. You'll crush it whether you want to or not. It will start the first time you go to sleep. You'll wake up, and Michaela will seem like a dream. She might be able to claw her way back, but after a few days she'll be no different from Jarhead and Larry. Just another set of memories, a few urges toward this or that predilection. Soon enough the need to jump will become overwhelming, and then, well, she'll be left to pick up the pieces."

I do not have predilections!

Jasper smiled.

"Michaela says to fuck off."

"Michaela should watch her mouth," Thomas said in an even voice, "before I cut her tongue out. And just in case you're wondering, Jasper, no, you can't grow her another. Regeneration, sadly, is one power the Mogran do not possess."

Jasper! Why aren't you running!

But Jasper didn't run. Not yet.

"I don't understand. If you're Mogran, why would you form an organization to hunt them down and kill them?'

"Because of the Covenant, of course."

"What's that? More of your pseudoreligious mumbo jumbo?"

"You're referring to the Ark of the Covenant, I assume? I can assure you, the Hebrews took the term from us, not the other way around."

"I don't care about etymology. I want to know what it *is*."

Jasper! Why are you talking to this guy instead of getting my tongue as far from him as you can?

"Nice use of the word etymology," Thomas said. "It's getting easier, isn't it? Accessing all the information in your consciousness? It's amazing what even a few badly educated specimens of middle-class America have been exposed to, especially in the age of radio, television, and the internet. All the ambient information that passes by everyone else's eyes is as present to you as your favorite book or your mother's name. You're hardly a seventeen-year-old boy anymore, are you?"

Jasper started to tell Thomas to get on with it, but the doctor waved him silent. "A long time ago, when it became clear that the proliferation of the Mogran was becoming problematic, both for us as well as for humanity, the original nine—the so-called Alpha Wave, if Q. told you about it—formed a pact to control the spread of our kind. In the first place, we elected to conceal the secret of our reproduction from our offspring, which it had taken us quite some time to learn ourselves, and, in the second, we decided to track down the nine hundred or so Mogran whom we had created in ignorance, and eliminate them."

"You're one of the original Mogran? But that must make you thousands of years old."

Thomas smiled. "I could tell you the number of days, the number of minutes and seconds even, but suffice to say that I was already ancient when the pyramids were built. I saw the walls of Troy come down, and the Tower of Babel, and the destruction of Pompeii."

Jasper waved a hand at the doctor's body. "You must've been in this body for at least a hundred years. How do keep yourself from jumping?"

"Such a practical boy! Your questions are almost startlingly banal. Listen, Jasper: no Mogran ever fully learns to resist the urge to jump. The seesaw of frenzy and lull is an incontrovertible aspect of our nature. This was one of the things that led to the Covenant in the first place. Our jumps were wreaking havoc. We carried information from one part of the world to another in the blink of an eye. The pace of technological innovation was vastly accelerated, far faster than the finite sensibilities of mortals could handle it. It was decided we would take the necessary steps to ensure that we never jumped again."

"You mean—"

Thomas nodded.

"I do."

What's he mean? Michaela said.

"Think about it," Jasper said out loud.

Ouch!

Jasper looked at the man in front of him. It seemed to him that the wound on Thomas's head had faded even more in the past five minutes. "How long *have* you been in this body?"

"The Covenant was negotiated over the course of about five hundred years and was finalized right after the first Council of Nicaea. So about—"

"Seventeen hundred years. Jesus Christ."

The doctor smiled wryly. "Idle minds in the Legion would have you believe he was one of us. I have worked the story myself from time to time. But Jesus was just another deluded young man who thought he was the Messiah. They were a dime a dozen back then. Or a dupondius a dozen, as the case may be."

"Wait a minute. If you signed on to this Covenant to eliminate all the other demons, then why did you tell Q. you wanted to capture Leo and use him to reveal the secrets of the Mogran to the world?"

"Jasper, Jasper, Jasper. You are hopelessly naive. I never had any intention of exposing the existence of Leo or you or any other Mogran, at least not yet. That was nothing more than a bit of misdirection, as the movie people put it. A plausible story that would cover my tracks, even as it convinced Q. to do what I wanted."

"I thought you convinced Q. to do what you wanted by hypnotizing him."

Thomas smiled wryly. "Like you, Q. possesses a certain stubbornness of will that almost resembles fortitude. Suffice to say that Leo forced my hand when he possessed Michaela, and I took the expedient route." Thomas's eyes roved up and down Michaela's body. "He did a nice job, by the way. On the remodel."

Jasper! I don't like the way he's looking at us!

Jasper ignored his host.

"Then why *did* you want to capture us? Why not just kill us?"

"Do you still not understand? You, who have already experienced three bodies in as many days? Who have felt the rush of an entire mind, an entire life, added to your own in a nanosecond? For seventeen centuries I have been trapped in this single, finite corpus. I want *out*."

Jasper raised Michaela's hands helplessly. "I don't get it. How can we help you with that?"

"Finally a pertinent question. Listen then: about twenty-five hundred years ago, it was discovered that the Mogran could occasionally be prevented from possessing a host by the use of the sigil. The original sigil," Thomas added, pulling at his necktie. "Of course, no one knew why it worked. In such an ignorant, not to mention superstitious era, it was assumed that the shape of the design had something to do with it, or the words spoken while one held it before the demon. This was in keeping with the idea that the Mogran were supernatural entities rather than some form of energy that had yet to be discovered or quantified."

"Q. said that!" Jasper said, excited despite himself. "He said that he thought the Mogran were just a kind of electricity."

"He said it because I told him. And I believe it to be true. But the only way to be sure, and to explore the various ramifications of that information, is to put it to the test."

At last Jasper understood. "You want to experiment on us! You want to find a way to extract yourself from that body without having sex!"

Thomas nodded his head eagerly, wincing slightly. "Still a little tender," he said, rubbing the back of his neck. "But think about it, Jasper. We would no longer have to force our hosts to do things they don't want to do, things they spend the rest of their lives puzzling over. Who knows, perhaps we can overcome our need for a human host altogether. Perhaps we can become a pure electronic intelligence, a true living computer, or be able to go back and forth between flesh and machine. The possibilities are extraordinary, Jasper, but we'll never know unless we investigate them."

Jasper's reaction to J.D. Thomas's words was not what he would have expected. Not relief at the thought of being freed from the need to steal other people's bodies, other people's lives, nor alarm at the idea of a new and even more powerful wave of Mogran loosed upon the world. Instead he felt a strange, almost indignant sense of outrage, as though Thomas were attempting to contravene a fundamental law of the universe. Mogran and mortals had cohabitated for as long as anyone knew. Surely this wasn't an accident. Surely there was a reason for such a state of affairs.

Deep inside him, Michaela's anxiety was palpable. *Where are you going with this, Van Arsdale?*

On the lawn, J.D. Thomas was still speaking.

"You understand there are other considerations as well?"

"What do you mean?"

"It has been said that the twentieth century was the century of physics, but the twenty-first will be the century of biology. With the breaking of the human genome, not to mention the genetic decoding of virtually every other life form, a new era is upon us. New species of plants are appearing almost every day. It is only a matter of time before the same is true of animals."

Jasper repeated Michaela's words aloud.

"Where are you going with this?"

J.D. Thomas laughed. "You sound so worried, Jasper! Don't you realize this affects you too? Who besides the Mogran are better suited to take advantage of these new technologies? With our control over virtually every bodily process, we can facilitate the merger of alien DNA with our own, augmenting our already prodigious physical abilities. Perhaps even more importantly, we may soon find a way to regain what we so foolishly removed all those years ago. Either through regeneration with the aid of stem cells, or transplant from another body, or assimilation of the same DNA sequence that allows salamanders to regrow their tails and starfish to regrow their limbs. One suspects the research would have been done already, had not the prudish forces of your conservative country held it up, as though altering the arc of human life were somehow playing God."

"Maybe they're right," Jasper said, trying to keep the fear out of his voice. "What do they say? If God wanted us to fly, he'd have given us wings."

"God *did* want us to fly!" J.D. Thomas said so forcefully that Jasper took a step back. "Who or whatever God is, it granted us the minds to unlock the secret of air travel, as well as a thousand other mysteries! This is just the latest, and by no means the last of our evolutions. I'll say it again, Jasper, a new age is dawning. The Covenant has succeeded. All the other Mogran are gone save you and Leo and the Alphas, skulking away in their caves and castles. It is time to forge a new relationship between mortals and Mogran, one based on cooperation and a recognition of our mutual interests. With the Mogran assuming their rightful place at the head of the species, we can create an era of peace and prosperity and universal harmony."

Michaela realized what Jasper was going to do even before he did.

Jasper, no!

Sorry 'bout this, Jasper said, *but someone's gotta stop this nut job.*

"Utopias never work," he said out loud, and launched the body of his beloved at the demon.

13

For one thousand eight hundred ninety-four years (not counting the ten pointless years of his fleshly existence) he has wandered the earth.

If he ever conceived of a destination, a goal—his own country, his own religion, his own home even—he has long since given up on it. Even before that happened, he convinced himself he never had a starting point either. Like the ancient river from which his kind take their name, he has no single source, but emerged imperceptibly from the movement of untold numbers of electrons. (Ah, but even the Nile was dammed, wasn't it, its eighty-four billion cubic meters of water converted into 20,000 megawatts of electricity annually, meaning the river is not simply his namesake, but a kind of cousin—a cousin who, like him, can be contained within borders, however briefly.) But no, the Germanic child who died when the Roman Empire stretched from the Tigris to the Tyne is no more the source of him than the addled gas jockey who now houses his ethereal essence.

He has possessed 46,881 people—the population of a good-sized city stretching from the wheat fields of Palestina to the apple orchards just outside the door that used to hang from these hinges. Many he took for less than a minute, one for almost a century, but in his memory there is no difference between them. He has complete recall of the shortest- and longest-inhabited of his hosts. At one point he thought of them as parents; then, when he came to understand that he left them in a rather different state from the one he'd found them in, he came to think of them as children. But for more than a thousand years he's just thought of them as meals. A new set of experiences, largely indistinguishable one from the other. There is an occasional skill to be learned—a language, a science—but these are tools. Any kind of emotional charge has long since vanished. It's been a thousand years since he gave serious thought to the idea of companionship, romantic or platonic. But when Foras came to him, Leo's mind went immediately to one idea.

A friend.

Not a lover. No, not love, for sex is the one thing destined to separate the Mogran from each other.

No, Leo wanted a companion. An ally. Someone to share eternity with. To toy with the Legion and whatever comes after them, as well as to engage in the larger battle with the Alphas and their ridiculous—selfish, really, positively flesh-centered—idea that the original nine are the only Mogran who deserve to exist. And why nine anyway? Why that cutoff? Did they have a problem with double digits?

Ah, too many thoughts. Leo hadn't been this introspective in centuries. It was all Jasper's fault. The fledgling had slowed him down. Made him think instead of act. Made him wish he'd never learned the secret—certainly he would think long and hard before attempting it again. But right now, he had loose ends to tie up. Starting with this one. *Qusay, Mohammed Jr.* A shame *his* soul hadn't been bound when Leo found him. He had more spunk than Jasper ever would, even if he possessed fifty thousands lives of his own. Although Jasper could still be useful to him, if only to distract the Legion and the Alphas.

But Leo didn't like to do things the easy way. And besides, he had a score to settle. A point to make. Jasper would die, by Leo's hand. And Q. would be the one to bring him here.

* * *

Q. heard the bucket filling after the fact. After the water splashed him in the face. Time seemed reversed: he felt the water, then heard the bucket fill. Felt the skull-splitting pain in his forehead, then realized his face was wet. A kaleidoscope of colors danced through his vision. He heard the demon speak, and then saw him standing in front of him.

"Oh, stop moaning, Q., and open your eyes."

Q. frowned. He knew he frowned because it made his face hurt like hell.

"I thought they were open."

The demon laughed as Q. concentrated, found his eyes, his eyelids, willed them open. It was hard. It felt as though weights had been anchored to them with fishhooks, and even after he got them open it was a moment before the kaleidoscope faded. But that didn't make things better, because then he had to look at Leo.

The demon sat on a barrel. Q. found it hard to focus to read the faint letters that disappeared around its curved side.

Van Ars—e

Q. looked around, his head throbbing painfully with each muscle contraction. He saw more barrels, a table strewn with uniformly rusty tools, a few hay bales, and a pile of machinery that looked like—and in fact was—a tractor that had been dissembled piece by piece. It was this last detail that brought him back. He and Jasper had taken the tractor apart four years ago for the simple reason that they wanted to see how many pieces there were. They had reached 1,276 before losing interest in the project.

He glanced back at the demon.

Van Ars—e

Only now did he notice that Leo held Ileana's watch in his hands, twisting the crystal round and round, listening to the faint clicks as the darts rotated beneath the dial.

"Neat, huh? If you could improve the range on it, it'd make a good weapon."

The demon placed the watch on the barrel beside him—right next to Q.'s phone—his real phone—which he picked up. "Heads up," he said, and tossed it to Q.

The demon aimed to Q.'s left, and the boy had to jerk his hand out to catch the phone. He thought his head would explode at the movement, but he was distracted from the pain by a light tap on his chest. He looked down and saw his other phone—the one he'd turned into a Solomon jar—dangling from a wire. He followed the wire up and found the metal band of the tiara circling his throbbing head.

"Ah ah ah," Leo said, waggling one of his host's fingers. "No touching, or I'm going to have to get rough. It looks good on you," he continued. "Who knows, maybe you can bring tiaras back into fashion for men. But that'll have to wait till another day. We've got work to do. Turn around, would you?"

"Look," Q. said, "would you just cut the theatrics and tell me what's going on?"

"But I *like* being theatrical. It makes things take up more time. And time is all I have."

"I really don't—"

"Turn, fucker."

Q. turned—and promptly jumped off the barrel, because his cheek had brushed against a man's leg. He followed the leg up, then staggered backwards until he tripped over a tractor tire and fell to the ground.

John Van Arsdale and his girlfriend Cakes hung from a pair of hooks screwed into the wall of the barn. At least Q. assumed it was them—their faces looked like they'd been chewed up, and what flesh remained was completely covered in blood. Cakes's throat had been ripped open, but Jasper's dad had gotten the worst of it. His right ear and cheek and most of his lips were missing, and his teeth leered out of his skull in a gaping, grisly smile.

"I have to be completely honest," the demon said in a nonchalant voice. "The dog did the best work. Apparently possession doesn't agree with canines."

Q. began pushing away from the corpses, but his hands and legs got tangled in tractor parts.

The demon was shaking his head.

"You really don't have the stomach for this, do you? Well, look, I'm not completely heartless. I mean, if you want to get technical about it, I *am* completely heartless, and armless and legless and tongueless, blah blah blah, but I was speaking metaphorically."

Q.'s eyes flitted back and forth between the demon and his two sacrifices. He saw that Leo had posed them hand in hand, the two appendages stuck together with their own drying blood.

"However, building a Solomon jar a week after you first learned of the existence of the Mogran *is* a pretty remarkable feat, although I have a hunch Dr. T. might've steered you in the right direction. Interesting theory, the Solomon jar. There were stories, back in the day—that would be King Solomon's day, which was even before my time. No one was ever able to make it work, though, or no one I ever heard of, but one suspects that was because the technology wasn't there yet. In the last few years, though, what we've learned about how consciousness functions and its concomitant implications about the nature of the Mogran have brought it closer and closer to reality. No doubt there are a dozen gatherers in as many countries who all have a version sitting on their mantel. Really, all that was needed was a test case. And now, finally, we have one."

Q. shook his head, felt the wires jiggle as he did so.

"I don't get it. Who? You?"

"Oh, hell no. I decided a long time ago that no one'll choose my final curtain call but me. And when I do go out, you can be sure it'll be with a bang—a big fucking bang. No, I was thinking of our mutual friend. The younger and much lamented Mr. Van Arsdale."

"Jasper."

"Unless John there has another son, then yes, Jasper. *Duh.*" The demon shook his head. "So what was the plan? I found the sleeping pills. Presumably you were going to drug JVA there and hook him up to the Solomon jar and then, what, try to get me to jump into him?"

"We thought you were in Dr. Thomas."

"Someone's in Dr. Thomas, and I've got about nine guesses who it might be." The demon laughed. "Were you going to make Michaela whore herself just to capture me? Maybe I misjudged you. That's genuine cold-blooded reasoning. You know how I love to fuck." The demon leered at the boy, licking his lips, then laughed again when Q.'s panic showed on his face. "Oh, not just yet, Q. Not just yet. First we have to find out if your little toy works."

Q. looked down at the circuit board. He thought about ripping it apart but the demon wagged a finger at him.

"I know what you're thinking, and it's a bad idea. Not only will I make you pay for doing something like that, but I'll also make Mommy and Daddy Qusay pay, and Michaela, and Michaela's family, and anyone else you ever had a pleasant conversation with in the course of your short, well-heeled life. Are we clear?"

Q. looked one more time at the bit of circuitry dangling on his chest, then lifted his eyes balefully. He nodded.

Leo smirked. "Another demonstration that the concept of enlightened free will is fundamentally sound. Now. Listen up, because I'm only going to say this once, and then I'm going to start breaking bones. You're going to call Jasper. You're going to tell Jasper that he needs to get out of Michaela's body, because his presence makes her a target of my anger. And you're going to tell Jasper to jump into you."

"I'm *what?*"

The demon rolled his eyes. "I knew I should've augmented your senses while I was in you. I *said,*" the demon raised his voice, "you're ... going ... to ... tell ... Jasper–"

"I heard what you fucking said. But why would I do something that stupid?"

Leo pointed to the bodies hanging from the wall.

"Okay, fine," Q. said. "But why would Jasper?"

"Because you're going to tell Jasper you've decided to step up.

You've taken the responsibility of being the Legion's new hunter on your young shoulders. Leo made you as invulnerable to injury as a human being can possibly be, and Jasper could make you even stronger. With Jasper inside you, you can eliminate all the big bad demons like Leo and the Alphas. And Jasper, with his all-too-human moral compass, will be as seduced by this idea as a normal Mogran is seduced by the well-rounded ass of a seventeen-year-old of either gender. He'll kiss Michaela goodbye and head for his bestest buddy in the world. And then, well, then we'll see if the Solomon jar theory is correct."

Q. stared at the demon. Leo sat on the jar of applejack, looking like a farmhand getting ready to head out into the field, save for the sneer that twisted his mouth. He seemed so sure of himself, like a poker player who's just drawn the ace that completes his royal flush.

"This—" Q. shook his head. What the hell was this? "This is crazy. Just *crazy*."

Leo licked his lips, but before he could answer another voice spoke.

"For once, Q.," Ileana said, "you and I are in total agreement."

Demon and human heads whipped toward the front of the barn. Ileana leaned heavily against the doorframe, her face ghostly white and dripping with sweat. But her mouth was set in a line as determined as the demon's, and, more to the point, her hands held a shotgun, shakily but firmly pointed at the demon astride his barrel of applejack.

"God bless the NRA," the huntress said. "It's easier to find a gun in America than it is to find a pyramid in Egypt."

14

Jasper was less than ten feet from J.D. Thomas when he leapt. He had no plan of attack, but even as his right foot left the ground a thousand memories flashed through his brain. The women's self-defense class Michaela had taken from a dykey-looking chick at the Y. The three months of jujitsu he'd taken when he was eleven, before his dad could no longer afford the bill. The thirty-seven Hong Kong martial-arts flicks Larry had watched (mostly in the common room in prison) as well as the more straightforward action movies Jarhead had taken in over the years. Every punch, snap kick, roundhouse, uppercut, karate chop, spinning back flip, and nameless pseudo-judo choreographed sequence that he or Michaela or Larry or Jarhead had caught even the tiniest glimpse of flashed instantaneously in his mind's eye. But it was more than that. It wasn't just pictures. The muscular action with which such moves were accomplished was also there. What had to flex, what had to relax. Where he needed to move, where he needed to be still. Where he needed to hit his target to do the most damage.

His right foot was off the ground. His left. His bent hips were a full five feet up in the air. His left heel was snapping toward J.D. Thomas's nose.

Oh my God, Jasper told Michaela. *We can do this! We can really do this!*

And then, so fast the motion was a blur even to Jasper's amplified senses, J.D. Thomas raised his hand. With what seemed like no effort he deflected Jasper's foot and turned it back at him. The force of Jasper's kick sent Michaela's body flying backwards at twice the speed with which it had come. Jasper wasn't even aware he'd done a backflip until he found himself somewhat unsteadily standing on his feet, right where he'd started.

He shook his head to clear it.

"Jasper, please. I have no desire to hurt you."

Jasper ran forward again. He tried fists this time. Right, left, right, left, right, left. To the head, to the gut, to the chest. J.D. Thomas needed only one hand to parry both of Jasper's. Jasper thought the man might actually yawn.

"I have had thousands of years to hone my skill at this sort of thing. In years gone by I have taken on Roman centurions and barbarian hordes, Apache war parties and Nazi stormtroopers. Trust me, Jasper. You don't have a chance."

Jasper dropped and did a leg sweep. By the time he'd reached the ground the doctor was no longer in front of him. He whipped his head around, just in time to see the doctor's hand race toward his face. He didn't even have time to blink.

But the blow didn't land. The doctor stopped his hand a millimeter from Michaela's nose.

"Are you ready to talk yet?"

Jasper somersaulted backwards and leapt up. Once again he charged.

He didn't even see the punch. Just felt Michaela's ribs crack as he flew backwards through the air.

J.D. Thomas sauntered to Jasper, who lay prone in his host's body, struggling to breathe.

"Three ribs broke. The upper right two, and the second from the top on the left."

Jasper looked inside himself. He nodded painfully.

Thomas shrugged. "You'll fix them."

Jasper's head whipped back and forth. He tried to get up, but one of the doctor's wingtips came to rest on his broken ribs. He applied a little pressure, and deep inside him, Michaela screamed.

"So that's it?" Jasper said when he could speak. "You're going to use me as a guinea pig? Take me back to your lab and rip me apart, find out what makes me tick?"

The Mogran picked a bit of lint or blood from beneath a nail. "As I tried to tell you several times, I have no intention of hurting you."

Jasper shook his head. "Huh?"

"I *did* want to conduct some experiments on you, but unfortunately too many people know about my lab now—Ileana and Q. and of course Leo. It would be difficult to kill them all without detection. I will need to relocate, assume a new identity, and build a new lab." He looked himself up and down. "It will be nice to shed this personality. I have grown so tired of playing the fop. I'm thinking of going a bit more 007. Then perhaps I'll come looking for you, to see if you can be of any . . . assistance." The doctor offered Jasper a slight but genuine-looking smile. "Who knows, if you've managed to make one or two or a hundred new Mogran by then, I'll have no need of you. You are a kind of first, after all. There is a certain rightness to your survival."

"You mean one or two or a hundred people murdered, just so you can experiment on their ghosts, rather than me? Yeah, I don't think so."

The doctor turned slightly, looked at the glow of the rising sun, pinkening the sky behind the distant Berkshire Mountains. The light gave his skin an orange tint, but it seemed to Jasper that the fire came from within the man's ancient body, as if his Mogran essence were attempting to burn its way out.

"It has been a long night, Jasper, but now the sun is coming up. It is time we both got on with our lives."

Jasper turned painfully, looked at the sunrise. "That's it? You're walking away?"

"Fighting is Leo's style, not mine. I have learned to be patient. Learned that there is more to being a Mogran than amusing oneself. But I would like one thing from you."

Michaela screamed inside him again, a cry of fear rather than pain. *Run!*

The doctor chuckled at Jasper's wince.

"*I* practically heard that. You should learn to keep her under control. But tell your lovely host that she has nothing to worry about. All I want is my sigil."

It hurt to reach into Michaela's pocket to retrieve the necklace. The rough metal glinted in the morning light like a single glowing eye. The eye of a Mogran. He studied its curves, compared them to the images he'd seen on Q.'s computer.

"Beleth?" he said. "That's your real name?"

Thomas shook his head. "I am Foras. Beleth was a . . . friend to me. In the same way that Leo attempted to be a friend to you."

Jasper shuddered. "Yeah, I don't need friends like that."

"I heartily concur."

The Mogran's hands closed over the sigil, and his skin touched Michaela's. Despite the fact that it was seventeen hundred years old, it felt just like normal skin. A moment later both hand and sigil disappeared into his pocket.

"It will be very hard for you to tell friend from enemy in the coming years, Jasper. But right now you have at least one real friend. I suggest you go to him, before Leo gets there first."

15

The demon held the huntress's gaze for a long moment. His face was slightly proud, almost paternal.

"*Iljana. Zdravo sestra.*"

Ileana said something in what Q. presumed was Croatian. "That means 'fuck you'," she translated helpfully. "Get out of here, Q."

The demon held his hand up. "You're injured."

"I have a gun," the huntress replied.

"Your hands are shaking."

"It's a shotgun."

"Ileana, wait," Q. cut in. "There's another way."

Ileana didn't take her eyes from Leo. "I don't have the energy for scruples, Q."

"You don't *have* to kill him, Ileana."

"Oh, but I do, Q. I have waited to kill this monster for more than a decade. Only my hatred for him has kept me going all these years."

"Not Leo. *Jarhead.*"

"Who?" Ileana blinked. "The host?"

In a voice still completely unperturbed, Leo said, "The boy has made a Solomon jar, huntress."

For one moment Ileana's face softened, and her whole body sagged. A far-off light filled her eyes as she contemplated what Leo had said. Then all at once she straightened, and her voice came harder than ever.

"A Solomon jar? Between the boy and the gatherer, I don't know who is more deluded. If he's made anything, it's a mousetrap in which he will be caught."

"I think you are wrong, huntress. I think it will work."

Ileana opened her mouth, closed it. She took a hand from the barrel of the gun to wipe sweat from her eyes, replaced it. Then:

"Perhaps someone who still believed there was a moral order in the universe would act differently. But a decade of hunting has taught me there is no such thing as justice. Only crime and vengeance. Often they occur at the same time. I have no doubt that each life I took in order to kill a demon was a murder. Unavoidable perhaps, in the absence of Solomon jars and exorcisms, but a murder nonetheless. Killing Mason West, though perhaps more callous, more expedient, will just be one more."

"Ileana, please," Q. begged. "Jasper will be here soon. He'll help us."

This time it was the demon who shot Q. down. "It's been one hundred and four minutes," he said, with the kind of accuracy only a Mogran could have. "Don't you think he'd've come by now, if he was really coming?"

"How many times do I have to tell you?" Ileana said. "There's no such thing as a good demon. Let him come. It will make my task that much easier."

"Ileana—"

For the first time the huntress took her eyes from the demon. "Unless you're prepared to kill me, Q., *shut up*."

"Allow me," Leo said. With unbelievable speed, he grabbed the only thing handy—Alec's watch—and hurled it at the huntress. At the same time, he rolled backwards, putting the barrel of applejack between himself and the huntress's gun.

The watch struck Ileana in the face, but she didn't flinch. Nor did she panic. She squeezed the trigger once. The side of the barrel exploded, and apple brandy spewed over the barn's concrete floor.

Q. didn't wait to see if the demon had been hit as well. He rolled to his left, grabbing for anything he could use as a weapon. The cellphone bounced around on his chest and his head throbbed within its metal circlet, but he forced himself to think past the pain. He grabbed the phone and yanked it free.

When he turned back to Leo, he saw that the demon had managed to put another barrel between him and the huntress. Q. glanced at Ileana. Her stitches must have ripped open, because a red stain was rapidly spreading across her abdomen. She didn't seem to have the strength to raise the shotgun to her shoulder, but held it braced against her hip. Gritting her teeth, she fired again, and the second barrel erupted in a flood of dark brown liquor. Her mouth opened in a cry of pain, but Q. could hear nothing over the gun's report echoing through the barn.

"That's two shots, Ileana. Three left, assuming the gun is fully loaded."

Q. turned back to Leo. The demon had made his way behind a stack of hay bales. Three feet of densely packed straw protected him from the huntress's gun, but he was still fully exposed to Q.

Q. looked down at the phone in his hand. He shrugged.

He put everything he had into the throw. Leo didn't even bother to look in Q.'s direction. He just stuck out his hand and caught the phone and hurled it over the bales at Ileana. The huntress shot it out of the air and it exploded like a clay pigeon.

"Very nice," Leo said, wiping bits of plastic from his hair. "You can thank me for those reflexes."

The huntress ignored him. "You're not helping, Q. Get the fuck out of here. *Now.*"

Q. didn't see how he could have left if he wanted to. The demon was between him and the door. All he could do was ease backward, look for something else to use as a weapon. He glimpsed a long saw hanging from the far wall on the other side of the barn, an axe, a pair of posthole diggers, hammers, shovels, drills, but the demon was between him and the tools as well. There were small tractor parts all around him, but throwing something else seemed like a bad idea.

"Two shots left, Ileana. Use them well."

The huntress was also looking around the barn. Left, right, down, up. Her eyes remained fixed on the loft for a moment, and then she nodded.

"I intend to."

With a grunt, the huntress raised the gun to her shoulder and pointed it toward the loft and fired. A barrel burst, and thirty gallons of applejack spilled down on the demon and the hay bales he hid behind.

"Are you trying to drown—"

"Death is in my sight today!" the huntress shouted over him, and fired her final shell. Another barrel erupted, another flood of liquor rained down on Leo. In the moment of stillness after the shot, the sound of Ileana's gun dropping to the concrete floor echoed through the barn.

The overpowering odor of apple brandy made Q.'s eyes water. Why in the hell had Ileana wasted her last two shots? And then, as a quiet *shtk* reached both his and the demon's ears, he understood just what Ileana was up to.

He whipped his head back toward her even as Leo stood up from behind his cover. The huntress had fallen to her knees, and blood ran freely from her stomach. One of her trembling hands held Alec's watch, but the other, more to the point, held a lighter, from which glowed the tiniest flame.

She tossed Q. the watch even as the demon launched himself over the hay bales, then dropped her lighter to the pool of alcohol on the floor. A sheet of flame ripped across the barn with a low rumbling *whoosh*.

No reaction showed on Leo's face. His right foot touched the flames, his left, and then he was up in the air again, still aiming for Ileana. But the hems of his pants were alight, and even before he reached the huntress a cloak of fire had engulfed his alcohol-drenched body. In eighteen hundred years, he had never looked more like a demon.

Even then he refused to scream, or stop, but continued barreling toward the woman slumped in the doorway. Ileana made no move to escape. One hand held her bleeding stomach, but her eyes were open and focused on the approaching demon.

The flaming figure touched ground, then leapt one more time—not *for* Ileana, Q. suddenly realized, but *over* her. Though his entire body was covered in flame, he was still thinking of escape. The river was two hundred feet downhill, but if anyone could make it there before the fire killed him, Q. supposed it was a Mogran.

Ileana wasn't about to let him go. Using whatever strength was left to her, the huntress pushed herself up to intercept the demon. But before she could reach him something shot through the door and Leo's forward motion came to as abrupt halt. For the first time he screamed. Not in pain but in pure rage. Q. could have sworn flames shot from his mouth along with his hatred.

"NO!"

He staggered backward into the flaming haybales, and only then did Q. see the dark pole wavering in front of him, the three tines disappearing into Jarhead West's torso. A pitchfork. An appropriate tool to kill a demon. But who—?

Q. looked at the door. Michaela stood over Ileana's prone body. Michaela and—

"Jasper?"

The figure in the door nodded, even as a grunt sounded to Q.'s right. He turned back to Leo. He was struggling to stand but couldn't. He looked down at the pitchfork sticking out of his host's chest.

"I . . . *made* . . . you!" he hissed.

"No," Jasper said. "*He* made me." And he pointed to the corpse of John Van Arsdale hanging from the wall.

There was a sudden bite of flame, and Leo's head fell back. His mouth was still open, and his eyes, and as Q. watched they seemed to melt and flow like wax. Even then Leo's fingers were twitching. Even then he was still struggling.

There was a *pop!* as something exploded in a shower of sparks. With a start, Q. came back to himself, realized that a wall of fire separated him from the door.

Jasper was pointing behind Q. "The wall! You have to kick it down!"

By now the fire was snaking toward the loft, where a half-dozen more barrels of applejack sat like powderkegs.

Q. turned and ran for the wall. Daylight glinted through the flimsy battens. He only hoped they were as weak as they looked.

His shoulder smashed into the wall and he bounced backwards, almost fell into the fire. But two planks had cracked. He slammed into them again and they snapped outward, making a hole about two and a half feet wide. His launched himself through it, the jagged wood tearing at his clothes and skin, catching on his pant leg. He ripped the fabric free and ran.

He felt the detonation before he heard it, a concussive wave that lifted him up and carried him through the air, then slammed him into the stony soil. A wave of heat surrounded his body like water, and he wasn't sure if he was on fire or not. Wasn't even sure if he was still alive.

Then the *boom* came. Even as Q. was wondering if he had really survived the blast, he knew with a certainty that defied contradiction that Leo had not. Leo was dead. Leo and Jarhead both. But what about Jasper and Michaela? And Ileana? Q. figured Jasper could have gotten away, but what of the huntress?

He pushed himself off the ground and turned back to the barn. The roof was gone, part of it blown out and flaming all over the yard, part of it collapsed into the building. The walls were solid sheets of flame shooting thirty feet into the air. Missing planks showed the interior of the barn, which was as full of fire as the inside of a volcano. There was no movement save for the dancing of the flames.

He got to his feet unsteadily, swatted at a few sparks littering his clothes, coughed black goo from his mouth. Other than soot, he seemed to be unmarked. He wondered if that was because of what Leo had done to him, or if he was just lucky.

He made his way around the barn slowly, not sure what he was hoping to see. The fire was a roar in his ears and its heat beat at him in palpable waves. Q. staggered as if he was drunk, realized the endorphin drain was making him woozy. Twice he almost fell.

"Jasper," he called weakly. "Michaela? Ileana?"

Only the flames answered him at first. But then, through the greedy, devouring roar, he heard a single loud crack.

A gunshot.

16

Q. broke into a run.

"Ileana! Don't!"

He rounded the corner of the flaming barn, immediately saw Ileana and Michaela–Jasper–*Michaela*–God, it was hard to keep it all straight–thirty feet uphill. The huntress held a pistol in both hands. The very gun Q. had left in the glove compartment of his car. You had to hand it to her. She thought on her feet.

Ileana's hands shook so badly she could barely hold the gun up. But Jasper was only a dozen feet from her, and Q. knew the pistol's clip held fourteen bullets. He had put them in himself. It seemed likely that at least one or two would find their target.

"Ileana!" he yelled again. "Don't shoot! He's different!"

As he ran up the hill, he saw the drag marks. Realized immediately that Jasper must have pulled Ileana from the barn.

"Jesus Christ, Ileana, he *saved* you!"

"Stay back, Q.," Ileana said as he got closer. "I will shoot you too, if you attempt to stop me." If anything, the weakness of her voice made her sound that much more dangerous. She didn't have the time or strength to fuck around.

"Stay back, Q.," Jasper repeated. "No sense in both of us dying." He blinked. "The three of us, I mean."

He poised on Michaela's toes, knees bent, eyes peeled, like a tennis player waiting for a serve. In his case, however, he wasn't trying to intercept Ileana's shot, but dodge it.

"Don't think you can save yourself by reminding me of the girl, demon. I have long since made my peace with that aspect of my job."

"I don't believe you," Q. said. He had slowed to a walk but still made his way toward the huntress. "You talk about how hard you are, but I know you still care. You wouldn't be hunting if you didn't care. If you weren't trying to save people."

"The girl is lost, Q. Between Leo and Jasper's possessions, there is nothing left of her."

"That's not true!" Jasper said. Or at least Q. thought it was Jasper. It sounded so much like Michaela. Not just the tone but the indignation. "I'm right *here!*"

"Michaela?" Q. squinted. "Can he let you out like that?"

Michaela didn't take her eyes from the woman with the gun.

"Listen to me," she said to Ileana. "You don't want to kill me."

Ileana peered at the girl in front of her, as if trying to decide if this was a trick on the demon's part.

"No? Will you take responsibility for all the lives the demon destroys after he abandons you?"

"I know you want to kill Jasper," Michaela said desperately. "Believe me, he wants to get this dying thing over too. *But you don't have to kill me to do it.*"

"Then who will I kill? This one?" She jerked her head sideways, toward Q. "Or perhaps Jasper will be so kind as to jump into me, and let me take my own life. *Someone has to die*, Michaela. I'm sorry it has to be you, but there is no other way."

"There *is* another way!"

"Q.'s Solomon jar? I'm starting to think you really *are* trying to play me."

"It could work, Ileana," Q. said. "We'll never know unless we try."

"Then we'll never know," Ileana said, and she fired the gun.

It seemed to Q. that Michaela moved even before the huntress squeezed the trigger. She rolled left, then again, then again, as the huntress fired two more shots. The hill was wide open here, nothing more substantial than the recently turned furrows of garden soil to hide behind. The gun bucked wildly in Ileana's hands, but Q. knew it was a matter of time before she hit her target. He didn't wait. He leapt at her.

All of her training tips filled his mind. The calm. The focus. He squeezed the chemicals into his bloodstream, felt strength and speed flood his limbs, forced himself to zero in on Ileana to the exclusion of everything else. He knew he would only get one shot.

Ileana continued firing even as she jerked an elbow backwards, but Q. was ready. He dropped and grabbed her ankle and pulled as hard as he could. The huntress refused to go down. She grunted in some combination of pain and rage and swung her gun around, looked straight in Q.'s eyes.

"I'm sorry," Q. said.

"Wha–"

He twisted the clasp on the watch and, with a tiny *phht*, the poison dart shot into Ileana's leg. There was a half second before the toxin took effect. A half second in which she could have squeezed the trigger and taken Q. out with her.

She didn't.

"You need to give her CPR."

"What the hell just happened?"

"Jasper–Michaela–whoever you are." Q. was fumbling with his watch. "You need to give Ileana CPR. *Now.*"

"It's me, Q." Michaela/Jasper ran up, fell to her/his knees, placed her/his hands over Ileana's heart and started pumping. "Thank God Larry was a paramedic."

Q.'s twitching fingers continued working the watch. He'd never actually rotated it before, and it seemed to be stuck.

"Jasper?"

Michaela's head nodded as she counted. "One-two-three-four.

One-two-three-four." She leaned over, blew air into Ileana's mouth, then pumped on her heart again.

"The last dart's supposed to have an antidote."

"Dart?" Michaela—Jasper—breathed into Ileana's lungs again.

"The watch. It's some 007 shit. Fuck!" Q. still couldn't get it to turn.

"Calm down, Q. You can't help her if you freak out. But you've got to hurry. She's completely gone."

"Finally!" Q. had pressed the chronometer on the side of the dial, and the mechanism began rotating with audible clicks. "One, two, three, four—shit!"

"What?"

"I can't remember how many darts I fired. There's only one dose of antidote."

Jasper pumped Michaela's shoulders up and down. "Isn't there an indicator?"

"It's not that high-tech. Fuck. Okay, one in the kitchen, and one just now. That's two, right? One and one makes two?"

"Q.!"

"Okay!" He moved the watch toward Ileana's wrist, then pulled back. "But what if she fired one before? These doses are designed to take a Mogran out. We're not gonna get her back if I shoot her up twice."

"We can't wake her up to ask—" Jasper broke off to breathe into the huntress's mouth, "—so you're just gonna have to risk it. Q.!" he said sharply, when his friend just sat there. "She's dying. You have to act *now*."

As Q. pressed the watch to Ileana's skin, he noticed how fair it was. Her face was fish white and slightly blue at the lips, but otherwise unblemished. Ageless. She could have been a teenager, just like him. He knew Leo had done this to her. Knew she thought the same thing every time she looked in a mirror. He wondered who she hated more in those moments. Leo? Or herself?

"I'm sorry," he said a second time, and fired the dart.

For a long time there was just the wheeze of Michaela's breath as

Jasper continued to perform CPR. Four times he stopped to breathe for her. Eight times. A dozen.

"Oh fuck," Q. said. "I killed her. Fuck, fuck, *fuck*."

"Sshh!" Jasper hissed.

"What?"

"I hear something."

"Is she—?"

But it wasn't Ileana Jasper heard. It was sirens.

"Fire trucks. Three of them. And one—no, two police cars."

"We have to get out of here."

"Not till she wakes up." Jasper pumped a little harder on Ileana's chest.

"There are bodies in the barn, Jasper. Not to mention Ileana."

"Jarhead was bad enough, Q. I'm not killing anyone else."

"*I* killed Jarhead."

Q. and Jasper looked down. The huntress's eyes were open, barely, and her voice seemed to float out of her mouth.

"You . . . saved me?" She was looking at Jasper, not Q.

"We did," Jasper said. "All three of us."

Ileana never took her eyes from Jasper's. The sirens grew suddenly louder as the first fire truck crested the hill south of the house. At length she nodded.

"Run," she said. "When I'm better, I'll find you."

17

A mile north of his father's house, Jasper walked Michaela's body to the river's edge.

"I'm going to take your shoes off," he told her. "I want to feel the water. One more time."

Michaela didn't say anything, but she didn't have to. Jasper could feel her emotions. Her wish that there was another way. Her acceptance that there wasn't.

"You and Q. are going to have to be the new hunters."

He felt her nod. Loosened his hold a little, so she could do it herself.

"Thomas—Foras—is still out there. And the rest of the Alpha Wave, and who knows what else."

I'm scared, Jasper. What if I can't handle it?

"If Q.'s Solomon jar works, you won't have to kill anyone."

Not that. Those memories Leo left in me. What if I can't control them?

"You can do it. You're strong."

Only because you made me strong.

"No." Jasper shook her head. "You. You're strong. You were always strong."

Jasper could feel her doubt. *Will you be there too?*

"Everything we had together. It'll always be there."

A long silence. The water was cold on Michaela's toes, but she didn't ask Jasper to step back. It was his last chance to feel it. To feel anything. She let him have it.

You're sure there's no other way?

"I have to end it. And this way I won't hurt anyone."

I know. I just wish—

"Don't. It's bad enough already."

Right. Okay then, let's do this.

They turned from the river. Q. sat on the grass a few yards up. There was soot on his face and hands, and his black hair waved in the breeze as if the top of his head were smoking. He looked at them expectantly.

"We're ready," they said.

Q. nodded. He stood up, walked over to them, stopped about a foot away. There was a sheepish grin on his face.

"What a morning."

Michaela and Jasper laughed quietly but didn't say anything. Another long pause. Q. reached a hand toward Michaela, then pulled back. He moved it toward his zipper, then stopped again. A nervous laugh gurgled out of his throat.

"Oh man. This is weird."

Inside Michaela, Jasper retreated. He felt the frenzy coming on him, but knew he had to let Michaela do this.

Michaela nodded. She reached out, caught Q.'s hand.

"I want you to touch me. Otherwise it would just be gross."

"Michaela? That you?" Q. said.

She nodded again. Drew his hand to her hip.

"It's just us, Q. Just us."

The words sounded like *justice* in Q's ears, and Ileana's words echoed faintly behind Michaela's. *There's no such thing as justice.* He would do his best to prove her wrong.

He looked into Michaela's eyes. Found Jasper there, swimming around like tiny phosphorescent fish.

"Close your eyes," he said to Michaela. "I don't want Jasper to see this."

Epilogue

S he's had a full life."

As the eldest surviving child (George had died thirty-four years ago, in Vietnam), Alison Myles felt it was her duty to say something. Felt it was important to use the present tense, even though the doctors had told her it was a matter of hours.

"Four children, including George, who I'm sure is up there with Dad waiting for her."

Nancy and Ellen, her younger sisters, met her eyes and nodded. It was good to remember George, and Dad too.

"Eleven grandchildren."

"Twelve," Ellen said, rubbing her stomach. Smiling.

"Twelve," Alison nodded. "And more friends than you could fit in a church."

"Here, here," Booker, Nancy's husband, said, although Alison wasn't quite sure what he meant by it.

Alison looked down at her mother. Courtney, Nancy's oldest, had come every day to do her hair, and a halo of soft mauve curls framed her mother's face. Her mother always did like her bluing. The ashen pallor of the last few days seemed to have faded a bit, and Alison wondered if Courtney had put a bit of makeup on her as well.

Someone coughed, and Alison pulled her eyes from her mother's face.

"This is probably the last time we'll all be gathered together like this," she said, "so if there's anything you want to say, now would be the time."

They started with Frank, Ellen's youngest, just four years old.

"Bye-bye, Grandma," he said in a grownup voice. "We love you."

She really did look lovely, Alison thought. As if she were sleeping, could wake up any moment.

The rest of the grandkids filed after Frank, then the husbands, then Uncle Sam and Aunt Glenda. As they crowded between Alison and her mother, she found her attention wandering to the empty bed. Her thoughts drifted to the girl who'd been there. Michelle—no, Michaela. Michaela Szarko. It was Courtney who'd found her awake when she came in to do her grandmother's hair. Not just awake but healed, restless even. She'd been walking around the room completely naked when Alison came in, pacing, trying to pry the cast from her broken arm. A miracle, the doctors said. Alison remembered the word, because it was what the doctors said after her mother's last round of chemo. *Only a miracle can save her.*

"Alison?"

Booker was looking at her with a slightly puzzled, slightly bored look on his face.

"Do you want to say goodbye?"

Alison made her way through the crowd of family. People touched her arm, her shoulder. She knew they expected her to make the right gesture.

She looked down at her mother's face. The pink cheeks, the little glow on her forehead. Courtney really had done an amazing job with the makeup.

Her mother's eyelids twitched and Alison started. The doctors had told her that was normal. She'll dream right until the very end, they said. That's why it was important to make sure she felt safe, loved. To keep her dreams safe as well. To ease the transition. But Alison found herself unnerved by how vital her mother looked. Better than she had in years.

Another cough. Booker really wasn't subtle, was he? She took a deep breath. She had thought about what she was going to say for a long time.

"Mom," she said. "We're all here, Mom." She took her mother's hand. "Whenever you want to let go, Mom."

Her mother's hand felt warm in hers. Hot even, and firm.

"Whenever you want to let go, Mom, we're here with you."

But Patricia Myles didn't let go. In fact Alison could've sworn she was squeezing back. She looked up at Nancy, smiled nervously.

"Whenever you want to, Mom," she repeated, a nervous tremor in her voice. "Whenever you, when you, when–"

"Alison?" Nancy said. "Is everything okay?"

"Ow!" Alison said. "Mom, stop! You're hurting me. Let go, Mom! Let go!"

"Alison! What's going on?"

Alison was desperately trying to pull her hand from her mother's. The old woman's arm jerked in her shoulder but she didn't release her grip.

"Mom, let go! You're hurting me! Let go, Mom! Let–aah!"

There was a wet snap then, less like knuckles cracking than balloons popping under water, as six bones in Alison's hand broke, and then Patricia Myles's eyes snapped open. A strange light swirled in their depths.

She didn't look at *all* happy to be alive.